HARLEQUIN A VE
COLL

It's time to turn up the heat this holiday season!

It all starts when these couples are tempted by a few sexy surprises under the tree. Whether it's being stranded with that superhot guy, reuniting with the one who got away or even assuming a different identity, these couples are reveling in their steamy, *private*, gifts.

This will be one sizzling Christmas they won't forget...especially when they discover that being naughty can be very, very good.

Indulge yourself with this special 2-in-1 collection of classic stories that brings the sexy into Christmas.

If you enjoy these stories, be sure to look for more red-hot reads in Harlequin Blaze.

LESLIE KELLY

New York Times bestselling author Leslie Kelly has written dozens of books and novellas for Harlequin Blaze, Harlequin Temptation and Harlequin HQN. Known for her sparkling dialogue, fun characters and depth of emotion, her books have been honored with numerous awards. Leslie lives in Maryland with her own romantic hero, Bruce, and their three daughters. Visit her online at lesliekelly.com.

Be sure to look for other books by Leslie Kelly in Harlequin Blaze—the ultimate destination for red-hot romance! There are four new Harlequin Blaze titles available every month. Check one out today!

New York Times **Bestselling Author**

Leslie Kelly
and
Samantha Hunter

WHITE-HOT REUNION

HARLEQUIN® A VERY SEXY CHRISTMAS COLLECTION

ISBN-13: 978-0-373-60967-3

White-Hot Reunion

This edition published by arrangement with Harlequin Books S.A.

For questions and comments about the quality of this book, please contact us at CustomerService@Harlequin.com.

Printed in U.S.A.

CONTENTS

IT HAPPENED ONE CHRISTMAS

Leslie Kelly

This one's dedicated to the Blaze Babes.

It's such a pleasure being one of you.

Merry Christmas!

CHAPTER ONE

Now
Chicago, December 23, 2011

WHEN LUCY FLEMING had been asked to photograph a corporate Christmas event, she'd envisioned tipsy assistants perched on the knees of grabby executives. Too much eggnog, naked backsides hitting the glass-topped copier, somebody throwing up in a desk drawer, hanky-panky in the janitor's closet—in short, a typical high-end work party where people forgot they were professionals and played teenager-at-the-frat-party, building memories and reputations that would take an entire year to live down.

She'd been wrong. Completely wrong.

Elite Construction, who'd hired her a few days ago when their previous photographer had bailed on them, had chosen to go a different, and much more wholesome, route. They were hosting an afternoon event, a family party for all of their employees as well as important clients, and whoever they cared to bring along—including small children. Catered food, from caviar to corn dogs, appealed to every palate. There were presents beneath a huge tree, pretty decorations, music filled with jingling bells and lots of smiles. It was almost enough to give a non-Christmas person like herself a little holiday tingle.

Oh. Except for the fact that she was working with a *very* cranky Kris Kringle.

"If they think I'm staying late, they can bite me. I got paid for three hours, not a minute more."

"We're almost done," she told the costumed man, whose bowl-full-of-jelly middle appeared homemade.

If only his nature were as true-to-character as his appearance. Though, she had to admit, right at this particular moment, his foul mood was understandable. He'd had to go dry his pants under a hand-dryer in the men's room after one boy had gotten so excited he'd peed himself. And Santa.

To be fair, Santa wasn't the only fraud around here this afternoon. Her own costume didn't exactly suit her personality, either. She felt like an idiot in the old elf getup, a leftover from her college days. But the kids loved it. And a happy, relaxed kid made for an easy-to-shoot kid…and great pictures.

All in all, she'd have to say this event had been a great success. Both for Elite Construction—whose employees had to be among the happiest in the city today—and for herself. Since moving back to Chicago from New York ten months ago, she'd been trying to build her business up to the level of success she'd had back east. Things were getting better—much—but a quick infusion of cash for an easy afternoon's work definitely helped.

Finally, after the last child in line had been seen

to, Lucy eyed the chubby man in red. "I think that's about it." She glanced at a clock on the wall. "Five minutes to spare."

"Damn good thing," he said. "God, I hate kids."

Lucy's mouth fell open; she couldn't help gawking. "Then why on earth do you do this?"

He pointed toward himself—his white hair, full beard, big belly. "What else am I gonna do, play the Easter bunny?"

Not unless he wanted to terrify every child on earth into swearing off candy. "Bet you can land a part in the stage version of *The Nightmare Before Christmas*," she mumbled. He sure looked like the Oogie Boogie man. And was about as friendly.

Lucy turned to the children lingering around the edges of the area that had been set up as "Santa's Workshop"—complete with fluffy fake snow, a throne and stuffed reindeer. Whoever had decorated for this party had really done a fantastic job. These kids had already had their turn on the big guy's lap, but were still crowded around the crotchety St. Nick. "It's time for Santa to get back to his workshop so he can finish getting ready for his big sleigh ride tomorrow night," she announced. "Santa, do you want to say anything before you leave?"

Father Friggin' Christmas grimaced and brushed cookie crumbs off his lap as he rose. "Be good or you won't get nothin'," he told them, adding a belly laugh to try to take the sting out of the words. His feigned heartiness fooled everyone under the age of ten, but certainly none of the adults. Waddling through the crowd toward the elevator, he didn't stop to pat one youngster on the head, or tickle a single chin.

Jerk.

For her part, Lucy found the little ones in their party clothes and patent leather shoes irresistible. Sweet, happy, so filled with life and laughter and excitement. There was one boy who was so photogenic he ought to be on the cover of a magazine, and she was dying to talk to his parents about a formal sitting.

You've come a long way, baby.

A very long way. To think she'd once vowed to never take a Santa photo, equating kid portraiture with one of Dante's circles of hell.

When she'd first set her sites on photography for her future, she'd argued with her brother over leaving Chicago to go to NYU to study. Then they'd argued when she'd decided to go from there to Europe, insisting she didn't want to take baby's-first-haircut pictures, dreaming instead of high fashion. Models and travel and exotic locations and *French Vogue* magazine covers.

She'd done all of that. Well, except for the magazine cover, though one of her shots had landed in a fashion week edition.

Yet, when all was said and done, she'd ended up finding her niche, her innermost talent and her satisfaction, back in the good old U.S. of A., working with children. It was, in this business, her claim to fame. Frankly, she was damn good at it. She'd made a name for herself in New York, her signature being the use of one color image in black-and-white shots.

A toy, a piece of candy, a shirt or bandanna…something bright and sassy that demanded attention. Just like her photographs did.

Now she needed to drum up the same level of business in Chicago—which, despite her having been gone for so many years, was still her hometown. No, she'd never imagined moving back here, but when her brother, Sam, had gone through a messy divorce and seemed so lonely, she'd decided family came before anything elsc. Shc was all hc had, and vice versa. So she'd returned.

Talk about changing your plans. Who'd have imagined it? Certainly not Lucy. And not her best friend from college, Kate, who still laughed about both her change in career path and in residence. Kate remembered Lucy's home-and-kids-are-boring stance in the old days.

Kate. She needed to give the other woman a call. Lucy hadn't seen her friend since she'd moved, though she and Kate kept in touch with frequent calls. Kate's two children were the ones who'd really opened her mind to the wondrous possibilities of tiny faces and hands and smiles, and she wanted to make sure their Christmas presents had arrived in time.

Those gifts—and working this party in the ridiculous getup—were about the sum total of her Christmas activities this year. Her brother had to work the whole weekend, cops not getting every holiday off the way civilians did. And though she was now back near the Chicago suburb where she'd grown up, she no longer had any close friends here who might have invited her over.

Not that she would have gone. Lucy avoided Christmas like the plague, and had for years. She'd just as soon pretend the holiday wasn't happening.

Most people would probably think that pathetic; Lucy found it a relief. Especially since the weatherman was saying a storm to rival the one at the start of Rudolph the Red Nosed Reindeer was on the way. It was supposed to roll in tonight and shut down the city with a couple of feet of the white stuff by Christmas morning. Sounded like an excellent time to be locked in her warm apartment with her Kindle and a bunch of chocolate and wine. Or chocolate wine—her new addiction.

Eyeing the gray sky through the expansive wall of windows, she began to pack up her gear. The party was winding down, only a dozen or so people remaining on this floor, which had been transformed from cubicles and meeting rooms to a holiday funland. She smiled at those nearest to her, then, seeing the glances at her silly hat, reached up to tug it off her head.

Before she could do it, however, she heard a voice. A deep, male voice—smooth and sexy, and so not Santa's.

"I hear that you did a terrific job."

Lucy didn't respond, letting her brain process what she was hearing. Her whole body had stiffened, the hairs on the back of her neck standing up, her skin tightening into tiny goose bumps. Because that voice sounded familiar. *Impossibly* familiar.

It can't be.

"It sounds like the kids had a great time."

Unable to stop herself, she began to turn around, wondering if her ears—and all her other senses—were deceiving her. After all, six years was a long time, the mind could play tricks. What were the odds that she'd bump into *him* here? And today of all days. December 23. *Six years exactly.* Was that really possible?

One look—and the accompanying frantic thudding of her heart—and she knew her ears and brain were working just fine. Because it was *him.* Ross Marshall.

"Oh, my God," he whispered, shocked, frozen, staring as intently as she was. "Lucy?"

She nodded slowly, not taking her eyes off him, wondering why the years had made him even more attractive than ever. It didn't seem fair, or just. Not when she'd spent the past six years thinking he must have started losing that thick, golden-brown hair, or added a spare tire to that trim, muscular form or lost some of the sparkle from those green eyes.

Huh-uh.

The man was gorgeous. Truly, without-a-doubt, mouthwateringly handsome, and every bit as hot as he'd been the first time she'd laid eyes on him. But he wasn't that young, lean, hungry-looking guy anymore. Now he was all fully realized, powerful, strong—and devastatingly attractive—man.

She'd been twenty-two when they met, he two years older. And during the brief time they'd spent together, Ross had blown away all her preconceived notions of who she was, what she wanted and what she would do when the right guy came along.

He'd been her first lover.

They'd shared an amazing holiday season. But after that one Christmas, they had never seen each other again. Until now.

Well, doesn't this just suck?

"Hello, Ross," she murmured, wondering when her life had become a comedy movie. Because wasn't this always the way those things opened? The plucky, unlucky-in-love heroine coming face-to-face with the one guy she'd never been able to forget while dressed in a ridiculous costume? It was right out of central casting 101—what else could she be wearing other than a short green dress with bells and holly on the collar, red-and-white striped hose, pointy-toed shoes and the dippy green hat with the droopy feather? The only thing that could make the scene more perfect was if she'd been draped across the grouchy Santa's lap, trying to evade his gropey hands, when the handsome hero came up to rescue her.

He did rescue you once. Big time.

Her heart twisted, as it always did when she thought about that... The way Ross had been there for her in what could have been a horrible moment. Whatever had happened later—however much she resented him now—she would never forget that he'd been there to keep her from getting hurt.

But that had been a long time ago. She was no longer that girl and she no longer needed any man's rescue.

"It's really you," he murmured.

"In the flesh."

"I can't believe it."

"That makes two of us," she admitted.

Her brain scrambled to find more words, to form thoughts or sentences. But she just couldn't. If she'd woken up this morning to find her bed had floated up into the sky on a giant helium balloon, she couldn't have been more surprised than she was right now.

Or more disturbed.

Because she wasn't supposed to see him again. Wasn't supposed to care again. Wasn't supposed to even think of getting hurt by him again.

She'd played this scene once, and at exactly this time of year. No way was she ready for a repeat.

She knew all that, knew it down to her soul. So why, oh why, was her heart singing? Crazy expression that, but it was true. There was music in her head and brightness in her eyes and a smile fought to emerge on her lips.

Because it was Ross. The guy she'd met *exactly* six years ago today. The man she'd fallen crazy in love with.

At Christmastime.

CHAPTER TWO

Then
New York, December 23, 2005

HMM. DECISIONS, DECISIONS.

Lucy honestly wasn't sure what would be the best tool for the job. After all, it wasn't every day she was faced with a project of this magnitude. As a photography student at NYU, she usually spent more time worrying about creating things rather than hacking them up.

Big knife? No, she might not get the right angle and could end up cutting herself.

Scissors? Probably not strong enough to cut through *that.*

Razor? She doubted her Venus was up to the task, and had no idea how to get one of those old-fashioned straight-edged ones short of robbing a barber.

A chainsaw or a hatchet?

Probably overkill. And killing wasn't the objective.

After all, she didn't really want to kill Jude Zacharias. She just wanted to separate him from his favorite part of his cheating anatomy. AKA: the part he'd cheated with.

Lucy didn't even realize she'd been mumbling aloud. Not until her best friend, Kate, who sat across from her in this trendy Manhattan coffee-and-book shop interjected, "You're not going to cut off his dick, so stop fantasizing about it."

Nobody immediately gasped at Kate's words, so obviously they hadn't been overheard. Not surprising—they were tucked in a back corner of the café. Plus, Beans & Books was crowded with shoppers frenzied by the realization that they only had one and a half shopping days left before Christmas. Each was listening only to the holiday countdown clock in his or her head.

"Have *you* stopped fantasizing about having sex with Freddie Prinze Jr. and Jake Gyllenhaal at the same time?" she countered.

"Hey, *that* could actually happen," Kate said with a smirk. "It's at least possible. Unlike the chance that you, Miss Congeniality, would actually go all Bobbitt on a guy's ass, even if he does totally deserve it."

It wasn't Jude's ass she wanted to…Bobbit. She knew, however, that Kate was right. Lucy wasn't the violent type, except in her fantasies. She might have fun playing a mental game of *why-I-oughta* but she knew nothing would come of it.

"Can't I at least wallow and scheme for an hour?"

"Sure. But we should've done it over beer or tequila in a dive bar. Coffee in a crowded shop just doesn't lend itself to wallowing and scheming."

True. Especially now that this place was no longer the same quiet, cozy hangout she'd loved since coming to New York three and a half years ago. It had once been her favorite place to meet up with friends, do some homework, or just enjoy the silence amid the scent of freshly ground arabica beans.

Since a recent renovation, though, it had turned from a cute, off-the-beaten-track coffee bar into a crazed, credit-card magnet, filled with overpriced gift books, calendars and stationery. Driven city dwellers who excelled at multitasking were flocking to the place to kill two birds with one stone. They could buy a last-minute gift for Great-Aunt Susie—a ridiculously overpriced coffee table book titled *The Private Lives of Garden Gnomes,* perhaps—while they waited for their Lite Pomegranate Vanilla Oolang Tea Lattes with whip.

Christmas had been reduced to expedience, kitsch and trendy drinks. Fortunately for her, she'd dropped out of the holiday a few years ago and had no intention of dropping back in.

"Face it, girlfriend, revenge just ain't your style. You're as violent as a Smurf." Kate grinned. "Or one of Santa's elves."

"Not funny," Lucy said, rolling her eyes. "*So* not funny."

Her friend knew how much she disliked the silly costume she had to wear for her "internship" with a local photographer. Intern? Ha. She was a ridiculously dressed *unpaid* Christmas elf wiping the drool off kids' chins as they sat on Santa's lap. What could be more sad to someone who dreamed of being a serious photographer? Someone who was leaving to study abroad in Paris next month, and hoped to go back there to live after graduation? Someone who planned to spend the next several years shooting her way across Europe, one still image at a time?

That girl shouldn't care about Jude. That girl *didn't* care about Jude.

But at this moment, Lucy didn't feel like that girl. For all the violent fantasies, what *this* girl felt right now was hurt.

"You know, for the life of me, I still can't figure out why I ever went out with him in the first place." She swallowed, hard. "I should have known better."

Kate's smirk faded and she reached over to squeeze Lucy's hand. Kate had been witness to what had been Lucy's most humiliating moment ever. Said moment being when Lucy had let herself in to her boyfriend Jude's apartment, to set up his big surprise birthday party that was scheduled for tonight.

Surprise! Your boyfriend is a lying, cheating asshat!

Jude had already gotten started on his birthday celebration. Contrary to his claim that he was going to "pop in" on his family for the day, Jude had apparently decided to stay in town and pop in on his neighbor's vagina.

At least, that's who Lucy thought had been kneeling in front of the sofa with Jude's johnson in her mouth when she and Kate had walked into the apartment. She couldn't be certain. They only saw the back of the bare-ass naked woman's head—oh, plus her bare ass and, uh, the rest of her nether regions. *Ew, ew, ew.* She was still fighting the urge to thrust two coffee stirrers into her eyes to gouge out the image burned onto her retinas. If she'd ever had any doubt she was strictly hetero, her response to that sight would have removed it.

"Maybe I should ask Teddy to beat him up."

Teddy, Kate's boyfriend, was as broad as a table, and could snap Jude like a twig. There was just one problem. "He's more of a pacifist than I am," Lucy said with a smile, knowing Kate had intended to make her laugh. Teddy was the sweetest guy on the planet. "Besides, we both know Jude's not worth the trouble."

"No, he's not." Then Kate grinned. "I am glad you got off a couple of good zingers, though. I still can't believe you asked him if the store was out of birthday candles and that's why he'd found something else that needed to be blown."

That, she had to admit, had been a pretty good line. It was a rare occurrence; the kind of one-liner she usually would have thought of hours later, when reliving the awful experience in her mind. Though, in this instance, since she was now feeling more sad than anything else, she might have been picturing herself asking him why he'd felt the need to be so deceitful.

If he'd told her it wasn't working out and he wanted to see other people, would she have been devastated?

No. A little disappointed, probably, but not crushed.

But to be cheated on—and to walk in on it? *That* rankled.

"Of course, I wouldn't have been able to speak.

I'da been busy ripping the extensions outta that ho's head," Kate added.

"She didn't cheat on me, Jude did." Then, curious, she asked, "How do you know they were extensions?"

"Honey, that carpet *so* didn't match those drapes."

Though a peal of laughter emerged from her mouth, Lucy also groaned and threw a hand over her eyes, wishing for a bleach eye-wash. "Don't remind me!"

Funny that she could actually manage to laugh. Maybe that said a lot about where her feelings for Jude had really been. This girlfriend-gripe session wasn't so much about Lucy's broken heart as it was her disappointed expectations.

She'd really wanted Jude to be a nice guy. A good guy.

Face it, you just wanted someone *in your life.*

Maybe that was true. Seeing the former man-eater Kate so happy was inspiring. But her brother Sam's recent engagement had also really affected her. Their tiny family unit—made even tinier when they'd been left alone in the world after the deaths of their parents—was going to change. Sam had found someone, he was forming a new family, one she'd always be welcome in but wasn't actually a major part of.

She'd wanted something like that, too. Or at least the possibility of something like that, someday. Heck, maybe deep down she also just hadn't wanted to haul her virginity along with her to Europe, and had been hoping she'd finally found the guy who would truly inspire her to shuck it.

Yes, that was probably why she'd let down her guard and gotten involved with Jude when she'd known he wasn't the right one in the long run. Being totally honest, she knew she was more sad at the idea of losing the boyfriend than at losing the actual guy. Not to mention continuing to carry the virgin mantle around her neck.

"Well, at least you didn't sleep with him!" said Kate, who'd had more lovers than Lucy had had birthdays.

"I'll drink to that," she said, sipping her coffee, meaning it. Because being stuck with a hymen was better than having let somebody so rotten remove it.

Something inside her must have recognized that about him, and held her back. Deep down she'd known there was something wrong about the relationship, even though he'd gone out of his way to make it seem so very right.

Maybe Lucy really was the oldest living virgin in New York—kept that way throughout high school by her bad-ass older brother's reputation, and throughout college out of her own deep-rooted romantic streak. Whatever the reason, she'd waited this long. So, as much as she wanted to know what all the fuss was about, she hadn't been about to leap into bed with Jude just because he'd said he liked her photography and opened the door for her when they went out, unlike most other college-aged dudes she knew.

Good thing. Because it had all been an act. The nice, patient, tender guy didn't exist. Jude had put on that persona the way somebody else might don a

Halloween costume, sliding into it to be the man she wanted, then taking it off—along with the rest of his clothes—when she wasn't around. He shouldn't be studying to be an attorney, an actor would be much more appropriate. God, could she have been any more gullible?

Maybe Sam was right. Maybe she really had no business living on her own in New York or, worse, going off to Europe. Perhaps she was a lamb in the midst of wolves. She should've just stayed in the Chicago suburb where they'd grown up, gone to community college, done first-communion portraits at Sears, married a nice local guy and gotten to work on producing cousins for Sam's future kids. At least then she wouldn't be sitting here all sad at being cheated on by someone she'd hoped was Prince Charming.

"More like King Creeper," she muttered.

"Huh?"

"Nothing. Just thinking about Jude."

Kate nodded, frowned and muttered, "Why are most men jerks? Other than Teddy, of course."

"Your guess is as good as mine."

"There have to be other decent men out there, right?"

"Sam's one," Lucy admitted. "And my Dad sure was."

"Mine is, too." Kate frowned in thought. "Your father managed a car dealership, didn't he?"

"Yes."

"And your brother, Sam, is a cop. My dad's in sales, and Teddy's a trucker. Hmm."

"Your point being?"

Kate tapped the tip of her finger on her mouth. "Most of the guys you've dated have been like Jude. Rich, future attorneys, politicians, doctors…and dickheads, one and all."

Lucy nodded, conceding the point.

"And that's the type I dated, before I met Teddy."

She started to get the picture. "Ahh."

"So maybe you need to look for an everyday guy, who works hard for a living, hasn't had everything handed to him."

That sounded ideal. Unfortunately Lucy couldn't remember the last time she'd met anyone like that. They sure didn't seem to be on the campus of NYU.

"A guy who's so hot he makes you stick to your chair when you watch his muscles bunch under his sweaty T-shirt as he works," Kate said, sounding lost in thought. She was staring past Lucy, as if visualizing this blue collar stud-muffin. "Who knows what to do with his hands, and has enough self-confidence that he doesn't have to show off in front of a woman."

Not used to Kate being so descriptive—but definitely liking the description—Lucy could only nod.

"Somebody like *him*."

This time, Kate's stare was pointed and her gaze speculative. Surprised, Lucy quickly turned to look over her shoulder, toward the front corner of the shop, and saw the *him* in question.

And oh, wow, what a him.

He was young—in his early twenties, probably, like her. But he didn't look much like the guys she interacted with on a daily basis at school. He had on a pair of faded, worn jeans, that hung low on his very lean hips. They were tugged down even further by the work belt he wore over them, which was weighted with various tools. Powerful hammers, long screwdrivers, steely drills. All hard. Strong. Stiff.

Get your mind out of his toolbelt.

She did, shaking her head quickly to get her attention going in another direction. Of course, there wasn't any other direction to go…he was hot any way you looked at it.

So she looked at it. Er, him.

Lucy lifted her gaze, taking in the whole tall, lean, powerful package. Though he wore the tools of the trade, he was not built like a brawny construction-worker type. Strong, yes, but with a youthful leanness—Hugh Jackman as Leopold, not as Wolverine.

Yum.

His entire body told tales of hard work An impressive set of abs rippled visibly beneath the sweat-tinged T-shirt. His broad chest and thickly muscled arms moved with almost poetic precision as he finished installing a new bookcase in the back corner of the shop.

He lifted one arm and wiped a sheen of sweat off his forehead, which just emphasized the handsomeness of his face, seen only in profile. He had a strong, square jaw, a straight nose. High cheekbones emphasized the lightly stubbled hollows below, lending his lean face an air of youth and power.

His light brown hair was longish, a little shaggy,

and he swept it back from his brow with an impatient hand. Seeing the strong hands in motion made Lucy let out a long, slow breath, and when he turned around and she beheld him from the back, she had to suck in another one. Oh, my, did the man know how to fill out a pair of jeans.

Apparently she wasn't the only woman who'd noticed. What she'd taken for shopper's distraction earlier she now realized had been female appreciation for the beautiful display of raw, powerful male in the corner. Every other woman in the place was either sneaking peeks or outright gaping.

She was a gaper. No peeking about it.

Finally realizing she was literally turned in her seat to stare, and probably had drool dripping down her chin, she swung back around to face Kate. Her friend wore a similar expression. "Wow," she admitted.

"Double wow. If I didn't love Teddy, I'd be over there offering to take care of his *tool* for him."

Lucy couldn't help being wicked when she was around Kate. "I bet it could use some lubrication."

"Atta girl!"

"But I think you'd have to stand in line."

"With you?" Kate asked, her eyes sparkling.

Lucy shook her head. "I don't think so. Cheated on and heartbroken an hour ago, remember?"

"Well, cheated on, anyway," said Kate, perceptive as always.

"Touché," Lucy admitted, not terribly surprised to realize she was already feeling better. What had felt like heartbreak ninety minutes ago had segued into a heart cramp. Now it was barely a heart twinge.

Kate glanced at her empty cup, and at Lucy's. "One more?"

"Sure."

"I got it," the other woman said, grabbing her bag. She stood up and walked toward the counter near the front of the shop.

Lucy sighed deeply, then forced herself to put Jude out of her mind. Time to forget about him. He hadn't been her lover, merely a boyfriend who'd gotten a hand down her pants just once in three months. Absolutely forgettable.

Besides which, she had other things to think about. Like Christmas, now just two days away. And the fact that she was spending it alone.

Your own fault. She'd made the choice. Kate was going away with Teddy tonight so the apartment would be empty. But Sam had begged her to come back to Chicago to celebrate Christmas with his fiancée's family. Lucy had refused, claiming she had too much work to do over the holidays.

Truth was, she couldn't handle a big family Christmas. The last traditional holiday season she'd experienced had been a week before her parents had been swept from her life by a stupid asshole who'd decided to celebrate a promotion by having a few bourbons, then getting behind the wheel of a car.

It had been just her and Sam for five years now, and each Christmas had been more nontraditional than the last. One year ago, they'd been in Mexico, lying on a beach, ignoring the merriment around them in favor of rum drinks and steel drums.

Though Sam was ready to dive back into the holiday spirit with his new fiancée, somehow, Lucy just couldn't face it yet. Honestly, she wasn't sure she'd ever be able to again. Christmas had once been her favorite holiday; it seemed almost sacrilege to enjoy it without the two people who had made it so special for the first seventeen years of her life.

Now she had another thing to add to her why-I-should-skip Christmas list: she'd been cheated on—right before the holiday. The angel on the top of Jude's tree had borne witness to the extension-wearing ho who went around sucking on dicks that belonged to other girls. Er, other girls' boyfriends.

"The whole holiday is just overrated," she told herself. "Better off just forgetting about it."

Not to mention a few other things. Like love. Romance.

And men.

"EXCUSE ME, SIR, can I ask you a favor?"

Ross Marshall heard a young woman speaking, but since he knew she wasn't talking to him, he didn't bother turning around. He instead remained focused on putting the finishing touches on the custom-made bookcase he'd been asked to install today. Thankfully, despite his concerns about the off-kilter walls in this old New York building, every shelving unit he'd built for Beans & Books had fit beautifully. Including this last one.

"Sir?"

Though curious, since the voice sounded a little insistent, again he ignored her. He tried to avoid the customers and usually didn't work until later in the evening when the shop was closed. The owner really wanted the final unit installed today, however—gotta have more shelf space to grab those crazy day-before-Christmas-Eve shoppers who'd be filling the aisles tonight. So he'd agreed to come in right after the frenetic lunch hour but before the five o'clock rush.

He'd still arrived just in time to listen to modern-day robber barons having power coffees while making let's-take-over-the-world deals via Bluetooth. Oh, and their trophy wives stopping by between Junior League meetings and museum openings to grab a Fat-Free Cappuccino with Soy milk and carob drizzle.

Manhattan was like a different planet. He preferred Chicago, which he'd called home for the first twenty-three of his twenty-four years. It was almost as big and half as pretentious.

"Hellooooo?"

Finally realizing the woman might actually be speaking to him, which he hadn't imagined since in New York nobody called hammer jockeys "sir," he turned around. The young woman *had* been addressing him—she was staring at him, her eyes narrowed, her freckled cheeks flushed and her mouth tugged down into a frown.

"I'm sorry, I didn't realize you were talking to me." He offered her a smile. "I'm not used to being called sir."

The blonde relaxed. "Oh, yeah. Sorry. Hey, listen, could I ask you a big favor?"

He stiffened the tiniest bit. He might not be used to being called sir around here, but he'd received a lot of suggestive invitations lately. It seemed men with calluses were, for some reason, catnip to the rich Manhattan types. "Yes?"

"See my friend over there at the table in the far corner?"

Ross glanced over, seeing the back of a woman seated in the shadowy rear corner of the place. Then he looked again, interested despite himself in the stunning, thick brown hair that fell in loose, curly waves halfway down her back. She stood out from every other female in the place—most of whom sported a more typical, reserved, New York professional-woman's blow-out or bun. Ross's hands started to tingle, as if anticipating what it might be like to sink his fingers into those silky strands.

He shoved them into his pockets. "What about her?"

"She's my best friend—we're both students. Anyway, she needs some help for this project she's working on. We've been sitting over there talking about it and trying to figure out what tool would be best." She lifted her shoulders in a shrug. "But we're both pretty clueless about that kind of stuff. Do you think you could go over and offer her your expertise?"

It sounded screwy to him, and the young woman looked like she was about to break into a grin. But something—*that hair*—made him curious to see more of the girl with the tool problem.

He looked again. This time, the brunette had turned a little, as if looking around for her friend, and he caught a glimpse of her face. Creamy-skin. Cute nose. Long lashes. Full mouth.

His heart-rate kicked up a notch; he was interested in spite of himself. "What kind of job is it?" he asked as he began to pack up his portable toolbox.

"Well, uh…it might be best if she explains that herself." As if sensing he was skeptical, she added, "She's a photography student, you see, and I'm in journalism. Between the two of us, we barely know the difference between a hammer and a chainsaw."

He shouldn't. Really. Even though he was finished here, he had some things to do for another project scheduled to start the day after Christmas. He needed to phone in a few orders, go to the lumberyard, go over the design he'd sketched out.

Of course, all that would have to come after he risked life and limb at the most miserable place on earth to be today: the nearest shipping store. He had to get his family's Christmas gifts sent off, via overnight delivery, obviously. Seemed in the past week he had gone from busy self-employed carpenter to forgetful procrastinating shopper. Bad enough that he wasn't going home for Christmas; if he didn't get a gift in front of his youngest sister, he'd never hear the end of it.

Yet even with all that, he was tempted to take ten minutes to see if the brunette was really as attractive as she looked from here. Not to mention seeing what this mystery project was.

"Please? I'm sure it won't take long. Besides, helping someone else will put you in the holiday spirit," the girl said, managing to sound pious, despite the mischief in her expression.

He chuckled at her noble tone. Her smile and the twinkle in her eyes told him something else was going on. She was probably playing some kind of matchmaking game. Hell, for all he knew, the brunette had put her up to this, wanting to meet him but not wanting to come on too strong.

That was okay. Because he suddenly wanted to meet her, too.

And if the blonde was on the up-and-up, and the woman did need some help, well, that was okay, too. Maybe doing something nice for someone—someone super hot with soft-looking hair he wanted to rub all over his bare skin—was just what he needed. Certainly nothing else was putting him in the holiday spirit. He was too busy working—trying to prove to himself and to everyone else that he could make it on his own and didn't need to go to work in the family business—to care much about celebrating.

His mom suspected that was why he wasn't coming home for Christmas, because he didn't want to get another guilt trip or have another argument with his dad. She wasn't entirely wrong.

"Okay," he said, seeing the shop owner smiling broadly at him from behind the counter, obviously thrilled that even more expensive holiday junk could be shoveled in front of potential customers within the hour. "Just give me a few minutes."

"Oh, thank you!"

The freckled blonde turned and headed not for her friend in the back corner, but toward the door of the shop. Like she was making herself scarce so her friend could make her move. He grinned, wondering why girls went through these motions. He would probably have been even more interested if the brunette had just come up to him herself and said hello.

Finishing up with a customer, the owner came out from around the counter. He offered Ross his exuberant thanks for having squeezed in this job so quickly. Ross accepted the check for final payment—which, he noted, included a nice holiday bonus—then shook the man's hand and picked up his tools. Then it was decision time. Head for the exit and get busy doing what he needed to do? Or take a few minutes out of his day to possibly be hit-on by a very pretty girl who'd gotten her friend to play matchmaker?

Hell. He might be hungry, might need work to pay his bills. But he was twenty-four, human and male. Pretty girl trumped food any day of the week.

Heading toward her table, he brushed some sawdust off his arms, nodding politely at the several women who smiled and murmured holiday greetings. The brunette hadn't moved from her seat, though he did see her look from side to side, as if she wanted to turn around to see if he was coming over, but didn't wish to be too obvious about it.

She so *set this up.*

Frankly, Ross couldn't bring himself to care.

He walked up behind her, about to clear his throat and introduce himself, when he heard her say something. She was alone, obviously, and had to be talking to herself. And what she said pierced a hole in the ego that had been telling him she'd sent a friend over to get his attention.

"You know you'd have been scared to even pick up a chainsaw," she muttered. "Or even an electric knife!"

Damn. She really was talking about tools? Some project that she needed to do?

Ross had to laugh at himself. Wouldn't his youngest sister—always his biggest critic—be laughing her ass off right now? He'd been all cocky and sure this sexy coed was about to come on to him…and she really was interested only in his toolbelt.

"Forget the electric knife," he said, intruding on her musings, the carpenter in him shuddering at the thought. "They're not made for cutting anything other than meat."

The girl swung her head up to look at him, her eyes rounding in shock and her mouth dropping open.

Big brown eyes. Full, pink-lipped mouth.

Then there was the perfect, heart-shaped face. And oh, that hair. Thick and shining, with soft brown waves that framed her face, and curls that tumbled well down her back. There wasn't a guy alive who wouldn't imagine all that hair being the only thing wrapped around her naked body; well, except for his *own* naked body.

He stared, unable to do anything else. She'd been pretty from across the room. Up close, she was beautiful enough to make his heart forget it was supposed to beat.

"Excuse me?" she said, shaking her head lightly as if she couldn't figure out what was happening. "What did you say?"

He cleared his throat. "I said, you need to use the right tool for the job. Electric knives are for cutting meat. Now what is it you were thinking about cutting through?"

"Meat," she replied, then quickly clamped her lips shut.

He laughed, admiring her quick wit. "Beef or pork?"

"I'd say pork loin," she replied, her mouth twisting a bit. "But I was joking. I definitely don't need to cut any meat."

"I figured," he said. Without waiting for an invitation, he walked around the table and sat in the vacant chair, facing her. He told himself it was because he'd promised her friend he'd offer her some construction advice. In truth, he just wanted to look at her a little more. Hear her voice. See whether she had a personality to go with the looks.

Most guys his age probably wouldn't care. Ross, though, did.

He might be young, but he wasn't inexperienced. And he'd learned very early on that a pretty face and smoking-hot body were enough before hitting the sheets. But after that, if there wasn't a great sense of humor, big heart and a brain to go along with the sexiness, he just couldn't stay interested. Some of his old college buddies used to joke about being happy with tits-on-a-stick. Ross preferred a real woman, from top to bottom.

She seemed like she had a brain. Right now, though, he was wondering about that whole personality thing. Because she just kept staring at him, her face turning pink, as if she didn't know what to say.

Or she was embarrassed.

Hmm. So maybe this wasn't about some mystery project. Because the way she was blushing made him suspect she'd had something wicked on her mind.

More interesting by the minute.

"So, what is this big project?"

"Project?"

"Yeah. Your friend came over, told me you needed some advice on tools for a project you're doing."

She sucked her bottom lip into her mouth and closed her eyes for a second, then whispered, "I'm going to kill her."

"Maybe that's why she left—she needed a running start."

"She *left?*"

"Yep. Right after she came to ask me to help you."

Groaning, she shook her head. "I can't believe this."

"So, she was trying to set us up?"

"I think so."

"What kind of friend does that?" he asked. "She doesn't know me—what if I'm some kind of serial killer or panty thief?"

Her brow went up. “Are you?”

“Am I what?”

“Either of those things?”

He grinned. “No on the first. I’ll take the fifth on the second until we get to know each other.” Certain he wanted that—to get to know her—he stuck out his hand. “I’m Ross.”

She eyed it, then reached out and shook. Her hand was small, soft. Fragile against his own. Having worked only with his hands for months, he knew he had calluses on top of blisters, but she didn’t seem to mind at all. In fact, she was the one who held on for a moment, as if not wanting to let go.

Finally, though, she pulled away, murmuring, “Lucy.”

“Nice to meet you, Lucy.”

“You, too. Especially now that I know you’re not a serial killer.” She flashed a grin. “As for the other, remind me not to walk into Victoria’s Secret with you…wouldn’t want to get arrested as an accomplice.”

“What fun would there be in stealing brand-new panties?” Then, seeing her brow shoot up, he held up a hand. “Kidding. Believe me, stealing underwear isn’t my thing.”

“Helping mystery girls with mysterious projects is?”

“Uh-huh. Now, mysterious girl, back to the mysterious project.”

“There isn’t one.”

“Your friend made it up?”

She shifted her gaze, those long lashes lowering.

"Not exactly. I was, um, wondering which tool to use to, uh, remove something. And she obviously thought it would be fun to bring you into my fantasies." She gasped, staring him in the eye. "I mean, I wasn't… it's not that I was fantasizing about you!"

"Aww, I'm crushed."

"If you knew the fantasy, you wouldn't be," she said, her tone droll.

"So why don't you tell me?" he asked, only half-teasing. What *did* a beautiful young woman fantasize about? More importantly, *who?*

"Believe me, you don't want to know."

"Oh, trust me on this, I definitely do."

She studied him for a moment, eyeing him intently as if to see if he was serious. Then, apparently realizing he was, she came right out and told him.

CHAPTER THREE

Now
Chicago, December 23, 2011

JUST BECAUSE ROSS Marshall hadn't seen Lucy Fleming for six years did not mean he didn't instantly recognize her. It did, however, mean his heart literally thudded in his chest and his brain seemed to flatline. The huge, open reception area of his office—decorated with lights and greenery—seemed to darken. It also appeared to shrink, squeezing in tight, crushing his ribs, making his head throb, sending him off-kilter. He couldn't form a single coherent thought.

Well, maybe one. *You cut your hair?* He had the presence of mind to notice that the long, riotous curls that had once fallen well down her back had been tamed and shortened. Then everything just went blank.

She couldn't be here, right? Could not *possibly* be here. This had to be a dream—he was still sleeping and she was visiting his nighttime fantasies, as she so often had over the years.

He couldn't resist, needing to grab the moment before he woke up. He lifted a hand, put it on her shoulder, felt the solid, real person beneath the elf costume. She didn't immediately pull away, and he leaned a little bit closer, breathing deeply, recognizing the scent that was uniquely Lucy. Not a perfume or a lotion or her shampoo. Just something distinctive and evocative that called to his memories, reminding him that she had been *the one.*

And he'd let her get away.

"You're not dreaming," she told him, her tone dry.

He dropped his hand and stepped back, needing to get his head back in the game. "Guess that means you're not, either."

"That thought did cross my mind," she said, her big brown eyes inquisitive. "I certainly never expected to run into you, today of all days."

He knew the day. Knew it well. Which just made the meeting all the more surreal. "Same here," he mumbled.

They both fell silent. Lucy appeared as stunned as he was.

Well, why wouldn't she be? They hadn't laid eyes on each other in years. Despite what had happened between them, what they'd shared over that one amazing holiday season, not one word had been exchanged between them since mid-January, nearly six years ago. Not a card, not a phone call. No chance of bumping into each other since, the last he'd known, she had been bound for Europe.

But here she was. Not just in Chicago, but in his office.

His freaking office!

"What are you doing here?" he asked, his brain not catching up yet. It should be obvious. Lucy had been studying photography when they'd met. Besides which, she was carrying a camera bag. And was dressed as an elf.

A smile tried to tug at his lips. He remembered that elf costume. Remembered it so well.

Suddenly he was remembering everything so well.

Some things *too* well.

"I'm working," she said, her head going up, that pretty mouth tightening. "Did you happen to notice the picture-with-Santa session that's been going on for the past couple of hours?"

He'd barely noticed anything that was going on, being too busy working to socialize. The employee Christmas party had been a long-standing tradition with Elite Construction, the company his grandfather had founded, and he now ran. That didn't mean the boss ever had much time to participate in it. He'd made the rounds, thanked his employees, greeted their kids and wives, then retreated back into his office for the last two hours, only coming out to say goodbye now that things were winding down.

"I noticed," he finally replied.

"Well, that was me behind the camera."

"I know that, I heard you did a great job and was coming over to meet you," he said, still knocked off-kilter by her mere presence.

"Sorry, Santa's gone. No more pictures. Though, if you want to sit on the chair, I guess I could snap a shot of you holding a candy cane and a teddy bear."

Still sassy. God, he'd always liked that about her.

"I meant, I was coming to thank you for agreeing to do the party on such short notice."

"You didn't know *I* was the elf until just now?" she asked, sounding slightly suspicious. As if wondering if he'd set up this little reunion.

Huh. If he'd known she was nearby, he might have considered doing just that—even though Lucy probably wouldn't have been thrilled about it, judging by the look on her face.

"I swear, I had no idea." He was suddenly very interested in talking to his assistant, wondering how she'd found Lucy. He also wondered if the motherly, slightly nosy woman had been doing a little matchmaking. He wouldn't put it past her. She was nothing if not a closet romantic.

"My real question was," he continued, "what are you doing here in Chicago? You swore you'd never live here. Hell, I figured you'd be in Europe."

That had been her dream, living overseas, being a world-traveling photographer. So what had happened? She had seemed utterly determined that she would never stay near home and take…Santa pictures of little kids.

He glanced at the velvet-covered chair, the fluffy fake snow, the tripod, and her, back in that elf suit.

How on earth had her life gotten so derailed?

"I was for a while, did my semester abroad and went back right after graduation," she said.

Just as she'd planned. Which was one reason he'd stayed out of touch, knowing an entire ocean was going to separate them, so why bother trying to make something work when geography said it couldn't?

"And?"

"And I wasn't happy, so I ended up back in New York a few years ago."

Years. She'd been on the same continent for years. A short plane ride away. The thought made him slightly sick to his stomach, especially considering the number of times he'd thought about her during that same time span. The curiosity about whether she'd kept the same cell phone number and whether it would work in Paris.

Maybe not. But it probably would have in New York. Damn.

"How did Chicago enter the equation?"

"You remember, I grew up in this area?"

He remembered, but she'd seemed adamant about never coming back here, associating it with her tragic loss. "I remember."

"Well, I moved back here ten months ago to be closer to my brother."

Even as another wave of shocked pleasure washed over him—she'd moved *here,* to the very same city—the brother's name immediately popped into his mind. "Sam?"

"Right. He went through a pretty bad divorce and I thought he could use some family nearby."

"That's a shame…about the divorce, I mean."

"Yes, it is. I really thought they'd make it."

"Does anybody anymore?" he mumbled before he could think better of it.

Her whole body stiffened, and he mentally kicked himself for going there. Because he and Lucy sure hadn't.

Then again, had they expected to? Hell, what had happened between them had been so sudden, so unexpected. Neither of them had been in the right place for any kind of relationship—mentally, emotionally, financially, or in any other way.

Except physically. Oh, yeah. There they'd been absolutely perfect together.

It had been so good during the incredibly brief time it lasted. Honestly, looking back, he could say it was the best Christmas Eve he'd ever had in his life.

Followed by the worst Christmas Day.

"How do you like being back in Chicago?" he asked, sensing she was trying to gracefully exit stage left.

"It's cold," she said with a shrug, not giving an inch, not softening up a bit. Hell, he supposed he couldn't blame her.

"You look like you've done well for yourself," she said, an almost grudging tone to her voice. She looked him over, head-to-toe, as if wondering where the jeans, T-shirt and tool belt had gone.

Some days—many days—he longed for them. Wearing a suit—even if he usually lost the tie and rolled-up his sleeves at some point every day—just didn't excite him the way working with his hands always had. "I guess. And you?"

She nodded. "I have my own studio."

"Still boycott Christmas?"

She glanced down at her costume. "As much as I possibly can, which isn't easy in my line of work. You still a sappy kid about it?"

He nodded, unashamed. "Absolutely." Even if, for the past five holiday seasons, he'd spent a lot more time wondering about Lucy—where she'd gone, if she'd stayed in Europe, become a famous photographer—than he had worrying about what present to get for which sister, niece or nephew.

As if they'd both run out of small talk for the moment, they returned to staring. Ross couldn't deny it, the years had been good to her; Lucy was beautiful. No perky little elf hat complete with feather could take away from that. Nor could the short dress, striped tights—oh, God, those tights, did they ever bring back memories—and pointy-tipped shoes.

She should look cute and adorable. Instead she looked hot and sexy, bringing wild, intense memories to his mind of the last time he'd seen her wearing that very same outfit.

He was suddenly—forcibly—reminded of how long it had been since he'd had sex.

Good sex? Even longer.

Fabulous, never-forget-it, once-in-a-lifetime sex?

Six years. No doubt about it.

He swallowed as memories flooded over him, having to shift a little. Lucy had always affected him physically. Damned if he wanted anyone to notice that now, though. The CEO wasn't supposed to sport wood at the corporate holiday party.

"I'm impressed that you can still fit into that," he

admitted against his own better judgment. "But not too surprised. You haven't changed a bit."

She flushed. "Maybe not physically. But I'm not the same sweet, wide-eyed kid anymore."

He barked a laugh. "Sweet kid? Aren't you the same person who was planning to dismember her ex-boyfriend when we met?"

"I didn't actually *do* it."

No, she hadn't. As he recalled, Ross had enjoyed the pleasure of taking her ex apart. And it had felt damn good, too.

"That's good—I'd hate to think you've spent the last six years in jail."

"Maybe if you hadn't stopped calling, you'd know where I spent the last six years," she replied, ever-so-sweetly.

Direct hit. He winced. "Look, Lucy..."

She waved a hand, obviously angry at herself for having said anything. "Forget it. Water under the bridge."

"You know what I was going through—why I left New York." Of course she knew, she'd been there when he'd gotten the call that brought him back home.

"I know," she said. "I understood...I under*stand.*"

Maybe. But that not-staying-in-touch thing obviously still rankled.

He'd probably asked himself a dozen times over the years why he hadn't at least tried to get back in touch with her once his life had returned to something resembling normal. Maybe a hundred times. It always came back to the same thing: he was stuck.

His life was here. Hers was…anywhere she wanted it to be. And she'd wanted it to be in another country, and a completely different reality from his, which was filled with contracts and workers-comp issues and the cost of lumber.

She'd been off to capture the world one still image at a time. He'd been boxed in, chained to the past, owing too much to other people to just go and live his life the way he had wanted to.

Not that it had turned out badly. He actually loved running the business and had done a damn fine job of it. He was glad to live in Chicago. He liked the vibe of this city, the people and the culture. So no, he didn't regret coming back here. He had only one regret. Her.

"And now here you are," he murmured, though he hadn't intended to say it out loud.

"Don't make a big thing of it," she insisted. "I had no idea you worked here."

"And if you had known? Would you have taken the job today, risked bumping into me?"

She didn't reply. Which was answer enough.

Lucy really was mad at him. Well, that made two of them; he was mad at himself. Plenty of room for regrets, with six years of what-ifs under his belt. But at the time it had seemed like he was doing the right thing—the best thing—for both of them.

Of course, he'd questioned that just about every day since.

"Excuse me, Ross?"

He glanced away from Lucy, seeing Stella, his administrative assistant, who he'd inherited from *his* father. Who'd inherited her from his father. Older than dirt didn't describe her. She had dirt beat—you'd have to go back to the rocks that had been worn down into the dirt to describe her.

You wouldn't know it to look at her. From the bottled black dye job to the floral-print dress, she could pass for fifty. But Ross knew she'd passed that milestone at least two decades ago. He dreaded the day she was no longer around to keep him organized.

Or to matchmake? He was going to have to have a talk with Stella about that. He knew his assistant thought he was stressed and lonely and spent too much time in the office. Plus, Stella knew about Lucy—she was one of the few people who did, having gotten Ross to reveal the story after one long, stressful day. But would she have gone to that much trouble—tracking Lucy down and getting her here? It seemed crazy.

If it was true, he would have to decide whether to give her hell for meddling in his private affairs...or thank her.

The way Lucy wasn't bothering to hide her dislike made him suspect the former.

The thought that he might be able to get her to change her mind? Definitely the latter.

He didn't deny he was still interested. Still attracted. Judging by the absence of a ring on her left hand, he suspected she was available—at least technically. So maybe it was time to take his shot. See if he could make up for six wasted years. See if there was any way she could forgive him for walking—no, running—away before they ever really had a chance to get started.

"Ross?" Stella prompted again. "Mr. Whitaker is about to leave, and he'd like to see you before he goes."

Whitaker—a client who'd sent a lot of work their way over the past several years. He wasn't somebody Ross could ignore.

"Okay," he said, before turning his attention back to Lucy. "Wait for me." It wasn't a request.

"No, I really have to go. It was nice to see you."

Said like she'd say it was nice to see an elementary school bully she'd loathed for decades. Damn. He'd screwed this up so badly. Six years ago, and today.

"Lucy, please..."

"Uh, Miss Fleming? If you'd step into the office, I can get you your payment right away," Stella interjected. "I'm sure you'd prefer not to have to wait until after the holidays."

Her lush bottom lip snagged between her teeth, Lucy looked torn. Ross glanced at Stella, wondering if she was intentionally using some stalling tactics to keep Lucy around. Then again, if she'd been trying to set them up, she probably wouldn't have interrupted about Whitaker, no matter how important a client he was. So maybe this whole thing had just been luck. Good luck. Incredibly good luck.

And maybe it meant he was going to have another chance with the woman he'd so foolishly let slip away.

HMM. MONEY OR DIGNITY? Go with the bossy assistant, or run like hell? *Decisions, decisions.*

Normally Lucy would have been heading toward the door the second Ross's back was turned. She had work to do, editing, photoshopping, cropping…plus all the stuff a small business owner was responsible for, but which often slipped through the cracks when the customers kept walking steadily through the door.

They wouldn't be walking through the door on Christmas weekend, though, so she should be able to catch up. And one thing she needed to catch up on was ordering. She had some equipment to buy, and paying for it by December 31 would make her tax bill a lot lighter come spring.

Which meant she should really stick around for the money. They'd offered her a *lot,* both for her time, and for the portrait packages the company had preordered for every family. It might even be enough money to get the new laptop *and* the new lens she needed.

Ross stared at her, not pleading, not ordering. Just asking her to wait, give them a chance to talk. To catch up on old times? Seriously, what was there to say except, *Hey, remember that time we had crazy wild sex in a pile of fluff in Santa's workshop?*

Good times.

Times that would never be repeated.

"I really should go," she said.

The administrator, who had a brusque manner that said she didn't like to take no for an answer, didn't take no for an answer. "Don't be silly, it won't take five minutes. It will save our accountants some trouble."

She eyed the woman doubtfully, suspecting this place did not keep their receipts and canceled checks in empty Amazon.com boxes the way she did.

"After the party, the offices shut down until New Year's. So I'd really like to get this taken care of today, clear the party off the books, if you will."

Huh. Sounded like every business had to deal with that pesky little IRS thing, even businesses as big as this one. Which, judging by the size of this brand-new six-story office building, and the fact that Elite Construction took up every floor of it, was very big, indeed. She wondered again what Ross did here. Obviously he no longer swung a hammer—he was dressed like a corporate guy.

She couldn't help wondering what had happened to his dream of someday buying a piece of property and building a house on it, every stone, every shutter, every plank of wood put there with his own hands. Had Ross given up his dreams? Or had they merely changed, like hers had?

As if realizing his presence was making her reluctant, Ross said, "I should go. It was great seeing you again, Lucy."

"You, too."

She forced a tight smile, wishing she could hit Rewind and go back a half hour to think of something else to say to this man. Something breezy and casual, something that wouldn't have revealed how she felt about not hearing from him after that one magical holiday. Something *other* than, "Well, if you'd called, you'd know where I'd been for the past six years."

Weak, girl. So weak. She could almost hear Kate's voice scolding her for making that snotty, hurt-sounding comment. Even though, now, there would be echoes of a baby and a toddler crying in the background as they had the conversation. Kate had married Teddy and started repopulating the planet.

Lucy, meanwhile, had managed only sexual affairs after Ross. But she hadn't come anywhere close to falling in love. Not after the one-two punch she'd taken at twenty-two. First Jude, then Ross—the latter being the one who'd truly taught her about love and loss. Her poor heart had formed an exoskeleton thicker than an insect's. Since then, she'd made love 'em and leave 'em a way of life, only substituting the *love* with *do*.

Even Kate had been impressed.

She watched him walk away, noting that he didn't look back. His departure should have made it easier to stick around for a few minutes to get paid. Instead it just pissed her off. Ross was always the one who got to walk away. One of these days she wanted to be the one to make the grand exit.

But grand exits didn't buy lenses and laptops. Money did. She'd spent a lot moving her studio from New York to Chicago. Yes, she was building a reputation and business was good. This one check, though, could do some nice things for her bottom line.

If she deposited the check tonight, then by this weekend, she could be happily shopping for laptops online while everybody else in the world unwrapped ugly sweaters and ate rock-hard fruitcake. She had bookings lined up all next week—a few of them big ones that could lead to some serious money. Plus, she was hoping to hear from a children's magazine in New York, to whom she'd submitted some work. She wanted to be ready if they called and said they wanted more.

"Okay, if you can pay me now, I'd really appreciate it," she finally told the administrator, who'd been waiting patiently, watching Lucy watch Ross.

"Excellent, come along."

Lucy put down her camera and lens bags, and followed the woman, who'd introduced herself as Stella when she'd called a week ago to hire her. They left the party behind, heading down a long corridor toward the executive offices. Lucy couldn't help noticing the opulence of this area, the thick carpet sinking beneath her feet, the beautiful artwork lining the walls. Somebody had spent a lot of time decorating this place and she suspected their clients ranked among Chicago's most wealthy.

At the back end of the executive wing was an enclosed suite, into which Stella led her. A broad receptionist's desk stood in the middle of a waiting area, blocking access to an imposing set of double doors. Stella breezed through them, into what looked like the head honcho's office. It was huge, a corner room with floor-to-ceiling windows on two walls. The building wasn't terribly high, but the location right on the water on the very outskirts of town meant nothing interrupted the beautiful view. The desk was as big as the kitchen in her tiny apartment, and in a partially blocked-off alcove, she saw an area for relaxation, complete with a refrigerator, TV and a fold-out couch…folded out. “Wow, is your boss a slave-driver? Do you have to be on call 24/7?”

The woman glanced around, then realized what Lucy was talking about. “That’s just for him. Our CEO is only hard on himself.”

“Does he live here or something?”

“It sometimes seems that way,” Stella said. “When we moved into this new building, he was spending so many hours here, I ordered the couch and make it up for him when I suspect he’ll pull an all-nighter.”

“That’s dedication.” On Stella’s part, and on her boss’s.

“It’s paid off. Elite is thriving when new construction is down nationwide.”

“I could tell by the party,” she admitted, knowing it must have set the company back a pretty penny. Few corporations bothered these days, and she suspected the happy atmosphere contributed to the company’s success.

Stella stepped behind the desk and picked up a pile of sealed envelopes, shuffling through a half-dozen of them before she said, “Ah, here we are!”

Lucy accepted it, tucking the very welcome check into her purse. “Thanks very much.”

“Thank *you.* Your photos were the hit of the party. I am actually glad the other company canceled. We’ve used them in the past and they’ve never had the response you did today. You're wonderful with children."

Lucy smiled, appreciating the praise. It was funny—six years ago, she probably would have been horrified at it.

Honestly, she wasn't sure herself how it had happened. She just knew that, after two years in Paris, photographing cold-faced fashion models had lost all appeal. Same with old, lifeless buildings and stagnant landscapes.

Then Kate had started having kids. Lucy had visited for summers and holidays, becoming a devoted godmother and falling head-over-heels for those babies. She had delighted in taking their portraits, finding in children's faces an energy and spontaneity she seldom found anywhere else.

So she'd gone back to New York. She'd set up a studio and begun exploring the amazingly creative world of little people. One thing had led to another, and then another. And soon she'd been getting calls from wealthy parents in other states, and had sold several shots to children's catalogs and magazines.

Who'd've ever thought it?

Not her, that's for sure. Nor would she ever have imagined that she'd really love what she was doing. But she did.

Life, it seemed, took some strange turns, led you in directions you'd never have imagined. It had taken her from the windy city, to the Big Apple, then to another continent. And now right back to where she'd started, in Chicago.

And back into Ross Marshall's life.

No, don't even go there, she reminded herself. She wasn't back in his life. She was in the same building with him for another five minutes, max. Then she could go back to forgetting about the guy. Forgetting how good he still looked to her. How his sexy voice thrilled her senses. How his touch had sent her out of her mind.

How he'd once seemed like the guy she could love forever.

CHAPTER FOUR

Then
New York, December 23, 2005

LUCY HAD TO give this very handsome stranger—Ross—credit. He didn't stand up and walk out of the coffee shop when she admitted she'd been fantasizing about separating an ex-boyfriend from part of his anatomy. He didn't yelp, cringe, or reflexively drop a protective hand on his lap. None of the above. Instead he simply stared for a second, then let a loud burst of laughter erupt from his mouth.

She smiled, too, especially because she hadn't *really* been fantasizing about maiming Jude when this guy had walked up behind her. In fact, she'd been laughing at herself for having thought about it earlier. Somehow, her whole mood had shifted from the time she'd walked into the coffee shop until the moment this incredibly handsome man had approached her.

Incredibly. Handsome.

Around them, others in the café glanced over. Lucy wasn't blind to the stares that lingered on him. Heaven knew, any woman with a broken-in vagina would stare. Heck, hers wasn't broken-in and she could barely take her eyes off the guy!

He'd been super-hot from across the room. Up close, now that she could see the tiny flecks in his stunning green eyes, the dazzling white smile, the slight stubble on his cheeks, well, he went from hot and sexy to smoking and irresistible. She'd actually shivered when their hands had met, unable to think a single thought except to wonder how those strong, rough fingers would feel sliding across her skin.

Gorgeous, sexy, strong. And a sense of humor.

Why couldn't she have met this guy on a day when she didn't loathe every creature with a penis?

You don't. Not every guy.

Truthfully? Not even one. She didn't loathe Jude. She would have had to care about him to hate him, and, honestly, having really thought about it, she knew she hadn't cared much at all.

"You're serious?" he asked once his laughter had died down.

"Not about doing it."

"But thinking it?"

"My turn to take the fifth."

"Why?"

"Probably because it's not very nice to admit you fantasize about dismembering someone."

"No, I meant why do you want to, um...dismember him?"

"I didn't, I was just indulging in a little mind-revenge. He wasn't the most faithful guy."

"I hate cheaters," he said, his voice both sympathetic and disgusted.

"Speaking from personal experience?"

"Well, not exactly," he admitted.

Yeah. Because any woman who cheated on him would have to have been recently lobotomized.

"Though, I did kinda get cheated on once…by a guy."

She didn't take the bait, knowing that there was no way Ross was gay. There wasn't one nonheterosexual gene in his body; you could practically smell the masculine pheromones that surrounded him like a cloud, attracting every woman in the place.

"Let me guess…your best buddy in first grade decided he wanted to play dodgeball instead of tag and left you alone in the playground?"

"Almost," he said, his eyes gleaming with approval that she hadn't gone where most would have. "It was in high school. I wanted my best friend to stick with the wrestling team, he wanted to do the school musical." He shook his head sadly. "I just couldn't understand what he was thinking. It wasn't until junior year that he finally told me the truth, and then I was so furious I didn't speak to him for a week."

Somehow disappointed in him, she stiffened slightly. "You were mad that he was gay?"

"Hell, no, he wasn't gay! He told me he left wrestling and went to drama because, let me see if I remember this exactly, 'Why would I want to roll around on the floor with a bunch of sweaty dudes, when I could be one of only a handful of guys surrounded by some of the prettiest girls in the school?' Man, some of those theater chicks were cute…and he never told me, he kept them all for himself!"

She laughed out loud, liking both the story, and that he had told it. He was obviously trying to distract her, to amuse her. It was a nice thing to do for a guy so young and good-looking.

"So, your first bro-mance ended up in a bad breakup."

"Yup. Now, back to yours…."

"Not a bro-mance, obviously. But also unpleasant. I only wish it were something as simple as him preferring *The Sound of Music* to pinning and undercupping."

His eyes widened. "Hey, you know wrestling!"

"Older brother."

"So is he going to kick this cheating dude's ass?"

"Sam? No. He doesn't live here, and even if he did, there's absolutely no way I would tell him about this."

"How come?"

"Because he's a cop. And he's extremely overprotective." Though she didn't usually discuss it, for some reason, she found this guy very easy to talk to, so she added, "He sort of became my father when our parents died."

Ross leaned forward in his chair, dropping his elbows onto the table. His fingers brushed against her hand, in a move that was as fleeting as it was sweet. A faint brush of I'm Sorry and How Sad and Hey, I Understand. All unsaid. All understood.

All appreciated.

She cleared her throat, feeling the lump start to rise, the way it always did when this particular subject came up. "Anyway, I don't need Sam to fight my battles. I can take care of myself."

"I don't doubt it," Ross said.

"Don't worry, I'm really not the violent type. This guy didn't crush my spirit, he merely dinged my ego."

He held her stare, as if assessing the truth of her words. Lucy stared right back, a tiny smile on her lips, relieved that she meant exactly what she'd said, hoping he realized that, too.

"I'm glad," he finally admitted, seeing the truth in her face.

"So am I."

"Still, if you change your mind and decide to get all saw-crazy on this boyfriend, remind me not to go with you. I wouldn't want to be arrested as an accomplice."

She chuckled as he turned her earlier words back on her, then clarified, "*Ex*-boyfriend." Shaking her head, she added, "Believe me, nothing could induce me to go back there." Then something occurred to her. "Oh, *no!*" Lucy put a hand over her forehead as she remembered something. Because she was going to have to make a liar of herself. "I'm so stupid!"

"What?"

"My brother's Christmas present to me. It came in the mail today—he sent it to Jude's place because he knows mail sometimes gets stolen from the building where I live and Jude's has a doorman." She felt moisture in her eyes, furious at herself for forgetting the gift, but also worried about what Jude would do with it. "He's probably already thrown it down the trash chute."

"Jude?" he said doubtfully. "Lemme guess—spoiled, rich punk?"

It might have taken a little while for the blinders to come off, but Lucy had to admit, that pretty well described her ex. "How'd you know?"

"Having a doorman in NYC is a pretty big tip-off. So's having a name like Jude. Plus, he must've done something pretty bad if you're fantasizing about chopping the head off his trouser snake, yet he'd still throw out a Christmas gift from your brother…meaning he's an immature, petulant brat." He spread his hands. "Or a spoiled, rich asshole."

"All of the above would cover it."

"And you're with this guy…why?"

"I'm not with him."

"But you were as of…"

She sighed deeply. "About two hours ago."

He whistled, leaning back in his chair, extending his long legs, crossed at the ankle. "Was it serious? I mean, were you guys exclusive?"

"Not according to him, apparently."

His jaw tightened a tiny bit. "And according to you?"

"Well, I thought so, but maybe I just saw things differently than he did. We'd been dating three months, but we hadn't even…you know. So maybe he cheated since he'd never gotten anywhere with me."

Ross coughed into his fist, apparently surprised

she'd admitted that. Maybe he was turned-off; some guys would be at the thought that a girl would wait three months before getting down to business. If so, better to find out now if he was one of them.

Why that should be, she didn't know. After all, she might never even speak to this guy again once she left this shop. Somehow, the thought made her heart twist a lot harder than it had earlier when she'd thought about not seeing Jude anymore.

"Good for you," he said.

Okay, so he wasn't one of *those* guys, apparently. The realization warmed her a little on this very chilly day.

"Let him eat his heart out, wondering what he's thrown away."

She liked that idea. "I hope twenty years from now he's still wondering if he missed out on the best sex of his life."

Their stares locked as the heated words hung there between them. They were having a very intimate conversation for two strangers, and now, she suspected, they were both thinking a little too much about certain parts of that conversation

Like sex. Great sex. She might not have had it—great, or otherwise—but that didn't mean she was immune to desire. Looking at the man sitting across from her, feeling the heat sluice through her veins to settle with quiet, throbbing insistence between her thighs, she knew full well she had a basic understanding of want.

Or more than basic. Because it wasn't just her sex

that was responding here. Every inch of her skin tingled as she thought of him touching her, pressing his mouth to all the more interesting parts of her body. Places that responded to the warm look in his eyes and how he opened his mouth to draw in a slow breath in a way they'd never responded to any guy's most passionate embrace.

His gaze dropped to her mouth and his voice was thick as he finally replied, "I almost feel sorry for the bastard."

She didn't. And she definitely didn't feel sorry for herself any longer. Not when, with one twenty-minute conversation, this complete stranger was introducing her to sensations her ex hadn't elicited in months of dating.

They remained silent for one more moment. Then, as if they both realized they were falling into something neither had anticipated—at the speed of light, no less—they shifted in their chairs and broke the stare.

Lucy forced a light laugh, trying to pretend she wasn't completely enraptured by the thought of pressing her mouth to the cord of muscle in his neck. "I'm not going to spare him any sympathy until I get my present back and make sure he didn't destroy it."

His gleaming eyes narrowed. "You really think he would?"

She considered it, remembered some of Jude's more spiteful moods. Not to mention his ridiculously misplaced indignation that she'd walked in on him today—as if it were all her fault because she'd caught him, not his that he'd cheated. "It's possible."

Ross's jaw clenched, a muscle flexing in his cheek. "Why don't you let me take care of this?"

"Why would you do that? You don't even know me."

"I know enough to know you shouldn't have to beg somebody who betrayed you to give you back something that's yours."

She heard the note of protectiveness in his voice, and found it strange. And very nice. Ross had just met her, yet he'd already been more thoughtful and considerate of her feelings than Jude had in the past three months.

"It's not that big a deal," she insisted, not wanting to drag somebody else into her troubles.

"It's from your only family member, Luce," he replied, shaking his head. "So of course it's a big deal. I want to make sure you get it back."

Lucy's breath caught. The soft way he'd said the nickname, Luce, seemed so tender. And the way he'd immediately understood why the gift from Sam was important to her, without her having to explain it…

Who are you? she couldn't help wondering. *Can you really be this nice a guy?*

"Do you think he'd really destroy your Christmas present?"

She didn't like to think so, but it was possible. "He was pretty mad when I left, mainly because I wouldn't stick around to listen to his explanation."

"Could there have been one?"

She snickered. "Sure." She tapped her finger on her cheek, as if thinking it over. "Hmm, okay, I have an idea how it could have, uh...*gone down.*"

A half smile lifted one corner of his oh-so-sexy mouth, as if he understood the reason for her inflection.

"So, his skanky neighbor was taking a bath, and she forgot she had no shampoo," Lucy explained. "Wrapped only in a towel, she came to his door to borrow some."

"Wait," he interrupted. "I bet I know what happened next. It just so happens, he was about to take a shower, too, so he was also only wearing a towel."

She giggled, wondering why she could already find this funny when it had brought tears to her eyes earlier today. More proof that her heart hadn't ever been involved in her relationship with Jude, she supposed.

"And then...hmm. Oh, I've got it," she said. "A pack of wild dogs somehow got into the building, rode up the elevator, burst into the apartment and ripped off both their towels. And in the ensuing struggle, slutty neighbor chick tripped and fell mouth first onto his sad, strange-looking little penis."

Ross winced. "Ouch."

"Ouch for her, or for him?"

"Well, mainly for you," he said, that gentle tone back in his voice. "For having to witness that." That sexy grin flashed. "But also ouch to him for having a sad, strange-looking little penis."

"Considering it was the first—and last—time I

ever saw it, I can only say I'm glad I made the decision not to sleep with him."

"Me, too," he admitted, sounding as though he meant it. Which was odd, considering she didn't even know him and neither of them had any idea if they would ever share anything more than this one conversation at this one particular moment.

She hoped they would. It was fast, and utterly surprising and the timing was pretty bad. But she already had the feeling this sexy, hardworking guy was someone special. And even if the timing was all wrong, she might be the one with lifelong regrets if she didn't at least give this more time to play out.

"So, do you always go around telling strangers about your sex life?" he asked.

She played with her coffee cup, tracing her fingers on its rim, not meeting his eyes. "You're the first," she admitted. Hoping she wouldn't reveal too much, she shrugged and added, "You just don't seem like a stranger."

He didn't. She felt like she was already starting to know him, or at least know the essence of him. The physical attraction had been instant. But there was so much more. Earlier, when she'd mentioned her parents, there'd been that warmth, the smile, the tender looks, that ever-so-gentle brush of his fingers against her hand. Then there was his reaction to her having been cheated on. His indignance over her lost Christmas present.

All those things told a story. A nice one. A good one.

A story she wanted to explore a little more. Or a lot more.

"Okay then, if we're not strangers, I guess that means we're friends," he told her with a tender smile. Then, without explanation, he pushed the chair back and stood up. She wasn't sure what he intended—to leave, to ask her out?—until he extended a hand to her.

"So, come on, friend. Let's go reclaim your Christmas present."

CONSIDERING HOW BEAUTIFUL Lucy was, Ross didn't expect her ex to be a total dog, even if he was a total dick. There had to have been something she'd found attractive about the guy. And even though he hadn't known her long, he already felt pretty sure it hadn't been the money. She just didn't seem the type. There wasn't a fake thing about her…and he should know. He'd looked. Hard.

Hell, it had been impossible *not* to look, not to try to get to know everything about her. Sitting across from each other at that coffee shop, they'd fallen into an easy, laid-back conversation that it had taken him a half-dozen meetings to achieve with other girls. Then things had gone from warm and friendly to hot and expectant.

He shouldn't have started thinking about Lucy's sex life, much less talking about it. Because it was damned hard to get it out of his mind—or to stop wondering about that look she'd had in her eye during the long silence they'd shared.

Walking outside to drop off his tools in his truck, then to the subway so they could ride up to her dopey ex's neighborhood, he found himself more surprised by her with every move she made.

She never stopped talking, but didn't jabber about stupid, inane stuff. He didn't once hear the word shoes. Or makeup. Or shopping.

She talked about the city—how much she loved the energy of it, the pace, the excitement.

She stopped to take pictures—things that would never occur to him to be interesting, like a pile of trash bags or an old rusty bike against a fence.

She talked about her plans to go to Europe after she graduated, to photograph anything that moved and lots of things that didn't.

She bought one of those disgusting hot dogs off a cart, and actually ate the thing.

She passed a five dollar bill to a homeless guy. She also dropped another five into a bell-ringer's bucket, even as she admitted she didn't really like Christmas, claiming her favorite response to anyone's "Merry Christmas," was "Bah, humbug!"

He had a hard time buying that one. She was too cute and sweet and generous to be a Scrooge. But he did see the shadow in her expression whenever she talked about the holiday and suspected she was serious about disliking it.

Other than that, though, she laughed a lot. She smiled at strangers. She turned her face up to meet the softly falling snow and licked its moisture off her lips. Sweet laugh, beautiful smile, sexy lips.

All in all, aside from totally attracting him, she charmed him. It was an old-fashioned description, but it fit. Lucy was, quite simply, charming. Plus adorable. And hot as hell. Every minute he spent with her made him like her even more…and made him more determined to ensure her cheating ex didn't get the chance to hurt her again.

She was, in short, fantastic. So, no, he definitely didn't see her hooking up with someone who had no redeeming qualities whatsoever. This Jude guy, who lived in a high-rise building with apartments that probably cost five times the rent in his own tiny place, had to have something to attract someone like Lucy.

Then he met the loser, face-to-face, and understood.

Jude Zacharias was spoiled, handsome and smooth—one of those old-money types whose family name probably hadn't been tainted by the stench of real work for a few generations. But the main thing about him, the thing that would suck in any girl, was the earnest charm.

He laid it on thick from the minute he answered the door and saw Lucy. He even managed to work up a couple of tears in his eyes as he told her how sorry he was that he'd let some skank trick him into doing something bad—*ha*—how much he wished he could take it back and how glad he was that she'd returned.

Then he spotted Ross, who'd been hovering just out of sight, near the hallway wall.

"Who the fuck is *he?*"

Stepping forward, Ross said, "He the fuck is Lucy's friend, Ross. We're here to pick up the package she left behind. Now, would you get it, please? We're in a hurry."

Yeah. Not because he had errands to run, but because he was in a rush to get Lucy away from this prick who'd hurt her, even if it had been her pride, not her heart that had been dinged. Honestly, he'd wanted to rip the guy's hand off when he'd actually reached out and tried to touch her. Fortunately, Lucy had stepped aside, out of reach.

The guy's jaw hit his chest. He gaped, then sputtered, finally saying, "Who *are* you?"

Ross looked at Lucy and shrugged. "Is he brain damaged or something? Like I said, I'm Ross. I'm here to make sure you give Lucy her package, and that you don't try anything."

"Lucy, are you serious? Did you bring this guy to throw in my face, make me jealous or something?" He reached for her hand. "Babe, you don't have to do that, you know I'll take you back."

"Dude, get over it. You've been dumped," Ross said.

Jude's glare would have fried an egg. "Mind your own damn business. Why the hell are you here anyway?"

Lucy stepped between them. "Ross is a friend."

"Yeah, sure, right. How long has he been your… *friend?*"

She tapped a finger on her lips, as if thinking about it, then cast a quick, mischievous glance toward Ross. "Oh, about an hour now."

Jude sputtered. Lucy ignored him.

"He just wanted to come along in case you decided to be a jerk about my package."

The guy sneered. "Oh, yeah? And what's he gonna do if I say you can't have it?"

Ross's fingers curled into fists and his jaw tightened. He took a step toward the door. He couldn't remember if he'd ever felt this anxious to punch someone but he didn't think so. Something about hearing the way this little asshole talked to Lucy brought out the overprotective he-man in him.

She put up a hand, stopping him. "It's okay. Jude, please don't be a pain about this. Can I just have my package?" She reached into her purse and pulled out a key ring. "And here, you should have this back."

He snatched the key out of her hand, cast one more glare at Ross, then stepped back into the apartment. He returned a few seconds later, shoving a small, paper-wrapped carton toward her. It was mashed, dirty, slightly torn.

Lucy stared at it, her bottom lip trembling, then took it. A small shake elicited a tinkling sound from inside. The paper in which it was wrapped was damp.

Whatever had been inside had contained some kind of liquid. And it was broken.

"You didn't," she whispered, her voice thick. Her eyes were wet with unshed tears.

Jude shrugged. "Hey, just figured it must not have been important if you left it here, so I was gonna pitch it."

It looked as though the bastard already had. Against a wall.

Furious, Ross took another step toward him. "You petty little douchebag." This time, Lucy was too distracted by the ruined gift in her hands to stop him.

Good. That left Ross free to grab a fistful of her ex-boyfriend's top and shove him back into his apartment. The guy tripped over a table, stumbling backward a few steps before falling on his arrogant ass.

"Take another step and I'll call the cops!" he shrieked. Obviously pretty boy wasn't used to anybody threatening his perfect, spoiled little self.

"I could knock out your teeth before they get here," Ross growled.

The other guy scrambled backward as Ross stalked him, step by step.

"Look, I'm sorry, okay?" he said. "Lucy, come on, you know I wouldn't do anything to hurt you. It was an accident."

"Accident my ass," Ross said as he leaned down and hauled the guy up by the collar of his J. Crew sweater.

His right hand curled into a fist but before he could let it fly, Lucy grabbed his arm. "Let him go. Please, Ross, let's just get out of here." She cast her ex a withering look. "Hey, he did me a favor. If there was any doubt in my mind that he's a disgusting, hateful person, this eliminated it."

"Babe..."

"Bite me, Jude," she snapped.

Ross grinned, then, for good measure, pushed the

dude backward until he hit the couch, sprawling out on it.

Ross glanced at Lucy, seeing she'd hugged the package to her chest, apparently not caring that it was wet. It was like seeing someone who'd lost their most prized possession. Nobody deserved to be cheated on, humiliated and then, to top it all off, have something important to them shattered. Remembering what she'd said about it being just the two of them after their parents had died, he felt his heart twist in his chest, knowing how much her brother's gift must have meant to her.

His own family drove him crazy sometimes—especially his overly controlling father—but he couldn't imagine life without them. She was so young to bear that kind of sadness. One thing he knew, Lucy Fleming had to be one hell of a strong young woman. And a forgiving one, if she was determined to stop him from kicking her ex's ass.

"Please, can we just go?" she asked.

Yeah. She seemed pretty determined. That was lucky for the ex, even though it didn't make Ross too happy.

"Fine," he told her.

He took her arm and led her to the door, glancing back over his shoulder before they walked through it. The ex still sat there on the couch, a sneer curling his lips. As if he were the injured party in this whole rotten mess.

The boiling well of anger inside him had rolled back to a slow simmer, and Ross knew he had to get out of here before it boiled back up. Mr. J. Crew dick-head had finally realized the merits of shutting the hell up, but that look on his face was seriously pissing Ross off. If he opened his mouth again, or if one single tear fell out of Lucy's eyes, he was gonna go postal on the squirmy punk.

Her hand tightened on his arm, as if she knew what he was thinking. So he wouldn't do it. But something wouldn't let him leave without one more parting shot. "Hey, dude, don't worry, I wouldn'ta hit you. Wouldn't risk damaging that pretty face of yours, 'cause it sounds to me like you really need it."

"What do you mean?" the other man snapped, starting to rise from his seat. Emboldened, perhaps, by the thought that Ross was admitting he wouldn't have hit him?

Just give me a reason, punk.

Ross shrugged as Lucy stepped into the hallway ahead of him. "I mean, it sounds like you need whatever help you can get. From what I hear, you not only have a scrawny neck, you have a scrawny dick as well." *Tsking,* he shook his head. "Even worse, a sad, strange-looking one."

The other guy's face erupted in scarlet, and he sputtered, but couldn't come up with anything to say. Which, in Ross's mind, confirmed what Lucy had said about him. A guy with an ounce of self-confidence would have laughed, or sneered. Jude just looked like he wanted to call Mommy and make the new kid stop saying mean things to him.

"Oh, by the way," he added. "Happy birthday."

Ross slammed the door, not waiting for Jude to come up with a crushing reply. Not that he could, really, because, man, any guy who couldn't defend himself against small-cock accusations didn't have much of a leg to stand on.

It wasn't until they were alone in the elevator, heading toward the bottom floor, that he looked down and saw Lucy's shoulders shaking. It was as if she'd held herself together, keeping her emotions in check until she got out of sight of her ex, but now that they were alone, her sadness over the day's events had come crashing down on her.

He turned her toward him. Ross fully intended to take her into his arms, awkwardly pat her back or whatever guys did to console crying women. But before he could do it, he realized he'd made a big mistake.

"Oh…my…God…" she said between gasps, which weren't caused by tears, but rather, by laughter. She looked up at him, her lips shaking, her eyes twinkling with merriment. "Did you see his face?"

"I saw," he said, smiling down at her, so pleased she wasn't brokenhearted over creepy Jude that he wanted to pick her up and swing her around in his arms.

"Thank you so much," she said. "You were my knight in shining armor."

He grinned and gestured toward his bomber jacket. "Carpenter in tarnished leather, at best."

Her pretty mouth widened in a smile. "Either way…my hero." Then, still looking playful, happy, appreciative, she rose on her tiptoes and reached up to brush her delicate fingers against his cheek. He had about a second to process what she was about to do before she pressed her soft lips against his.

It was a thank-you kiss, he had no doubt about that.

Sweet. Tender. Simple.

Incredibly good.

It should have been nothing but a three-second brush of skin on skin, an expression of gratitude between two people who didn't really know each other yet but definitely wanted to.

But damned if Ross was willing to let it go down that way. Once he felt Lucy's mouth, shared her sweet breath, impulse took over. He lifted both hands, cupping one around her cheek. The other he tangled in her long, thick hair, taking pure pleasure in the softness of it, letting it glide through his fingers like water.

He deepened the kiss, sliding his tongue out to tease hers. Lucy groaned slightly, taking what he offered and upping the ante even more by tilting her head and widening her mouth. *Thank you* and *you're welcome* turned into *I-want-you* and *where's the nearest bed* in about ten seconds flat. Sweetness faded and heat erupted as their tongues thrust and twined.

"Ahem."

It took a second for the voice to intrude. But another throat-clearing and a titter finally invaded his Lucy-infused consciousness. It appeared they'd arrived at the bottom floor. The door had slid open and they were providing quite a show for the people waiting in the lobby.

Filled with regret, he pulled away, looking down into her pretty, flushed face, seeing the way her long lashes rested on her high cheekbones. She kept her eyes closed a moment longer, swaying a little toward him. But the box pressed against her chest prevented her from melting into his body.

And their sudden, unwelcome audience prevented him from moving the box.

"We're here," he whispered.

Her eyes flew open. Seeing the strangers watching them—two young men with their arms around each other's waists, both grinning widely, and an older, white-haired woman whose grin was, if possible, even wider—Lucy stammered an apology.

"No need to apologize," one of the men said, waving his hand as Lucy and Ross exited the elevator.

The other nodded in agreement. "Tell me this means you ditched 6C."

Lucy's jaw fell open. "Wha…?"

"He's a bad egg," the woman said, jumping into the conversation as if they had all known each other for years. In truth, Ross suspected they were complete strangers to Lucy. "A total fart-weasel."

Ross coughed into his fist at the description, but the two men were already nodding in agreement. "He sure is."

"Have we met?" Lucy asked, shaking her head in confusion, confirming Ross's suspicion.

"No," said the darker-haired man. "But we all live

on six, too. And honey, 6C is just *nasty.* So not your type!"

"Thanks," she murmured, looking even more embarrassed than before. Considering complete strangers were dissecting her love life, he could see why.

The light-haired man eyed Ross. "Did you beat him up?"

"No."

Ms. Elderly Busybody sighed heavily. "That's too bad. I've been hoping somebody would. That boy could benefit from an ass-whupping."

"Well, given what I know of him so far, I have no doubt that someday your prayers will be answered," Ross said.

He and Lucy murmured goodbyes to their three new friends, then headed for the door. As they approached him, the doorman offered Lucy a conspiratorial wink, as if he agreed with the other residents' opinion of her ex. Which was nice, but probably had to be making Lucy feel even worse about ever having dated the fart-weasel in 6C.

He reached for her hand and squeezed it. "Don't beat yourself up about it."

She sucked in a surprised breath, and stopped halfway across the lobby. Looking up at him, she appeared shocked that he'd been able to figure out what she'd been thinking.

"He's a con artist, Luce," Ross said with a simple shrug. "He became what you wanted him to be."

"Yes, he did," she murmured. "But how did you know?"

"Guys do it all the time, especially with girls who won't, uh…." He didn't want to be crass enough to say *put out,* though that was what he meant.

"Gotcha," she said. "And thanks for not telling me I was a complete idiot for not seeing it sooner."

"You *did* see it," he told her, not liking that self-recrimination in her voice. "Which is probably why you wouldn't, uh…"

This time, during the pregnant pause while they both mentally filled in the blank, Lucy actually laughed. "You really are a nice guy, aren't you?"

"I have a few ex-girlfriends who would disagree, but my parents like to think so."

"I think I'll have to side with your folks on that one."

"I'll be sure to tell them that," he said with a grin.

She grinned back, then, without another word, slipped her hand into his and turned again toward the exit.

As her soft fingers entwined with his, Ross's heart jolted. He'd kissed her, touched her…but this was a little bit more. It wasn't just a simple touch. That clasped hand was so easy and relaxed, like she already trusted him, as if they'd known each other for weeks rather than hours.

He honestly wasn't sure what was going to happen when they walked out of this building. He'd done what he'd set out to do—escorted her to her ex's place to retrieve her present. But now what? They'd made no other plans. It was the day before Christmas Eve, the streets were a madhouse, he had a million things to do. But as they walked into the bracing December day, alive with the thrum of city life, laughter, and energy, all he could think was that the very last thing he wanted was to say goodbye to her.

CHAPTER FIVE

Now
Chicago, December 23, 2011

THOUGH HE KNEW Stella had the checks for the subcontractors ready, Ross was hoping it would take a while for her to find Lucy's. While there were still people in the building, it would be far too easy for her to slip away. The longer it took, the better the chances were that she wouldn't be able to avoid him on her way out.

Yet somehow, she nearly pulled it off. He didn't even realize she was leaving until he spotted a thick head of dark hair—topped by a merry green, feathered elf cap—getting onto the elevator. "Damn it," he muttered.

"What?"

Seeing the surprised expression on the face of one of his project managers, who'd stopped to chat after Mr. Whitaker departed, Ross mumbled, "I'm sorry, I just remembered something I forgot to take care of."

Like getting Lucy's address, phone number and her promise to get together very soon so they could talk. Exactly what they'd talk about, he didn't know. Six years seemed like a long time for a how've-you-been type of conversation. So maybe they'd skip how've-you-beens in favor of what-happens-now?

Then he remembered that Stella had hired Lucy. She had to know how to get in touch with her. Plus, Lucy had mentioned she lived here, worked here—it shouldn't be hard to find her online.

So, yes, he could be reasonable and mature and patient about this. Could wait until after the holidays, then call her sometime in January to say hello and see if she'd like to meet.

But something—maybe the look in her eyes when she'd said he would know what she'd been up to if he'd called during the past six years—wouldn't let him wait. He couldn't have said it in front of anyone at the party; wasn't sure he'd have found the words even if they'd been left alone. Still, Lucy deserved an explanation from him. Even if she thought it a lame one and decided to keep hating him, he'd feel better if he offered it.

Then he'd get to work on making her not hate him anymore.

"Thanks for the party, Mr. Marshall," his employee said. "The kids really loved it."

"I'm glad. Hey, you and your family have a great holiday," Ross replied, already stepping toward the enclosed stairs that were intended for emergencies.

This was one. The elevator could have made a few stops on the way to the lobby—there were still employees on other floors, closing down for the holiday break. If he hustled, he might beat her to the bottom.

He might not be slinging a hammer and doing hard

physical labor ten hours a day anymore, but Ross did keep himself busy in his off hours. So the dash down six flights of stairs didn't really wind him. By the time he burst through the doors into the tiled lobby of the building—surprising Chip, the elderly security guard—the elevator door was just sliding open, and several people exited, some carrying boxes, bags of gifts, plates of food, files to work on at home.

One carried nothing, but wore a silly hat.

Lucy saw him and her mouth dropped. "How did you…?"

"Staircase," he told her. "Were you really going to leave without saying goodbye?"

"Did you really stalk me down six flights of stairs?"

He rolled his eyes. "Stalking? That's a little dramatic."

"You're breathing hard and sweating," she accused him, stepping close and frowning. "Don't even try to tell me you didn't run every step of the way."

He couldn't contain a small grin. "Busted."

"The question is, why?"

"Here's a better one. Why'd you leave without saying goodbye?"

"We said our goodbyes a long time ago," she retorted.

He whistled.

"What?"

"You're still really mad at me."

Those slim shoulders straightened and her chin went up. "That's ridiculous."

Lucy was obviously trying for a withering look, but with that silly hat and the droopy feather hanging by her cheek, she only managed freaking adorable. He couldn't resist lifting a hand and nudging the feather back into place, his fingertips brushing against the soft skin of her cheek.

She flinched as if touched with a hot iron. "Don't."

"Jesus, Lucy, do you hate me?" he whispered, realizing for the first time that this might not be mere bravado. Was it possible that over the past six years, while he'd been feeling miserable even as he congratulated himself on doing the right—the mature—thing, she'd been hating his guts?

"Of course I don't hate you," she said, sounding huffy. As if she was telling the truth, but wasn't exactly happy about that fact.

So she *wanted* to hate him?

"Can we please go sit down somewhere and have a cup of coffee?"

A wistful expression crossed her face, as if she, too, were remembering their first meeting in that New York coffee shop.

"I can't," she murmured. "I need to get to the bank before it closes, and before the snow starts."

"I'll walk with you."

"I'm driving."

"I'll ride with you."

She huffed. "You're still persistent, aren't you?"

"Only when it's important."

"And when did I become important to you?"

The day we met. He didn't say the words, but he suspected she saw them in his face.

"Look, Ross, I swear, I am not holding a grudge," she said. "So you don't have to go out of your way to try to make up with me."

"That's not what I'm doing. I just...I've missed you. A lot."

"How can you miss someone you knew for only a weekend, years ago?"

"Are you telling me you don't feel the same way?"

If she said she didn't, he'd make himself believe her. He'd let her go. Chalk this up to one of those life lessons where a memory of a time you'd considered perfect turned out to be something less than that to the one you'd shared it with.

Lucy didn't respond at first. Not wanting her to breeze over this, to reply without thought, Ross lifted a hand. A few strands of her silky, dark hair had fallen against her face. He slid his fingers through it, sending heat all the way up his arm. Her eyes drifted closed, the long lashes stark against her pale skin. And he'd swear she curled her face into his hand for an instant.

Ross groaned, as helpless to resist her now as he'd been that first day, in the elevator. Ignoring the surprised stare of the guard, who was the only other person in the lobby, he bent to Lucy and brushed his lips against hers, softly, demanding nothing more than a chance.

She hesitated for the briefest moment, then melted against him. This time there was no crumpled box separating their bodies; he was thrilled to discover she still fit against him as perfectly as ever. Her soft curves welcomed his harder angles, her feet parting a little as she brushed her legs against his and arched into him.

Sweetness flared into desire, just like it had the first time they'd kissed. Ross dropped his hands to her hips and held her close. Sweeping his tongue into her mouth, he dared her to go further. She, of course, took the dare, accepting what he offered and upping the ante by lifting her arms to encircle his neck. Their tongues thrust together, hot and languorous and deep, leaving Ross to wonder how he'd ever even imagined kissing any other woman had been as good as kissing this one. Everything about her was as intoxicating to him as it had been then. Maybe more so—because Lucy was no longer the sweet-faced co-ed. She was now every inch a woman. And he'd had the intense privilege of making her that woman.

Maybe that's what made this kiss different from their first one. Then, there'd been curiosity and wonder, riding on a wave of pure attraction.

Now they knew what they could be to each other. Knew the pleasure they were capable of creating together. Knew what it was like to be naked and hot and joined together as sanity retreated and hunger took over every waking thought. And many sleeping ones.

She lifted her leg slightly, twining it around his, and Ross echoed the tiny groan she made when she arched harder against him. There was no way she couldn't feel his rock-hard erection, any more than he could miss the heat between the thighs that instinctively cradled him.

Six years fell away, along with time, place and any concerns about an audience. There was just this, just the two of them, exploring something that had been missing from their lives for far too long.

Though he felt lost to everything else in the world except Lucy, Ross did finally become aware of a throat-clearing—Chip?—followed by a dinging sound that indicated the arrival of the elevator. A *swoosh* of the door was followed by a dull roar of laughing voices; the last few partiers…i.e., his employees, were about to make their way home.

He and Lucy quickly ended the kiss and stepped apart. "Déjà vu all over again," he muttered. Only this time, they'd been caught on the *outside* of the elevator.

She actually laughed a little, that sweet, warm laugh that was so distinctly hers. Over the past several years, he'd listened for that sound, always expecting to somehow hear it again, even though he'd never really let himself believe he would.

"Hopefully we're not going to hear some old lady say the guy on six is a fart-weasel."

"Hey, my office is on six," he said with a chuckle, pleased to realize Lucy remembered as much about that day as he did.

A group exited the elevator. "Have a happy holiday!" said one of his workers, who walked with his pregnant wife.

Ross nodded at the couple, and at the three others

who'd come down with them. "Same to you. Be careful out there—it's supposed to be a bad one."

Murmuring their goodbyes, the group headed for the exit. They were escorted by Chip, who turned a key to operate the intricate, electronic locks that turned this place into a fortress. With the offices closed to the public today, Chip had been kept on his toes playing doorman, letting employees in for the party, and, now that it was over, back out.

Fortunately the guard never complained. Not even about the fact that he had to work all night, during an impending blizzard, right before Christmas Eve. They might not have state secrets to be stolen, but some of their competitors would risk a lot for the chance to get at prebid documents. With millions of dollars in high-end construction projects at stake, corporate espionage had never been more of a danger. Plus, Elite had invested a hell of a lot of money in computers and equipment. Keeping security on-site 24/7 was one place where Ross had stood firm against his penny-pinching father, who loved to keep a hand in the business even though he was technically retired.

"Wait, I'm leaving, too," Lucy said as Chip began to relock the doors.

"Lucy…"

She held up a hand and brushed past him. "Please, Ross, I really need to go."

Hell, she sounded more determined to leave than she had before he'd kissed her. Not that he regretted it. Not one bit.

Chip glanced toward Ross, as if asking what Ross

wanted him to do. He nodded once. He couldn't keep Lucy here against her will. Nothing had changed; he'd taken his shot, and he'd lost.

But just for now.

Definitely. They'd been caught off guard, taken completely by surprise when they'd bumped into one another today. Now, though, he knew Lucy was living in Chicago. There was no longer any geographic reason for him to bow out. Nor was he young enough—angry and resentful enough—to let outside situations and demands make him walk away from her for a second time.

It was as if she'd been delivered back into his life, like the best kind of Christmas gift. The one you never expected, didn't realize you needed, but, when you tore off the paper, suddenly understood that it was exactly what you'd been waiting for.

No, he wasn't about to let her get away again, but he knew the old saying about picking your battles. Lucy had her guard up, she was uncomfortable here on his turf and hadn't had a moment to evaluate what all this meant to her. So he'd give her a few days to figure things out, then try again. And the next time he asked her to hear him out, he would not take no for an answer.

"Goodbye, Ross," she said, not even turning around to face him. Her voice was soft, low, and he suspected she was trying desperately not to reveal her emotions.

He had to let her go. Had to trust that was the right thing to do in order to get her back.

"Goodbye," he replied. "And Lucy?"

She hesitated, then glanced back at him over her shoulder.

"Merry Christmas."

A brief hesitation, then a tiny smile widened her perfect lips. "Bah humbug."

And then she disappeared out into the gray twilight.

IT USUALLY TOOK twenty minutes to get to the nearest branch of her bank. But today, Lucy was dealing with Friday evening, holiday weekend, impending-blizzard traffic. So she didn't reach the drive-thru until right before they closed at seven.

Thick flecks of white started to appear on the windshield of her Jeep as she waited in the long line of cars. New York got the white stuff by the foot, but here, the Snow Miser seemed to delight in sending wicked, bone-chilling winds along with his icy droppings. The flakes weren't the sweet, delicate ones that gently kissed your bare face. These were big, sloppy and wet, landing like punches, instead.

Once she'd made her deposit, Lucy headed right home. Luckily she had believed the weatherman's warnings and gone shopping yesterday. Having stocked up on chocolate, Diet Coke, and DVDs, she looked forward to a weekend inside, chomping on junk food, watching disaster movies, and shopping online.

Her trip home was difficult, even though the Jeep had 4-wheel drive. Her main concern was seeing through the swirling blanket of white in front of the windshield. Chicago was usually a bright city, even at night; yet this kind of snowstorm didn't reflect the light the way some did. It instead sucked it in, making streetlights hard to see.

It took almost two hours. By the time she arrived at her apartment building, she was not only cold and tired, she was actually jumpy from having been so on-alert.

Once inside her place, she wrenched off her coat and headed for the bathroom. A hot bath sounded like the perfect way to de-stress. She promised herself that, once in that bath, she would not spend one minute thinking about Ross. Or about that kiss.

Why did you have to go and kiss him back?

Probably because she'd been curious, wondering if her memories had been faulty. Could their brief relationship really have been as intense as she'd told herself it was? Had every other man she'd been with really paled in comparison, or was it wishful imaginings of the one that got away?

That kiss had answered all her questions: she hadn't imagined a damn thing.

"Stop thinking about it," she ordered herself as she got into the tub. The hot water stung her skin at first, but she welcomed the sensation, welcomed anything that would take her mind off the man she'd been kissing just a couple of hours ago.

It didn't work. Ross became more prominent in her thoughts. Not just the Ross of today, but the one she'd known before. The guy with whom she'd been so incredibly intimate.

The warmth, the fragrance of the bubble bath, the darkness of the room, lit only with candlelight—all seduced her. The sensation of water hitting every inch of her—between her thighs, caressing the tips of her breasts—made all her nerve endings leap up to attention.

But when it came to really turning her on, her brain did thc heavy lifting. It was too easy to remember the magical feel of his hands on her body, the sweet, sexy way he kissed, the groans of pleasure he made when he came.

Her hand slid down, scraping across her slick skin, teasing the puckered tip of one breast. The contact sent warmth spiraling downward, until her sex throbbed. Her eyes closed, her head back, it was easy to think *his* hands were on her, *his* fingers delicately stroking her clit until she began to sigh.

She gave herself over to desire, and let her mind float free. Memories gave way to imagination and her body, starved of physical connection for many months—since she'd left New York—reacted appropriately. Before too long, a slow, warm orgasm slid through her. She sighed a little, quivering and savoring it. But the deliciousness went away far too quickly.

It just couldn't compare to the real thing. To Lucy, getting off had never been the point; it had been sharing the experience that she loved. And she couldn't deny it, even after all these years, after the silence and the regret, she wanted to share that experience with him.

She quickly finished her bath, replaying the day's events as she washed her hair. As she thought everything over, including the way she'd tried to skulk out of the building when his back was turned, something started to nag at the back of her brain. She couldn't put her finger on it at first, just feeling like there was something she had forgotten. Something important.

It wasn't until she was dressed in a comfortable pair of sweats, with her hair wrapped in a towel, that she realized what it was. "Oh, no!" she yelped.

Lucy ran to the living room of her apartment, seeing her purse on the table. Alone. "You *idiot!*"

Because, though she hoped and prayed she'd just forgotten to bring it in from her Jeep, she seriously feared she'd left her most precious possessions at the Elite Construction office: her camera bag and her very expensive specialty lenses.

She perched on a chair, trying to picture every moment. She remembered putting her equipment down on Santa's seat before leaving with Stella. When she'd returned, she'd seen Ross. Desperate to get away without being seen, she'd hurried onto the elevator. Without stopping to grab her camera bag and lens case.

"Damn it," she snapped, trying to decide if this was just bad or catastrophic. She had some big jobs lined up next week. Monday's was with a very wealthy family, who wanted to sit for a holiday portrait at their home. They were the kind of people who could really give her a leg up with the Magnificent Mile set.

Unfortunately Lucy remembered what Stella had said about the Elite office: after tonight, they'd be shutting down until January.

She glanced at the clock—almost ten. Then out the window. The snow still fell steadily, but it appeared the wind had died down some. She could actually see down to the parking lot, could make out cars slowly driving by on the main street, which had been plowed, though the lot itself hadn't been.

If the office was downtown, or as far away as the bank, she probably wouldn't risk it. But it was close, maybe two miles. And the security guard could still be working. There was no guarantee that would be the case on Monday, especially if the whole city was snowed in until then.

Of course, if that happened, her own portrait appointment could be canceled as well. But if it weren't—if the weatherman had overestimated this time, and everything was fine Monday—did she really want to risk not having the equipment she needed to do the job?

Convinced, Lucy raced to her room and changed into jeans and a thick sweater. Adding boots and her warmest coat, she headed outside. The snow on her car was heavy and wet, and every minute she spent clearing it reminded her she was crazy to go chasing after a camera at the start of a blizzard.

Fortunately, as soon as she exited the parking lot and got onto the slushy road, she could tell things were better than when she'd come home an hour ago. The snow was heavier, yes, but she didn't have to crane forward and press her nose against the windshield to see out. It appeared old man winter was giving her a break—a short, wind-free window. She only hoped it didn't slam shut until after she got back home.

The drive that had taken her a few minutes this morning took her fifteen tonight. But when she reached the parking lot for Elite Construction and saw the security vehicle parked there, plus the warm, welcoming lights on the first floor, she was glad she'd taken the chance.

Parking, she hurried to the entrance and pounded on the door. The man inside was so startled, he nearly fell off his stool. He came closer, calling, "We're closed!"

"I know," she said, then pulled her hood back so he could see her face. Hopefully he'd remember her, if for no other reason than that she'd been making out with one of his coworkers a few hours ago. "Remember me? I was here earlier."

He nodded and smiled. Pulling out a large key ring, he unlocked the door, and ushered her in. "Goodness, miss, what are you doing out on a night like this?"

"I wouldn't be if I weren't desperate." She stomped her feet on a large mat. "I need to get upstairs to where the party was held. I forgot something and I have to get it tonight."

"Must be pretty important," he said, his gray eyebrows coming together. "It's not a fit night out for man nor beast."

She chuckled, recognizing the quote from a show she'd loved as a kid. "Do you think you could let me go look for my things?"

"I'll take you up. Gotta make my rounds, anyway."

He escorted her to the bank of elevators, and punched in a number on a keypad by the nearest one. The light above it came on, and the door slid open. Pretty high-tech stuff. Of course, she'd noticed earlier today that the new building had all the latest bells and whistles.

Arriving on the sixth floor, Lucy hurried to the area where the photo booth had been set up. It had been dismantled. Santa's chair was gone, and so were her bag and case. "Oh, hell."

"Some stuff was left in the break room," he told her. "If it's valuable, it's possible somebody locked it up for you."

"Could be. Stella saw me leave my camera and lenses here."

"Let's check her office first, then," he said, leading her down the hallway to the executive suite. He preceded her inside, but before she even had a chance to follow, she heard him exclaim, "Oh, no, watch it, mister!"

Following his stare, she looked out the window to the street below, and saw a car spinning out of control. It skidded off the street, hydroplaning across the parking lot where the Elite Construction security truck was parked. She winced, doubting the driver could regain control.

He didn't.

"Dang it all," said the guard. He cast her a quick look. "Do you mind looking by yourself? I should run down and make sure that driver's all right. If your stuff's not here, check the break room, back down the hall, fourth door on the left."

"Of course," she said, then watched the elderly man hurry away. She quickly scanned the office area. No luck. She wasn't going to go snooping through Stella's desk drawers or file cabinet, even if they weren't locked. Her things wouldn't fit, anyway.

She next spent several minutes searching the break room. It was piled with boxes of decorations, and containers of unopened food. Lucy looked through every bag and box, to be sure nobody had tucked her things in there for safekeeping.

Growing frustrated—and worrying somebody might have picked up the camera and lenses and given themselves an early Christmas present—she opened a free-standing cabinet and at last, struck pay dirt. "Yes!" she exclaimed, spying the familiar bag and case.

So relieved she felt like crying, she scooped them up, hurried toward the elevator and pushed the call button. She waited. And waited. And waited. Nothing.

Apparently the guard needed to again enter the code on the keypad so she could get down. Wondering if he could still be outside after all this time, she went to the front window and looked down toward the parking lot.

What she saw surprised her. An ambulance, its lights flashing, was parked beside the two vehicles involved in the fender-bender. She hadn't realized the crash had been so serious, but apparently the driver had been hurt. They were putting him on a gurney and wheeling him over to the ambulance.

Suddenly that gurney was pushed under a streetlight, and she had a better view of the person on it. Even through the snow and the darkness she could make out the grizzled gray hair, not to mention the uniform.

It wasn't the driver of the other car. It was the guard.

"Oh, God!" she muttered, wondering what had happened.

He'd gone out to help the accident victim—had he slipped and fallen? Or, maybe he'd been trying to help dig the vehicle out of a snowbank. Considering his age, and knowing even the healthiest of men could be affected when they tried to shovel too-heavy snow, she prayed he hadn't had a heart attack.

Then she began to wonder something else.

What if she was trapped in this building?

Her heart started thudding as she replayed everything in her mind. The conscientious way the man had carefully locked the door this afternoon, even though people were still leaving. And the way he'd obviously kept the elevator turned off tonight, despite knowing she was up here.

Would he really… "No," she muttered, certain he wouldn't have locked her in when he went to help the other driver.

There was only one way to be sure. Remembering how Ross had beat her to the lobby today, she found a door marked Stairs and headed through it. Six flights down was not fun, but it was better than sitting in somebody's office all night.

Reaching the entrance, she held her breath and pushed the nearest door. It didn't budge. Neither did the one beside it, or the next. She really was locked in here.

"Every building has an emergency exit," she reminded herself. She just had to find it. How difficult could that be?

Not difficult at all.

At least, she didn't think so…until the power went out.

CHAPTER SIX

Then
New York, December 23, 2005

AS THEY WALKED the busy streets of the city, Ross glanced at his watch and saw it was almost four o'clock. He began to do some mental calculations. What time did the shipping place close? How many people were lined up there already? How long would it take to get back to his place and pick up the wrapped presents?

Eventually he just started to wonder how much money he had in his checking account. He needed to know that, since he suspected he wasn't going to make it to the mailing store today to send off gifts to his family. He had lost track of time with Lucy; plus, he hadn't even picked up something for his nephew yet. So it looked like he'd be paying a king's ransom to send it tomorrow and arrange for a Christmas Day delivery. If there was such a thing.

For some reason, though, that didn't bother him as much as he'd have expected. It seemed worth the price since it had let him spend more time with Lucy Fleming. After the unpleasant scene with her ex, followed by that amazing kiss in the elevator, he hadn't been about to say *nice meeting you* and walk away. Errands could wait. Plus, if worse came to worst, he could always send the family e-gift cards tomorrow. Having twenty-five bucks to spend at Amazon would make even his bratty youngest sister squeal; she was really into those teen romance books.

With a fallback plan in place, he let himself forget about everything else—missing the holidays with his family for the first time in his life. The job he was starting next week. The tense phone call he'd had with his father last week. It was sure to be repeated on Christmas Day, when talk would shift from turkey and Mom's great stuffing to the same-old question: *When are you going to give up that vagabond lifestyle and come back home to work for the company where you belong?*

Gee. He could hardly wait. *Not.*

So an afternoon spent with a beautiful young woman whose gold-tinted brown eyes actually sparkled as she looked in delight at the softly falling snow sounded like a great idea to him. The best one he'd had in ages—the last being when, after graduating from Illinois State, he'd decided to come to New York for a while rather than going home to work for Elite Construction. He didn't regret that decision. Especially today. Today, he was very happy to be right where he was.

"Do you want me to carry that?" he asked as they snaked up the street, weaving around street vendors and harried shoppers.

Lucy glanced down at the rumpled box containing her broken gift from her brother. She was still clutching it against her chest. Every once in a while, a distinctive tinkle of broken glass came from within. Each one made her wince.

His hands reflexively curled every time he saw her pain. He so should've laid-out her jerk of an ex. "Are you okay?" he asked, stopping in the middle of a sidewalk, earning glares from a dozen people who streamed past them.

She nodded. "I'm fine, really. Thanks for the offer, but I'd rather hold onto this for a while."

She'd probably like to find a quiet place where she could open her gift, but that wasn't going to happen here.

Taking her arm as they were nearly barreled into by a power broker yammering into his cell phone, he led her down Broadway. Manhattan at Christmastime was a world of mad colors, sounds, and crowds, and this area felt like the pulsing center of everything. It might not have all the high-end shop windows up on Park or Fifth, with their fancy displays that dripped jewels and overpriced designer clothes. But it had a million little electronics stores with huge Sale signs in their windows, kitschy tourist shops, street performers, barkers, camera crews and vendors selling everything from scarves to hot dogs.

It also had so much life. Walking one block up Broadway brought words from a half-dozen languages to his ears. While the city often got a bad rap for being unfriendly, Ross had never heard so many

Merry Christmases. Even Lucy, who'd sworn she was a Scrooge about the holidays, seemed caught up in it.

"This is the worst place in the world to be today, you do realize that, right?" she said, laughing as they wove through a crowd of Japanese tourists loaded for bear with shopping bags.

They'd just headed down into a subway station, Ross having suddenly realized exactly where he wanted to go. "Nah. Maybe the second worst. Just wait till we get to our destination—that's number one."

"Uh-oh. Dare I ask?"

Grinning, he remained silent as they crammed into the subway car. Despite her pleas for clues, he didn't say anything, not until they were actually across the street from the store he most wanted to visit. Then he pointed. "We're here."

Her jaw unhinged. "You've got to be kidding! You seriously want to go into the biggest toy store in the universe *today?*"

"Come on, it'll be fun."

She took a step back. "It'll be insane. There will be a gazillion kids in there."

"Nah. Just their frenzied parents."

"Who are worse than the kids!"

"You'll like this, I promise. Come on, Miss Cranky Ass."

She gaped.

"Look, I need to get a present for my nephew. I know he'd love this walking, roaring dinosaur toy I've seen commercials for. My sister told me he's spent the last month with his arms hidden inside his shirt, waving his little hands and roaring at all his preschool classmates."

"Velociraptor?"

"Yup."

"Okay, at least he's got good taste in dinosaurs. They're my favorite, too."

"I always preferred the T-rex, myself."

"Not bad," she said with a shrug. "So I guess that means we're a couple of carnivores."

He nodded, liking the banter, especially liking that the bad mood her ex had caused appeared to have completely disappeared. "I guess so. Though, I don't suspect it would take a whole pack of you to bring me to my knees." No, he suspected Lucy would be quite capable of that all on her own.

He didn't elaborate, letting her figure out what he meant. When she lowered her lashes and looked away, he figured she had.

What could he say? He was affected by her, had been at first sight. The feelings had grown every minute they'd spent together. Not that she was probably ready to hear that from a guy she'd met a few hours ago. Nor, honestly, was he ready to say it. Knowing she was amazing, fantastic—and that he wanted her, badly—was one thing. Admitting it this soon was another.

So he went back to safer ground. "Anyway, that store's probably the only place I'm going to find the dino-toy I'm looking for today. It walks, it roars, he'll love it!"

"Preschool-age appropriate?" she asked, sounding dubious.

"Hell, no." He grinned. "But that's for his parents to deal with. I'm just the cool uncle who buys it."

Considering the present might be late, he wanted to make it a good one. No internet gift card could ever satisfy a four-year-old, and since Ross was the boy's godfather, and his only uncle, he had to do right by him.

"So, what do you say?"

"I dunno…"

"We're talking about going into FAO Schwarz, not Mount Doom and the fires of Mordor."

She rolled her eyes. "At least there are no screaming little ones on Mount Doom, unless you count the Hobbits."

He liked that she got the reference. He wasn't a total geek but couldn't deny being a LOTR fan. "None in there, either. They're all home being extra-good, hoping Santa will notice."

"How about I wait outside?" she offered, looking horrified by the idea of going in, but also a bit saddened by it.

Lucy was obviously serious about that not-liking-Christmas thing. Though, he wondered if it was the holiday she didn't like, or the memories that were attached to it. Given the few things she'd said about her parents, and the happy childhood she'd had before she'd lost them, he suspected that might be it.

Well, bad memories never truly went away, but

they could certainly be smacked into the background by good ones.

"Your call," he replied, tsking. "But remember, you don't have to shop. Don't you think you'd have fun watching the crazed parents fighting over the last Suzy Pees Herself doll, or the My Kid Ain't Gonna Be Gay Monster Truck playset?"

Lucy laughed out loud, as he'd hoped she would. "When you put it that way, how could I possibly refuse?"

"You can't. Anyone with an ounce of schadenfreude in their soul—which I suspect you have, at least when it comes to Christmas and oddly-penised exes—would race me to the door."

Mischief danced on her face and a dimple appeared in her cheek as she offered a self-deprecating grin. She didn't deny it. That was something else he liked about her. Most other women he knew kept up that I-love-puppies-and-kitties-and-everyone front, at least at the beginning of a relationship. Lucy hadn't bothered. Hell, she freely admitted she hated Christmas, and had been fantasizing about cutting off a guy's dick when they'd met. Talk about not putting on some kind of nice-girl act. Was it any wonder he already liked her so much?

"Okay, Mount Doom, here we come," she said, taking his hand.

It was cold out—very cold—yet neither of them wore gloves. His were tucked in his pocket, and he knew she had some, too, since she'd worn them when they'd first left the coffee shop. But neither of them had put them on once they'd left her ex's place…once she'd taken his hand. Her fingers were icy cold, and he suspected his were too. But it was worth it.

Slowly making their way through the crowds outside, they ventured into the hell that was called a toy store the day before Christmas Eve. The moment they entered, they were assaulted with heat and noise and color. Any kid would have thought they'd entered wonderland—the whole place was set up to inspire thoughts of childhood fantasy. Well, if your fantasy included being pressed jaw-to-jaw with strangers. Oh, and getting into the spirit of the season by elbowing each other to get closer to the front of the long lines at the cashier stations.

"You've got to be kidding me!" she said when she realized it was worse than she'd predicted. Not a square foot of floor space seemed to be unoccupied. The merriment from outside hadn't worked its way in here. These people were shopping like they were on a mission: *Nobody gets between me and my Bratz dolls.*

"I think we've just entered shark-infested waters," she said, raising her voice to be heard over the loud music and the general thrum of too many people packed in too small a space.

"Stick close to me, minnow."

"Gotcha, big white. But please tell me this dinosaur you're looking for isn't the hottest toy of the season."

"Nah, that's the Suzy Pees Herself *and* Drives a Monster Truck doll."

"My kind of girl. Uh, other than the peeing herself part."

"Whew!"

Finally, after one too many stomps on her foot, Lucy reminded him she wasn't the one shopping. She ducked into a corner and waved him off. Every time he caught sight of her, watching the hysteria that surrounded her, he noted the expression on her face—amusement, yes. But also, he suspected, relief that she didn't have to actually be a part of this.

Maybe one day she'd want to. One day when she didn't have just her brother, and a single broken gift to look forward to for the upcoming holiday weekend.

And me.

Ross was reaching around a glowering man—who was arguing with a sharp-tongued woman over what was apparently the last Barbie doll in Manhattan—when that realization struck him. He was here, alone, with plans to do nothing more than eat Chinese food and watch *National Lampoon's* Christmas Vacation this weekend. And Lucy was going to be here alone, too.

His mind didn't go where it might have gone a year or two ago, when he'd been more focused on what happened at the end of a date with a girl than during it. He didn't immediately picture the two of them naked under the mistletoe.

Well, it wasn't the *only* thing he pictured when he thought about spending Christmas with her. But mainly, he thought about seeing her smile, hearing her laugh, touching her soft skin and that amazing hair.

Even if they spent the weekend pretending Christmas didn't exist, he really wanted to spend it with her.

After some hunting, Ross found the Robo-Raptor toy he'd been seeking. The thing was expensive, but, considering it would likely be late, he wasn't going to quibble over the cost.

Grabbing it, he made his way back to Lucy, finding her not too far from where he'd left her. She stood by herself, having found another quiet corner, and was gazing at a display in the games area. A huge Candyland display, with nearly life-size gingerbread men game pieces and tons of pink fluff that looked like cotton candy.

Lucy's expression was definitely wistful. As he watched from several feet away, she reached out and touched a large fairy-type doll—he couldn't remember the name, it had been a long time since his board game days. Her hand shook slightly, but the touch on the pale blue hair was tender. Sweet. As if she were reaching out and stroking the gossamer wings of a beautiful memory that flitted in her subconscious. Having noticed the hint of moisture in her eyes, he suspected she was.

As he approached, he noticed her reach up and swipe at her face with her fingertips, confirming that moisture had begun to drip. Ross dropped a hand on her shoulder. "You okay?"

She nodded. Her voice low, she explained, "This is so pretty. I loved this game as a kid."

"I was more of a Chutes and Ladders fan, myself."

She barely smiled, and he regretted making light of it when something was on her mind.

As if knowing he was curious, she admitted, "I used to beg my mother to play with me all the time. She ran the business with my Dad, and had more time at home than a lot of moms, so I assumed that meant she was mine 24/7."

"I think every kid feels that about their mom."

"Well, I was pretty relentless, and eventually we had to start negotiating. 'Just let me finish this paperwork, and I promise we'll play *one* game of Candyland.'"

"Kinda like how my parents negotiated with me—eat one more green bean and you can have ice cream after dinner."

She nodded. "Exactly. I outgrew the game, of course, but one day when I was older, it occurred to me that every time we had played, I would *always* get the Queen Frostine card within the first couple of hands. So I always won."

He glanced at the board on display, seeing how close that particular character was to the winning space, and smiled slightly. "Quickly."

She laughed. "Exactly. I was a world champion Candylander. My mom was a world champion cheater for fixing the deck so I'd get that card and win the game super-fast every time."

"Did you confront her about it?"

"Uh-huh. When I was eleven or twelve." Her laughter deepened. "She totally confessed, saying she'd never break a promise to me, and always played when she said she would. But that didn't mean she couldn't speed up the process a little."

Her eyes, which had been sparkling with tears a few minutes ago, now gleamed with amusement. The warmth of the good memory had washed away, at least temporarily, whatever sadness she'd been feeling.

"I miss her a lot," she admitted simply. "My dad, too. It'll be five years Tuesday."

He sucked in a surprised breath. She'd lost both parents, together, which could only mean some kind of tragedy. And just two days after Christmas… No wonder she'd just rather skip over the whole holiday season. Talk about mixing up happy thoughts with sad ones. "I'm so sorry, Lucy."

"Me, too." She glanced around the crowded store. "I guess you've figured out that's why I'm not a big fan of the season."

"Yeah."

"That's why my brother and I have unconventional holidays."

But this year, she'd already told him, she wouldn't be seeing her brother. And her roommate was going away. She would be entirely alone, surrounded by a merry world while she sunk deeper into memories of the past.

Not if he could help it. She wanted unconventional? Fine. One good way to start—how about Christmas with a near-stranger?

He lifted a hand to her face and brushed his fingertips across her cheek. "Well then, how about we make a deal? I promise not to sing any carols or serve you any eggnog…if you promise to spend this holiday weekend with me."

A FEW HOURS later, after having shopped a little more and laughed a lot more, they grabbed some dinner, then headed back toward Lucy's place. The tiny apartment she shared with Kate wasn't too far away from Beans & Books, where Ross had left his truck. She told herself he was just escorting her home and would then leave. But in the back of her mind, she couldn't help wondering just how *much* of the weekend he'd meant when he talked about them spending this holiday together.

And how much she wanted him to mean.

It was crazy, considering she'd dated Jude for three months and had barely let him onto second base, with one unsatisfying attempt to steal third. But she already knew she wanted Ross to hit the grand slam. What she felt when she was with him—savoring the warmth of his hand in hers, quivering when his arm accidentally brushed against her body, thrilling to the sound of his voice—was undiluted want. She'd heard it described, but now, for the first time, she *felt* it.

She knew she should slow it down. But something—not just the instant physical attraction, but also his warm sense of humor, his generosity, the sexy laugh—made him someone she didn't want to let get away. So, when they got back to her building, she intended to invite him up for a drink. And then see what happened. Or make something happen.

She and Kate shared a small efficiency, whose rent was probably as much as a mortgage payment for places outside the city. Right now, the apartment was empty. Kate had left for the holidays—she'd called two hours ago, right before Teddy was picking her up. So the place was all Lucy's for the weekend.

Hmm. Was it possible she was within hours of getting *it* at last? She didn't mean getting laid, she meant finally understanding. Finally grasping what it was like to be so overcome by pleasure that you lost track of the rest of the world.

Her steps quickened. She was so anxious to get home, to start finding out if the weekend included nights or only daytime hours, she didn't notice when Ross stopped walking. She finally realized it and looked over her shoulder, seeing him a half-dozen steps back. He stood in the middle of a crowded Sixth Avenue sidewalk, and was gazing up toward the sky.

No. Not the sky. Those twinkling lights weren't stars. Instead, thousands of tiny bulbs set the night aglow, their gleam picked up by a sea of sparkling ornaments gently held in the arms of an enormous evergreen.

"Can you believe this is the first time I've seen it?" Ross asked, staring raptly at the Rockefeller Center Christmas tree.

"Seriously?"

He nodded. "It's my first Christmas in the Big Apple, and I haven't happened to be over this way for the past few weeks."

Lucy might be Ebenezer's long-lost twin sister,

but she couldn't be a scrooge when it came to seeing Ross with that delighted expression on his face. He looked like a kid. A big, muscular, incredibly handsome, sexy-as-sin kid.

She returned to his side, looking up at the tree. It was beautiful against the night sky, ablaze with light and color. Even her hardened-to-Christmas heart softened at the sight.

Saying nothing, Ross led her toward an empty bench ahead. It was night and the crowds had thinned to near-reasonable levels.

She sat beside him on the bench, giving him time to stare at the decor. But to her surprise, he instead looked at her. "Since this is probably as close to a tree as you're going to get this year, do you want to open your present now?"

She glanced at the tattered box, which she'd lugged around all day. She could wait and open it when she got home, but somehow, this moment seemed right. "I already know what it is."

"Really?"

"Well, not specifically." She began plucking the still-damp packaging paper from the box. "Sam and I have this tradition."

"I suspect it's a nontraditional one."

"You could say that." She actually smiled as she tore off the last of the paper and lifted the lid. Jude might have broken her gift, but it was the joy of seeing what Sam had found that delighted her. No broken glass could take that away from her.

"Oh, my God," Ross said, staring into the mound of tissue paper inside the box. "That is…is…"

"It's the ugliest thing I've ever seen," Lucy said. She lifted her hand to her mouth, giggling. Jude's petty destruction hadn't done much to make this thing less appealing, because it had already been pretty damned hideous. "Isn't it perfect?"

His jaw dropped open and he stared at her. "Seriously?"

"Oh, yeah," she said with a nod. Then she lifted the broken snow globe, now missing glass, water and snow, and eyed the pièce de résistance that had once been the center of it. Sitting on a throne was the ugliest Santa Claus in existence. His eyes were wide and spacey, his face misshapen, his coloring off. His supposedly red suit was more 1970s disco-era orange, and was trimmed with tiny peace signs. Beside him stood two terrifyingly emaciated, grayish children who looked like they'd risen from their graves and were about to zombiefy old St. Nick.

Hideous. Awful.

She loved it.

"Oh, this is so much better than what I got him—a dumb outhouse Santa complete with gassy sound effects."

"Do you always give each other terrible presents?"

"Just for Christmas. He gives me snow globes, I give him some obnoxious Santa, often one that makes obscene noises."

He chuckled. "My sisters would kill me if I did that."

"It started as a joke—a distraction so we wouldn't have to think too much about the way it used to be. And it stuck."

She couldn't be more pleased with her gift—unless, of course, it weren't broken. But she wouldn't let Sam know about that part. The center scene was the key.

Smiling, Lucy tucked the base of the globe back in the box, trying to avoid any bits of glass. But when she felt a sharp stab on her index finger, she knew she hadn't been successful. "Ow," she muttered, popping her fingertip into her mouth.

"Let me see," he ordered.

She let him take her hand, seeing a bright drop of red blood oozing on her skin.

"We should go get something to clean this."

"It's okay, we're not too far from my place…as long as you're ready to leave?"

He rose, reaching for the now-open box, and extending his other hand to her. She gave him her noninjured one, and once she was standing beside him, he dropped an arm across her shoulders. Ross took one last look at the famous tree. Then, without a word, he turned to face her.

"I know this is cheesy and right out of a holiday movie," he said, "but I'm going to do it anyway."

She wasn't sure what the *it* was, but suddenly understood when he bent to kiss her. People continued to walk all around them, street musicians played in the background, skaters called from the icy rink below. But all that seemed to disappear as Lucy opened her mouth to him, tasting his tongue in slow, lazy thrusts that soon deepened. It got hotter, hungrier. Both of them seemed to have lost any hint of the restraint that had kept them from getting this intense during their previous kiss.

Ross dropped his arm until his hand brushed her hip, his fingertips resting right above her rear, and Lucy quivered, wanting more. A whole lot more.

"Get a room!" someone yelled.

The jeer and accompanying laughter intruded on the moment. Sighing against each other's lips, they slowly drew apart.

"Thank you," he said after a long moment, during which he kept his hand on her hip. "I can check that off my bucket list."

"Kissing in front of the Rockefeller Center Christmas tree?"

"No. Kissing *you* in front of the Rockefeller Center Christmas tree."

She couldn't keep the smile off her face as they began walking the several blocks to her apartment building. Ross carried not only the bag with his robotic dinosaur, but also her snow globe. He had insisted on wrapping a crumpled napkin around her fingertip, but she didn't even feel the sting of the cut anymore. Because the closer they got to home, the more she wondered what was going to happen when they arrived. That kiss had been so good, but also frustrating since she wanted more.

Much more.

Unfortunately once they reached her building, and

she looked up and saw what looked like every light in her apartment blazing, she realized she wasn't going to get it. Damn. "I guess Kate didn't leave, after all," she said, wondering why her friend had stuck around. It was nearly 10:00 p.m.; Kate and Teddy were supposed to get on the road hours ago.

"Your roommate's still here?"

"Sure looks like it. No way would she leave all the lights on—she's a total nag about our electric bill."

Ross nodded, though he averted his gaze. She wondered if it was so he could disguise his own disappointment.

It wasn't that she hadn't had dates up to her place before; Jude had been over numerous times. It was just, she'd wanted to be alone with Ross. *Really* alone. And there was no privacy to be had in her apartment. She slept in one corner on a Murphy bed, with just a clothesline curtain for a wall, and Kate used the daybed that doubled as a couch the rest of the time.

Being with him in a confined space, under the amused, knowing eyes of her roommate, would be bcyond torturous.

He seemed to agree. "What time should I come tomorrow?"

She raised a brow.

"You promised me the holiday weekend, remember?"

"You really meant that?"

He lifted both hands and cupped her face, tilting it up so she met his stare. "I absolutely meant that."

Then he bent down and kissed her again. He kept

this one light, sweet, soft. Still, Lucy moaned with pleasure, turning her head, reaching up to tangle her fingers in his hair. Once again, the damned box was between them, and now, a dinosaur was, too. But maybe that was for the best. Kissing him—feeling the warm stroke of his tongue in her mouth—was too exciting. If his hot, hard body were pressed against her, she'd be tempted to drag him up the stairs and see just how much privacy a clothesline curtain offered.

Ross ended the kiss and stepped back. "Good night, Lucy Fleming. I'm really glad I met you."

"Ditto," she whispered.

"See you tomorrow."

"Tomorrow."

Then, knowing she needed to get away now, while she had a brain cell in her head, she edged up the outside steps. She offered him one last smile before jabbing her finger on the keypad to unlock the exterior door, then slipped inside.

Her heart light as she almost skipped up the stairs, she felt like whistling a holiday tune. For the first time in several years, Lucy was actually looking forward to Christmas Eve. Because she had someone so special to share it with.

As she opened the apartment door, she looked around the tiny space for her roommate. "I thought you'd be long gone by now," she called.

Kate didn't respond. Lucy walked across the living room to the galley kitchen, peering around the corner, seeing no one. Then she noticed the thin curtain that shielded her bed from the rest of the apartment shimmy. *Strange.* "Katie?"

The curtain moved again, this time fully drawing back. Lucy's mouth fell open as she saw not her pretty roommate but someone she'd truly hoped to never see again. "Jude?"

"Where have you been? I've been waiting for hours."

"What do you think you're doing here? How did you get in?"

"Had a key made a couple of weeks ago." He smiled thinly, stepping closer, a slight wobble in his steps. *Drunk.* "It's my birthday. You never gave me my present. I've been waiting for it a long time and expected to get it tonight."

He stepped again. This time, Lucy saw a gleam in his eye that she didn't like. Jude suddenly didn't look like a drunk boy. More like a determined, vengeful man. One who might like her to think he was a little more intoxicated than he truly was.

She edged backward.

"Where you going? C'mon, you're not *really* mad, are you? You know I don't care anything about that skank. I was just frustrated, waiting for you. Guys have needs, you know." He stepped again, moving slightly sideways, and she suddenly realized he was trying to edge between her and the door.

This was serious. Kate was gone, her next-door neighbor was practically deaf and few people were out on the street in this area this late. And Jude knew all of those things.

"I still can't believe you got some dude to come with you to my apartment," he said, his eyes narrowing and his mouth twisting. "That was wrong, to bring some stranger into this."

Ross. Oh, God, did she wish she'd invited him up!

Lucy's thoughts churned and she went over her options, none of which included intervention by a knight in shining armor, *or* a carpenter in brown leather. Her brother had drilled college rape statistics into her head before she'd ever left home. He'd also taught her a few defensive moves. But better than trying to physically fight Jude would be to get him to leave.

She began thinking, mentally assessing everything in the apartment, knowing the knives in the kitchen were none too sharp. He now stood between her and the door. Her cell phone was in her purse and they didn't have a land line—not that anybody she called, including the police, would get here for a good ten or fifteen minutes. In that time, he could do a lot. And, she suspected, that's exactly what he intended to do.

"What's the matter?" he asked, a sly smile widening that petulant mouth. "Don't you want to give me something for my birthday? After making me wait all this time, you owe me."

"I don't owe you anything," she snapped, curling her hands into fists, deciding to go for the Adam's apple.

"Yeah, bitch, you do," he snarled, the mask coming off, the pretense cast aside. Any hint of the sloppy drunk disappeared as he rushed her, the rage in his expression telling her he was fully aware and cognizant of what he was doing.

But so was Lucy. She sidestepped him, kicking at his kneecaps with the thick heels of her hard leather boots. He stumbled, fell against the daybed and knocked over a lamp.

Not wasting a second, she headed for the door, hearing his roar of rage as he lunged after her. His fingers tangled in her hair and she was jerked backward. Ignoring the pain, she spun around and slashed at his face with her nails.

"Little cock-tease," he yelled.

Then there was another roar of rage. Only this one didn't come from Jude. It came from behind her, from the door to the apartment, which she'd neglected to lock when she came in.

Ross. He was here. Against all odds, for who knew what reason, he'd come up and gotten here just in time.

Stunned, Lucy watched as he thundered past her, tackling Jude around the waist and taking him down. A handful of her hair went with them, but she was so relieved, she barely noticed.

"You slimy sack of shit!"

The two guys rolled across the floor, knocking over furniture. Jude squirmed away and tried to stagger to his feet. Ross leaped up faster, his fists curled, and let one fly at Jude's face. There was a satisfying crunching sound, then blood spurted from that perfect, surgically enhanced nose.

Jude staggered back. "Dude, you broke my nose!"

Ross ignored him, striking again, this time landing a powerful fist on her would-be rapist's stomach. Jude doubled over, then collapsed onto the daybed, wailing.

Ross gave him a disgusted sneer before turning his attention to Lucy. "Are you all right? Did he…"

"No, I'm okay," she said, shaking as it sunk in just how bad this could have been. "Thank you."

"I was a block away, when I realized I was still holding your present from your brother." He gestured toward the floor, where the package lay. "I heard yelling from outside. Fortunately I remembered the numbers you hit on the keypad."

Thank God.

"I'm gonna have you arrested for assault!" Jude raged as he staggered back to his feet.

"Okay, sure. We'll share the back of the police car as you're hauled in for attempted rape," Ross replied, fury sparking off him as he took a threatening step toward Jude.

The other man dropped his shaking hand, eyeing Lucy, his mouth quivering. "Wait, I didn't mean…I wouldn't have…"

"Yes, you would have," she replied, knowing it was true. "And I am pressing charges."

"Don't—my parents…I could lose my internship! I'm sorry, I guess I just went a little crazy."

She didn't feel any sympathy for him. But she was worried about Ross. He was a carpenter, a flat-broke out-of-towner, and Jude was the only son of a rich corporate shark. Lucy only had her word to convince anyone that Jude had attacked her.

Well, that and a probable bald spot.

She needed to think about this. "Just go," she said, suddenly feeling overwhelmed.

"Thank you!"

"I'm not promising you *anything.* At the very least, I'm reporting you to campus security and to the dean's office."

Jude's bottom lip pushed out in an angry pout. But Ross cut him off before he could say a word. "Get the fuck out, before I hurt you some more."

Shutting his mouth, Jude beelined for the door, giving Ross a wide berth, as if not trusting him not to lash out. Probably a good call, considering Ross was visibly shaking with anger.

Just before he left, Jude cast Lucy one more pleading glance. She ignored him, focused only on Ross. Her knight in shining armor, whether he saw it that way or not.

Lucy had never been the kind of girl who wanted to be rescued. Nor had she ever thought she'd need to be. But tonight, that Galahad riding in on the proverbial white horse thing had come in incredibly handy.

Once they were alone, Ross strode to the door, flipping the lock. When he returned, he didn't hesitate, walking right to her with open arms. Lucy melted against his hard body, letting go of the anxiety of the past ten minutes and just holding on, soaking up his warmth and his concern. He kept stroking her, running his fingers through her hair, tenderly rubbing tiny circles on the small of her back. Murmuring soft words into her ear.

It was, quite honestly, the most protected and cherished she'd felt in years.

"It's okay, Luce, he's gone. He's gone."

Finally, after several long moments, he pulled back a few inches and looked down at her. "You shouldn't stay here alone."

No, she probably shouldn't. "He said he made a key..."

"You're *definitely* not staying then." He mumbled a curse and stiffened, and she knew he was mad at himself for not getting the key back before Jude had left.

"I guess I could go to a hotel..."

"Screw that," he muttered, looking at her with an incredulous expression, as if she'd said something absolutely ridiculous. "Pack a bag, you're coming home with me."

CHAPTER SEVEN

Now
Chicago, December 24, 2011

Ross was at his parents' house outside of the city when the call came in about Chip being taken to the hospital. The caller told him the elderly man had gone outside to deal with an accident, and the exertion of helping to push a car out of the snow had apparently caused a heart attack.

The police officer who called didn't have any more information, but that was enough to send Ross back into town. He didn't have the phone numbers of the other guards with him, nor could he be sure they'd be able to go in to the office. He had no idea whether Chip had even locked the main doors when he'd gone out to help the driver, so somebody had to get in there. And the buck always stopped at the boss's desk.

The drive would be bad, and he already knew he'd have to spend the night at the office. Fortunately Stella had made up the fold-out sofa in his office. Besides, while everyone was disappointed—especially his older sister, who'd just arrived with her family for the holidays—he couldn't deny he wouldn't mind getting away from all the holiday cheer. He hadn't been able to take his mind off Lucy, and the longer he stayed, the more likely it was somebody would notice. He just didn't feel like explaining his mood to a nosy sibling or parent.

It was nearly 2:00 a.m. by the time he arrived—the trip had taken three exhausting, stress-filled hours. The plows were barely managing to keep up with the thick snow—he'd earned a few scolding stares from their drivers as he followed them down newly plowed stretches of highway.

The private parking lot wasn't plowed, of course, and he was glad he drove a monster SUV that could clear the already foot-high drift. Parking, he bundled up, then stepped outside, his body immediately battered by the wild wind. It howled eerily in the night and the snow seemed to be moving in all directions—up, down, sideways. Not that he could see much of it in front of his face, and he suddenly realized why.

There were no lights on. Not anywhere.

Blackout. Wonderful.

Fortunately the building was well-insulated and plenty warm. He had a couple of extra blankets for the foldout; he'd be fine overnight, and hopefully the power would be back on in the morning.

Hunching against the wind that tried to knock him back with every step, he made his way through the wet snow to the entrance, finding the doors locked. He had a master key, and used it to get in. Emergency reflective lights cast a little illumination in the lobby, and he cautiously made his way to the security desk, knowing a few industrial-strength flashlights were stored back there. Grabbing one, he headed for the stairs, trudging back up six flights, mere hours after he'd raced down them. Going up definitely took longer.

By the time he got to his floor, he was ready for sleep. It looked like he might be snowed in for a couple of days, so he'd have plenty of time to work. Right now, he was weary—physically and emotionally—and just wanted to call it a night.

Once inside his office, in familiar territory, he turned off the flashlight. Hopefully the power would be on tomorrow, but if not, he wanted to conserve the battery. Stretching, he stripped off his wet coat and kicked off his shoes, then walked across the office to the small, private sitting area.

Ross moved cautiously; it was even darker in this corner, since there were no windows. He still managed to bump into the edge of the foldout, and muttered a curse. Then, glad the day was over, and that it couldn't get any crazier, he lifted the covers and climbed into the bed.

A noise split the silence. A low sigh.

What the hell?

The sound surprised him into utter wakefulness. Carefully reaching out, he patted the other side of the bed…and felt a body under the covers.

"Ross?" asked a soft, sleep-filled woman's voice.

A familiar woman's voice.

"Lucy?" he whispered, shocked.

Could it really be her? He knew that voice, and

could now smell the sweet cinnamon-tinged scent she always wore.

She mumbled something and shifted, scooting closer as if drawn to his warmth. His eyes had adjusted a little, and he was able to make out her beautiful face. The creamy skin, the strand of dark hair lying across her cheek, the perfect mouth drawn into a tiny frown.

And she'd said his name in her sleep.

His heart pounded as he realized it was real. Lucy Fleming was asleep in his bed, in his office, in a building that was supposed to be deserted. It made absolutely no sense, was probably the last thing he'd ever have expected to happen. Considering how determined she'd been to get away without even talking to him earlier, climbing into this bed and finding the real live Santa Claus seemed more likely.

He frantically thought of the scenarios that might have landed her here. She had to have come back sometime after the building closed—when he'd left at seven-thirty, everybody had been gone except the guard. Why she'd returned, he had no idea. Maybe she'd forgotten something? Whatever the reason, Chip had to have let her in, probably recognizing her from this afternoon.

Beyond that…what? Had she offered to stay in the building when he was taken away by ambulance? That sounded incredibly far-fetched, and the officer who'd called hadn't mentioned it.

The doors. Shit. When the locking mechanism was engaged, they couldn't be opened, even from the inside, without a key. If Chip had gone out to help the motorist, he must have locked up behind him.

"You got locked in," he murmured, suddenly understanding.

And she had no way to call for help. The building was notorious for its poor cell phone reception even in the best weather, and the phone system fed off the power, so regular phones wouldn't have worked. The internet would be out, of course, plus all the computers in the building were password protected.

He could almost picture Lucy banging on the doors, trying to get someone's attention. But with the dark night, the swirling snow and the lack of people venturing out, it must have seemed like a hopeless proposition. She'd have known she was stuck here until at least morning.

So, like Goldilocks, she'd found a bed and crawled into it.

He was glad he hadn't followed his first instinct, leaped to his feet and bellowed, "Who's that sleeping in my bed?"

Lucy Fleming is who's sleeping in my bed.

A smile tugged at his mouth. What were the odds? Six years ago tonight she'd slept in his bed, too.

Remembering everything about that night—seeing the parallels—he had to laugh softly. If he were a more new age kind of guy, he might see fate having a hand in this. But being a realist, he knew the fault lay with a blizzard, a blackout and a strong security system.

That didn't, however, mean he wasn't thankful as

hell for it, as long as Chip was going to be okay. Because, trapped as she was with him in this building, it wasn't going to be easy for Lucy to walk out of his life again.

He could hardly wait until morning to see just how much snow had fallen. How long they were going to be stuck here.

And what Lucy would have to say about it.

LUCY WAS HAVING the nicest dream. In that state between asleep and awake, she somehow knew it was a dream, but didn't want to give it up.

She was lying on a beach, cradled by soft, sugar-white sand. The turquoise waters of the Caribbean lapped in gentle waves, caressing her bare feet, the crash of the surf steady and hypnotic. Above, the sun shone bright in a robin's egg blue sky. Occasionally a puffy white cloud would drift across it, providing a hint of shade, but mostly she just felt warm and content.

Except her nose. That was really cold.

Actually, so were her cheeks. She lifted a hand, pressing her fingers against her face, wondering how her skin could be so cold when she was lying in such deliciously warm sunshine.

Beside her, a man groaned, as if he, too, was loving the feel of the sun, and the island breeze blowing across his skin. The sound was intriguing, and she moved closer. He was hot against her, big and powerful, with sweat-slickened muscles that she traced with her fingertips. She kept her eyes closed, not needing to see his face, somehow sensing she already knew who it was.

Or, maybe a little afraid she wouldn't see the face she wanted to see.

"Mmm," she moaned as she pressed her cheek against his chest. Languorous heat slid over her; she was lulled by his rhythmic exhalations, and by the sound of his steadily thudding heart.

Wait. Too scratchy. He should be bare-chested.

She waited for the dream to change, waited for the feel of slick, male skin against her face. Instead her cheeks just got colder, and the texture against her jaw scratchier. Not smooth, slick skin. Something like…wool?

Though she desperately wanted to grab the dream and sink into it again, she'd passed the tipping point into consciousness and knew it was no use. The dream was over. She was awake. Her face was cold because she was trapped in a building with no power and no heat. It was scratchy because…because….

She opened her eyes. Waited to let them adjust to the darkness. Saw a shape. A body. A scratchy sweater on which her cheek had been resting. A neck. A face. *Oh. My. God. Ross. Ross?*

She froze, unable to move a muscle as she tried to understand. She'd gone to sleep alone, worried, angry, wondering what would happen tomorrow if nobody came to check the building.

And had woken up in bed with Ross Marshall.

It was him, no doubt about it. The guy who'd broken her heart, the one she'd sworn would never get close enough to hurt her again, was sleeping beside her in the fold-out bed! Not just beside her, but practically underneath her. Apparently, in her sleep, she had curled up against him, raising one leg and sliding it over his groin, her arm draped across his flat stomach, her face nestled in the crook of his neck.

She was practically humping the guy.

And he was sound asleep.

Lucy's first instinct was to leap up and run. Her second, to grab a pillow and beat him over the head with it, demanding to know what the hell he was up to.

But then her brain took over.

Because, as far as she could tell, Ross hadn't been *up* to anything except sleeping. She'd been the one getting all creepy-crawly, sucking up his warmth while she'd dreamed of exotic beaches and blazing sunshine. Probably not too surprising, considering Ross was still just about the hottest man she had ever laid eyes on. Even in the nearly pitch-black room, it was impossible to miss the sensual fullness of his mouth, the slashing cheekbones, that angular, masculine face. His lashes were sinfully long for a guy, hiding those jewel-green eyes.

All the coldness she'd been feeling, at least on those parts, which weren't covered by Ross, dissipated. There was only warmth now. In fact, certain places of her anatomy throbbed with it.

She was suddenly very aware of the position of her arm across his waist, how it dipped low on his hip. Her leg had slipped so comfortably between his, she was almost afraid to move, lest she wake him. But staying like this was torturous.

Because it was simply impossible to have her legs wrapped around him, to feel him pressed against her, without remembering the past; all the ways he'd delighted her, pleasured her, thrilled her. The man had taught her things about her body she hadn't even known were possible.

While one day ago she would have sworn she was not the least bit susceptible to him anymore, the woman who'd had to get herself off in the bathtub a few hours ago would say otherwise. As would the one who now felt totally at the mercy of her girl parts.

Her nipples were tight and incredibly sensitive against his chest. The barest movement sent the fabric of her soft sweater sliding across them, and since she'd been in a hurry and hadn't grabbed a bra, the sensation was definitely noticeable.

That wasn't all. Her thighs were quivering, and between them, her sex was damp and swollen. The urge to thrust her hips nearly overwhelmed her, and she had to forcibly remind herself it was not polite to rub up against a sleeping man just to get a little satisfaction.

Though, to be totally honest, she suspected—no she knew—he could give her a *lot* of satisfaction.

She closed her eyes, took a deep steadying breath, willed her body into standby, then tried to extricate herself. Bad enough to have to wake him up and ask him what the hell he was doing here—or explain the silly story about why she was. But to do it when he knew she'd been using him as both a heating blanket and a potential sex toy was more than she could stand right now.

Holding her breath, she lifted her bent leg, drawing it back off his groin. Slowly, oh, so carefully. But when she shifted a little too low, and her jean-clad thigh brushed against the money-spot on the front of his trousers, she stopped with a gasp. Because those trousers were not flat anymore. Definitely not.

He was hard, erect, aroused.

And, she greatly feared, awake.

He confirmed it by dropping a big hand onto her arm, holding her right where she was—right against him.

"Stop."

"Uh…how long have you been awake?"

Please don't say long enough to know I've been climbing all over you in your sleep. Though, judging by the ridge in his pants—the big, mouthwatering ridge—that seemed pretty certain.

"I just woke up a few seconds ago," he claimed.

He could have been telling the truth, the gravelly note in his voice hinted at sleep. So maybe his body had just been doing its nocturnal thing. Perhaps the fact that her thighs were spread and practically begging to be parted further didn't factor into the big erection pressing against the seam of his pants.

Stop thinking about his pants. And what's in them.

Yeah, fat chance of that. Every cell she had was on high alert, and her blood roared through her veins. She might have told herself a thousand times that she never wanted to see Ross again. But being here, in his arms, knowing his body was reacting to her even if his mind didn't know it, was the most exciting thing she'd experienced in ages.

There was no sense denying it, at least to herself. She wanted him. Against all reason and all common sense.

Or maybe not. What if it *was* reasonable? Maybe it made *perfect* sense to take this unexpected moment and wring whatever she could from it.

She and Ross had been a perfect sexual match once. Lucy had spent six years learning that was a pretty rare thing. Other men had given her orgasms… nobody else had made the earth shake. Plus, she was no longer the inexperienced twenty-two year old who confused sex with love. She and Ross didn't need to love each other to experience pure, undiluted pleasure in each other's arms.

At least…as long as he *wanted* to. His body apparently did, but his mind had to be engaged in the decision-making process. Ross had walked away without a backward glance once before, so maybe this tension she was feeling didn't mean as much to him as it did to her. If not, she needed to know that before deciding whether to slide onto him and kiss his lips off, or roll over, get out of the bed and demand that he let her out of the building. Facing a blizzard sounded more appealing than admitting she wanted him and finding out he didn't really feel the same.

"You could have woken me up when you realized I was here. Why didn't you?"

"Maybe because I just wanted to sleep with you one more time," he admitted.

Nice.

Then, with a sigh, he added, "Plus I knew if I woke you up you'd put all those defenses back into place and insist on leaving in the middle of a blizzard."

She ignored the comment, since she'd pretty much just decided to do exactly that.

"So you just crawled in and curled up next to me?"

"As I recall, you were the one doing the curling," he said, his tone lazy and amused. Which confirmed he'd been awake a little longer than he'd let on. Hell.

"So," he continued, "what'd you forget?"

"Excuse me?"

"I think I put everything together—you must have forgotten something this afternoon, come back to retrieve it, then gotten stuck in the building when Chip went outside and had a heart attack."

"Oh, no! Is he okay?"

"The cop who called me said he thought he would be."

"I hope so. He was very nice, letting me come back in because, yes, I did forget something." Embarrassed to admit it, since every photographer considered their camera an extension of their own body, she explained, "I left my camera bag and my specialty lens case."

He chuckled softly, obviously reading between the lines, knowing he'd flustered her enough to make her forget her equipment. The man had always been a little too perceptive. Damn it.

This conversation wasn't going the way it was supposed to. She'd broached the topic, hoping to hear him say he'd climbed into bed with her because he wanted her so desperately.

Now they were talking about cameras and cops. Ugh.

The wind howled, and though the temperature hadn't fallen too much inside, she instinctively curled closer to Ross. They both fell silent, as if totally comfortable with the fact that they'd ended up in bed together by accident—which she still wanted to discuss, by the way.

But later. Not now. Not when he was so warm and strong, when his breath teased her hair, and his hard thigh fit so nicely between hers. Not when she was trying to breathe ever deeper, intoxicated by the warm, spicy scent of his skin.

Not when she needed to know if he really wanted her—Lucy Fleming—and not just the female body that happened to be beside him in the bed.

If he did, Lucy intended to let herself *have* him. Ross would be the ultimate Christmas present. Just this once, just for tonight.

As if he knew she had no intention of putting some distance between them, Ross lowered his hand to her wrist, lazily tracing circles on the pulse point. Like he had every right to touch her. Lucy sighed, shocked at how evocative that touch felt. Her already moist sex grew hotter, wetter, as she remembered how those strong but gentle fingers used to slide across her clit, making her come with a few deliberate strokes.

Stretching, he shifted a little, and she felt the flex

of the powerful muscles in his shoulder. She'd noted earlier that his body had changed—he was bigger, broader across the chest and shoulders, though his lean hips would still be easily encircled by her thighs.

It was far too easy to visualize that. To visualize everything. In fact, she was having difficulty focusing on anything else.

Without warning, Ross moved his hand, dropping it to her hip, tugging her more tightly against his body. For warmth? For old time's sake? Because he had nothing better to do?

Oh, God, he was driving her crazy!

He continued with that steady, even breathing, remaining silent, and didn't reveal by word or deed whether he was just killing time or trying to start something.

Finally, unable to take it anymore, she sat straight up in the bed and glared down at him. "Well, are you going to do something about this?"

She was asking a lot more than that. *Are you interested? Do you feel this? Do you want me?*

He didn't respond for a second, didn't reply with a confused, *Like what?* But then, just when Lucy was about to launch herself out of the bed and call him an idiot, he moved, quickly and deliberately.

Between one breath and the next, Ross sat up, pushed her onto her back and slid over her, his powerful body pressed hard against hers. His face lowered toward her, and Lucy's heart thudded with excitement as she saw the hunger in his expression.

Then he said two words…the only two she wanted to hear.

"Hell, yes."

After that, no words were needed. Her heart flying, all thoughts disappearing, she rose to meet his lips with her own. Their tongues plunged together, frantic, hungry for a connection.

There was nothing slow and quiet about it. Only driving need and demand. Their hands raced to touch each other, and Lucy hissed when he moved his mouth to her neck and sucked her nape. He nipped lightly and she quivered, wanting that mouth, that tongue, those nibbling teeth, on every inch of her body.

The Ross she'd made love with all those years ago had been slow, tender and deliberate. This Ross was wild. Desperate. She felt his driving need, and answered it with her own. Emotion had been chased away by lust, and she realized, suddenly, that she'd been waiting for this since long before the moments they'd just spent in his bed.

She'd longed for years to feel like this, through other affairs and other men. She'd wanted to experience the intense, nearly animalistic passion she felt right now. Deep down, Lucy knew she'd been waiting for him. Ross. Waiting until they met again—as if knowing someday they would—to truly let go of every inhibition, every doubt, every question about her own desirability. To know she was someone's sexual obsession, if only for one night, one moment in time.

And she was. He wanted her with every fiber of

his being. His desperate touch proclaimed it and her own body was already screaming a silent *Yes* to every little thing he might ask of her.

They separated only far enough to remove their clothes. His sweater came off, revealing the golden-skinned chest beneath, and she had to reach out and run the tips of her fingers across his impressive abs. He was built perfectly—broad chest, lean at the waist and hips. Like he'd been the model used to create the prime example of man.

When his hands touched her waist and began yanking her sweater up, Lucy arched toward him. She heard his low groan when he realized she wasn't wearing a bra, and even in the near-darkness, could see the look of pure appreciation as he visually devoured her.

Lucy had been built a little differently six years ago. She'd been more girlish, more lean. Now she was curvier, carrying an extra ten pounds in all the right places...places he obviously liked. A lot.

"God, you're gorgeous," he muttered. Then he bent to her breast, no warning, no hint, his mouth landing on her nipple and sucking hard. As if he couldn't help himself, had to quench his ravenous thirst with the taste of her.

"Oh, yes, please," she groaned.

She sunk her fingers into his hair, pressing him even harder, needing to feel it, deep down. And with every deep pull of his mouth, she did feel it. All the way down to the throbbing center of sensation between her thighs.

He leaned over to give her other breast the same attention. Plumping it with his hand, he rolled her nipple between his fingertips before he blew lightly, then suckled her. Lucy cried out at how good it felt. Savoring his attention, she kissed his neck, his shoulder, raking her nails down his bare back, wondering how he could possibly be so strong when he appeared to now be a suit-and-tie kind of guy.

She wanted to cry when he moved his mouth away again. But she got with the program when he kissed his way down her midriff to the waistband of her jeans, which he quickly unfastened. He backed away, kneeling on the edge of the bed and straightening her legs. Lucy lifted her hips, arching up toward him, helping as he tugged the denim away.

Thank God she'd been in too much of a hurry to put on long johns or something equally as hideous before she'd left home. Her pink panties weren't Frederick's of Hollywood worthy, but they were cute and sexy. And Ross seemed to like them. A lot.

Or maybe not. Because without a word, he ripped them off her, tearing the fabric. She didn't give a damn. The hunger in his every movement excited her beyond anything.

"Gotta taste you, Luce."

She had a second to prepare, then his mouth was on her, licking at her core. She actually shrieked, shocked by the raw intimacy. He didn't carefully sample her, he dove deep, thrusting his tongue into her opening, then up to her clit, then back again. She was whimpering, her hips bucking freely, helpless to do anything but take what he wanted to give. Her first orgasm smashed into her like an earthquake, making her whole body quiver. He didn't stop, merely holding her hips in his big hands, continuing to lick at her as if he couldn't get enough.

Then came the aftershocks—the tsunami—wave after wave of hot, electric delight, popping in little explosions that made her head spin. Colors, instruments, spinning lights—a whole freaking carnival seemed to be taking place all around her, all calliope music and the thrill of spinning and riding until you were breathless and just couldn't take anymore.

She couldn't take anymore.

"Stop," she ordered dazedly, knowing she'd reached that point. Pleasure overload. She could barely breathe, her heart was pounding hard enough to burst out of her chest, and she was almost hyperventilating from all the gasping.

Mostly she was stunned. Shocked.

Awakened.

They hadn't had a lot of time together six years ago, and oral sex was one intimacy they hadn't shared. She'd been young, a virgin, and he'd been tender and incredibly patient. She suspected that if Ross had ever used his mouth on her like that, she would have stalked him to Chicago.

Now, she wanted him to feel that same unadulterated freedom. Wanted to give him what she'd never given him before. Not just to please him, but also to make him as absolutely crazy as he had made her.

More, though, she wanted that intimacy for her

own sake. She'd never viewed oral sex as anything more than foreplay, a tit for tat return on a guy's earlier tongue investment. This time, though, she wanted to take that thick ridge of male heat into her mouth and explore the flavors of his body. Wanted to taste him, explore him, suck his cock until his willpower gave out, or his legs did.

She scooted away, grabbing his hair and pushing him up. He eyed her from between her legs, his eyes glittering, his mouth moist. "You taste good," he growled.

Licking her lips, she murmured, "I bet you do, too."

Sitting up, she became the aggressor, stalking him to the end of the bed, until he hopped off it. Eyeing her hungrily, he said nothing as she scooted to the edge, parting her thighs around his legs.

She was eye level with that wonderful, thick ridge straining against his zipper. Though she felt just as desperate to tear his clothes away, she hesitated, holding her breath. For that moment, she felt like she was about to open a Christmas present—just one, on Christmas Eve, the way she always had as a kid. The excitement of choosing the right one, and the certainty that there would be so many more good things to come all washed over her.

Catching her lip between her teeth, she unbuttoned his jeans, then eased the zipper down. He hissed as her hands brushed against the cotton of his boxer-briefs. Burying his hands in her hair, he held her tightly, not painfully, yet more forceful than she'd ever expect from him. It felt possessive. Demanding. Unlike the tender Ross she'd known, but perfect for the hungry man who'd eaten her like he'd been served his last meal.

Pushing the jeans and briefs down, she took a second to admire his cock—strong, erect and powerful. Lucy moistened her lips, then leaned forward and kissed the tip of it, hearing him groan as skin met skin.

That groan egged her on. She parted her lips, taking him into her mouth, swirling her tongue over and over. She swallowed the hint of moisture his body released, liking the salty taste, wanting a mouthful of it. She didn't worry that taking him to the edge would cut into what she wanted from him later. Ross was young and vital, and right now he looked like he could easily do her all night long, take a coffee break, then get right back in there and bang her brains out another half-dozen times.

Her thighs clenched, moisture dripping from her sex, still swollen, maybe even a little sore, from the thorough attention of his mouth.

She gave him the same attention, sucking hard. He swayed a little, which she took as a good sign. So she took more of him, deeper into her mouth, until she could take no more. Reaching between his legs, she carefully cupped the taut sacs, timing each stroke of her hand with one of her mouth, pulling away, then sucking him deep, over and over.

His groans deepened. The pace quickened. She

knew by the tenseness of those powerful muscles that he was close.

He stopped. "Uh-uh. I've waited six years. No way am I coming in your mouth."

Pulling back, he reached into his pocket and grabbed a condom. As he hurriedly donned it, she considered telling him she had the birth control covered. But she figured they should err on the safe side when they were being so impulsive, so crazy.

Ross shoved his pants completely off, then reached for her. Lucy let him lift her, wrapping her legs around his waist. He held her easily, her bottom cupped in his hands, then backed her against the wall, bracing her between it and his chest.

She sunk her fingers into his hair, tugging his mouth to hers for a deep kiss. He plunged his tongue deep…then did the same thing with his cock.

Oh, yes.

He didn't move at first, just stood holding her there, impaled on him. She felt her body soften and adjust, taking him completely. Savoring the fullness, she rocked against him, signaling him that he didn't need to go slow.

She didn't want him to go slow.

"Next time," he promised.

"Whatever," she panted

Then there were no words. Just hard thrusts of his body into hers. Deeper and deeper, he reached heights no one ever had before. Or maybe she was reaching those heights. It certainly felt like she was flying, almost out-of-body with sensation.

Moisture fell on her cheeks. Lucy realized she was crying. But not sad tears, God-it-feels-so-good-and-I've-waited-so-long tears.

She closed her eyes, dropped her head back and just took and took and took. The rocking of his groin against hers brought just the right friction and she felt all that familiar pressure boiling up again. Her clit throbbed and swelled. Then the dam burst and she came again.

"Oh, yes, God, yes."

Her words? His? Both?

She didn't know. She just knew they were both crying out, both sweating and twisting and thrusting. And finally, both coming.

He groaned, suddenly growing very still. Lucy kissed him. She could feel his pulse thundering, both against her chest, and where he was inside her, and she found herself wishing she had told him not to bother with the condom. She wanted all that heat bursting into her.

Fortunately, however, they were just getting started.

They had time. Plenty of it. Because, judging by the wind battering the building, and the dark snow swirling around the windows, they weren't going anywhere anytime soon.

CHAPTER EIGHT

Then
New York, December 24, 2005

THOUGH ROSS HAD wanted Lucy to call the police right after Jude had slithered out, he had sensed her desperation to get out of her apartment. She didn't just *want* to leave, she *needed* to. He suspected the place suddenly felt tainted to her, and had to wonder how long it would take before she ever felt safe there again.

That definitely wouldn't happen until he got her locks changed. And no way in hell was she staying there alone until then.

So, after she'd thrown a few things in a bag, they'd headed for his place. After a short walk to his truck, and a long drive out of the city, they arrived in Brooklyn. Every mile put the ugly scene further into the past, and Ross was finally able to begin clearing his mind of the mental images of what might have happened had he not shown up when he did.

The very idea made him sick. And violence surged up within him when he so much as thought Jude's name.

But now it was time to think about something else.

Making sure she was okay and felt safe, for one. Wondering what the hell had happened with his life in the past twelve hours for another.

Nah, he'd think about that tomorrow.

"Here we are," he said when he pulled up outside the tiny rental house where he lived. It wasn't much to look at, but it was a place of his own—a place nobody had helped him get. He didn't love the location, but he loved not feeling like he owed anything to anybody. Especially his father.

"I can't tell you how much I…"

"Forget it," he said, waving off her thank-you. Probably her twentieth since they'd left her place.

Reaching into the tiny back compartment of the truck, he grabbed her small suitcase and her camera bag, then got out, going around to open her door. She didn't wait, hopping out before he had made it around the bumper. "What a cute house!"

He raised a brow. "Seriously?"

"Sure. You have a yard and everything. I can't tell you how much I miss backyard barbecues in the summer."

"The last tenant left a grill. Maybe I'll cook up some burgers tomorrow."

She laughed. "In the snow?"

"You call this snow? Yeesh. Until you've experienced a lake effects winter, you don't know the meaning of snow."

"I have," she told him. "I grew up in Chicago."

Shocked, he almost tripped. "Seriously?" The woman he had begun to suspect was the girl of his dreams had grown up in the same city, and he'd never even been aware of her? That seemed wrong on some cosmic level.

"Uh huh. And even the thought of that windy winter reminds me why I'll never go back."

His heart twisted a little at that admission, but he pushed aside the disappointment. "Yeah, I can't say I'm missing it right now, either."

"Do you think you'll ever go back?"

"Yeah, I think so."

Actually he didn't just think it, he knew it. One of these days, he was going to have to return and face up to his responsibilities. His father wasn't getting any younger, or any healthier, and not one of his sisters showed any interest in construction.

Ross, on the other hand, genuinely loved it. He'd had a toy tool set as a kid, had built his first birdhouse at four. By the time he was ten, he had constructed a four-story Barbie house for his kid sister. He just had a real affinity for building things, and had never wanted to do anything else. Some even called it a gift.

Going away to college, then to grad school, and learning drafting and architecture had just made him better at his craft. More than that, he truly *wanted* to run the company one day, as his grandfather and now his father always said he would.

He just didn't want to be forced to work there under his father's watchful eye *now.* Having spent every summer and school holiday building things for Elite Construction, and knowing he'd end up doing that for much of his life, he just wanted some time to himself. To be free, to go somewhere new, to be totally on his own. That wasn't too much to ask, was it?

Well, it was according to his father.

"Ross?"

Realizing he'd fallen into a morose silence, he shook his head, hard. "Hold on a sec," he told her, going to the back of his covered truck to retrieve the robotic dinosaur and the bags of presents he'd been supposed to mail today. He'd told Lucy about them on the way home, and she'd promised to help him package them up tonight, then find a UPS store tomorrow.

Once inside, he flipped on the lights, and zoned-in on the thermostat. No, this wasn't a Chicago winter, but it was still pretty damn cold. Plus the house was old and drafty.

He jacked up the heat, then turned back to Lucy, who looked a lot less shell-shocked than she had when they'd left the city. He didn't try to hide his relief, glad for that strong, resilient streak he'd sensed in her from the moment they'd met.

Right now, she acted as though she didn't have a care in the world. In fact, she was wandering around, comfortable enough to be nosy and check out the house. "Oh, my God, is that really a lava lamp?"

"Like the grill, also left by a former tenant. As was the couch and the ugly kitchen table."

Lucky for him. After laying out cash for a security deposit, plus first and last month's rent, he hadn't had much money for furnishings.

Kinda funny, really, how he was living now. He'd been raised in a house with ten bedrooms on twenty acres. His sisters had each had a horse in the stable, and he'd had his choice of car when he'd turned sixteen. He hadn't necessarily been born with a solid silver spoon in his mouth, but it would have to be called silver-plated.

And now he lived in a drafty, tiny old house with hand-me-down furniture and an old analog TV that got only one station, and that only if there wasn't a cloud in the sky. He drove a five-year-old truck whose payments were still enough to make him wince once a month. Ate boxed mac-and-cheese and Ramen noodles, the way a lot of the scholarship kids in college had.

Most shocking of all? He liked it.

You do this and you're on your own, totally cut off! Don't expect a penny from me!

His father's angry voice echoed in his head. But so did an answering whisper: *But I did it anyway, didn't I? And I'm doing just fine.*

"What about the bean bag chair?" Lucy asked, interrupting his thoughts of the angry scene last summer, right after graduation, when he'd decided not to move back home.

He admitted, "What can I say? I bought that one. It seemed to go with the decor."

"Lemme guess…thrift store shopping spree?"

"Bingo." Shrugging, he added, "I was on a budget."

"I think my groovy, peace-sign Santa would fit in very well here."

"Don't even think about pawning that thing off

on me. Even if it weren't broken, I wouldn't let that drugged-out St. Nick and those zombie-kids anywhere near my Christmas tree. It might lose all its needles in pure fear."

She finally noticed the small tree, standing in the front corner near the window. Her smile faded a little, as if she'd suddenly remembered it was Christmas Eve, albeit very early on Christmas Eve—only about 1:00 a.m.

It was a sad-looking thing. He'd bought it on impulse—it had been the last one on a lot up the block, scrawny and short, with half its needles already gone. It had reminded him of Charlie Brown's tree…in need of a home. So he'd shelled out the ten bucks and brought it here, sticking it in a bucket since he didn't have a tree stand.

Nor had he had any real ornaments to put on it. Right now, an empty aluminum pot-pie tin served as a star on the top, and a bunch of picture hangers and odds-and-ends hung from the few branches.

As she stared at the pathetic thing, Lucy's sadness appeared to fade. She shook her head, a slow, reluctant smile widening her pretty mouth. "Are those beer can tabs?"

"Just a few," he admitted. "I was experimenting. I'm not a big drinker, so I only had a few cans in the fridge. I finally raided my toolbox."

Putting a hand on her hip and tilting her head, she said, "And you had the nerve to criticize my Christmas decorations?"

"Hey, mine's pathetic, not terrifying."

"My snow globe from last year wasn't terrifying."

"Oh, no? Let me guess. A tiny female elf wearing pasties and a G-string?"

Her eyes rounded. "Ooh, that sounds fabulous! But, no, it was just a North Pole scene."

He crossed his arms, waiting.

"With a clown that popped out of Santa's chimney like a Jack-in-the-Box."

Shuddering, he said, "Clowns are terrifying. What's wrong with Jack?"

"Why would a Jack-in-the-Box be in Santa's chimney?"

"Why would a clown?"

"Well, that's the point," she said, laughing at the ridiculous conversation. "None of it makes any sense!"

"Which makes it perfect to you and your brother. Merry Christmas to the Scrooge siblings."

"Exactly!"

Liking that her good mood was back, he asked, "Hey, are you hungry? I've got frozen pizza, frozen bagels, frozen burgers…."

"Typical single guy menu, huh?"

"Yep. Oh, if you want some wine, I think I have a box in the back of the fridge."

She snickered.

"It was a housewarming gift from a neighbor."

One pretty brow went up. "Oh? Not a basket of muffins?"

"Let's just say my neighbor's of the cat persuasion."

Her brow furrowed in confusion.

"The cougar variety." Frankly whenever his neighbor came over, he felt like putting on another layer of clothes.

"Never mind," he said, waving his hand. "So, why don't you help yourself while I go get cleaned up."

"You look clean to me."

"Under these clothes is a layer of sawdust—I'm itchy all over. I need to take a shower."

"Help yourself," she said, waving a hand as she headed to the kitchen, already making herself at home. "Want me to make you something?"

"Whatever you're having."

"Filet mignon it is."

He snorted. "Hungry Man Salisbury steak frozen dinner, if you're lucky."

Still smiling, glad her good mood had returned and thoughts of her vicious ex—who still had a lot of bad stuff coming to him—were gone, he headed for his room. The bed was unmade, clothes draped across it, the dresser drawers open. It looked like a single guy's room. Considering he intended to offer Lucy the bed, and take the couch for himself, he took a few minutes to straighten up.

As he did so, he couldn't help thinking about how much different his life seemed now than when he'd left this morning. He'd figured he'd be coming home to a quiet house, a solitary holiday, maybe a turkey sub from Subway. And he'd been okay with that. Not happy, but okay.

But he had to admit, in recent days, as the holiday season zoomed in like a rocket ship, he had really begun to think about his family back in Chicago. He had a few friends here, but not the type you'd share Christmas with. Being from a big family—which got bigger with every sister's marriage and the births of new nieces and nephews—he began to realize there were times living alone wasn't so great. As December marched on, he'd resigned himself to a lonely, kinda pathetic holiday weekend.

Wow, did things ever change on a dime.

Still thinking about those changes, he headed into the bathroom—spent another few minutes cleaning it—then got in the shower. He hadn't been kidding about that sawdust; the stuff had filtered into his clothes as he'd maneuvered the custom-made bookcase into place at Beans & Books.

Finally, his hair damp from a quick towel-dry, he pulled on a clean pair of jeans and a T-shirt and headed back out to the living room. Smelling something—popcorn?—his gaze immediately went to the kitchen, but didn't see Lucy there.

After a second, he spotted her in the one place he had not expected her to be, doing something he had *never* expected her to do. "Lucy?"

She looked up and smiled at him, a little self-conscious. "I couldn't take it anymore, it was just sad."

Ross could only stare. It appeared she had gone all Linus on his Charlie Brown Christmas tree, and had decided to give it a little love—how appropriate for a *Lucy.* What had been just sticks, needles, picture-hangers and beer can tabs an hour ago now at least resembled a bedecked evergreen.

"Where did you..."

"I just used stuff that was lying around. Hope you don't mind, but I cut up a couple of mac-and-cheese boxes...the packets are still in the cupboard. I assume you've made it often enough that you didn't need the directions?"

"Not a problem," he mumbled, still a little shocked at how much she'd done, how quickly she'd done it, and how good it looked.

"I'm glad you're the healthy type and your microwave popcorn wasn't buttered. That would have been sticky," she said as she plucked another piece out of a bowl and stuck it on the edge of a needle. A whole thread full of them dangled on her lap. "Oh, and I hope you don't mind me digging through your kitchen drawers. I was pleasantly surprised to find that sewing kit."

"Old tenant," he murmured, still a little stunned.

"Well, thanks to the former tenant then. Unfortunately he didn't happen to leave any twinkle lights or pretty red bows behind. But luckily, I hadn't cleaned out my camera bag," she added. "I had picked up some construction paper, glitter and glue to make decorations for the studio where I'm interning."

She'd used all those things to full advantage. Right now, glittery snowmen and Santa shapes dangled from several branches, apparently with directions for making mac-and-cheese on the other side. She had also managed a long strand of construction paper garland, like the kind he'd made as a kid. Red, green and white loops encircled each other, making a colorful chain that draped around the tree.

But that wasn't all. His pot-pie pan-topper had actually been cut into a star shape. And there was some kind of red-and-white fabric tucked around the bucket, creating a tree skirt. Having no clue where she could have gotten that, he quirked a questioning brow.

She chuckled. "My elf tights. I had two pair in my bag."

Good God. Tight, shimmery fabric, usually used to encase what he suspected were a pair of beautiful legs, was now hugging a dirty bucket at the base of an old, dead tree?

"I didn't have any lights, obviously, but I think this'll work. Hold on."

He watched as she crawled around the baseboard and fiddled with something on the floor. Suddenly the tree was bathed in a soft, reddish light from below. "Glad I had the red gel on me!"

Not knowing what she meant, he bent to peer at the light, which he realized was a camera flash with a sheet of red plastic over it.

"Voilà!"

He reached for her hand, pulling her to her feet and together they stared at her masterpiece. She'd taken a pretty pathetic stick, added a bunch of random objects and MacGyvered the whole thing into a work of art.

"Wow," he whispered, genuinely impressed. "It's amazing."

She shrugged. "But it's still not exactly traditional."

He heard the tremor in her voice and knew where her thoughts had gone—to that dirty word, *traditional.* For four years, she'd tried hard to distance herself from happy holiday traditions, keeping those sweet memories at bay for fear they'd be accompanied by sad ones. Yet now, she'd stepped out of her comfort zone, doing things she probably remembered doing with the parents she'd lost, even though it was painful for her.

And she'd done it for him.

He turned to her, dropping his hands to her waist, pulling her close to him. Lucy looked up at him, her eyes bright, shining in the holiday light, and he'd swear he had never seen a more beautiful face in his life.

"Thank you," he whispered. Then he punctuated the thanks by dropping his mouth to hers, kissing her softly.

She reached up and wrapped her arms around his neck, pressing her soft body against him. He'd kissed her earlier, but they'd both been wearing coats, and layers of clothes. Now, with just his T-shirt and her blouse, he was able to feel the fullness of her breasts against his chest. She moaned lightly, moving one leg so their thighs tangled.

As if needing to feel his skin, Lucy moved her hands under the bottom of his shirt, stroking his stomach. He pulled away enough for her to push it up and over his head, liking the way her eyes widened in appreciation as she began to explore his chest. She scraped the back of her finger over his nipple, and

Ross hissed in response. This time, when he pulled her close to kiss her again, he could feel the rigid tips of her breasts, separated from his bare skin by only by that silky blouse.

Saying nothing, Lucy began to pull him with her, toward the couch. Rather than follow, he bent and picked her up. Cradling her in his arms, he crossed the room and sat down, keeping her on his lap. They never broke the kiss. It just went on and on, slow and deep and wet.

Unable to resist, Ross reached for her stomach, trailing his fingertips over the blouse, hearing her purr in response. She arched up to meet his touch, telling him she wanted more. He tugged the material free of her pants, almost shaking in anticipation, knowing he'd been dying to touch her since they'd met.

As he'd expected, Lucy's body was silkier than her clothes. He took pure, visceral pleasure in the sensation, delighting in the textures against his callused hand.

"Oh, yes, more," she whispered against his mouth.

Glad for the invitation, he began to slide the buttons open, exposing more of her warm, supple skin. Lucy shifted a little, helping him tug the blouse free of her pants, so that by the time he unfastened the last button, the shirt fell open completely.

Ross stopped kissing her long enough to look at her, soaking in the breathtaking sight. Her breasts were high and round, every inch of her creamy smooth. Her lacy bra did nothing to conceal the tight, puckered nipples. And the way she arched up toward him told him what she needed.

He happily complied, covering one taut peak with his mouth, before tasting her with his tongue through the fabric.

She jerked, tangling her hands in his hair, pressing his head harder to her breast. Ross heard her tiny, raspy breaths, the little whimpers she couldn't contain, and knew she was loving every bit of this.

So was he.

With care, he lowered one of her bra-straps, releasing her breast and catching it in his hand. Her tight nipples demanded more attention, and he licked and kissed her there, sucking deep until she was squirming on his lap.

That squirming drove him a little crazy. His cock was rock-hard beneath her sexy butt, and the way she slid up and down on him told him she knew it. It also told him she wanted to keep going.

Needing to feel her heat, to see if she was as tight and wet as he suspected she was, he unsnapped her pants and slid the zipper down. He was careful in his movements, intentionally scraping his hand against the skimpy yellow panties she wore beneath. *Satin over silk.*

She didn't pull away, instead pushing against his hand, practically demanding that he touch her more thoroughly. *As though he needed to be asked?*

His mouth still on her breast, he could feel the raging beat of her heart and knew she was almost out of her mind with excitement. Breathing deeply to inhale that musky, feminine scent that practically drugged him into incoherence, he tugged the elastic away and moved his hand to the curls covering her sex. She whimpered, digging her nails lightly into his bare back. She was begging for more, though she didn't say a word.

Needing more, too, he slipped his finger between the warm, soft lips of her sex, almost groaning at how slick and wet she was.

"Oh, God," she cried, her eyes flying open. "Please, don't stop."

As if.

"Okay, time for the clothes to go," he growled.

He helped her push the pants all the way down and off, and once she was naked in his lap, he had to just pause and visually drink her in. She was perfect, from head to foot, laid out in front of him like a feast. He didn't know where to start, he just knew he already didn't want it to end.

He reached down to the front of his jeans, unfastening them, wanting to get naked and pull her leg across his lap to straddle him. Sitting there, looking up at her while she rode him sounded like the perfect way to start this night.

"Ross?" she whispered.

"Hmm?"

"Um…there's something you probably should know."

"Unless the house is on fire, there's nothing I really need to hear right now," he said as he unzipped and pushed the jeans down his hips. His body was already on fire, and as he pushed his shorts away, too, and his cock came into contact with her bare hip, he groaned.

She gasped. "Oh, my goodness."

"Give me another five minutes and it will be both *yours,* and *good,*" he told her as he stopped to kiss her breast, and stroke that sweet, quivering spot between her thighs.

"Ross, uh, really, I need to tell you something."

Hearing the quaver in her voice, and feeling the slight stiffness of her body, he finally shook off the haze of lust in his head. He lifted his mouth from her perfect breast and slid his hand into safer territory down on her thigh.

"What's wrong?"

She lowered her head, eyeing him through a long strand of hair. Lucy's cheeks were pink, like she was embarrassed. Well, hell, they'd known each other less than a day and now she was lying naked on his lap. But she wouldn't be embarrassed for long, not once he showed her how much he wanted her.

"Um…I just wanted to say…"

She bit her lip, shook her head slightly. Which was when a thought—a shocking, crazy one—burst into his head. His whole body went stiff and he leaned back into the couch.

"Lucy, are you trying to tell me you've never done this before?"

A hesitation, then she slowly nodded. "That's what I'm trying to tell you."

Holy shit. She was naked in his arms, thrusting

into his hand like she needed to come or die and she was a virgin?

Well, honestly, the needing to come or die made sense. Seriously, how many twenty-two-year-old virgins were out there? He'd certainly never met one. The beautiful, sexy woman had to be a seething mass of sexual frustration.

Something he could well appreciate right now.

"I mean, you said you and Jude had never…but, seriously, nobody else, either?"

"No. Never."

"That's incredible."

"I guess right around the time most girls were giving it away in the backseats of their boyfriends' cars, I was grieving and helping my brother figure out what to do about our parents' business, their house, their lives. And ours. It just sort of…never happened."

He nodded, understanding. She hadn't been thrust into the role of sexual grown-up while in high school. She'd landed in the adult world through one brutal tragedy.

That, as much as the fact that he was not a ruthless bastard like Jude, was enough to make Ross find the strength to do what had to be done. Knowing he'd have blue balls tonight, he still cleared his throat and carefully pushed her off his lap.

"Okay. It's all right, Lucy, I understand."

She grabbed his arm before he could get off the couch and head toward the bathroom for an icy cold shower.

"No, I don't think you do." Reaching for his face,

she cupped his cheeks in her hands and leaned close, her soft hair falling onto his bare shoulders. "I want you, Ross. I want you to be my first. Now. Tonight."

LUCY HAD THOUGHT a lot about the moment when she'd finally have sex. She'd pictured it being with someone she knew, someone she'd dated for a long time, someone she trusted.

Well, one out of three wasn't bad, right?

She didn't know Ross that well. She'd never dated him.

But she trusted him. Oh, did she trust him.

Telling him the truth about herself hadn't been easy, but she certainly wasn't going to try to fake her way through her first time having sex. Not only was that unfair to herself, it was unfair to him. He deserved the chance to say, "Thanks but no thanks." After all, some guys just didn't seem to want to deal with the drama of it.

She would have predicted Ross wouldn't be one of those guys.

She wouldn't have predicted the incredibly tender, loving way he kissed her, then stood and took her by the hand to lead her to his bedroom. As if now that he knew the truth, the responsibility of it was weighing on him, and he didn't want a quick lay on a couch. Like she deserved the whole package, big bed and all.

The walk to the bedroom seemed incredibly long. And while her whole body was still burning from the incredible way he'd touched her, she couldn't deny a faint trepidation, the tiniest bit of self-consciousness.

After all, she was naked. He still wore jeans. And she'd just told him she was a virgin.

"It's okay," he told her when they'd reached his room, standing by his bed. He brushed her hair off her face, then touched her cheek. "It's gonna be fine."

She smiled. "Do you think I'm afraid?"

He eyed her, visibly unsure.

"I'm not scared, Ross. Maybe a little embarrassed about being so…exposed."

He stepped back and looked at her naked body, shaking his head slowly and rubbing his jaw, as if he just didn't know what to say. Then he said exactly the right thing. "If there's any such thing as a perfect woman, Lucy Fleming, you're her."

She went soft and gooey inside, everywhere she wasn't already soft and gooey. As she'd already suspected, she'd most definitely chosen well.

"Thank you."

"So don't be nervous, Luce, I won't do anything to hurt you," he added, tenderly cupping her cheek.

"I won't. I swear to you, my only fear is that it won't be as good as I've made it out to be in my head."

A slow smile curled those handsome lips upward. He shook his head, then sunk his hands in her hair and dragged her close.

"It'll be better. I guaran-damn-tee it."

He pushed her down onto the bed, and set about proving it.

Lucy honestly hadn't known sex could be both incredibly hot and amazingly tender. He kissed her deeply, slowly, like he wanted to memorize the taste of her mouth. And his hands did magical things to her, gliding across her breasts, offering her barely there caresses that left her a quivering pile of sensation.

But then, his control would slip a little. He'd groan as he nipped her breast, or shake when she reached out and brushed her fingertips against the soft head of his erection. Lucy wanted to do more, longed to explore his body, but he seemed determined to make this all totally and completely about her.

Which was wonderful…and incredibly arousing.

"Please," she said on a sob when he again teased her clit with his fingers, giving her light touches that made her long for firmer ones. Her hips thrusting, Lucy was on the verge of going over the top, she knew that from her own explorations of her body. And she was dying for it.

As if knowing he'd teased her as much as he could before she smacked him, Ross murmured something sweet and unintelligible, then slid a finger inside her. She practically cooed; the unfamiliar invasion felt *so* good. He moved his thumb back to her clit and this time, there was no teasing. Just slow, deliberate caresses, with just the pressure she needed.

Her breaths grew choppy. Sighs turned into gasps when he slid another finger into her channel, using both to stretch and fill her, even while he continued stroking her clit.

Then it came, sweet, warm relief. She quivered as the orgasm rolled over her, amazed at how much stronger it was when shared. She cried out, let her body shake and stretch, then sagged back into the pillows.

"You're gorgeous," he whispered.

"So are you," she said, absolutely meaning it. Ross's body was delicious—so hard and muscular, all power and steel. When combined with the thoughtfulness, the boyish smile, the twinkle in his green eyes, he was an absolutely irresistible male package.

She smiled at him, wrapping her arms around his neck. "I want you now."

He didn't ask if she was sure, as if knowing they were way past that. Reaching for a drawer in the bedside table, he took out a condom. Lucy caught her lip between her teeth, watching as he maneuvered the tight sheath over his thick, powerful erection. Seeing the rubber stretch to accommodate him, she felt the first thrills of nervousness. But they were immediately drowned out by utter excitement.

Just watching him sent even more heat to her sex and she had to drop her legs apart, the skin there was so engorged and sensitive. Ross looked down at her, masculine appreciation written all over his face, then moved between her thighs.

"Tell me if..."

"I will," she said, cutting him off. Then she lifted her hips, wrapping her arms around his shoulders and staring up at him.

They didn't kiss. They didn't blink. They barely breathed.

Lucy's heart skipped a beat when she felt his rigid warmth probing into her, nuzzling between her folds and into the slick opening of her body. He moved slowly, so carefully, so tenderly. Each bit of himself he gave her just made her hungry for more.

She arched her hips toward him, silently telling him to continue. Seeing the clenched muscles in his neck, the sweat on his brow, she knew he was hanging on tightly to his control.

"I'm fine," she insisted. "Please, Ross, please fill me up."

He bent to her, covered her lips with his and kissed her deeply. And with each stroke of his tongue, he pushed into her, filling her, inch by inch, until he was buried inside her.

There had been only the tiniest hint of pain; now there was just fullness. Thickness. A sense that she'd finally been made whole and didn't ever want to go back to feeling empty again. Like he was exactly where he was meant to be.

"Okay?" he asked.

"Definitely."

She slid her legs tighter around his, holding him close. Ross began to pull out, then slowly thrust back in, setting an easy pace. She caught it, matched it, giving when he took, taking when he pulled back. It was, she realized, like dancing...one step he led, then she did. Only no dance move had ever felt so good, so sinfully delicious.

"You're so tight," he groaned, picking up the pace.

She knew his control was slipping. Frankly she marveled that he'd been able to maintain it this long. Every molecule in her body was urging her to thrust and writhe, to just take in so much pleasure that she'd never remember what it was like to not feel it. She knew he had to be feeling the same.

The rhythm sped up a little, his thrusts deepening. Lucy met him stroke for stroke, clinging to his broad shoulders, sharing kiss after kiss. Reality had faded, there was nothing else except this feeling, this rightness. This perfect guy on this perfect night.

And then, the perfect moment. Warm delight spilled through her as she climaxed again, differently than she ever had before. It started deep inside and radiated out, a ripple widening into a wave.

Even as she savored the long, deep sensations, she heard Ross's shallow breaths grow louder and felt him tense against her.

"Beautiful, you're so beautiful," he muttered as he strained toward his own release.

His low cry and the deepest thrust of all signaled that he'd found it. He buried his face in her hair and continued to pump into her, as if every bit of him had been wrung dry.

Though she knew he had to be totally spent, he didn't collapse on top of her. Instead, Ross rolled onto his side and tugged her with him. They were still joined, and she slid her thigh over his hip, liking the connection.

His eyes were closed, his lips parted as he drew in deep breaths. When he finally opened them, she didn't even try to hide her smile.

"What?"

"I liked it."

He chuckled. “I’m glad.”

“When can we do it again?”

His chuckle turned into a deep, masculine laugh. “Give me a half hour.”

She stuck out her lower lip in a pretend pout.

“Okay, okay,” he said, reaching down and stroking her hip. “Twenty minutes.”

“I guess I can live with that,” she said, with a teasing smile. She rubbed against him, stealing his warmth. The bedroom was cool, but she definitely hadn’t noticed it before. Ross gave off a lot of heat… whether he was right beside her or across the room.

She much preferred him right beside her.

They fell silent for a few moments, just touching each other, exchanging lazy kisses. She loved the way he kept a possessive hand on her, as if making sure she didn’t disappear on him.

That wasn’t going to happen. Definitely not. In fact, she was already wracking her brain, wondering how on earth they could make this work for a lot longer than this one weekend. He hadn’t said he wanted to, neither had she. But she definitely felt it.

Yet, she was leaving for Europe in three weeks. She’d be gone for months, then had intended to come home only long enough to graduate, then go back again.

None of that had mattered when she’d been with Jude. Not even when she’d been thinking about sleeping with him.

Now, though? With Ross? The very thought was devastating. How could she possibly walk away when, for the first time in her life, she'd met someone she wanted desperately to hold on to?

"Is there anything you need?" he whispered, his voice breaking the silence in the shadowy room.

"Like what?"

He shrugged and looked away, as if not wanting to embarrass her. "I mean, you know, are you hurting?"

"Definitely not. Honestly, I don't know that I have ever felt better." Unable to help it, she yawned. "Okay, maybe I do need something—a catnap. A twenty-minute one."

He laughed softly and tugged her even closer, until she was actually lying on his chest. He kissed her brow, stroked her hair, whispered sweet things about how good she'd felt to him.

Lucy's cheek was right above his heart and she not only heard its beat, she also felt its steady, solid thrum. His words lulled her, his touch soothed her. Quite honestly, she couldn't recall a more perfect moment in her life.

Not ever.

She only hoped there would be many more to come, and could hardly wait to see what tomorrow would bring.

CHAPTER NINE

Now
Chicago, December 24, 2011

THEY WERE SNOWED IN. Totally trapped in a world turned white.

Standing at his office window and assessing the situation Saturday morning, Ross could only shake his head in wonder. He hadn't seen a storm like this in a lot of years, probably not since he was a kid. He tried to estimate how much of the white stuff had fallen; judging by the way it climbed up the side of his SUV, he'd say at least three feet so far. And still it came down, swirling, spinning, blowing up and down and sideways.

This might be one for the record books.

"You left and took your body heat with you," Lucy grumbled from the foldout.

"Sorry."

She'd been asleep when he'd slipped out of bed a few minutes ago. Now she was curled on the side he'd vacated, the blankets pulled up to her nose, like she was trying to suck up any residual warmth.

She looked both adorable and sexy as hell.

And a little chilly.

Though it wasn't freezing, by any means, the temperature had definitely dropped below what it normally was in the building. Not that they'd really noticed during the night. God, had they *not* noticed. In fact, Ross would have sworn there was an inferno blazing in this little corner of Chicago. Because he and Lucy had redefined hot throughout the long, erotic hours after she'd awakened to find him in bed with her.

"How does it look out there?"

Shaking off the sultry images in his mind of the ways they'd explored and pleasured each other in the darkness, he smiled. "Like Santa decided to move here and brought the North Pole with him."

"Oh, that's just perfect," she said, sounding sarcastic.

"What's the matter, did you have big plans for the day?" He somehow doubted it. Lucy didn't seem any more of a Christmas fan now than she had been six years ago.

She thought about it, then shook her head. "Actually, no. Sam's working all weekend. I was figuring on staying in, being lazy, going online and spending that money your company paid me yesterday."

Well, she couldn't do any shopping, but staying in and being lazy sounded ideal. Especially if they were lazy between bouts of being as energetic as they'd been last night.

Damn. Lucy had become a wild woman.

Seeing her shiver, he clarified that—a *cold* wild woman.

"Here," he said, walking over to the bed, carrying two cups of coffee, which he'd just brewed.

"So the power's back on?" she asked, appearing both relieved and disappointed.

"'Fraid not," he said, shaking his head. "Fortunately, we get a lot of vendors coming in here. One of them makes a battery-operated coffeemaker and suggested we get them for sites that aren't wired yet. We did—and they gave us a few for the office as a thank-you for the contract."

"Thank goodness for free samples," she said, sitting up and letting the covers drop to her lap. Ross managed to not slosh hot coffee all over her. Seeing her in the daylight—as murky as it was—was enough to make the earth jolt. Not to mention his dick.

He hadn't realized it was possible to be so insatiable about another person. They'd had sex three or four times during the night, and he was ready to have her again. It had been dark—now he wanted to watch her face pinken as she came, see the perfect body as he licked every inch of it.

"Wonderful," she murmured as she sipped, then blew on the steaming rising from the mug. "Cream, no sugar—you remembered."

"Of course I did," he murmured. He remembered everything.

It was funny, considering he'd tried so hard to put Lucy out of his mind over the years. But she'd refused to leave, haunting his memories through other women—two of them serious—and so many other changes.

Lucy glanced at him and their stares held. She didn't try to lift the blanket, didn't blush or feign embarrassment at sitting right in front of him so beautifully naked. He'd worried she would feel some kind of doubts or uncertainty in the cold light of day. But he'd been wrong. She looked confident—serene even. Like she didn't regret a damn thing.

He smiled at thc realization.

"What?"

"I half expected you to leap up, wrap the sheets around your body and accuse me of molesting you during the night."

She snickered. "I think I was the one who molested you. Although, you did creep into my bed while I was sleeping."

"*My* bed, Goldilocks. Speaking of which, I don't have any porridge to offer you for breakfast, but there's a ton of leftover party food in the break room."

She didn't seem to care about the food, instead focusing on the first part of his statement. "*Your* bed? Are you serious?"

"As a heart attack."

She looked around the office, taking note of its size and furnishings. It was, he knew, probably bigger square-footage wise, and better furnished than his entire rental house had been back in Brooklyn.

"So if the bed is yours, I guess that means this office is yours as well? I mean, I don't suppose you were just sneaking into your boss's bed since you got stuck here, too?"

"It's mine," he said with a laugh. "I'm assuming you didn't notice the nameplate on the desk."

She glanced over. Even from here it was easy to make out the "CEO" before his name. Her eyes wide, she turned her attention back to him. "You really run this place?"

"I really do."

"Wow," she said, sagging back against the pillow. "I mean, I knew you were talented, but going from handyman to CEO in six years? That's pretty remarkable."

Ross put his cup down and sat in a chair opposite her. Lifting his jean-clad legs, he used the end of the foldout as a footrest, crossing his bare feet there. "Not that remarkable, really. I inherited the position. It's my family's company."

Lucy's mouth rounded into an O. "Your father..."

"Yeah."

"How is he?" she asked. "Did he..."

"Pull through? Yes, he did. It took a long time, a lot of rehab and he still doesn't have full use of his right side, but he made it." Chuckling but only half-joking, he added, "He's still the same demanding tyrant he always was."

It would take more than a massive stroke to get his old man to stop being bossy, pushy and opinionated. And Ross should know; he dealt with that bossy, pushy opinion every damn day.

His name might be on the letterhead of Elite Construction, but his dad still held a lot of shares. They'd had a few major battles once the elder Marshall had started feeling like his old self again. It had only been lately, in the past year or so, that he'd conceded Ross was doing an excellent job, and stopped questioning every little decision.

Not that Ross wasn't very grateful his dad had lived, of course. Though they hadn't been getting along at the time, he'd been shocked and devastated by his father's massive stroke six years ago. Though he'd only been fifty-five, nobody had thought he would make it, not the doctors or the industry. Nobody except his family, who knew Ross Marshall, Sr. was too stubborn to do what everyone predicted he would.

"I'm so glad he survived," Lucy murmured.

"Thanks."

He didn't doubt she meant it. But he also didn't doubt Lucy's mind had gone right where his had—to the timing of his father's stroke. She'd been there when he'd received the frantic phone call from his sister at the crack of dawn on Christmas morning. After a weekend of pure excitement and happiness with Lucy, his world had come crashing down with one conversation.

His entire life had changed on a dime. Before that, he'd known he would someday go back to Chicago and take his place beside his father in the business. But he'd thought he had time—a couple of years, at least—to live the life he wanted. Hell at that particular moment, he'd even been considering asking Lucy if she thought he might be able to pick up some carpentry work in France for a year or two. They'd gotten *that* serious *that* quickly.

Then the phone had rung. His sister's sobs had finally made sense, and he'd left for the airport right away. As much as he'd hated bailing out on Lucy on Christmas Day, she'd been completely understanding. Hell, if anyone would understand, it would be her—she'd received her own horrifying phone call one holiday season.

He'd wasted no time packing, not even a single bag. He'd been desperate to get back to Chicago, convinced his father was on the verge of death. And horrified, realizing that the last words they'd exchanged had been angry ones.

The vigil at the hospital had been long and difficult. He'd dealt not only with the worry, and with his family, but also with stepping right in to look after the company. That, in itself, had been a battle, considering he was so young. But he hadn't been about to let the whole thing founder while his father fought for his life.

Despite being so busy, he'd found time to call Lucy every day that first week—especially knowing she had a tough anniversary of her own to contend with. During each call, she'd expressed concern about his father, but inevitably the conversation would turn to her preparations for her upcoming trip. Her plans for her future. Her great life.

Then a couple of days went between his calls.

Then a week.

Then it was almost time for her to leave for her semester abroad.

And he'd stopped calling.

"I never stopped thinking about you. I swear, you were on my mind constantly." He got to the point, the main thing he wanted to say. "I'm sorry, Lucy."

"For?"

"You know what for. I couldn't stop thinking about you…but I couldn't bring myself to call you, either."

She stiffened, didn't reply for a second, then tossed off a casual, "Hey, don't sweat it. The phone lines were notoriously unreliable that year."

He saw through the feigned humor. She'd been plenty hurt yesterday; no way had she gotten over it in one single night.

But, maybe last night had at least opened her to the possibility that he wasn't a user who'd taken her for the ride of a lifetime then dropped her flat.

"You know, I never went back to New York."

Her brow went up. "What about your house? Your things?"

"I hired somebody to take care of it that winter, once it became obvious that not only was my dad going to have a long recovery ahead of him, he would almost certainly never be able to work again."

"That must have been really tough."

"Tough doesn't begin to describe it." He swiped a hand through his hair and sighed. "Anyway, I didn't mean to get into all that. I just brought it up so I could finally tell you what I meant to tell you then and never got the chance to say."

She eyed him warily. "And that would be?"

He held her gaze, daring her not to believe him. "That I fell in love with you that weekend in New York."

She sucked in an audible breath, and slowly shook her head.

Ross nodded, not worrying about looking like a fool or fearing any kind of rejection. Maybe something great would happen between him and Lucy now. Maybe it wouldn't, and last night would be his final memory of a relationship he'd once thought would define his whole life. But no matter what, he owed her the truth about the past.

"It's true. I was crazy in love with you."

"You might have told me..."

"To what purpose?"

Rolling her eyes and looking at him like he was an idiot, she said, "Maybe just because the words would have been nice to hear once in my life?"

He couldn't imagine no man had ever fallen in love with the beautiful woman in front of him. But he didn't particularly want to think about her with anyone else. The very idea made his stomach heave.

"Maybe I should have," he said with a simple shrug. "But I was trapped."

She tilted her head in confusion.

"Lucy, you were about to leave to go grab the world by the balls."

She didn't try to deny it, but a wistful expression crossed her face, as if she were remembering the feisty, passionate girl she'd been. One of these days, hopefully, he'd find out what had brought her back here, why she was photographing children when she'd sworn she would do anything but.

Right now, though, he had his own story to tell.

"But me? Dad was on his deathbed, my family was falling apart, and I was the one who had to hold them—not to mention this business—together." He rose from his chair and walked to the foldout, sitting beside her and reaching out to stroke a silky strand of her hair. "My life was here. It *is* here. Yours was—" he waved a hand "—out there. We were going to be living in two different worlds and as much as I wanted you in mine, I knew that wasn't going to happen. Just because my dreams fell apart didn't mean I could ask you to give up yours."

"So…you let me go?"

A simple nod. "I let you go."

Moisture appeared in her eyes, though no tears spilled from them. Sniffing, she curled her face into his hand, rubbing her soft skin against his.

They remained silent for a long time. The room was quiet enough that he could hear the plink of tiny, icy snowflakes striking the window. Then, with a low sigh, Lucy looked up at him and smiled.

"Thank you for telling me," she whispered.

"You're welcome."

Nothing else. No promises. No requests. It was as if they'd just wiped clean the slate and could now start again, fresh. And see where the road took them.

"I've got to admit it, Papa Bear, this beats porridge any day."

Lucy licked a few cookie crumbs off her fingers, sighing in satisfaction at the strange Christmas Eve brunch they'd just shared. Cookies, eggnog, cheese and crackers, chips, chocolate and fruit.

The food at the party had been plentiful and delicious. It had also kept very well in the large refrigerator, which was doing a pretty good job holding its temperature despite the power outage. Though, if they were going to be stuck here much longer, they were going to have to ditch the eggnog in favor of unopened bottles of soda or fruit juice.

"I think there's even some leftover sliced turkey for Christmas dinner," he replied. "If it comes to that."

Judging by the way it continued to snow, it could definitely come to that.

She should be bothered by it. Should be worried about being trapped, should at least be freaked out about not having a spare pair of underwear—not that she expected to wear them for long.

But the truth was, she didn't care. She had no obligations to anyone else, didn't have holiday plans, other than shopping. Her brother had already been scheduled to work all weekend, and with the weather, she doubted he'd have time to even drop by before Monday or Tuesday.

So why not spend a few days trapped in a secure building with plenty of food and water, and someone to provide plenty of entertainment. If, that was, she could survive that much…entertainment.

"I guess this meets your requirements for a non-traditional Christmas, huh?"

"Hey, I ate a bell-shaped cookie, didn't I?" Then she chuckled. "Though, believe it or not, I've gotten a little less stringent about that."

"Seriously?"

"Kate has kids now, and I actually went and spent Christmas with them a couple of years ago. It was… nice."

More than nice. It had been lovely. Sweet and wholesome and fun. And yes, a bit painful. But after many years, Lucy had been able to let down her guard and let some of the magic of the season back into her heart. She wasn't ready to go out and chop down a tree or download a copy of *Now That's What I Call Christmas #948* to her MP3 player. But she could at least hum Silent Night—her mother's favorite Christmas carol—and not want to break into tears.

"You must know I'm curious…"

"About?"

"Paris. Europe. Photographing Fashion Week, landing the cover of *Vogue?*"

She sighed, remembering that girl, those dreams. How important they'd once seemed, when she was running away from anything resembling the life she'd once had and so painfully lost. Changing her plans completely had helped her evade the memories for a little while, but not forever. Eventually she'd had to face them.

She explained that to him, as best she could, wondering if the explanation would make any sense to anybody else.

When she was finished, Ross nodded slowly. "And now that you know you don't have to go halfway across the world to keep from caring too much about anyone or anything…are you happy?"

Wow. He'd obviously read between the lines. She hadn't mentioned anything about not wanting to care about anyone. But she couldn't deny it was true.

"I'm happy," she admitted. "I love what I do—you remember how I swore I'd never work with kids?"

"Even though you were great at it."

"Exactly. I guess I was the last one to see it. But I love it, and I'm good. I've had more success with my kid portraiture than I ever did with adults. I actually had a photo in *Time* magazine last year."

He whistled. "Seriously?"

"Yep. I've had shots picked up by the AP, and magazines and catalogs. I actually just submitted a photo essay for Parents Place Magazine as well, and I'm hoping they'll take me on for more freelance work."

"Sounds wonderful," he told her, sounding like he meant it. "I'm really happy for you."

"Thanks." Suddenly remembering something, and knowing he'd be interested, she said, "Oh, guess who I ran into a year or so ago in New York?"

He raised a curious brow.

"Remember Jude the jackass?"

His sneer said he did. "Please tell me he ended up in prison being some Bubba's bitch."

"No, but his daddy did."

Ross's jaw dropped.

"His family ran one of those businesses that was 'too big to fail.' Only, it failed during the financial meltdown. Daddy went to jail, the family lost everything. Jude was very humbled—and very poor—when I ran into him."

"Couldn't have happened to a nicer guy."

Almost unable to remember the girl she'd been when she'd thought Jude could be "the one," she said, "I guess that catches you up with what's been going on with me."

And he'd already caught her up on what his life had been like. It had been full of family and work and duty. Not much downtime, from the sound of it, although he had apparently had time to start building that dream house of his—oh, she would love to see it.

As for his personal life, though she hadn't pried, not wanting to be nosy, she had sort of rejoiced when he admitted he hadn't had any romantic relationship that had lasted longer than six months. That made two of them.

"Wait, what about your brother?" Ross asked. "Does he still give you ugly snow globes every Christmas?"

She chuckled, thinking about the collection that she set out every single year. With the exception of the broken groovy Santa, she still had each and every one.

"I put out my entire collection every holiday season."

"*All* of them?" he asked, his voice soft and serious.

She knew what he was asking. Knew he wondered if she'd kept the one and only Christmas present he'd ever given her. Considering she'd been heartbroken shortly after he'd given it to her, the answer probably should have been no. But in truth, she'd never been able to part with that special gift, even though, every time she took it out of its box, she'd wondered about Ross. Where he was, what had happened to him.

Now she knew. He'd been living his life as best he could…after having freed her to follow her dreams.

"Yes, Ross," she murmured. "Every one."

"I'm glad."

"Me, too." Then, wanting to keep the mood light, she added, "The one my brother got me last year had to take the prize for kookiest ever."

"Do tell."

"Sam found one from some weird cult that believes the three wise men came from another planet. Balthazar had green skin and claws. Melchior had a spiked tail. And the other one was furry all over."

Tossing his head back, Ross laughed. "Please don't tell me the baby Jesus was an alien, too."

"No, but he looked terrified."

"Is it any wonder? I mean, with the cast of a bad episode of *Star Trek* standing over him?"

Snorting as she realized that's exactly what the three kings had looked like, she got up and began clearing away the plastic dishes they'd used for their late-morning feast. They'd eaten in the break room, since it was closest to not only all the food, but all the supplies, too.

"So, you ready to go down and check things out?" Ross asked.

They'd agreed that, after eating, they would head downstairs to the lobby and try to get a better idea of what was going on outside. From up here on the sixth floor, it looked like they were trapped in a spaceship that had landed on a marshmallow planet.

"Ready when you are."

Though they didn't expect to get anywhere, the two of them dressed warmly. They had raided a coat closet to add layers to their own clothes. There were a few jackets, scarves and hats that had been left behind over the years—enough so that they shouldn't freeze if they dared to step outside.

Once they trudged down the six floors to the lobby, and saw that the snow had drifted almost all the way up the glass doors, though, Lucy realized they needn't have bothered.

"This is crazy!" she said, standing up on tiptoe to try to see over the white mountain. "Can you see the parking lot?"

Ross cupped his hand around a spot of glass that wasn't obscured by snow. "There are three lumps out there—I assume your car, mine and the security truck. It would take a sled and a team of dogs to get us to them, though."

Meaning, even if the power came on and the streets were cleared, they weren't going anywhere until Ross's private snow removal contractor showed up to clear the walks and the parking lot. And who knew when that would be?

"We're not going anywhere, are we?"

"Nuh-uh." He turned to face her. "Is that okay? I mean...you're not scared about being trapped here, are you?"

She scrunched her brow. "Have you turned into a cannibal sometime in the last six years?"

He wagged his eyebrows. "You complaining about what I like to eat?"

Good Lord, she was never going to complain about that for the rest of her life.

"Never mind," she said, knowing she sounded off balance.

The man was good at distracting her, putting wild thoughts in her head. He was good at a lot of things. Making her laugh, making her sigh, making her crazy. Giving her incredible pleasure.

At twenty-two, she'd found Ross Marshall to be the sexiest guy she'd ever met. Now, six years later, she knew he was more than that. Still sexy, oh, without a doubt. Probably even more so, actually, because he had a ton of confidence and a man's mature personality to go along with the looks and charm.

But she now saw him as a whole lot more than a broke carpenter with a bean bag chair and a lava lamp. He was successful, very smart, and incredibly likable. She'd seen the way he talked to all those people at the party yesterday; now, knowing he was their employer, she was even more impressed.

"Seriously, you're not too worried, are you?" he asked. "We have plenty of food, the building's secure. And I don't think it's going to get unbearably cold. If it does, we can move to an interior room with no windows."

She shook her head. "Honestly, I'm not worried. The only question is, what on earth are we going to do to occupy ourselves?"

She accompanied that question with a bat of her eyelashes.

Ross stepped closer, dropping his hands onto her hips. Even through the padding of her pants, sweater, somebody's hoodie, somebody else's jacket and her heavy coat, she felt the possessive weight of it.

"I'm sure we'll think of something."

She gazed up at him, licking her lips and smiling. "I already have thought of something."

"Oh?"

She leaned up on tiptoes, brushing her lips against his jawline and whispered, "Close your eyes."

He did. Immediately.

"Count to twenty."

"Uh…why?" One eye opened and she immediately frowned. He closed it again. "Sorry. Counting. One."

She stepped away. "No peeking. Keep counting."

"Two."

A smile crossed his face, as if he were picturing her stripping out of her clothes, laying herself out naked on the security desk. Hmm. That could be kind of interesting. Though they couldn't possibly be seen through the drifts or the still-falling snow, it sounded extremely daring.

"Three."

She shook her head and tiptoed backward toward

the closed stairwell door. He was saying four as she carefully pulled it open and five as it swung closed behind her. Hopefully, by the time he reached twenty, she'd be back up on the sixth floor.

Hide-and-seek in a six-story office building. Sounded like a good way to kill some time.

Especially if she made sure she was naked by the time he found her.

CHAPTER TEN

Then
New York, December 24, 2005

As much as Lucy would have liked to stay in Ross's little house and learn everything there was to know about making love, she had to work on Christmas Eve. The photographer for whom she was interning had families coming in for holiday portraits and she needed to be there with bells on.

Literally. Jingle bells. They were attached to the curled-up toes of her silly elf shoes and she tinkled with every step.

One day, when she was a world-famous photographer, she'd laugh about this. But not now. It was just too ridiculous and embarrassing. So much for wanting to seem like a cool, collected, mature woman during her first-ever "morning after." Ross was going to look at her and think he'd spent the night with a teenager.

"Please tell me you'll wear that outfit tonight," Ross said, not attempting to hide his amusement when she emerged from the bathroom early Saturday morning.

"Ha ha."

"I mean it. You're totally hot. Hermie would never have left the North Pole to become a dentist if you were around."

"Dork."

"Elf." He grabbed her by the hips and pulled her close, laughing as her bobbing red feather poked him in the eye. He was still laughing when he pressed his mouth against hers for a deep, good morning kiss.

Lucy wobbled on her feet a little. Somehow, she suspected Ross's kiss—or even just the memory of his kiss—would *always* make her wobble.

"Are you ready?"

"Don't I look ready?" she said with a disgusted sigh. Then she added, "You're sure you don't mind driving me all the way back up to the city?"

"I told you, I have errands to run."

They'd spent time this morning wrapping and packing up his holiday gifts to his family. But she suspected there had to be shipping stores somewhere closer than Manhattan.

"I could take the train."

"Forget it," he said, ending the discussion.

The traffic heading into the city wasn't as bad as it would have been on a weekday. Most cars were heading out—obviously people who'd been stuck working right up until the twenty-third leaving for holiday weekends with family.

They reached the studio about a half hour early, and Lucy, who had a key, led him inside. "You really don't have to stay," she told him as she turned on the lights.

"I'm staying," he insisted, immediately stepping to a front window to glance back out at the street.

She knew why. Ross didn't trust Jude not to come here and harass her. Not that either of them really thought he'd try anything violent in broad daylight, while she was at work. But she wouldn't put it past him to come in and try to talk to her about why she should let last night's ugly incident go.

She wouldn't. In fact, this morning, with Ross's encouragement, she'd already called and spoken to someone at the police precinct near her apartment.

"Are you usually here alone in the mornings?" Ross asked, when, after ten minutes, nobody else had arrived.

"My boss is always late." Rolling her eyes, she added, "He's the irresponsible, creative genius type."

"So I see," he said as he followed her into the studio, where a holiday scene had been laid out. A large sleigh with velvet cushions stood in a corner, in front of a snowy backdrop. Surrounding it were mounds of white fluff that looked like snow. Woodland creatures, decorated trees, candy canes and icicles finished the scenario. "This is cute."

"Thanks," she said, pleased at the compliment, since she was the one who'd designed the whimsical scene. Her employer had never done more than drop a snowy screen behind a stool before she'd come onboard, and he'd already complimented her on the increased amount of traffic, telling her she had a knack for this kind of thing.

Funny, really, since she never intended to do it

again. Surprisingly, though, as she stood looking at the results of her creativity, she felt a pang of sadness at the thought. She'd put a lot of effort into this and had actually enjoyed doing it.

Forget it. Paris fashion beats North Pole kiddieland any day.

Right. Definitely. Even if she did love hearing the squeals of delight of some of the littlest children who came in for holiday sittings, she would almost certainly love the squeals of millionaires as they eyed the latest fashions on the catwalk.

Hearing her cell phone ring, Lucy retrieved it, recognizing the studio owner's name. "Uh-oh," she mumbled, hoping this didn't mean the man would be later than usual.

A few seconds into the conversation, she realized it was worse than that. "You're not coming in today at *all?*"

"I'm sorry, it can't be helped! I fell last night and hurt my knee. I can't walk."

Huh. Considering the older man liked to dig into the spiked eggnog by noon, she had to wonder how he'd fallen.

"We only have a few appointments—you can handle them."

Lucy sputtered. She was an intern—an unpaid one at that. And he seriously wanted her to do his job, on Christmas Eve?

"I know this is going above and beyond," he said. "But I'd be so grateful. I will absolutely compensate you for your time."

She could just imagine what he'd consider fair compensation. Considering she had worked like a slave for three months without earning a penny, she'd be lucky to make a hundred bucks.

But hell, she was here. She was a photographer. And even if she didn't ever want to take the kinds of photographs he took, it was her chance to work professionally. So she agreed.

After she disconnected, and explained the situation, Ross offered to stay and help her. Lucy appreciated it, but knew he had things to do. Insisting that he go mail his packages, she added, "I'll check the book, but I think there are only appointments between ten and one. If you can get back by then and greet people as they come in, I'd really appreciate it."

Then she'd be finished for the day, and they could go do...whatever two lovers, who were strangers a day ago, one of whom didn't do Christmas, did on Christmas.

She could hardly wait.

"You're on," he promised as he headed toward the door. Before exiting, he said, "Keep this locked until ten, okay?"

She nodded. "I swear. Don't worry."

He gave her one of those devastating smiles that lit up his green eyes. "Can't help it, Lucy."

The way he said it, the warmth in his expression, made her smile for several minutes after he'd gone. But eventually, she had to set up for work.

Given the freedom to experiment, she decided to try out a few ideas, as long as the paying customers were willing. So by the time the first was scheduled to arrive, she'd already played around with some lighting effects, as well as a couple of her boss's specialty lenses.

Ross arrived back right on time, and with his help, she spent the next couple of hours enjoying the heck out of her job. For the first time, she wasn't just signing people in, collecting checks, selling overpriced packages, and trying to make cranky, wet little kids laugh, while nodding at every single idea her boss had. She was creating, trying new positions and lighting and special effects. She could feel the energy as she worked, and suspected these images would turn out to be something special.

By the time she'd finished with the last customer, it was after two. Ross had been a huge help, and once they were alone in the front office, she threw her arms around his neck and kissed him. "Thank you so much—what a fun day!"

"It was," he told her, laughing as he dropped his hands to her hips and squeezed her tighter. "You were fantastic. I don't know that I've ever seen anyone as great with kids as you are."

She rolled her eyes. "I wouldn't go that far."

"I would," he insisted. "You were really amazing. You should specialize in this."

"Fat chance," she snorted. "I have other plans. Big plans."

"Like?"

They bcgan to clean up, getting ready to shut the studio down for the next few days. And while they did, Lucy told him about her upcoming study abroad trip. About her plans to photograph her way around the world. About the bright, exotic future she envisioned for herself, which had nothing to do with Santas or reindeer or chubby-cheeked infants.

He broke in with a few questions, but for the most part, just nodded, agreeing that her future sounded wonderful. But when all was said and done, he still murmured, “I still say you’d be great doing this, too.”

“Not happening,” she told him, knowing he didn’t truly understand. How could he? She hadn’t come right out and told him that her need to escape to somewhere far away had a lot in common with her need to avoid Christmas and all the happy family trappings that came with it.

Lucy had loved photography from the time she was twelve and her parents had given her a “real” camera. She’d been the family photojournalist from that moment on, recording every event and capturing every wonderful smile.

But then the family and the smiles had disappeared. Their loss had been almost more than she could bear. So going out into the world and seeing exotic places and people through the lens of her camera sounded ideal to her, now that she could no longer see the people she’d always loved. Exciting, of course…but more, it sounded a lot less painful. Her heart wasn’t going to be broken if a shot didn’t land on the pages of a magazine. Not caring as much about her subjects was the smart choice, the right choice. The perfect way to live her life.

Ross's voice suddenly jolted her out of the moment of melancholy. "So, little girl, have you been good all year?"

Spinning around, she saw him sitting on the sleigh, patting his lap suggestively, like the world's sexiest Santa.

"Hmm," she said, sauntering over. "That depends on your definition of good."

He pulled her down on top of him. "After last night, you are my definition of good," he told her. "They should just put your picture on the G page in Webster's."

"Are you sure I'm not a little bit bad?"

He nuzzled her neck. "Only in the very best way."

Feeling soft and warm all over, she dropped her head back, inviting him further, loving the feel of his unshaven cheek against her skin. When he pressed his mouth to the hollow of her throat, she sighed. And when he moved lower, to tease the V-neck of her blouse, she leaned back even further. So far, she fell off his lap, onto a mountain of white, fluffy fake snow.

"Ow," she said, even as she laughed at herself.

He leaped off the seat and knelt beside her. "Are you okay?"

"I'm fine."

"You'd better let me check you all over and make sure you're not hurt."

Hearing the naughty tone, she feigned a deep sigh and sagged back into the fluff, which cushioned her like a giant feather bed. "Maybe you should. I do feel a little weak."

His eyes gleaming, Ross did as he'd threatened. Slowly, gently, he caressed her neck, brushed his thumbs over her collarbones, cupped her shoulders. As if he couldn't be certain using just his hands, he began kissing his way down her body as well. Every time she sighed, or flinched, he'd look up at her and ask, "Did that hurt?"

"Definitely not," she mumbled, rising up to meet his mouth.

He didn't tease her for long. Neither of them could stand that. As if he couldn't wait to be with her again—though it had only been hours since they'd left his bed—Ross unbuttoned her blouse, pulling it free of her flouncy skirt. He kissed his way to her breasts, bathing the sensitive tips through her bra.

"Mmm," she groaned, wrapping her fingers in his thick hair.

She loved that he was so into her breasts, loved the way he slipped the bra strap down and plumped each one with his hand before sucking deeply on her nipples. Each strong pull of his mouth sent a jolt of want through her body, and her tights felt even more restrictive than usual.

"Luce?" he mumbled as he pulled her skirt up around her waist and cupped her thigh.

"Hmm?"

"Since tomorrow's Christmas, does that mean you don't need this costume anymore?"

"I guess so," she murmured.

"Good."

He didn't explain what that meant, he simply showed her. Rising onto his knees, Ross reached for the crotch of her tights and carefully yanked. They tore open, exposing her sex completely, since she'd been wearing nothing underneath.

"Good God," he muttered, sitting back on his heels to look at her.

Seeing that shocked delight in his face gave her such a feeling of feminine power. She deliberately spread her legs, revealing more of herself, loving the way his hand shook as he lifted it to rub his jaw.

It wasn't shaking when he reached out to touch her, though. She hissed as his long, warm fingers stroked her, delving into the slick crevice between her thighs. She was wet and ready, wanting him desperately.

Fortunately, Ross had brought a condom, and she laid back in the fluff, watching him push his jeans out of the way and don the protection. She lifted a leg invitingly, knowing he'd like the feel of the silky fabric of the tights against his bare hip.

She imagined he'd like it in other places, too. But his hips and that amazingly tight male butt were a good start. Without a word, she pulled him down to her, inviting him into her warmth.

She was still new enough at this to gasp when he entered her, but Ross kissed away the sound. His warm tongue made love to her mouth as he pressed further into her body, until they were fully joined. Lucy wrapped her legs around him and rolled her hips up in welcome.

He lengthened his strokes, filling and stretching and pleasing her so much she cried out at how good it felt. He was so thick and hard inside her, and she was used to this enough to want him harder, faster. Deeper.

"More," she demanded. "You're being so careful… you can stop. I want it all, Ross. Give it to me."

He groaned. Then, as if he'd just been awaiting the invitation, pulled out and slammed back into her. Hard, deep. Unbelievably good.

"Oh, yeah. More."

"You're sure."

"Absolutely," she insisted. "Give me everything you've got."

He didn't reply with words. Instead, to her surprise, Ross pulled out of her and reached for her hips. His face a study in need and hunger, he rolled her over onto her tummy, then wrapped an arm around her waist and pulled her up onto her knees. Lucy shivered, more excited than she'd ever been in her life.

She was wet and hot and ready, and when he thrust into her from behind, she threw her head back and screamed a little.

Still buried deep inside her, he grabbed her tights again. It took just one more tug and he'd ripped them completely in half from waist to thigh, baring her bottom entirely. Filling his hands with her hips, he drove into her again. Heat to heat, skin to skin.

Lucy just about lost her mind. She loved it sweet and slow and tender. But oh, did she ever love it hot and wild and *wicked.* In fact, she realized, she loved each and every thing Ross Marshall did to her.

Especially that. And, oh, *that.*

They strained and writhed, gave and took, and soon, a stunning orgasm tore through her. As if he'd just been waiting for her to reach that point, Ross immediately buried his face in her hair, kept his arms wrapped tightly around her waist and let himself go over the edge, too.

They collapsed together on the fluff. He rolled onto his side, tugging her with him, spooning her from behind. Lucy had a hard time catching her breath, but oh, God, was it worth it.

Finally, when their breathing had calmed down a bit, Ross said, "So, since you're finished with work, was that the official start of the holiday?"

"If so," she said, sounding vehement, "then merry Christmas to us!"

He hugged her closer. "And to us a good night."

THEY HAD A hell of a good night. An amazing night, as far as Ross was concerned.

After he and Lucy had cleaned up the studio and left, they hadn't headed right back for Brooklyn. Instead they'd tooled around the city a little bit. He'd even managed to convince her to go up to Rockefeller Center and go ice skating. Sure, they'd been blade-to-blade with a thousand other people who had the same idea, but it was worth it.

They'd walked past every decorated window on Park and Fifth Avenues, had gone down as far as Macy's and jostled a place in line to see those, too. Lucy grumbled a lot, but beneath the complaints he'd heard something that tugged at his heart. A sweetness, an excitement, a longing she hadn't verbalized, but was there all the same.

Underneath it all—the vibrant, gonna-go-see-the-world, and I-don't-care-about-Christmas veneer—was a pretty innocent twenty-two-year-old. One who had lost her anchor at a young age and didn't trust the world not to slam her again. Hard.

He wouldn't have admitted it, but Ross really liked trying to get Lucy to enjoy the holiday season, despite her own best efforts to dislike it. And while he wasn't totally certain she'd like the gift he'd bought her before going back to help at the studio this morning, he hoped she at least understood the intentions behind it.

"That was great," he said as he set his fork onto his empty plate. They'd just finished dinner at his tiny kitchen table.

Lucy had insisted on cooking for him, though she'd warned him she wasn't up to anything fancy. Still, it had been the first real "home-cooked" meal he'd had in ages, and he didn't think meatloaf had ever tasted so good.

He stood to clear the table and clean up the kitchen.

"Let me help you," she said, starting to rise.

"You cooked," he told her. "Go sit down and relax for a while. I've got this."

"You're sure?"

"Of course." It struck him, suddenly, how domestic

the whole thing was. Which was pretty bizarre, considering they'd known each other for a day and a half.

The best day and a half ever.

That was a crazy realization, but it was true nonetheless. He couldn't remember a better time than he'd had since meeting Lucy Fleming. Honestly, wondering what was going to happen next had him more excited than anything in a very long time.

Cleaning the kitchen quickly, he went into the other room, and found Lucy sitting on the sofa, with her head back and her eyes closed. She'd turned on the stereo and Christmas music played softly in the background. He was about to open his mouth to tease her about breaking her own rule when he saw the teardrop on her cheek.

Saying nothing, he joined her on the couch, tugging her against him so that her head rested on his shoulder. They sat there for a long time in silence, listening to the music, watching the way the silly camera flash—now covered with a green sheet of plastic—cast glimmers of light on the Christmas tree.

Finally, she shifted in his arms and looked up at him. "This is the nicest Christmas Eve I've had in a very long time."

"I'm glad. Not *too* traditional for you?"

"No. It's perfect." She licked her lips. "I know you're very close to your family, and this is all probably hard for you to understand..."

"I can understand it with my brain," he told her, meaning it. "But my heart doesn't even want to try to understand. I just can't imagine what it must be like."

His father drove him crazy, but Ross still loved him, and his mother. He couldn't even fathom having his world yanked out from under him like Lucy had, couldn't comprehend getting a phone call telling you the people you'd always assumed would be there were suddenly gone.

People expected to outlive their parents, that was natural. But not until they reached at least middle age. Not until their own kids had gotten a chance to meet their grandparents. His own parents were pretty young, only in their early mid-fifties, and Ross fully expected another twenty to thirty years of arguing with his Dad and being fussed over by his Mom. He wouldn't have it any other way.

"I can tell you what it's like," she said. "It's like waking up one day and realizing someone's torn half your heart out of your chest. Your life is no longer about the number of years you've lived, or the ones you have in front of you. It becomes measured by before and after that one moment."

He understood. It broke his heart, but he definitely understood. He hugged her close, smoothing her hair, kissing her temple.

"But then," she whispered, "the hole starts to fill in. You remember the good times from before that moment, and also start to acknowledge the good ones that come after." She shifted on the couch, looking up at him. Her beautiful brown eyes were luminous, but no more tears marred her cheeks. As if she wanted him to see that she was melancholy, but not heartbroken. "This weekend, you've given me good moments, Ross. And I'll never forget them."

He bent to her, brushing his mouth across hers in a tender kiss. She kissed him back, sweetly, gently, then smiled up at him.

"So," he said, knowing the time was right, "is it okay if I give you your Christmas present now?"

She eyed him warily.

"It's not much," he told her as he got up and went to the tree. He'd hidden the wrapped package behind it when they'd arrived home earlier this evening.

"You shouldn't have gotten me anything," she insisted. "I don't have anything for you."

He winked and raised a flirtatious brow. "I'm sure I'll think of something you can give me later."

"Hmm...why don't we see what's in here, then I'll decide just what you deserve to get in return." She took the present, and though a shadow of trepidation crossed her face, and she nibbled her lip lightly, he would also swear he saw a glimmer of a smile.

He sat on the opposite end of the couch, watching her unwrap the box. As she opened the lid, and stared down in silence at the gift inside, he couldn't help wondering if he'd made a mistake.

Maybe it was too soon. Maybe she wasn't ready. Maybe she'd think he didn't understand, after all.

She reached in and pulled out the snow globe, shaking it gently, watching the white glitter swirl around the scene inside.

It wasn't anything funny, like her brother would give her, and certainly wasn't intended to replace the peace sign Santa that had been broken. Instead it was simple, pretty—traditional. A house with a snowy roof and a wreath on the door. Warm, yellow light coming from the windows, where a family could be imagined to have gathered. A car parked outside. A tree-studded landscape. It portrayed a quiet Christmas night, when all was calm and bright.

"I just thought, since your other one was broken..."

"It's beautiful," she whispered. "Absolutely beautiful."

She twisted the knob on the bottom, and Deck The Halls began to play. Smiling, Lucy carefully set the globe down on the table. "Thank you."

"You're welcome, Lucy."

The song on the radio ended, and an announcer came on to mention the time—midnight on the nose.

They looked at the tree, then at each other. With no more sign of those tears, Lucy whispered, "Merry Christmas, Ross."

She rose from the couch and extended her hand. Ross took it and together they walked to his bedroom. They exchanged langorous, intimate kisses as they slowly undressed. Throughout the long night hours, they didn't have sex, they made love. He had never been sure of the distinction before, but now, he finally got it.

He fell asleep with a smile on his face, and was pretty sure it stayed there all night long. Because he was still smiling hours later, on Christmas morning, when he woke up to a naked Lucy wrapped in his arms...and a ringing phone.

"What time is it?" she asked in a sleep-filled voice.

He glanced at the clock. "Only six-thirty."

There would only be one person calling this early. His kid sister was always the first one up on Christmas, and she'd probably already checked her email and seen the cyber gift card he'd ordered for her.

Checking the caller ID on his phone, and seeing his parents' phone number, he chuckled and opened it, fully expecting to hear his sister's joy-filled, chattery voice.

"Hello?"

A pause. A sob.

Then the bottom fell out of his entire world.

CHAPTER ELEVEN

Now
Chicago, December 25, 2011

LUCY WOKE UP Christmas morning feeling nice, warm and toasty. That wasn't just because of the incredibly hot, sexy, naked man against whom she was lying, but also because the heating vent right above the foldout was blowing out a steady stream of warm air.

The power was on. *Hallelujah.*

She lay there for a few minutes, relieved, but also a tiny bit sad. Power was good. Great, in fact. But it signaled something: a return to normalcy. The real world was knocking at the doors of their romantic little love nest, reminding them it was really a six story office building in Chicago.

For thirty-six hours, they'd been able to pretend the rest of the world didn't exist. Now that they were wired again, however, they were just a phone call away from everyone.

She should make use of that and call Sam, who might be worried. Hopefully he had been too busy to try to reach her. But at the very least she needed to call and wish him a merry Christmas…or at least a *bah, humbug.*

She wondered if it would be merry for her. Before yesterday, she would have laughed at the idea. Now, though, she honestly wasn't sure.

It would probably be smart to cut her losses, grab the memory of the gift she'd already received this holiday season, and get out while the getting was good. She and Ross had shared a magical Christmas Eve—for the second time in her life. But they'd already proved once that they couldn't last much beyond that. So what kind of fool would she be to let him back into her heart again, the way she'd let him back into her arms?

Anybody could make a lovely, romantic memory out of the holiday season and some snow. They'd never had to try to exist out in the real world.

And maybe they shouldn't. Maybe they weren't meant to.

Saddened by that thought, she slowly sat up and stretched. She peered over Ross's shoulder toward the wall of windows and realized that not only had the snow stopped, but the sky was trying to be all blue and sunny. There was also a distinct sound of some kind of motor nearby.

Curious, she climbed out of bed and went to the window, which overlooked the parking lot. To her surprise, it was already half-cleared. A truck with a plow was working on the lot, and a small skid loader was taking care of the mounds of snow on the walkways.

"Damn," she whispered. Not only were they now

connected electronically with the world, it looked like their "snowed-in" status was about to change, too. Their private holiday adventure had come to an end.

"Merry Christmas," he said from the bed, his voice thick with sleep.

Though she wanted to respond in kind, the words stuck a little in her throat, which had thickened with every second since she'd awoken. "Good morning."

"Does it feel warmer in here, or is it just because I'm staring at you and you're naked?"

She laughed softly and returned to the bed, bending to kiss him as she crawled in beside him. "Power's on. And the parking lot's almost cleared."

He frowned. "Remind me to fire that snow clearing company."

Ross didn't sound any happier about being "rescued" than she felt. Maybe because, like her, he wasn't sure what was going to happen when they returned to reality.

Did they have what it took to go beyond this weekend? To actually work in a day-to-day relationship? With his ties to his family and this business and this city…and her sometimes whimsical need to change direction and explore new opportunities, were they really cut out to be together?

She had no idea. Nor did she really want to talk to him about it yet. She had some thinking to do. And it would probably be best to do it alone.

"I guess you ought to call your family and let them know you're okay," she said. "They've probably been very worried."

He nodded. "Listen, why don't you come with..."

She knew what he was going to ask and held a hand up, palm out. "Thanks, but no thanks."

"I'm sure they'd love to meet you."

"Bah humbug, remember?"

"Lucy..."

"Please don't," she said as she got up and reached for her clothes and began pulling them on. As much as she'd like to stay naked in bed with Ross, she knew things had changed. She felt a lot less free and a lot more worried than she had last night. The presence of the rest of the world in their strange relationship had thrown her off-kilter. Where a few hours ago she had been filled with nothing but contentment and satisfaction, now the only things that filled her head were questions and concerns.

"I need some time," she told him. "I'd really just like to go home and take a shower."

"What about Christmas dinner?"

Turkey subs out of the break room had sounded just about perfect. Going with him to his parents' estate for a grand meal with a big family? Not so much.

"Please don't push it," she said, hearing the edge in her voice and getting mad at herself. He was trying to share something special—his family's holiday.

"Okay," he said. "I understand."

Since she didn't understand herself, she doubted that, but didn't want to argue with him. Not after the wonderful day they'd had yesterday and the beautiful, amazing, incredible nights in that narrow foldout bed.

"You can use the phone on my desk if you want

to call Sam," he told her. "If the power's on, the lines should be working. Just dial 9 first."

Thanking him, she finished dressing and went to the desk. She got Sam's voice mail and left him a message. She checked her cell phone—still no reception—and decided to call her home phone and see if there were any messages.

She dialed home, then entered the security code. When she heard she had two messages from Friday, she winced, realizing she'd never even listened to them when she got home the other night. She'd been too busy masturbating in the bathtub while thinking of Ross.

A voice she didn't recognize came on the line. "Ms. Fleming, this is Janet Sturgeon, I'm with *Parents Place* magazine. I'm sorry for calling right before the holidays, but we really wanted to reach you. Everyone in the office just loved your photo essay."

She sent up a mental cheer. But the voice wasn't finished.

"And of course we all remember the great work you've done for us in the past. Anyway, we're making some changes here at headquarters and were wondering if you might be interested in coming to New York to discuss a more permanent working position with us? We're looking for an artistic director. We all really like what you do and think you would be a great fit with our staff."

Lucy's jaw had slowly become unhinged while she listened. She'd been hoping for a *Yes, we'll take your work and pay you X dollars*. But a job offer? At least, the offer of an interview for a job? She'd never imagined it.

Well, that was a lie, of course she'd imagined it. She'd thought many times about getting out of the self-employment wading pool and into the bigger publishing ocean. And *Parents Place* was a huge part of that ocean. The chance to work for them, to be an artistic director for a major national publication…honestly, it was like someone had just handed her the winning prize for a lottery, when she'd never bought a ticket.

Her mind had drifted off, and she'd missed the phone number the caller had left at the end. Lucy saved the message to listen to again when she got home and thought about what to say when she called the woman back tomorrow.

"Lucy? Are you okay?"

Ross was watching her from the alcove. He'd finished dressing, and swept a hand through his thick, sleep-tousled hair, looking perfect and sexy and gorgeous. Her heart somersaulted in her chest, as it always did when she looked at the man in broad daylight. Or, hell, in pitch darkness.

Only now, there was a faint squeezing sensation in her heart as well.

Don't be silly, you don't even know if you'd actually get the job yet. Or if you'd take it.

True. She couldn't let herself get upset about what could possibly happen in the future, and what it meant for her and Ross. For all she knew, there was no her and Ross. This weekend had been amazing and wonderful...but she had already acknowledged there might not be more than that.

There won't be if you're in New York.

Which made her wonder—would he care if she left?

Would he ask her not to go?

"Lucy? Is everything okay? Was it Sam?"

She shook her head slowly and lowered the receiver back onto the cradle. Trying to keep her voice steady, so she wouldn't reveal either her excitement, or her incredible turmoil over what this could mean for them, she told him about the phone call.

Ross didn't react right away. He didn't immediately smile and congratulate her. Neither did he frown and insist that she couldn't possibly think about leaving now, when so much between them was up in the air.

So maybe it's not. Maybe everything was settled in that bed in the past thirty-six hours, and it's all over and we are both supposed to just go merrily on with our lives.

God, did she not want to believe that. But it was possible. To Ross, this may have just been a one-time thing. Maybe he couldn't care less if she went. She just didn't know. And honestly, she wasn't sure how to ask.

"I see. Well, that's exciting," he finally said.

"It could be," she replied carefully.

"When would you go back to New York?"

Yell, damn it. Show some kind of emotion.

"She said they wanted to interview me immediately, this week if possible."

"I don't imagine the airports are going to be open for a day or two. Maybe by late Tuesday, or Wednesday."

"Maybe," she said, wondering how he could be so calm, why he wouldn't reveal a thing about what he was thinking.

Why he wasn't telling her he didn't want her to go.

But he didn't. Instead, still calm and reasonable, as if they'd just finished a dinner date rather than a thirty-six hour, emotionally-charged sexual marathon, he helped her straighten up the office and the break room, hiding evidence of the wild weekend idyll that had taken place there. Everything went back in its spot, the borrowed coats returned, the food neatly put away. Even the foldout was made and folded up. No evidence that they'd been here at all.

The realization made her incredibly sad. But there was nothing she could do about it.

Finally, with nothing left to do, they dressed in warm clothes, and headed downstairs. They had no problem getting out to the parking lot, and Ross paid his contractor a little extra to dig out their cars. So, by twelve noon, they were ready to go, neither too concerned about their drive, considering the plows and salt trucks had been out in force most of the night.

Chicago was a city that was used to dealing with snow. Despite the wicked Christmas Eve blizzard, things would likely get back to normal pretty easily. If anything was ever normal again. Right now, Lucy wasn't sure about the definition of that word.

"You sure you're okay to drive home?" he asked.

She nodded. "I'll be fine, it's only a couple of miles."

He opened her car door for her. It was warm inside; she'd let it idle for a few minutes while they stood outside saying goodbye. Or, not saying goodbye. So far, they'd said anything but.

She wasn't sure what she was waiting for him to say. Or if he was waiting, too. Or what either of them could say that would make this all right, make them both understand where they'd been and where they were going.

In the end, they didn't say much of anything. Ross simply leaned down and brushed his mouth across hers, their breath mingling in the icy air. Then he whispered, "Merry Christmas, Lucy."

She managed a tremulous smile and nodded.

"Bye, Ross."

Her heart was screaming at her to say something else. Her brain was, too. But she couldn't find the words, didn't know what he wanted to hear.

So she simply got in her car, watched him get into his, and then they both drove away.

AFTER GOING HOME to change and shower, and call the hospital to check on Chip—who was going to be all right—Ross headed out to his parents' place. His family had been holding their celebration until he got there. So he tried to pretend he gave a damn about the holiday and wasn't utterly miserable.

He didn't think he succeeded. His smile was tight, his laughter fake and the strain had to be visible. He couldn't keep his mind on the games, got lost in the middle of conversations and generally walked around in a daze for most of the afternoon.

All he could think about was Lucy. The time they'd spent together…and the way they'd parted.

He just couldn't understand it, couldn't begin to comprehend how she could have spent the weekend with him, doing everything they'd done, saying everything they'd said, then casually talk about moving back to New York. It made no sense.

He would have bet his last dollar that she loved him, that she'd always loved him, as he'd always loved her. But the words had never come out of her mouth, not even when he'd told her how he'd felt about her all those years ago.

You're the one who left her. You did the heartbreaking, a voice in his head reminded him. So maybe it wasn't so surprising that she wasn't going to just rush right back into this.

But to rush to the east coast instead? What sense did that make?

"So, are you going to tell us who she is?"

Ross jerked his head up when his kid sister Annie—who was no longer a little kid, but instead a college junior—entered the room. "Excuse me?"

"Come on, everybody can tell you've got woman troubles. We haven't seen you this mopey about a girl since you moved back home from New York after losing that girl…Linda?"

"Lucy. Her name is Lucy," he muttered, looking away and frowning.

Hearing Annie's surprised gasp, he wished he hadn't said a word. "Wait, are we talking about Lucy now?"

"What makes you ask that?"

"Well, you said her name *is* Lucy. Plus, the way you say her name, bro. It's like going back in time six years. I remember exactly how you were when you first got back after Dad got sick. I've never seen you so hung up on anyone."

There was a good reason for that. He'd never *been* so hung up on anyone else.

"So what's the story? Why didn't you invite her over for Christmas dinner?"

"I did. She…doesn't really like Christmas." He didn't want to share any details of Lucy's private life, but did explain, "She has some pretty bad memories of this time of year."

"So where is she? Is she here in Chicago?"

"Yes, she moved here. She's home at her apartment now."

"Dude! Harsh!"

He rolled his eyes, still not used to hearing his sister talk like an eighteen-year-old guy, which seemed to be how all young women talked now.

"You left her sitting at home, alone in her apartment, on Christmas?"

"Like I said, I asked her to come here. She wanted to go home. Alone."

Annie's eyebrows wagged, which was when he realized he'd slipped up. Again. "*Go* home, huh? As in, she was with you for the past couple of days during your big trapped-in-the-snow emergency?"

"Shut up," he muttered.

She laughed. "Look, all I gotta say is, if I was seeing someone, and he left me sitting at home all alone on Christmas, I'd feel absolutely sure he didn't give a damn about me."

"You're not Lucy," he muttered.

"Good thing for you," she said, getting up and sauntering toward the door. "Because if I were, I'd have said later, dude, and made you think I didn't care any more about you than you did about me."

She left the room, leaving Ross sitting there alone. But his sibling's words remained. In fact, they somehow seemed to get louder…and louder.

He knew Lucy wasn't the type to play games. But he also knew she had to be feeling very unsure about them—about him—right now. Considering he'd walked out on her Christmas Day six years ago and had stopped calling her shortly thereafter, why wouldn't she have doubts? Why wouldn't she have questions?

Why wouldn't she expect that he wouldn't give a damn if she decided to move back to New York?

In trying to be calm and rational and fair, had he made her think he didn't care? Had hiding his fear of losing her again made it that much more likely to happen?

No. That just wouldn't do. No way was he going to let her think he didn't want her. Lucy might want to leave, she might view this great career move as the next logical step in her life. But he wasn't going to let her make that decision without making sure she knew how he felt.

Which meant he needed to go talk to her. And this time, there would be nothing left unsaid.

OF ALL THE sucky Christmases Lucy had ever experienced in her life, this one had to rank right up there among the suckiest.

Oh, it had started off great. Magically, in fact. She'd awakened this morning in the arms of an amazing man, sure she'd never been happier in her life.

But since she'd arrived home—alone—and moped around her apartment—alone—and eaten a frozen dinner—alone—Lucy couldn't find a single positive thing about it.

She'd tried doing her online shopping—boring. She'd cleaned her apartment—more boring. She'd answered a few emails, checked her appointment book, looked into flights to New York.

Boring. Boring.

And heartbreaking.

Heartbreaking, because she didn't want to fly to New York. Not under these circumstances, anyway. Not without knowing how Ross felt about it—whether he gave a damn.

This morning, when she'd first heard the message about the potential job offer, oh, it had been exciting, a great validation. Thinking that a major magazine was seeking her out for her talent was a huge ego boost and a true reinforcement that she'd made the right choice when switching gears in her career.

But she didn't particularly want to move back to New York. She liked Chicago. She liked living near her brother again. She liked the people she'd met and the studio she'd rented and the life she was living.

Most of all, she liked being near the man she loved.

"Hell," she whispered that evening as she sat on her couch, listening to Christmas music on an internet radio station.

She loved him. She loved Ross Marshall. She always had. He'd entered her heart six years ago and had never left it, despite time and distance and other relationships.

Some people could fall in and out of love. Some loved only once in a lifetime. She suspected she was one of those people. Which would be wonderful, if only she didn't love a guy who didn't seem to care if she moved a thousand miles away.

Feeling truly sorry for herself, she almost didn't hear the knock. At first, she assumed her neighbors' kids were banging around with all their new Christmas toys. They'd been filled with joy and laughter all day, and she'd smiled at the sounds coming through the thin walls. But the sound came again, and she realized someone was at her door.

She glanced at the clock, seeing it was after eight. She'd finally reached Sam this afternoon, and he'd told her he was working all night again. But perhaps he'd managed to swing by on a break or something.

She went to the door and opened it with a smile.

The smile faded when she saw not her brother, but someone she'd never expected to see at her doorstep tonight.

"Ross?"

"Can I come in?"

Stunned, not only because he'd told her he was going out to his family's, but also because, as far as she knew, he'd had no idea where she lived, she stepped aside and beckoned him in. "How did you..."

"Stella. She had both your work and your home addresses in her BlackBerry."

"Is everything all right? Your family?"

"Fine. By now they're probably engaged in the annual Trivial Pursuit Christmas marathon."

Still unsure why he'd come, and not knowing what to say, she quickly asked, "And your security guard?"

"He's going to pull through," he said.

"I'm so glad." Twisting her hands together, she finally remembered her manners. "Can I take your coat? Would you like to sit down?"

He took off his coat, but didn't sit in the chair to which she gestured. Instead, sounding and looking somber, he stared into her eyes and said, "If I ask you a question, will you answer me truthfully?"

"Of course."

"Okay." Stepping closer, close enough that she smelled his spicy cologne and felt his body's warmth, he asked, "Do you want to move back to New York?"

Talk about putting her on the spot. She crossed her arms over her chest, rubbing her hands up and down them and thought about her answer. Her first instinct was to answer his question with a question—*do you want me to stay?*

But they'd played enough games, lost enough time dancing around the truth or making decisions for each other without benefit of a real, genuine conversation. So she would be nothing but honest, both with him, and with herself.

"No. I don't."

He closed his eyes and sighed, so visibly relieved, she almost smiled.

"My turn to ask you a question," she countered.

"Okay."

Drawing a deep breath, and hoping her voice wouldn't quiver, she asked, "Do you want me to stay?"

He didn't hesitate, not even for an instant. "Oh, *hell* yes."

Though pleased by his vehemence, she tilted her head in confusion. "Then why did you act like you didn't care earlier?"

"Why did you let me think you wanted to go?"

Neither answered for a second…then they both replied in unison. "Because we're idiots."

Laughter bubbled between them, then Ross stepped closer, dropping his hands to her hips and tugging her to him. She lifted hers to his shoulders and looked up at him, seeing the warmth and the tenderness in his green eyes. Even without the words being said, she knew what he was thinking, what he was feeling. What his heart was telling him.

Because her heart was telling her the same thing.

They were meant to be together. They always had been. Time and circumstance had separated them, yes. But, maybe that was how it had to be. They'd been young and impulsive. And she hadn't truly been ready to accept love and happiness, to offer the kind of trusting, loving relationship Ross deserved.

Now she was ready. And they'd found their way back to each other. It had taken years, and moving to another city, but their lives had come full circle and this week, they'd re-created the past.

Only, this time, it would end differently. They weren't going to let anything come between them.

This time, they would make it work.

"I love you," he said, and her heart sang.

He lifted a hand to cup her face. "I let you go once. I wasn't about to make the same mistake again."

"What if I had said I wanted to go to New York?"

"I would have said fine, when do we leave?"

She started to smile, at least until she saw he meant it. Then she could only stare at him in shock. "Are you serious?"

"Very serious."

"But how—"

"I talked to my father when I was out at the house today. I told him I had let you get away once, but it wasn't going to happen again. And that while I'd like to stay at Elite, if it came down to it, I was going to do what was right for *me* for a change. Live my life for myself, since I've been living it for everyone else for the past six years."

"How did he react?"

He looked away. "I think that's the closest I've ever seen my father to tears."

She sucked in a breath.

"Not because he was upset, but because he finally had the chance to tell me how damned grateful he is for everything I've done, and how much he wants me to be happy." Ross shook his head slowly. "To tell you the truth, I couldn't believe it. He's never said anything like that to me before."

Knowing how much that had to have meant to him, Lucy rose on tiptoe and brushed her mouth against his. "I'm so glad."

"Me, too."

"But your father doesn't have anything to worry about, and neither do your shareholders."

"We can go if you want to," he insisted.

"I don't," she insisted back, being completely honest. "I'm finished running off to do new things, in new places, just to avoid having to ever expose myself to pain and hurt again. There's no love without risk…but there's no life without love."

Then, realizing she had never actually said it, she gave him the most honest, genuine present she could think to give him. "I love you, Ross. I always have, I always will."

He smiled tenderly, then bent to kiss her, slowly, lovingly. And having those words on their lips made it taste that much sweeter, made it mean that much more.

When they finally ended the kiss, they remained locked in each other's arms, swaying slowly to the holiday music playing softly in the background. "Joy to the World."

How fitting. For the first time in what seemed like forever, her life felt filled to the brim with joy. Because Ross was in it. And she knew, deep down to her very soul, that he always would be.

"Merry Christmas, Lucy," he whispered against her cheek.

"Merry Christmas, Ross."

She tightened her arms around him, wanting to capture this feeling and imprint it in her mind forever, like a beautiful photograph. The first moment of the rest of their lives.

There would be many more, she knew. Some beautiful, probably some sad.

But no matter what, they would all be filled with love.

EPILOGUE

Two Years Later

CURLED UP TOGETHER on the sofa, Lucy and Ross watched out their front window as the first flakes of Christmas snow began to fall. The weatherman wasn't predicting a major storm—nothing like the one that had trapped them in Ross's office building two years earlier—aka the best blizzard of all time. No, this was quiet and sweet, a nighttime snow as gentle and peaceful as the carols playing softly on the stereo behind them.

Wrapped in the arms of the man she loved, here inside the beautiful home they'd finished building together and had moved into last spring, Lucy didn't mind if it snowed all night. She had everything—and everyone—she needed, right here within these walls.

"Here it comes," he murmured, tightening his arms around her.

"Mmm-hmm."

They remained silent for a moment, watching the white flakes drift down, slowly at first, then more steadily. Lucy suddenly realized, looking out that huge front window that overlooked the water, that this must be what it was like to be inside a snow globe. Perhaps the very one Ross had given her all those years ago, which now had a place of honor on the center of the mantelpiece. She was tucked inside that happy home, with the warm yellow light in the window and the cars in the driveway and the snowy evergreens all around.

She smiled, loving the image, thinking back to that Christmas Eve. What, she wondered, would that girl, that twenty-two-year-old Lucy, have thought if she could have foreseen this future? She probably wouldn't have believed it, and it would have scared her to death. But, deep down she knew she would have been very hopeful—because that day had opened her eyes to a world of possibilities.

All because of the man holding her so tenderly, humming Silent Night as he kissed her temple.

She looked up at him, so handsome in the glow from the fire, and whispered, "Merry Christmas, Ross."

He smiled back and brushed his lips against hers. "Merry Christmas, wife."

No more *bah humbug* for Lucy. No more building walls against things like memories, and holidays… and love. That part of her life was over.

Ross stretched a little and chuckled. "Am I rotten for being glad my parents and your brother decided to stay home and come over tomorrow, after they see how much snow falls?"

She laughed softly, understanding him so well.

"Not unless I'm rotten, too, because I feel the same way."

It wasn't that either of them begrudged the visit—she actually adored his family, and her brother's new girlfriend. They certainly had plenty of room for everyone in the huge house. But she couldn't deny being happy things had worked out this way. Now they would have tonight and tomorrow morning for themselves, getting a start on creating holiday memories and traditions of their own.

She was ready for that. Ready to incorporate the ghosts of her Christmases past into her present and her future. Ready to open her heart to the magical season of giving that she'd once loved so very much… and move forward, molding it, changing it, shaping it into something that was just hers, and Ross's, and their family's.

"It's not that I don't love them…"

"It's just because tomorrow's so special," she replied.

Very special. Not just because it was their first holiday season in their new home. Not just because it was the first Christmas since they'd gotten married last year, on Christmas Day. Not just because they were still wildly in love and so incredibly happy. Not even because Lucy had become a fan of Christmas again.

No, they were glad to be alone because they both wanted to savor and rejoice in the early present they'd received ten days ago. Well, two presents.

They were sleeping upstairs in matching cribs, one with a blue baby blanket, the other pink. Scott and Jennifer—Jenny—named after the grandparents they would never know.

When Ross had suggested the names, she'd thought her heart would break. Not with sadness, but because of how happy her parents would be to see her so deeply loved by such an amazing man.

That, she knew, was the greatest Christmas gift she would ever receive. And she'd be getting that gift every day for the rest of her life.

* * * * *

SAMANTHA HUNTER

lives in Syracuse, New York, where they have very cold winters, so she likes to write hot books! When she's not writing, Sam spends time on numerous hobbies and projects, and she enjoys traveling and spending time with her husband and their pets. She's also an unapologetic TV addict. You can learn more about her books, current releases and news at samanthahunter.com. You can also email her at samhunter@samanthahunter.com and look for her on Twitter and Facebook.

Be sure to look for other books by Samantha Hunter in Harlequin Blaze—the ultimate destination for red-hot romance! There are four new Harlequin Blaze titles available every month. Check one out today!

I'LL BE YOURS FOR CHRISTMAS

Samantha Hunter

Happy holidays and Happy New Year to all of my readers, editors, to my agent, my husband, friends and family. I hope Santa treats all of you very well this year!

CHAPTER ONE

ABBY HARPER'S EYES clung to the man who stood not twenty feet away, dressed in an expensive silk suit that glided over his broad chest and muscled arms like water over rock.

Reece Winston.

She frowned, watching the restaurant hostess sidle up a little closer than necessary, making sure Reece had a clear view down the deep V of her low-cut blouse.

Abby couldn't blame her, not really, taking in the impressive figure Reece made as he turned, noticing the way the tailored pants clung to a perfect masculine ass that had her fingers itching to reach out for a squeeze.

She knew just how it would feel. She'd been there, done that.

Almost, anyway.

Once, a long, long time ago. How unfair—or pathetic—was it that she could remember the feel of one man's backside from eight years before?

To his credit, Reece barely seemed to notice the hostess, as he was deep in conversation with a small, hawkish man who stood beside him. Abby had heard

Reece was home but hadn't seen him around, even though he lived next door.

That wasn't unusual. He'd come home a few times over the years since he'd left for life in Europe, but their paths had never intersected. She'd been off to school, or busy working at her parents' winery, and Reece had his life as a famous race car driver on the Formula One circuit. With the differences between their two lives, the half a mile between their homes might as well have been a thousand.

This was the first time she'd actually seen him anywhere but in a local newspaper or television sports report. Her heart beat a little too quickly for her liking. So she turned her attention away, though she wasn't really looking at the crowds milling around the Ithaca Commons, the artsy, outdoor shopping plaza in the heart of the small central New York city.

It was almost a month before Christmas, the Friday after Thanksgiving, which she had spent catching up on inventory. Abby and her friend Hannah were meeting here for lunch, something Abby had been looking forward to all week. Some downtime and a chance to forget about work for an hour or so.

Some light snow fell, blowing and circling around the booted feet of shoppers and local shopkeepers who were moving around the walkway. She hardly noticed. Her mind insisted on reminiscing about Reece.

She'd only kissed him once, on a crazy, wine-drenched evening one summer when he'd been home from college, the semester before he took off for Europe. They were both at the same lakeside party given by a mutual friend. Even then, Reece ran with a crowd way out of Abby's league.

Abby had been seeing Josh Martin back then, a graduate student from Cornell Veterinary College who helped out at their vineyard, where they also hosted a small petting zoo with goats and sheep. Josh was a great guy. Cute.

Abby had been lying in wait by a dense hedgerow, intent on seducing her date. When she pulled the man she thought was Josh into the quiet, dark spot, she didn't give him a chance to say anything. She kissed him in clear invitation before he could say a word.

Abby discovered early on that she liked some kink with her sex, and Josh had a kind of quiet reserve that she took as a challenge. Sex outdoors at a party, with people right on the other side of the hedge, was an exciting thought for her, but she knew her mild-mannered date would have to be convinced.

She had pretty much made her way around second base heading for third when she told him how pleased she was with his sense of adventure and wondered what other experiments he might be up for.

Reece had chuckled softly and whispered in her ear that he would be happy to try anything she wanted to suggest.

She'd recognized his voice, and her mistake, immediately.

It had been *so* humiliating. Even now, her cheeks burned to think of it. She'd popped out from the hedges without even fixing her clothes, much to the amusement of some onlookers in the yard. Reece walked out, too, completely unapologetic with his shirt still unbuttoned, his eyes hot and the top button of his jeans undone. The button she had been undoing when he'd spoken up.

Worse, as furious as she was, she'd wanted to go back behind that hedge and finish what they'd started. Reece smiled and told her to lighten up, that he wouldn't have let it go too far. She imagined he and his buddies had a great laugh about it later.

Then he told her that Josh had received an emergency phone call and had to leave suddenly. Josh had asked Reece to find Abby and let her know. He'd started to say something else, but Abby had turned and left, and that was the last time she'd seen him, until now.

Reece had been her tormentor since childhood. The boy who always hid her lunchbox in the wrong locker, who tugged her pigtails and always, always rubbed it in that his parents' vineyards were bigger, more profitable and better than her family's smaller organic operation.

Though Reece teased her, he was never really mean. When she was fourteen, in fact, he defended her when another boy had been needlessly cruel about her braces, making her cry. Reece had almost punched the other boy, she remembered. Abby hated to admit it, but a secret, nasty little crush on him developed in that moment.

And he knew it.

And she knew that he knew, even when they both

emerged back out from behind the hedge and he'd smiled at her so *knowingly.*

"Hey, earth to Abby?" The voice finally broke through as Hannah Morgan, her best friend since high school, returned to the table, sliding back into her seat.

Abby shook her head clear and blinked the past away.

"Sorry, lost in thought."

"Yeah, I saw Reece at the door. From the roses blooming in your cheeks, I assume you did, too."

Abby grunted. "It's just warm in here."

Hannah grinned widely. "Warmer since Reece walked in," she said without shame, watching him where he sat across the room from them. "I guess he's home because of what happened with his dad."

"I'm kind of surprised to see him, really. He had a bad crash last spring and has been recovering ever since—it was really serious," Abby said, shuddering as she remembered seeing the replay of the accident on the news. Reece had been on his way to superstardom, living a glamorous and high-profile life as a race car driver until the crash.

Hannah cocked an eyebrow. "I'd heard, but didn't realize you followed racing that closely."

"I just watch the news. And I might have read a few things online."

"Well, he looks healthy and hale to me," Hannah said with a playful leer.

Abby knew better than to look again, but did anyway, and sure enough, as soon as she peeked, Reece turned his head to look directly at her.

The shared look nearly sucked the breath out of her.

The years disappeared, and she was the crush-stricken teenager again. His eyes narrowed, and she knew that he recognized her, too, even though she was now twenty-five pounds lighter and her previously plain, boy-short brown hair was now long and layered, curling softly with honey-blond highlights, her one indulgence.

"Why does he have to be so *hot?*" Abby mumbled, deeply annoyed and digging in to the beautiful salad that a server set before her moments ago. Shoving a forkful of spinach and various greens, fresh pears, walnuts and blue cheese into her mouth, she barely tasted it. Reece's fault.

"Hey, I think he's coming over," Hannah whispered across the table, looking up with a big smile as Reece approached them.

"What?" Abby sputtered, swallowing a mouthful of greens, promptly choking on her food as she saw Hannah was right. Abby coughed, reaching for her water, but suddenly strong hands had her from behind, spanning her rib cage and pulling her back against a rock-solid chest.

"I'm okay, I'm okay!" she insisted. She could sense the heat from his hands on her skin in spite of the sweater she wore over her blouse. His hold released, and she took a few breaths, composing herself.

"Abby?" he said in a voice that was deeper than

she remembered, his breath just brushing the back of her neck.

She didn't turn around, not yet. Picking up her water, she took a sip, using the moment to focus. Then, smoothing the front of her sweater, she faced him with a bright smile.

"Reece. How nice to see you," she said, and was yet again flung back to those hedges as his gray eyes sparkled with warm recognition. He was remembering it, too, she could tell. Damn it. "Thanks for the first aid, but I really was okay," she said.

"Glad to help," he said. "So, Abby Harper, all grown up. No more pigtails or braces," he said with a smile and a wink.

Her cheeks heated and she wanted to kick Hannah for grinning so broadly.

"I'm sorry to hear about your father. I hope he's doing well," Abby said, meaning it, determined to act like an adult.

She noticed a network of thin scars, recently healed, that ran along the side of his neck, and what looked like another behind his ear. "And you, too," she continued. "That was an awful accident they showed on the news. I'm so glad you're up and around. You look great," she said, proud of herself for sounding so mature, like an old friend who was happy to see him again.

Reece's expression became more serious. She thought he looked bigger now, more muscular than she remembered. She assumed that all race drivers kept to a rigorous fitness regimen and needed to be physically fit to withstand the physical and mental pressures of racing, but…wow.

Those beautiful, thick-lashed eyes were the same, as were the sharp cheekbones and full lips. She'd always loved how his pin-straight, raven-black hair had fallen in his eyes, a little long in the front, but now he kept it cropped short, which only accented his features all the more.

"Thank you. Dad's recovering well. Doctors are very optimistic."

He obviously didn't want to discuss his own near miss, and she couldn't say she blamed him. Regardless of his celebrity status, it couldn't be fun to have your private life and health problems made into entertainment news.

Abby nodded. "Is he still at the hospital? I imagine he'd probably be happy to be back to work when he can."

Reece frowned. "Actually, he won't. The surgery was remarkably fast—they can do amazing things these days. He and Mom were only home for a few days, but they're down with Ben now, in South Carolina. The doctors advised it, so that he'd be in an easier climate, closer to hospitals. They'll live with Ben and his family for a while, which will make it easier on Mom. Then they plan to find a new place down there."

"Oh," she said, her reaction part surprise and part regret. She liked the Winstons and would have liked to have seen them before they left. They'd been good neighbors. "Who's taking over the vineyards? You?"

It was what she'd done when her parents retired. They were off catching up on all of the travel they had put off all those years. Abby was happy for them and she loved the updates they sent her and posted on their Facebook pages. Her parents—world adventurers.

"Not exactly," Reece said, looking cautious. "We've decided selling is the best option. I'm taking care of the details, though, and I have some buyers interested, but—"

"You're selling?" she interrupted, in shock.

"Yes, I'm afraid so."

"But, I thought…now that you're not racing…"

Her misstep was reflected in the tightening of his expression.

"I want to be back to racing next year," he said shortly. "As soon as possible, really. So there's no choice but to sell. Which reminds me," he said, glancing over at his table, "I have to get back to my meeting. I just wanted to say hello."

"Oh," was all Abby managed to say.

Reece's expression shifted from cool to friendly again. Maybe a little too smoothly, in Abby's estimation.

"It's good to see you, though. Maybe we'll get a chance to have a drink together over the holiday, catch up on old times. I should be home for the month, to see the sale through and finish things up here," he said.

"Yeah, sure," she responded, but he'd already turned to walk away. This time, she did notice a slight hitch in his gait and wondered about his injuries. Things might be happening behind the scenes that the public didn't know about…still, she'd thought from what had been reported in the news and online that he was out of the sport.

"Wow, I can't believe he's selling," Abby said again, her mind returning to that bombshell. There were some new start-ups along the lake, and some of the vineyards had closed over the years, but Maple Hills and Winston Vineyards were the two oldest in the area. "All the news said he was out of racing. His accident left him with injuries that simply won't allow him back in."

"He seems to think differently," Hannah said absently.

Abby watched Reece sit down at his table and then turned to see Hannah worriedly chewing her lip.

"What?"

"I hope he hasn't been talking with the Keller Corp. rep. The same guy who bought out Stevens and Harvest vineyards last year."

Abby put her fork back down, her hands turning cold.

"No."

"It's a possibility."

"He…can't. He can't sell to them. It would ruin Maple Hills!" As if selling wasn't bad enough, selling to Keller would be a disaster.

Keller was a housing developer that had been buying up lakeside property and building cookie-cutter housing developments that ruined the area's natural appeal. They didn't care about the watershed or about the long tradition of wineries in the area. They didn't care about anything, except for making money.

The runoff from pavement, lawn chemicals and the potential for septic leaks and so forth, would be awful for her business, ruining her land. Not to mention scarring the beautiful view of the lake.

"Every wedding couple we book wants to be married out on the vineyard, with the view of the lake. We'd lose them all if the backdrop is a bunch of prefab houses," she said, shaking her head.

Even in the economic hard times, people still got married, and these days many of them decided to do so locally to save money. Her wedding bookings were up considerably, and that helped when wine sales were down. In fact, she was preparing for a wedding reception that was scheduled for two days before Christmas. Weddings and other special events had become a big part of her bottom line.

Harvey Winston, Reece's father, hadn't been an organic farmer, not strictly, but he used the least harmful methods available and made sure to observe a buffer between her grapes and his. And all of the vineyards worked to maintain the beauty of the landscape, as it was to their collective advantage.

No way would Keller Corp. care. In fact, if they drove her out, they would buy up her family business, as well.

"He can't do it, Hannah."

"Well, he can, sadly. And probably will if he wants to sell fast and for a good price," Hannah said flatly, making Abby sit back in her chair, utterly losing her appetite altogether.

"There has to be some other way. I should talk to him, maybe we can work something out."

"I'm sorry, hon, but I do your accounting, and there is no way you can afford to buy him out. Speaking as your friend, without Sarah, you already have more than you can manage alone. Maybe if you hire someone..." Hannah said sympathetically.

"I planned to, in the summer. I don't have time for interviews now. But if he sells, none of it will matter."

Sarah had been her manager and her second-in-command. She'd known the winery and their vineyards inside out, had been with them since her parents ran the place, but finally had also decided to retire a few months before. It had been tough finding a suitable replacement. Abby had been running in circles handling everything.

"What are you thinking?" she asked Hannah, who had that look that told Abby her friend was clearly cooking up something as she smiled mysteriously.

"Well, he was awfully eager to get his hands on you—no way were you choking badly enough for him to jump in and Heimlich you."

"What are you saying?"

"I'm saying you two always had some chemistry, always had a little push and pull between you. Maybe that's something you could use to your advantage."

"You're deluded."

"You know it's true. You said yourself that he was

a great kisser and you wish that snafu behind the hedgerow had gone further. So…"

"No fair. I said that when I was really drunk."

"And we know alcohol is like truth serum for you. But why not give it a try?"

"Are you seriously suggesting I sleep with Reece in order to get him to change his mind about selling?"

"I wouldn't put it that way. Just…strike up your old friendship, flirt a little, see if you can make him more sympathetic to your cause. Or at the very least, keep your enemies closer so you know what's going on. He seemed interested in meeting up for a drink, and well, it can't hurt, right?"

Abby narrowed her eyes. "I don't believe I've seen this side of your personality. Very *Desperate Housewives.* But it's not for me. Besides, that incident behind the bushes was a mistake. Before that, the only chemistry we had was him tormenting me since second grade."

"Boys always punch girls in the arm when they like them."

"You've been watching *Brady Bunch* repeats again, haven't you?" Abby accused, and both of them collapsed in laughter for a moment, before Abby sighed, sobering again.

"I'm afraid we'll have to come up with some other plan."

"Maybe it's for the best," Hannah suggested. "I know the developments suck, but you haven't had a vacation in almost two years, and have you even been out on a date in that time?"

"One," Abby challenged.

Though that hadn't been so much of a date as a disaster.

"All you do is work. Your parents never meant for you to have no life when they turned the place over. Maybe if you sold it, you could—"

Abby looked at her in horror. "How can you even say that? My parents risked everything, worked their entire lives to make this business a success, and at a time when organic farming had hardly been heard of, let alone been popular. How can I just sell out on them?"

Hannah shrugged. "It's worth thinking about, from a practical perspective, hon. Things change. Sometimes you have to change with them."

Abby knew she had been working too hard, almost constantly since Sarah retired, and Hannah was right on one score—as her parents' only child, they were delighted to give her the business, but they were also huge believers in balance. They would be the first ones to tell her to ease up—yet they would also never sell to somebody like Keller, Abby knew that in her heart of hearts.

There had to be some way she could talk to Reece, find an alternative or get him to change his mind. Short of sleeping with him, not that the idea didn't have some appeal. He was gorgeous, undeniably.

"I guess I could at least talk to him," she said lamely, watching Reece deep in conversation with his business associate over big sandwiches. Thinking about those strong hands on her rib cage and the hot kisses they had shared, she wondered if Hannah wasn't on to something.

Maybe her friend was right. Why not? They were old friends—sort of—but they were both grown up now. She hadn't had so much as a kiss good-night in months. She knew for a fact that kissing Reece wouldn't be any sacrifice at all, and if it would get him to listen to her…

All of her appetites kicked back in, and with a dash of hope she dug back into her salad.

Hannah's lips twitched and she had a self-satisfied look. "You're thinking about it, aren't you?"

Abby couldn't resist a smile. "Hey, you're the one who wants me to go out on a date. Besides, it's not like I would let it go too far," she said, echoing Reece's words from so long ago. "I wouldn't trade sex for him selling the place to me or anything tawdry like that, but as you said, maybe just some flirting, spending time together, might help him see my side of things a little better."

"Exactly. Just be careful. Remember from eleventh-grade chemistry what happens when you put two volatile substances together," Hannah warned, but her eyes were twinkling with mischief.

"Maybe," Abby said, but her mind was racing ahead, intrigued by the idea of flirting with Reece. "But what a way to go."

REECE WAS HAVING a hard time focusing, and it had nothing to do with the injuries he'd sustained nine months before and everything to do with the unbelievably sexy woman sitting across the room. He could hardly believe that was Abby Harper.

Seeing her had been the first pleasant surprise he'd had since coming back to help with his family's affairs. Life had been one long string of disasters for the past year. First, two members of his racing team had to be replaced at the start of the season, after which they'd lost a major sponsor, and then he'd had his accident at the end of March, right when he'd been about to turn a major corner in his career.

Everyone told him he was lucky to be alive and in one piece, walking and talking again, and he supposed that was true. He'd been in a coma for three days, followed by six months of language and physical therapy after he had emerged from the coma, his head injury leaving him with a broken memory and speech problems. He'd overcome it all. Mostly.

Some of the guys he'd known hadn't made it through crashes that left them with lesser injuries, but there were a lot of days when Reece didn't feel all that lucky, especially since they told him there would be no more racing, not until a neurologist cleared him. Then his dad had a major heart attack. It had been one thing after another, and Reece found his time split between his recovery and wanting to get back to racing and having to help out his family. They'd been there for him, and there was no way he'd leave them in the lurch now, but it sure didn't make things easier. His life was an ocean away.

For months his mom and dad had been traveling back and forth to Europe, where Reece lived just outside of Paris. It was too much strain for them to try to run the winery and travel so often, and his father's illness was proof of that. He felt responsible, and although they'd bent over backward to tell him it wasn't his fault, guilt demanded he stay here and help in any way he could.

He'd been here, in central New York State, for a few weeks, though he had spent most of the time at the hospital, in hotels and then getting his parents to his brother's home down South. He couldn't help the feeling that his real life was passing him by. He could only be absent from racing for so long. There were always new guys coming up, ready to take his place, and sponsors had short memories. Few drivers came back after a crash like his; hell, few survived.

But Reece wasn't ready to retire yet. He just had to sell the winery, to do the best he could by his parents and get back to France ASAP. At thirty-one, he didn't have too many years left to get back into the game.

Though some guys raced into their forties, it was getting to be less and less the case, so he needed to still show he could do the job. The doctors were apprehensive, but he planned to prove them wrong. He'd come this far, he was going the rest of the way.

He thought again of Abby's shocked face when he'd said he was going to sell the winery. His parents weren't thrilled, either, but they'd long ago accepted that both of their boys had other lives now.

Still, Reece was bothered by the clear disapproval in Abby's gorgeous brown eyes when he'd made the announcement.

"So, I can bring the Keller representative by tomorrow, if you like," Charles said.

Charles Tyler was one of the premiere real estate agents in the area, and he was also a shark—if anyone could sell the place for the best price, it would be him.

"They'd be a last resort. I thought I made that clear."

Charles sighed, smiling slightly at the pretty server who delivered their lunch. "Well, if you want it sold for the asking price and fast, they are the best bet. They'll jump at a property as large as yours."

Reece frowned. They'd also tear down the renovated farmhouse he grew up in, and they'd flatten the vineyards, rows of Riesling, Chardonnay and Pinot Noir grapes, paving them over with cul-de-sacs and driveways. He'd been away, but he kept in touch, and he'd seen the changes along the lake since he'd come back, few of them good.

"Some of those vines have been around longer than my parents have been alive, planted by my grandfather," Reece murmured, not realizing he'd said it out loud.

"Well, you might be able to sell to another winery, but it won't go for nearly as much, not in this economic climate," Charles said with a sigh, no doubt disappointed that sentimentality could get in the way of a larger commission for him. "And it could take quite a bit longer."

Reece nodded, thinking. "Keep Keller on the line, but let's not move too fast. If they want it now, they'll want it a month from now, but let's see what comes up in the meanwhile," he said, his eyes drifting back to Abby.

"Who's the girl?" Charles asked, following Reece's gaze.

"Abby Harper. An old friend, her family owns the winery next to ours, Maple Hills."

"More than a friend?" Charles asked.

"No. Just a girl I knew in high school," Reece said.

"Any chance she might be interested in selling, as well? I could get you a sweet deal if you two went in on a sale together—that could significantly up the price Keller would offer."

"I doubt she would ever sell, and definitely not to Keller," Reece said.

"They're not the devil," Charles said dryly. "They just build developments, nice ones, which tend to fill up very quickly."

"I know what they do," Reece said absently, his attention still on Abby.

Charles picked up the check and changed the subject, droning on about local real estate markets or some other big sale he had just completed, all of which Reece tuned out.

Abby was in close conversation with her friend, whom he only vaguely remembered from school. He and Abby hadn't really belonged to the same crowd, even though they grew up next door to each other and shared a common interest between their families.

Her folks were always a little different than everyone else on the lake—more iconoclastic, with their organic methods and sustainable farming beliefs, the petting zoo and homespun lifestyle. Those things were all the rage now, of course. Maple Hills could ask twice for a bottle of wine what other non-certified organic vineyards could.

While they were still primarily a small family business, Maple Hills had broadened its distribution and marketing quite successfully in recent years, so his father said. Probably Abby's doing. She had a good head for business and was growing it well.

She'd taken a lot of ribbing in school—she and her parents being called hippies and so forth—and quite a bit of that had been from him. He hadn't meant any of it, not in a mean-spirited way, but even then, Abby had been fun to tease. He could never resist.

Her cheeks turned pink if he even looked at her, and he'd always thought it was cute. He'd never suspected she would be as hot and as daring as he had discovered that night at the lake party.

It was the last time he'd seen her until now. Though he'd kissed plenty of women in between—including a few A-list celebrities—the memory of Abby Harper pressed up against him and kissing him for all she was worth, her hands everywhere, was as clear to him as if it had happened five minutes ago.

He'd wanted to drag her back behind the hedge that night, and he'd regretted making light of it afterward. She'd bolted before he could ask her out. On a date. So they could do it right.

He wanted to make up for what he'd been too much of an immature idiot to do in high school. He'd always liked her, but when he was young, he was too worried about what his friends would think. Typical teenage boy stuff.

A few years later, on that night by the lake, he didn't care what anyone thought, but Abby was clearly not interested as soon as she found out whom she'd been feeling up behind the bushes.

He'd known, in some corner of his mind, that she hadn't been in real danger of choking at her table earlier, but seeing her had somehow led to the immediate need to touch her. He'd become semihard from the way her pretty backside pressed against him when he'd been trying to help her, his wrists just brushing the undersides of her full breasts when he'd wrapped his arms around her.

Sad, when emergency Heimlich was your excuse to get close to a woman, but Reece hadn't had sex since before his accident and, apparently, his body was more than ready for some action. Despite lingering effects from his injuries, that part of his nervous system seemed to be in fine working order.

What if he decided to pursue that drink with Abby and see if they could pick up where they'd left off by the bushes? She hadn't been interested back then, but he could swear he'd felt her respond to his touch today, and not just in a panic about choking.

It was fun to think about, and it might be worth seeing the look on her face if he asked. He couldn't resist the idea of teasing Abby, even now, though the way he wanted to tease her had taken on a whole new dimension.

He chuckled to himself, feeling better than he had in weeks.

"Something funny about that?" Charles asked, obviously peeved, either because he knew Reece wasn't listening, or because Reece had just laughed at something he shouldn't have.

"Oh, no, sorry. I was just thinking about something else," he said vaguely.

"Okay, well, I'll start pushing the property and see what we can do to hold Keller off for a while, but unless you want to wait longer, they may be the best deal in town," Charles repeated.

"I'll talk to them, but I just want to see what other offers we get. I'll be living at the house, so you can get me there. You have my numbers," Reece said.

"I'll do my best." Charles stood and shook Reece's hand firmly, an action that sent a buzz of numbness rushing up his arm, making him wince and reminding him all of the problems from his accident that still remained.

The short-lived nerve reaction ticked off a bit of desperation, nearly making him tell Charles to sell to Keller now. Reece had to get back to Europe, had to get better and had to race again. It was the only life he knew or wanted.

But Charles was on his way out, and Reece took a breath, calming down. It would be okay. He'd healed faster than anyone thought he would, and he'd be on the track again before next summer. Still, the sooner he could conclude his business here, the better, he thought with a small pang of regret as he took one more glimpse of Abby before leaving the café.

CHAPTER TWO

THE NEXT DAY, Abby was busy from the moment she woke up, barely able to keep up with everything she had to get done, even though it was a weekend. Weekends—Saturdays, anyway—were busier than weekdays for her, and today was no exception.

She'd waited all morning only to be stood up by an electrician who was supposed to show up during the week, but had rescheduled and then stood her up again. Some overhead lights kept flickering intermittently in the main room of the winery, and she needed it fixed yesterday.

Today they'd had three tastings and tours offered at ten o'clock, noon and two, and in between that she was fielding online orders, wedding prep and Christmas decorating that should have been done two weeks ago. The guests were fewer than they had been over the summer, or on holidays like Valentine's Day, when they did their wine-and-chocolate parties. Still, they'd had a respectable showing for each tour.

Right now she was in the middle of the last tasting, and while she was exhausted, her mind running in a million directions, she focused on smiling, explaining the type and origin of each wine and its story.

All of their wines had stories, background about how old the vines were, where they came from, who planted them and anything fun or anecdotal that happened while the wine was being made. It personalized the experience and made people aware that the wine they sipped wasn't just any generic wine, but a drink with a specific history, made by real people.

"This peppery Baco Noir," she said, finishing her presentation, "is called 'Just the Beginning' and it is one of our classic vintages. One summer night almost forty years ago, two lovers walked over the fields behind us, and the man asked the woman he was with to marry him. They didn't have enough money for rings, but he handed her a small plant, the beginning of the Baco vines from which these grapes still grow. Those people were my parents and, yes, eventually he did buy her a ring," Abby said warmly, smiling as she did every time she told the story.

A chorus of appreciative comments and chuckles about the ring followed. She discussed nuances, taught newcomers the basics of wine tasting and then moved to the desk where people purchased their wine and other goodies from the small gift display.

It was a good day, and she'd enjoyed her guests. By six, though, she was ready for bed. Her other employees were gone for the day, and they rarely had guests staying in their few upstairs rooms, used mostly for wedding parties in the winter. So, she closed up shop and thought of what needed to be done next.

She did need to get the trees decorated—three gorgeous Fraser firs that graced the tasting room, the entry to the winery and the first floor of the main house. Her home, a private residence, was built off the central rooms where they hosted tastings, receptions and sold their wines. In the back of the property, above the vineyards, were the animal barns and the building where they made and stored the wines. Their specialty was Baco Noir.

The trees were set up, the lights were on, but they needed ornaments, all of which had to be pulled out of storage at the house and carried over. She also needed to take care of her horses for the night.

They no longer had the petting zoo, unfortunately, but Abby could never part with her horses. Riding them along the lake was one of her favorite ways to relax. Her parents had given her these two colts when she was fifteen. As she headed down to the barn and looked out over her land, the sight always took her breath away in any season. Today, there'd been a light snow all day long, and it was shining like diamonds in the moonlight.

This was hers. It was home. Like her parents, she'd love to travel more, but she'd never really wanted to live anywhere but here.

All of the stress and work that went with it was hers, too. Lunch with Hannah yesterday had left her with a lot of food for thought and a lot of worry for the future.

Inside the barn she was greeted by soft, muffled welcomes, and she grabbed feed buckets, hay and fresh water and took care of business, which included much brushing and stroking.

"Hey, babes," she crooned, feeling guilty that she hadn't done more than put them out in the field that day. "I promise tomorrow you'll both get some good exercise. I'll get Hannah and we'll see you both early in the morning for a nice ride."

After long moments of petting warm muzzles and feeling more relaxed than she had when she walked in, she locked the doors and said good-night, turning back toward the house. Her gaze drifted down over the landscape to the Winston property. She noted some lights on in the house, although the winery was dark. Was Reece really going to sell?

She shivered, pulled her thick wool coat tighter around her and stared at the upstairs light. Reece? In his room? Was he there alone? She shivered for a different reason.

She'd been all fired up yesterday, having fun with Hannah, but she was crazy to think she could seduce Reece into...what? Not selling his land? No doubt he would think that was very funny; she was still out of his league, always had been.

But she *was* going to talk to him. She had no idea what she'd say to try to convince him to hold off, but if he didn't rush into a sale with Keller, maybe she could help find someone who would buy in with her. It was a huge gambit, but not impossible. Not entirely. She had money saved, and she'd have to mortgage her home to the hilt, but what other choice did she have?

She had to do whatever she could to protect her home and business. Keller would ruin the entire area.

The little hamlet that had sprouted up around the

wineries a few miles up the lake from the city of Ithaca offered a coffee shop, a few quaint boutiques, a gas station and a convenience store, and all of her friends were here. Unlike Reece, who had gone away as far as he could as soon as he was able, she'd gone to college locally, at Cornell, and she went down into the city a few times a week. They sold many of their wines in local stores, as well as all over the region.

She wished she could go inside, open a nice bottle of wine, make some dinner and sit in front of the fireplace in the living room, then finish decorating her trees without it feeling like work.

It would be even nicer to not have to do it alone.

Maybe she wouldn't have to. Biting her lip, she walked faster toward the house and didn't think too much about what she was contemplating. If she did, she'd lose her nerve.

Entering the warmly lit kitchen that hadn't changed too much since she'd grown up, she went carefully down the cellar steps to the room where they kept their private stock and grabbed a bottle she had been saving for a special occasion.

Back upstairs, she pulled two glasses from the shelves and a wedge of Brie and a few other goodies from the fridge.

The trees could wait. Her talk with Reece could not.

If she didn't do it now, she could lose her chance as well as her nerve. Setting aside her doubts and worries, she started out walking across the land between their homes, a windy half mile, her eyes focused on the lit windows. The snow and moon illuminated everything, making it easy to walk, and she covered the distance quickly. As she neared the house, her eyes focused in on a form in the upstairs window.

Her mouth went dry and she dropped the bottle of wine, which didn't break, thank goodness, but landed softly in the snow.

She picked it up again and walked closer. It was Reece. He hadn't pulled a shade or a curtain, thinking—rightly—that no one would be looking in his windows from the field side of the house.

He was nude. Completely. Stretching his arms up over his head, and then bending at the waist, she couldn't see everything, but she saw enough to make her heart slam against her rib cage as he did something that looked very much like yoga.

He was strong. Muscled, but graceful in his movements.

Gorgeous.

She forgot to move forward, entranced, but then as she realized where she was and what she was doing, she averted her eyes—though she couldn't erase what she'd seen. How could she? The strong line of his back, the muscles of his shoulders and arms were stunning. She could imagine running her hands over him and wondered what it would be like to have those slim, strong hips settling in between her legs....

"Oh, no," she said to herself, breathless with lust, her hands trembling as she almost dropped the wine again.

She hovered for a second on the porch. Reece was

home, alone and naked, and she was standing here at his front door with a bottle of wine. Her courage flagged. Maybe she should talk to him another time, like during the light of day, or at a bar with a lot of other people around.

Don't be a coward, Abby, she scolded herself. She sucked in a deep breath and pressed the doorbell before she could change her mind.

REECE STEPPED GINGERLY out of the shower, wrapping a large towel around his waist, wincing from the pain in his left leg, where pins and needles shot back and forth along his thigh, causing weakness in his stance.

Each pinprick was like an individual jab, reminding him that he couldn't get in a race car again and do the thing that he loved most. Headaches had come back earlier that afternoon as well, and he'd spent most of the day on the sofa with an ice pack.

What if this never went away? What if they never signed off on letting him race again? At this point, doctors gave him a fifty-fifty shot, but he had to be one hundred percent, his reflexes perfect, completely reliable before he could race.

The betrayal of having his own body prevent him from doing what he loved most was utterly unacceptable. He'd gotten through the worst of it, and he'd defeat this, too. There was no alternative other than… what? Staying here?

Not an option.

Crossing the hall, he walked into the guest room and dried off. His mother had long ago, with his blessing, turned his old room into a place where she did her sewing and other crafts. He came home for holidays and a few short vacations but not often enough for his parents to have preserved his room. At the moment, he was glad they hadn't. He'd been feeling strangely sentimental about the old place, and that wasn't like him. He supposed it was because of the close call with his dad. Almost losing someone—as well as almost losing your own life—made you see things differently.

He loved his family, but this was just a house, he reminded himself. A building. One he couldn't get away from fast enough when he'd been a teenager looking for something more exciting.

He started going through the stretching routine that he'd been taught by his last physical therapist to relieve the pins and needles. Focusing on his breathing, his form, he drove away unwanted thoughts. The hot shower had helped loosen him up, but it still hurt like hell at first to push through the moves and hold them, though the symptoms lessened after a few repetitions.

He felt better as he relaxed, going through the rest of his exercises for good measure. He'd talked to his neurologist earlier in the day for the umpteenth time, and he had been reassured yet again that it was all normal.

Easy for him to say.

Reece turned to grab a pair of jeans when the ring of the doorbell caught him by surprise. Who would be here now?

Surely not Charles with someone to see the house. No one had called.

Pulling on his jeans and grabbing a shirt, he rushed down the stairs and pulled open the door, unable to believe his eyes.

"Abby?"

He took in her pink cheeks and tousled hair, and stepped back, inviting her in as the frosty air nipped at his bare toes.

"C'mon in. It's freezing out there," he said.

"Thanks, it is," she said, moving quickly. Her eyes flew to his chest. He hadn't had time to completely button his shirt.

"Oh, sorry…just got out of the shower."

Her cheeks turned even pinker and she didn't meet his eyes. He wondered why she was here holding wine, two glasses and some other foods.

Reece prompted her again. "What's all this?" he asked, looking down at the stuff she still held in her arms. One glass was tenuously dangling from her fingertips.

"Let me take that for you," he offered, and reached forward to take the flute. When his fingers caught with hers around the stem, her hand jerked away and they fumbled the glass, nearly dropping the fragile crystal.

Reece frowned. "Are you okay?"

She finally smiled. "Yes, I'm fine. Sorry to intrude on your evening, but I saw your lights on and felt like some company. You said you wanted to have a drink, so…" She shrugged, holding up the bottle. "Unless this is a bad time?"

He remembered saying something about having a drink when he'd seen her at the restaurant. This wasn't exactly what he meant, but maybe it was better.

He'd had a rough day, and having a bottle of wine with a pretty woman might be exactly what he needed.

"It's a perfect time, actually. I'm really glad you decided to stop by," he said, smiling and taking the rest of the things she was holding so that she could shuck her jacket. "You walked all the way over, in the dark?"

"It wasn't that dark, with the snow and the moon. Very nice, actually," she said lightly, handing him her coat just as she met his eyes and a spark flared as his hand touched hers.

She shifted uncomfortably, looking away and turning pink again. Reece didn't remember her being so… wait.

She'd come across the field on the side of the house whcrc the guest room was. Where he'd been doing his stretching, with the curtains open. With no clothes on. He never closed the drapes, since no one was likely to be lurking out in the fields

Silence hung at the end of her comment, and he had to smother a smile. She had to have seen him. Reece wasn't shy and had to resist the urge to tease her about it.

So Abby was a bit of a voyeur? It didn't bother him. He'd be happy to let her look all she liked, he thought, his grin breaking loose as he turned away to hang her coat.

Maybe this evening would go even better than he thought.

"Grab that bottle and we can go put the food together in the kitchen, then sit by the fire," he said casually, though he wasn't feeling casual at all. All of his worries were pushed back by a surge of unexpected lust, and it felt great. He wanted to hold on to it, ride it and see where it took him.

"Oh, that would be nice," she said, walking with him to the kitchen. Dressed in jeans and a sweater that accentuated her curves, he leaned forward and pulled something from her hair. He could swear she sucked in a breath when he did, becoming perfectly still.

Hmm.

He presented a straw of hay to her with a smile. "Been down with your horses, I take it?"

She rolled her eyes and snatched the hay from his hand, but couldn't hold back a laugh, which made her even prettier. He'd always thought she was pretty, even as a little girl, but now...she was incredible. She always looked so natural and fresh, and he wondered what her skin tasted like.

"Yes, I was closing them up for the night when I saw your lights on my way back from the barn."

"Do you still have just the two? Buttercup and Beau?"

She paused, looking surprised that he remembered. He was a little surprised, too.

"Yes. Wow, you know their names," she said

bluntly, taking the plate he handed her to open the Brie so they could heat it up in the small toaster oven he pointed to.

"Why so surprising? We went to the same school, rode the same bus," he said. "Must've just stuck in my mind, I guess."

"Huh. I didn't think you knew I was alive unless you were poking at me about something," she said, and it was his turn to be a little surprised.

"I always liked you. I teased you, sure, but did you feel like I picked on you? Really?" A small frown creased his lips. He didn't like thinking he had hurt Abby's feelings or been mean to her.

Taking the food, they made their way to the main room and set the dishes down on the coffee table, placing a platter with green grapes, crackers and apples and the warmed Brie between them. All perfect to go with the Baco, but Reece waited for her answer before moving to the fire.

She looked him in the eye and sighed lightly. "Well, you have to admit, aside from teasing me or pulling my hair, you didn't give me reason to think you knew I existed, let alone that you would remember details of my life."

"Hmm," he said thoughtfully, rubbing his chin slowly. "I remember some things very clearly," he said with a teasing wink.

"You can't even resist now, can you?" she said accusingly, but a smile twitched at her lips.

She remembered what happened between them that night at the lake as clearly as he did, he'd bet.

And, no, he wasn't sure he could resist, or wanted to. But there was time. He backed away, letting it drop for now.

"Let me put a few more logs on the fire and we can eat. Suddenly I'm starving."

He was, though he wasn't sure the food on the plate was what he had a taste for, but it would have to be enough for the moment.

They spent the next two hours eating and talking in front of the crackling fire, when Abby suddenly looked around the room.

"You don't have a tree or any Christmas decorations up," she observed.

He shrugged. "There hasn't been any time, or much point, I guess. I'm the only one here, and Charles, the real estate agent, thought it was better to show the place without a lot of decorations. Let people imagine their own lives here and all that."

"Oh," she remarked, her expression turning serious. "That's kind of what I wanted to talk to you about," she said carefully.

"Christmas decorations?"

"No, that you're selling. I was hoping—"

Reece put a hand up. "Abby, I'd be happy to sit down and talk business with you at some point. But not right now, okay?"

"But—"

"It's been kind of a tough day. I'd really like to relax, catch up with an old friend," he said.

He geniunely didn't want to talk business with Abby. He knew she'd want to convince him not to sell, or something like that, and he didn't want to discuss that with her. It was a done deal, and that conversation was sure to put a damper on the heat building between them.

She bit her lip and looked reluctant, but nodded. "I can understand that," she said, looking down at her wine. "I know things must have been hard for you this year," she said vaguely, inviting him to say more, but he didn't want to talk about any of that, either. Maybe that wasn't fair, but he needed a night off from all of it.

"Yeah," he said, and changed the subject. "But how about you? You live in the house alone now?"

Nothing like discreet fishing before you tried to seduce an old friend, he thought. Hopefully there wasn't another guy in the picture, though looking at her, it was hard to believe they weren't lined up.

She shook her head, and his relief was immediate.

"Nope, just me now. Sarah retired, and Mom and Dad are traveling all over the world. I still have a small part-time staff, of course, to help me get things done, but I handle most of it myself."

"They don't come home for the holidays? Your parents?"

"It would be difficult. They send gifts, and we video conference on the computer a lot. Last year they were in India, helping local people build a school. This winter, they've been helping down in Haiti."

"Really? I thought they were tourists now?"

"They mix their pleasure travel with activism. It's

just their way, and they have always been more like explorers than tourists."

He nodded, smiling. "I remember."

"I know what they're doing is important, and I'm a big girl. We're busy enough through the holidays that being alone at Christmas gives me a quiet day or two to relax, read, sleep in, that kind of thing."

"Your parents were always so progressive," he said admiringly, but really he was thinking about Abby sleeping in, under the covers, warm and soft, curled up in something slinky with a book. Then he imagined taking the book out of her hands and slipping the lacy bit of nothing from her shoulder....

"Reece?" she said, and he realized he had gone blank, lost in his fantasy. "Are you okay?"

She seemed worried, and it bothered him. Of all the people he didn't want worrying if he was healthy and ready to go, she was first on the list at the moment.

"Sorry. You just made me remember that summer when your parents decided to try to add selling goat cheese to the winery business, and all of the goats got loose one weekend and ate some of my dad's vines," he lied, unable to look away from her face. Her eyes had landed on the scar behind his ear—the skin graft had healed, but it was visible. Did it bother her?

The definite sparkle of interest in her eyes said no, he assumed.

She laughed then, breaking the bond. "He was pretty nice about it, considering."

Her honey-brown hair was soft and slightly curled,

pushed back in a haphazard way that made him want to reach out and weave his hands into it. She didn't wear makeup, which he found refreshing. She didn't need to. Her skin was flawless, her cheeks pink and kissable. And those lips…

"Did you ever wonder?" he heard himself ask.

Her cheeks turned rosy again, her lips parting slightly, as if she knew exactly where his mind had gone.

"Wonder what?"

He paused. They'd had a nice evening, two old friends talking over high school times and getting reacquainted. Did he really want to step into other waters? He was only back for a month or so, or however long it took to sell the winery. And the faster, the better. Abby wasn't one of his pit stops.

The women he knew in Europe were aware of his commitment-free lifestyle, his focus on his racing. They knew the score. They also had their own agendas, liking to be seen with a well-known driver, having their picture show up in the next day's entertainment news.

Abby had no agenda. She was just…Abby.

He still had to ask the question.

"What it might have been like if we didn't stop that night at the lake?" he said and noted the slight catch in her breath, but she didn't look away.

"Sure, I wondered," she said simply.

"I was about to ask you out, back then, when you took off," he admitted.

"You were?"

"Yeah. I wanted to know what it would be like to be with you, for real," he said. "I always liked you, Abby. A lot."

"Oh" was her only response, sounding slightly breathless. He took that as a good sign and plunged ahead.

"Still want to find out?" he said, in spite of every bit of better judgment he had.

Her eyes widened in surprise and she stood suddenly, setting down her wine, her movements fluttering and nervous.

"I should go. We're just tired. There's the fire and the wine, and it's easy to be caught up in old times, but really…I should go," she repeated, and walked to the door.

Reece shot up, moving after her.

"I'm sorry," he said, catching her arm, turning her to him. "I didn't mean to scare you off."

He wasn't sure if he was talking about eight years ago or two minutes ago. He was sure he didn't want her walking out the door.

They were close, and she looked up at him, her eyes somber.

"Listen, Reece, as much as I might be…curious, too, it wouldn't be a good idea—"

"You're curious?" His mind selectively honed in on the one thing he wanted to hear and he stepped closer. "About me?"

She licked her lips nervously, making his cock jerk, semihard already, against the rough fabric of his jeans. In his hurry, he hadn't even pulled on briefs, so all that held him back was a bit of thin fabric.

"I—" She had started to say something, but he saw the pulse beating hard at the base of her throat, the desire in her eyes.

"What else are you curious about, Abby? I seem to remember you liked the excitement of being there, by the hedge, in public. Are you still up for that kind of adventure?"

He remembered how aroused she had been, and it had been just as hot for him, too. Did she still want that?

Reece liked risk, too. Hell, it defined him. He also had fantasies that not all of his lovers had satisfied.

What kind of sex was Abby into? He knew about her fondness for public places. Bondage, maybe? Something more creative? Role-play, perhaps?

He wanted to find out, imagining Abby tied to his bed or dressed in black leather. What if she wanted him tied up?

He could probably live with that. He was open to anything short of real pain or multiple partners—Reece wasn't sharing Abby with anyone.

"Let's just see, Abby, what it could be like between us," he said, needing to know and pulling her to him, his hands traveling up her back and into her hair, as he'd thought about.

It was like silk. He wanted to feel it trailing over his stomach and his thighs, her mouth on him.

The thought made his kiss less introductory, less tentative, than it might have been otherwise. He took her soft lips and opened her wider, invading and rubbing his tongue against hers with a deep moan. She felt so right, like she had before, but better, the flames leaping between them.

Her arms went around his neck, and she rubbed back with her tongue, her lips and the rest of her body as she strained against him.

Green flag, he thought, but resisted accelerating, instead maintaining the steady heat of the kiss, learning her taste, her touch, until neither of them could take it any longer.

When her hands started undoing the buttons on his shirt, he walked her back against the wall by the window, pressing his hardness against her, moving his hands up to cover her breasts. She was firm and soft in his palms, the nipples budding hard.

Touching wasn't enough, he needed to taste.

Moving his hands up under her sweater, he set the flimsy lace of her bra aside and bent to take one tight, beaded nipple in his mouth. He drew on it hard, murmuring encouragingly as she arched away from the wall, her hand at the back of his head, keeping him there.

He replaced his lips with his fingers, rolling the warm buds between his thumb and forefinger as he kissed her again, wanting to be everywhere at once.

He stood back, staring down into her flushed face, her passion-drenched eyes, raising a finger to touch lips that now looked like crushed cherries.

"Abby, I want you, but..." He let the question hang.

He wanted her, but he'd back off now if she wanted him to, no matter what.

"Yes, please," she said, her breathing short and hard.

She was incredibly sweet. He planned to take his time with her, he thought, and pressed her back, sliding a thigh between her legs, pinning her to the wall. He wanted to make her come as many times as he could before he got inside her, because once he was, he knew he wouldn't last long. Not this first time.

He took her lips again and massaged those pretty breasts with both hands, moving against her until she was whimpering and grinding against him. Without warning, she arched, coming hard, moaning into his mouth as she rode it out. And he didn't even get her clothes off yet, he thought with raw hunger, wanting more.

He pulled back, taking in her bemused expression, the surprised satisfaction he saw there making him swell harder.

He thought she might be shy, embarrassed, but she linked her arms around his neck and leaned in, nipping at his lower lip.

"More" was all she said as she looked him in the eye.

"Oh, honey," he choked out. "There's plenty more."

Swinging her up into his arms, he turned to take her back to the fireplace, planning to dim the lights and strip that sweater off in the warm glow of the flames, when he stopped, his gaze drawn out the window.

He stared, uncertain what had caught his eye, but a bad feeling overcame him and he let Abby slide to her feet. He walked closer to the window that looked out over the field.

"Reece? What is it?"

Sirens screamed in the distance, and the glow in the air over the field that had attracted his attention was not a figment of his imagination.

Her winery was on fire.

CHAPTER THREE

ABBY RESTED HER HEAD against Buttercup's soft neck and just thanked the heavens that the barns hadn't caught fire, too. That was something she couldn't even bear to think about.

Her house was badly damaged, unlivable after water from the hoses had ruined what fire had not, but the main rooms of the winery were reduced to cinders. The horse seemed to nuzzle her in comfort as she tried to hold her tears back, but couldn't, sobs racking her body.

What now?

The flickering light that she'd been trying to have fixed ended up being wires that the fire investigator said were probably chewed through by a mouse or squirrel in the wall. When the tree lights had been plugged in, she hadn't thought twice about it, but the circuit had been overloaded and started the fire. It had spread inside the walls before consuming the entire winery.

If she'd been home, she might have been killed if she had been sleeping or overcome with smoke, although she had detectors everywhere. On the other hand, if she had been there, she might have been able to call the fire department sooner, and maybe it wouldn't have been so bad, such a complete loss.

Instead, she'd been at Reece's, in his arms, ready to say yes to anything he asked, while her family's legacy burned to the ground.

She had to get away from the swarm of people. The firemen were still keeping watch, even though the fire was officially out, the insurance and other investigators were there, along with some neighbors, friends…and Reece. Everyone wanted to help, but she'd insisted on being alone for just a few minutes.

She needed the peace to think about what she would say to her parents, how she could tell them what happened.

Guilt assailed her. How could she explain why she hadn't been there? That she'd been so busy, and so distracted by thoughts of Reece, that she hadn't thought twice about the tree lights or the electrical problem?

She groaned, standing straight, wiping the tears away. No time for this now.

She had to get the insurance settled and cancel the wedding they'd been planning—that would be another tough phone call. The couple wouldn't likely find another venue with only weeks until the wedding, but there wasn't anything she could do about that. Abby would have to refund their deposits. That was going to hurt.

She'd see if Hannah would let her move in for a while, though it would mean driving back and forth to Ithaca daily, or maybe her insurance would pick up a room at the local inn, for a while at least.

"I thought you might be down here," a familiar voice said behind her.

"Hannah," she said, trying to sound normal, but her voice cracked under the weight of her exhaustion, being up all night, dealing with it all.

Hannah was across the barn, holding her arms out and Abby didn't hesitate.

She held on to her friend, just for a minute, but it was Reece's arms she knew she'd been seeking. Remembering how good it had been, not just the sexual part, but the way he'd held her against his hard chest later, when they'd watched the firemen work, had kept her from losing it altogether. She wanted that comfort back.

No, no, no. That was how she'd gotten into this mess, sort of.

"You okay?" Hannah asked, stepping back and smiling as two of the barn cats wound their way around her ankles.

"Yeah. I'm just so thankful the barns are far away from the house," she said, stroking Beau's silky nose. All of the animals were okay.

"That is a good thing," Hannah agreed, chuckling softly as Buttercup snorted happily in response to more scratching. "Everything else can be replaced. It was a straightforward electrical fire. The insurance agent is already on it. Things can be rebuilt."

"True, but I don't know if that will be enough," Abby said, too discouraged to be optimistic. "They can't start rebuilding until after winter, which means we're not only losing the Christmas events, but the spring wedding season and tastings as well. We lost almost all of the Riesling casks. With Reece selling, this could just be a killer blow," Abby said tightly, her throat constricting at the thought.

"How am I going to tell Mom and Dad? I feel so much like I've let them down," Abby said, sucking in more tears.

Hannah knew just what to do to drive the tears away.

"Speaking of Reece…he seemed awfully involved in helping you last night. And I couldn't help but notice when we went inside that at first his shirt wasn't buttoned up quite right. You know, like it had been put back together in a rush," she said, with mischief in her tone that made Abby's tears completely evaporate.

Abby groaned. Did everyone know where she'd been and what she was doing?

As if reading her mind, Hannah added, "He said he saw the fire from his house, got dressed and rushed down to help. Don't worry—he didn't give anything away, though I sure hope you're going to share details with your very best friend in the whole wide world, right? You know, about why Reece was really getting dressed?"

Unbelievably, Abby had to laugh. Leave it to Hannah, even in the middle of utter loss. When all Abby had left was this barn and what was in it, her friend found a way to lighten the mood.

Reece had been wonderful. He hadn't left her

side until Hannah had arrived. He jumped in, talking to the firemen, police and the other people milling around, even opening up the main room of his winery for people to come in, get warm and have coffee. At some moment when she'd been talking to the fire investigator, Abby had lost track of him and assumed he had gone back home.

"Thanks, I needed that," she said, taking a breath and feeling a bit better. "And there aren't many details to share. Not really. I went down to Reece's, brought some wine, hoping to talk…one thing lead to another, but before it went too far, he noticed the fire. That was pretty much it," she said, shrugging.

"Oh, I doubt that's it. The man's interested—he couldn't take his eyes off you, especially when that hunky fireman was talking to you, and standing a little too close, by the way," Hannah said.

"You're imagining things. Reece was just helping out. We're old friends and we shared a moment—instigated by a bottle of wine. It's best forgotten. I have enough to worry about now." Abby's attention snapped to the barn doors, where outside, she heard a woman's voice, and then sharp, shrieking words. She couldn't make out what was being said, but several colorful curses punctuated the diatribe.

Abby headed out of the barn to find Sandra Towers, the Christmas bride-to-be, standing in the middle of the yard in front of the blackened mess of Abby's winery, wild-eyed and in tears. She spotted Abby then and marched across the lawn, obviously ready for a confrontation.

Great, just what she needed right now. Abby sighed. She shouldn't bother with having quiet time in the barn. She should have been on the phone doing damage control.

Too late, she admitted, as Sandra met her, almost standing nose-to-nose, and Abby backed up slightly.

"Sandra, I am so sorry. I was about to make phone calls—"

"I saw this on the news and couldn't believe it. I had to see for myself. This is a nightmare! How could you let this happen?" the prospective bride yelled, clearly not thinking straight.

Abby tried to be patient. This was hard on everyone, and brides were under a lot of stress in general. Sandra wasn't finished, obviously.

"What am I going to do? The invitations are all sent! Everything is scheduled! How are you going to fix this?" she demanded, and Abby pulled in a deep breath, closing her eyes, reaching for patience.

"Sandra, I know it's terrible, and I wish there was better news, but I'll definitely refund all of your down payment and try to help you find another—"

"The wedding is twenty-five days away! There is *no* other place," the young woman wailed. "I know, I checked them all. We have family coming in from Europe! You had better fix this or…or…we'll *sue!*"

Abby was quite sure the normally pleasant woman was just distraught, and also was sure—mostly—that she had no basis for a lawsuit whatsoever. Still, it was hard to remain calm, and she was digging her nails into her palms in her effort to do so.

Suddenly, Reece appeared, putting his large hand on her shoulder. She looked up in surprise, noting the circles under his eyes. He was obviously exhausted, too.

"Abby, could I talk to you for a minute?" he said politely. "Excuse us for just a moment," he said to Sandra with a smile. Amazingly, the young woman didn't pitch yet another fit.

Abby walked with him to a spot about twenty feet away and wondered how she could still feel his touch when she was wearing her coat and he had put on a pair of heavy gloves. Maybe the same way she'd had a scream-worthy orgasm against his thigh—apparently clothes were not a barrier to sex with Reece Winston.

"First things first," he said, dragging her away from her thoughts and producing a steaming travel cup to her. She could smell the aroma of the hot coffee inside. She took the cup, took a sip and peered at him over the top, thanking him with a look of bliss.

"I came out to bring you that and heard the shouting. I guess you had a wedding planned soon?"

She groaned and nodded. "Two days before Christmas."

"And that is the blushing bride," he stated more than asked.

"Yes." Abby sighed. "I don't blame her for being upset, but I didn't expect her to come out here and go nuts.... Still, I can imagine it's a mess for her, too."

Reece nodded. "She's obviously missing the point that you lost a lot more than she did last night," he said in a hard tone, peering over to where Sandra stood, arms crossed, watching them.

Abby didn't say anything, but took another sip of the strong coffee so the heat would scorch away the tightening in her throat. He was sticking up for her again, just like he did when the mean boy had picked on her about her braces.

"Thanks, but I have to find some way to compensate her. Now is as good a time as any. Then I have to find out what our exact losses are and call my parents. That is going to be so awful…" she said, and didn't dare meet his eyes, lest his sympathy weaken her resolve not to cry again.

Normally Abby never cried, not even during sappy movies, but she was overwrought and exhausted. Right now, she needed to concentrate on business.

"I have an idea," Reece said.

"If we try to lock her in the barn, I don't think anyone will believe that she's a runaway bride," Abby tried to joke, but it fell flat.

Reece smiled slightly. He tipped her chin up with his fingers, making her meet his eyes, which were sympathetic, but not in a bad way. In a silvery, soft way that made her remember his kiss.

"What?" she asked, almost panicked that amid everything, she could still lust for Reece.

"Use Winston wineries for the wedding, and for any other events you have this month. You can move your wines down to our room, and we'll feature both vineyards, if you don't mind—yours and ours. I need to clear out inventory before we sell, so it could work out for all of us."

Abby stared. Had he just offered for her to use his winery?

"But…you're selling," she said blankly. What if the place sold quickly? She'd only become reaquainted with Reece two days ago—could she trust him? She couldn't make promises that she'd break again later on.

"Don't worry about that. I can work it out so that whoever buys us, they don't close until after the wedding, at least. If it takes longer, we can figure it out as we go, but in the meanwhile, you're welcome to run your business out of our front rooms."

Abby was stunned and unsure what to say, but she couldn't think of one good reason to say no, except what had happened between them the night before. What had *almost* happened. If she and Reece were going into business together, even temporarily, she couldn't let that happen again.

"I don't know what to say…it's so generous of you," she admitted. "It would save me so much, not having to refund the deposit on this wedding. And all you want me to do is sell your wines, too?"

That wouldn't be hard; the Winstons made spectacular wines, and she had lost several barrels in the fire, so this could be the perfect solution.

As long as they could keep their hands—and wonderful, muscular thighs—to themselves, she thought silently.

"I thought you said your Realtor wanted you keeping the property empty, neutral? I'd have to decorate, and there would be people around all the time…."

Reece didn't look concerned. "I know. I'm sure he can work around it. The place is just sitting there. I already sent the staff home and was going to run the main room myself for a few weeks, but you obviously could use it."

Her heart lightened as she considered, and she felt hopeful for the first time all morning. This could save her, in more ways than one.

"We'd have to, um, keep things strictly business, though," she said, hoping he got her drift.

This would also give her the perfect opportunity to talk with Reece about selling. Maybe she could convince him there was a better way…and give her time to figure out what that was.

"Whatever you want, Abby. I'm just a friend, trying to help. No strings attached," he said, though she could tell from the heat in his eyes that he was remembering the night before, too.

Could *she* keep things "strictly business" with Reece?

"I guess I could ask Sandra," she said, though she couldn't imagine it wouldn't be an acceptable option. Winston wineries was far fancier than Abby's reception room, and with the same beautiful views.

"I could try booking rooms for the wedding party at Tandy's Inn, and I'll need one, too," she added, thinking out loud.

"We have some rooms upstairs. Mom used them more for guests, but they would work for your wedding party to dress or spend the night. You should stay at the house. You're more than welcome."

"I don't think that's a good idea," she said. "I mean, I don't want to intrude. You're being kind enough as it is."

He looked at her as if she was talking nonsense. "It's a big house, Abby, and you'd be near your barns and the winery. There's no reason to pay for a room when we have six empty ones upstairs in the house."

Abby chewed her lip, feeling like she was jumping into the frying pan after the fire, but her house wouldn't be habitable for quite some time. Staying at Tandy's, even though it was right there in the village, wouldn't be as convenient as being at Reece's.

Or as tempting.

Steeling her resolve, she nodded. *Put on your big girl panties and do this, Abby,* she mentally nudged herself. *Just be sure you keep them on.*

Ha. Like panties would matter.

"What?" he said.

She coughed, realizing she might have said that under her breath.

"Uh, nothing." She looked up at Reece. Surely last night was a fluke, the result of wine and reminiscing. They could do this. "Thank you, Reece. You have no idea what this means to me."

"It's my pleasure, Abby. Just let me know anything you need," he said.

His pleasure? Anything she needed? Ohmygod, this was a bad idea.

With another squeeze to her arm before he turned

away, he walked back toward his house. Where she would be sleeping tonight.

But not with him.

Abby groaned as she went to talk to Sandra. Hannah was absolutely going to love this.

REECE STOPPED AND looked back, watched Abby walk away, her stride lighter than before. That made him feel better, too, that there was something he could do to help.

She chatted with the young woman whom he had heard yelling at the top of her spoiled, self-interested lungs when he had arrived with coffee. The two women chatted a few seconds, and the bride threw her arms around Abby. Apparently his solution worked for her.

He nodded in satisfaction, strolling the rest of the way to his place. This path over the field would get a lot of wear back and forth over the next month, he thought.

Surprisingly, suddenly, he was looking forward to Abby's company in the big house. Normally being alone didn't bother him. In fact, he preferred it, but this could work.

He hoped.

He might be losing his mind, actually, but what was done was done. It hadn't even occurred to him until he'd heard the woman yelling about suing Abby, and he'd taken in the exhaustion that bruised the pale skin under her eyes and the strain that pinched at her as she tried to maintain her composure.

How could he not offer her the use of the winery? It's what any decent neighbor, and old family friend, would do.

Right?

Right. It really wasn't an excuse to spend more time with Abby while he was here, or to hopefully have her in his bed, even though she warned him they wouldn't be mixing business with pleasure.

He hoped to change her mind on that score. Soon.

He'd have to call Charles, who wasn't going to be happy, not at all, but Reece knew his parents would agree—this was the neighborly thing to do.

Especially when his neighbor was as sexy as Abby, with lips like satin and a body that moved against his like she was made for him.

As much as he meant his promise of a no-strings arrangement, he knew she wanted him, too. He could feel it every time he touched her.

And he planned to touch her. A lot.

His cell phone started ringing as soon as he got through the door, and he saw it was his brother, Ben. Immediately concerned that something was wrong with his father, fantasies about Abby disintegrated and Reece answered the call, tense.

"Ben, what's wrong?"

"Whoa, brother, calm down. Everything's fine—but you sound upset. What's going on?" he asked sharply.

Ben had fallen in love with the game of golf when he was a kid, though he was never more than an average player. But he never gave up on his dream of being involved in the sport, and landed a graduate degree in landscape architecture, with a specialization in designing golf courses. He'd spent years working with some of the best designers, building his name, and finally accumulated the backing to open his own course, his own design. Then he met his wife, Kelly, and they had two beautiful kids now. Ben had a stable, solid life.

Reece, unlike Ben, had lived a more precarious, adventure-driven existence. He'd finished college, but the business admin degree was something he'd pursued because he didn't really know what else he was going to do with his life. Reece had always bragged that he liked not knowing what was around the next corner. He never stopped moving, until recently.

"Sorry. I guess I just assumed something was wrong with Dad," Reece said.

When had his love of adventure turned into him expecting a disaster every time the phone rang? Was this part of the post-traumatic stress disorder that his neurologist had warned about—and that Reece had dismissed—that was often the result of serious car crashes?

"He's fine. Mom, too. But they're worried about you, up there, alone, especially for the holidays. I offered to come up. I can book a flight today if you want some help getting things done there, arranging the sale, the move, whatever. We could have some serious brother time," Ben said. "Go ice fishing or something."

Reece smiled. "That would be great, but I don't

want to take you away from Kelly and the kids so close to the holidays. I'm good, and in fact, things have taken an interesting turn," he said, going on to explain about the fire and offering use of the winery to Abby.

Ben whistled. "Wow. Never boring for you, is it?"

Reece laughed. "Yeah, you could say that. Could you fill in Mom and Dad? I assumed they wouldn't mind."

"I'm sure they'll be fine with it. More than fine even," Ben said and Reece closed his eyes, hearing the grin in his brother's voice.

"Don't start, Ben, and don't make them think this is anything other than what it is."

"They'd just love for you to move back, whether it's to run the winery or not. And I saw Abby when we were there for Christmas last year. She filled out nice, huh?"

Reece's hackles raised, hearing his brother's frankly admiring tone. But he wasn't surprised. A man would have to be gay or dead not to notice Abby.

"Yeah, but it's not like that."

Yes, it was.

"Really? I know you, Reece. And I know you've had a thing for her ever since you were about six years old."

"How could you know that? You were only four," Reece said with a scoff.

"Yeah, well, I remember all the years after that, too. I never could figure out why you just didn't ask her out. Hell, I almost did, just to make you jealous," Ben said, laughing at his brother's expense.

And it might have worked, Reece acknowledged. But that was then. They were only kids.

And he wasn't Ben. Reece didn't do permanent with anything, not when the real love of his life was getting behind the wheel of a car and driving two hundred miles an hour for a living. He'd seen too many racers leave families behind, after they had sacrificed everything to the sport, including their lives.

"Ben, seriously, please make sure it's okay with them. I'm still planning to sell and to move back to France. I want to race again. It's all I want."

Except for Abby.

He shook his head of the thought. Sure, he *wanted* her—in his bed—but his life was still on the track, on the other side of the Atlantic.

Ben's disappointment was carefully veiled behind a general remark, but he agreed to what Reece asked. After some more discussion about the winery and its future, Reece put the phone back on the mahogany table by the window. Right there, the night before, he'd pressed Abby up against the wall with every intention of making her his.

For the night.

He still planned to do that—for a week, or a month—and he'd make sure she knew that up front, too. She'd use Winston to get through the holiday and the wedding, and they'd share some good times to make up for what they missed back in high school—or not, if Abby stuck to her guns about business only—then they would both go on with their lives. It was that simple.

Reece ignored the mocking laugh in his head as he went upstairs to get a room set up for Abby.

CHAPTER FOUR

TWO DAYS LATER, Abby drove up the lake road, returning from a day of shopping. The sun hung low on the horizon, and she figured she had about an hour of dusky daylight left. Even with the shorter days, the snow helped keep things brighter longer. She turned into her driveway out of habit, forgetting that she meant to go to Reece's and unload her goods, but since she was here, figured she could check in on the horses. When she spotted the barn doors open, she froze.

Though they weren't susceptible to much crime, and though she was just across the field, she'd been worried about her horses. She'd barely had time to take care of Beau and Buttercup, having had to break her promise of a long ride and settle for leaving them out in the pasture.

But that door shouldn't be open. She knew for a fact that she'd locked it when she left that morning.

The stale scent of smoke from the fire still clung faintly to the crisp winter air as she hopped out of the car and made her way down to the barn. Slowly opening the door, she peered inside and saw no one but Shadow, their black lab, who came bounding to greet her, and Buttercup. But no Beau. The door to his stall was wide open, though it appeared undamaged.

Abby's heart fell to her feet and she stepped inside, instantly noting that Beau's tack was gone as well.

Frowning, she pulled out her cell phone.

"Hannah? Are you riding Beau?" she asked as soon as her friend picked up, though usually Hannah would let Abby know if she was coming by. Also, Hannah typically rode Buttercup, who was somewhat smaller.

"Uh, no, why would you ask?"

Abby put a hand to her forehead, closing her eyes to stave off panic, and walked back out the door to breathe in the cold air and calm down.

"Beau's not here, neither is his tack, and I've been gone all day—"

She stopped midsentence as she caught sight of a figure getting closer, down by the edge of the field. Hannah was upset, too, and told her to hang up and call the police, but a few moments later, Abby saw with a wash of relief that that wouldn't be necessary.

"It's Reece. Reece has him," she said into the phone, and then hung up as the rider and the horse came closer.

Abby had never seen Reece on horseback. She didn't even know he could ride. His family always had dogs, but never horses.

"Reece!" she called, waving, and he waved back, heading toward her.

He looked like every cowboy fantasy she'd ever had, sitting tall on Beau, his camel-colored coat and hat contrasting with the steed's dark chestnut coloring as they approached her. Beau whinnied in welcome, and Abby was so relieved he was okay she realized she was shaking.

"Hey, are you all right? What's wrong?" Reece asked as he came up next to her.

"I—I saw the door open and Beau gone… I didn't know where he was. I thought maybe someone stole him. The police told me to be careful about people poking around here, which I guess some people do when they find out about burned buildings…." She trailed off, petting the horse's soft cheek with a sigh of relief.

"Ah, damn, Abby. Sorry about that. You left the barn keys on the counter, and I was feeling antsy. I knew you hadn't had any time to get them out for a ride, so I figured I'd do it for you," he said, clearly apologetic.

"That's so good of you, Reece. I guess I didn't think of you because I didn't even know you rode," she admitted.

"I learned in France. Haven't had the chance to ride in a while, but it felt good."

"Did you ride both of them?"

"No, I figured I'd give them both a short turn around the field, so I was just coming back for Buttercup."

Abby nodded. "Let me grab a saddle and I'll join you, if you don't mind. They can have a longer ride that way, and I could use some fresh air, too."

"Sure, that would be great," he agreed, and a little

while later Abby was on Buttercup, riding alongside Reece on the lake path, more relaxed than she had been in days.

"I needed this. I'm glad you had the idea to take them out," she said. "I feel so guilty when I can't tend to them like I always did, but it seems like the winery takes over my life sometimes."

"I hear you. I thought I would like to get some pets at home in France, but I don't want to kennel them or pay pet-sitters when I'm away, which is usually a lot."

The easy companionship between them seemed enhanced by the quiet of the trail and the rhythmic gait of the horses.

"You have a house there?" she asked.

"Yes, outside of the Talence, near the Bordeaux region. There's a lot of industry there, as well as wine and some universities. I found a house outside of the town that allowed me to go into the city if I wanted to, but to retreat when I needed to, as well. It's an older house, and I have been fixing it up slowly, when I have the opportunity."

"Bordeaux? So you left wine country to live in wine country?" she said with a soft laugh, so he knew she wasn't criticizing.

"I guess so. I did intend to study wines when I went there, and then I discovered racing."

"Funny how you had to go that far to find it, when we've lived with the Glen under our noses all our lives."

"I know. But we never really went to the races when we were kids. Ben and Dad spent more time playing golf, which I never took to. I went to a few races at the Glen, but at that point in time I was more interested in making out with whatever girl I met there instead of watching the race," he said with a self-effacing grin.

She laughed. "That's changed?"

"Mostly. I rarely date in season. I can't afford the distraction, not that there aren't plenty of offers."

"You're modest, too," she teased.

"Hey, it's true. Groupies follow racing just like any sport, and some of the guys take advantage, but it's never been my thing."

"So you don't date?"

"Not in season, not really," he said, and she considered that, leaving the subject alone for a while. She hadn't intended to turn her questions into a fishing expedition about his love life.

So he wasn't saying he didn't see women, he just didn't see them while he was driving. She guessed that made sense. She never assumed he was a saint.

"How about you?" he asked.

"What?"

"You date much?"

"Now and then, nothing serious. I've been so busy with the business since Mom and Dad left. It takes up all of my time, really."

"Lucky for me," he said, almost under his breath, and Abby blinked and shot him a look, unsure she had actually heard that. She decided not to ask for clarification, and they stopped talking for a while, making their way back up the far end of the trail, and across the fields to the barns.

"I'll get the door," she said, dismounting easily and making her way over to pull the doors open.

It was darker by the time they returned, and in the soft, golden light that spilled out of the barn, he looked even more handsome, she thought. He smiled, but there was something tight about it. He didn't dismount, and Abby wondered what the problem was.

"Are you okay?" she asked, unsure what to make of his sudden silence. Beau shifted and snorted, dancing under Reece, eager to be brushed and fed now that he'd worked off some energy.

"Yeah, I'm fine," Reece almost growled between clenched teeth, and in the next second, he swung his leg over to the ground. Abby was horrified to see that as he landed, his leg gave way and his other foot never quite made it out of the stirrup, making Beau jump sideways nervously.

"Reece, oh, no," she breathed, steadying Beau and making her way over to help him up so that he could get his foot out of the stirrup to regain his balance.

"Are you okay?" she said, looking down and stepping carefully. There was no ice.

Reece was on his feet now, his expression reflecting stifled pain, and he walked forward, taking Beau's reins as he limped into the barn without a word.

Abby frowned, following. "Reece? Are you okay?"

He paused, his posture stiff. "I'm fine, Abby. My leg just fell asleep."

"Oh. I thought it might be the injury from your

accident," she said, knowing that now she *was* fishing. He knew it, too.

He rested his forehead on his hand, where it lay on Beau's back, as if he was looking for patience, or a way to escape.

Finally, he straightened and looked at her again. "It is. It's not serious. I kept my leg in the same position for too long and it went numb. No big deal."

"It could have been a big deal if you couldn't get back up or if Beau had taken off in a panic or trampled you," she said. "Does this happen often?"

"I don't need the third degree, Abby. I just should have been more careful dismounting. Can we leave it? Okay?"

"I'm concerned," she said, refusing to feel guilty. If that had happened when he was alone, he could have been badly hurt.

"I know," he said, sounding tired. "But it's fine."

She didn't think so, but she bit back any more comments. The easy mood they'd had all evening was now replaced with tension, and she nodded, grabbing a brush and getting Buttercup set for the night.

Reece didn't say anything more, and he was still limping, if a little less severely, as he put Beau away and left, walking back to the house without another word. She would have offered to drive him, since she had to take her car back anyway, but somehow she didn't think that would help.

Obviously falling from the horse hadn't only reminded him of his injuries, it had probably dented his ego to fall in front of her. Silly, but she knew men were like that sometimes.

"I guess I stepped in it," she said to Buttercup, petting the mare's sleek coat. The horses looked at her with calm patience, and Beau snorted again.

Abby smirked at him. "Oh, sure, take his side," she said affectionately to the animal, locking the barn and making her way back to the house, as well.

THE FOLLOWING AFTERNOON, ABBY had done little more than run back and forth to Ithaca and Syracuse, dealing with insurance issues and setting up contractors. Today, she'd caught up on more personal needs, purchasing a stash of clothing to replace some basics that were ruined in the fire, taking what she could salvage to the cleaners and loading up some food for Reece's kitchen.

He hadn't really stocked the kitchen, probably because he didn't think he'd be there long, and he would probably eat out, she figured. But Abby liked to cook and she liked to eat, so food was a necessity. She also needed supplies for tastings—crackers, chocolates and cheeses. She wanted to make up for her snafu the evening before, when Reece fell. She couldn't blame him for being embarrassed, and she had been too nosy.

She planned to make him a nice dinner—it was the least she could do, given his generosity. Visiting markets in the city to find the ingredients she needed had been the first fun she'd had in days.

She'd also taken time to walk around a bit, enjoying the atmosphere and having a moment to herself. Ithaca was such a lovely little city, a neat combination of funky college town with an active arts community and working-class neighborhoods.

Set at the southern edge of Cayuga Lake, Ithaca hosted two colleges, including the famous Cornell University, her alma mater. The city also had more eateries per capita than New York City. It was surrounded by beautiful hillsides, vineyards, gorges and waterfalls, and the town had a wonderful underground mall by the Commons, the famous Moosewood restaurant and the farmer's market, where she shopped every week. She loved what every season had to offer, and the place was as woven into who she was as much as anything else in her life.

How could Reece have wanted to leave so badly? She had everything she needed here, and though everyone enjoyed a vacation away, Abby always liked coming home.

Her worries about staying at his home had been groundless—she'd been gone so much, usually working, and apparently he was busy doing things, too, so they'd barely seen each other long enough to say good morning since the horse-riding incident.

She had to walk past his room, trying not to notice the light on under the door, and continue down the hall to a large guest bedroom that looked out over the lake. The guest room was twice the size of her own bedroom in her house, and she loved the view of the lake, facing the opposite direction of her burnt buildings. She appreciated Reece being so thoughtful as to spare her the reminder.

Still, even with the beautiful view and the big bed, she hadn't slept great since the fire. It was hard to not think about everything looming over her, and she hadn't been able to contact her parents yet, which was weighing on her. Then there was the itching desire for Reece, the need to touch him, to be close to him, that she couldn't quite stop fantasizing about.

She finally finished putting everything away and left out only what she needed for dinner—a lovely pork roast, vegetables and potatoes, the perfect comfort meal for a winter evening.

She planned to make some appetizers as well, and of course, open some wine.

She paused as she started the roast—would Reece take this the wrong way? She merely wanted to do her part, to thank him for his help and to feel at home as much as she could. As much as she was tempted to give in to her fantasies, doing so would only make everything so much more complicated, and right now the last thing she needed was more complication in her life.

On second thought, maybe she shouldn't open any wine.

The phone on the wall next to her rang, and without thinking she picked it up.

"Hello?"

"Um, hello?" a heavily accented woman's voice responded, obviously confused. "I am looking for Reece?"

"He's not home. May I take a message?" Abby asked, reaching for a pen.

A heavy sigh met her request. "And who is this?" the woman asked, her "this" sounding more like "theese."

None of your bees-niss, Abby felt like saying, feeling annoyed. "I'm a friend of Reece's. May I take a message?"

"A friend, eh? You may tell him Danielle called," she said, a bit huffily, Abby thought. Maybe it was the accent.

"Danielle…last name?"

"He will know," she said with an aggravatingly sexy laugh.

"Sure."

"Be sure he receives the message, please."

"Of course," Abby said. "Goodbye."

She set the phone down, wondering why she felt so peevish. It was obviously just a friend of Reece's from Europe calling. Abby sighed, shaking it off.

She bet that Reece had *lots* of friends with sexy accents back in France. Plopping the roast into the Dutch oven a little more forcefully than she planned, she splashed stock on her shirt and shook her head.

Ridiculous to be this put out by the idea of Reece with other women. Sexier, more sophisticated, French women.

Well, she couldn't compete and didn't want to, she decided, tying on an apron to avoid further damage. Putting the woman and her snooty accent out of her mind, she turned on the radio and focused on cutting vegetables and making her appetizers.

She quickly worked her way out of her snit and was shimmying across the kitchen, singing at the top of her lungs to Mariah Carey's version of "All I Want For Christmas Is You." She was on her way to put the tray of cheese and fruit in the refrigerator, but nearly dropped it all when she met Reece's amused expression as he stood, propped in the doorway, grinning from ear to ear.

"Reece!" she said, fumbling and blushing to the roots of her hair. "How long have you been standing there?"

He pursed his lips thoughtfully. "Mmm…about from the first chorus," he said lightly, still smiling.

"Oh, God," she said, covering her face, shaking with embarrassed laughter.

"I have to admit, the apron adds a certain panache to your performance," he teased.

She looked down at the sexy apron she wore, a Cheetah print with red ruffles and a bow at the neckline. Hannah had bought it for her birthday as a funny gift, and it had never been worn, especially since an embroidered patch on the pocket read Hot Stuff.

As if this wasn't embarrassing enough.

It was one of the few items from the kitchen pantry that didn't get ruined. She hadn't thought twice when she'd donned it, unused to an audience while cooking.

"It was a gag gift," she explained. "From Hannah."

Reece scanned her up and down appreciatively and walked over to where she stood.

"What smells so good?"

"I thought I would make us dinner, as a thank-you…and also because I like to cook. It destressed me," she said, trying to keep her voice level as he ran a finger over the edge of the bow, the tip of his finger brushing against her skin at the edge of her shirt.

"That's nice of you. I haven't had a home-cooked dinner in a while," he said sincerely, but there was a glint in his eye.

"This is every man's fantasy, you know," he said, tugging at the bow to pull her forward against him. "A sexy woman in the kitchen making him dinner after a long day."

She rolled her eyes. "Puh-leese. I can't imagine you ever having a fantasy that mundane," she said, and then shook her head.

Why was she still standing here, so close to him?

He lowered his head and nibbled at her earlobe, making her yelp.

"Reece! What are you doing?"

He chuckled against her skin. "Just having a taste," he said, nibbling again. "I think you splashed something on your neck. Let me get it," he offered.

It was news to her that the nerves in her earlobes were connected directly to her knees, which seemed to turn to water. She planted her hands against his chest and tried to push. The man was rock-solid.

"I have appetizers," she said breathlessly.

"Not what I'm hungry for," he said against her neck, nipping at her speeding pulse.

"Reece," she said as calmly as she could. "We agreed we had to keep things only business."

"You said that, but I only agreed out of politeness," he whispered, his breath against her lips. "I said I'd do whatever you want," he added, brushing a thumb over a very hard nipple, making her gasp, his eyes meeting hers. "You want?"

Oh, did she ever.

"It's not a good idea," she said lamely, still unable to force her feet to move. He just felt too damned good.

"Abby," he said, laughing softly, "it's just me."

That was like saying, "It's just dynamite," to her mind.

He proceeded to cover her lips with light, soft, teasing kisses that made her grab on to him, curling her fingers into his jacket as she sought more. He didn't accommodate her until she groaned and worked her hands up to his neck, holding him still as she kissed him, taking what she needed.

She was weak, but she just couldn't work up the energy to care.

"I guess you're not angry at me anymore for the other night?" she asked, breathless.

His brow wrinkled, as if he was surprised. "I never was angry with you. Just frustrated, and a little embarassed. I'm sorry if I let you think otherwise," he said. "Let me apologize properly."

Reece walked her backward as they kissed hungrily, lifting her almost without her noticing until she sat on the kitchen counter. He settled in between her thighs, deepening the kiss until breathing was unheard of and—as far as Abby was concerned—completely unnecessary.

"Nothing mundane about this fantasy from where I'm standing," he said when he broke the kiss, her face framed in his hands, his eyes devouring her.

He'd tugged the tie of the apron loose and continued to trail kisses down her throat. Slowly his hand moved down to cover her breast before pushing up the edge of her blouse, and Abby was beyond arguing. She wanted the frustrating barrier of their clothes gone and to know his touch on her bare skin.

The sheer idea made her dizzy.

He had her shirt off in a split second. She reached behind to unclasp her bra, his hands covering her, spilling over with the fullness of her bare breasts.

"Damn, babe, where were you hiding these in high school?" he said appreciatively, bending to nuzzle her intimately, her hand slipping into his hair to press him close. She wanted his mouth on her in the worst way.

"I've lost a little weight since then," she said with a chuckle, "and I guess I filled out in other areas. Late bloomer," she finished on a sigh. He'd taken her aching nipple into his mouth, sucking hard, then laving with his tongue until she was writhing on the counter.

"You're so sweet," he said, working his lips over her stomach and taking her hand, placing it to her own breast as he watched. His eyes darkened intensely as she touched herself, tweaking and pulling as he slowly unzipped her jeans while he watched and kissed.

She stopped, and put her hand on his.

"You first. You have far too many clothes on," she said provocatively.

He nodded and stepped back, not breaking the gaze between them as he took his jacket off and threw it on the island behind him, then made quick work of his sweater.

She gasped.

He was gorgeous. Lean and muscled, his tanned skin proved he'd spent the majority of his winters in sunnier places, and she loved how his shoulders and biceps flexed as he tore the garment off.

Then she realized he'd stilled, looking at her strangely, more tensely.

"I'm sorry. I didn't think to warn you," he said, glancing down, and only then did she even notice some of the scars, remnants of a burn by his shoulder, and what looked like thin lines from surgery a little lower.

"That wasn't what I was staring at," she said, wanting nothing more than to touch him, thinking only of that. "But it doesn't bother me at all. Come here," she commanded softly.

He walked over to her and pushed his hands into her hair, pulling her up hard against him. Her breasts crushed delightfully against his hard skin, his mouth plundering hers.

She managed to retain enough focus to move her hands to the front of his jeans, undoing the buttons, and sliding her hand down inside.

Now it was his turn to gasp, breaking the kiss. He

leaned his forehead on her shoulder as he trembled beneath her touch. He was hard, thick and hot in her hand. She stroked him, loving the friction of his skin against hers.

His breathing was labored as he ground out, "No, stop." His teasing tone gone.

She froze. Had she hurt him? Done something wrong?

"What?" she asked.

"I'll come," he said tensely. "It's been months, since before the accident, and this feels too good," he explained, pushing away a stray hair that had landed in her eyes.

Abby couldn't think of a single thing he could have said that would have turned her on more.

She smiled, feeling feminine, powerful.

"Seems like you're well overdue then," she said, closing in for a kiss. She continued stroking him, rubbing her thumb over the slippery head of his cock and mimicking the rubbing motion with her tongue against his.

In mere seconds he exploded, thrusting into her hand, groaning deeply into her mouth as he came. When he broke the kiss, his beautiful chest heaved with hard breaths, his cheeks flushed and his eyes were still hot as he looked at her.

"I don't think anything in my life will ever feel better than that did," he said, still catching his breath.

She smiled again. "Maybe we should go upstairs and find out."

She was more than ready to take him to bed, and

she didn't want to wait. To hell with complications. Complications could feel damned good, from where she was sitting.

"What about dinner?"

"That roast has a couple hours yet. It can just simmer," she said, the last word coming out more sexually than she intended.

She would take the memory of the way he looked at her—a gaze rich with lust, gratitude and anticipation—to her grave.

The loud sound of an engine and the hissing of air brakes made her jump, and they stared at each other in confusion before she looked at the clock and realized.

"You're expecting someone?" Reece asked.

"Yes! I completely forgot—it's the trees," she said, scrambling to get her bra on and trying to find her blouse before the nursery delivery guy came to the door.

"Trees?"

"Christmas trees. I completely forgot he was bringing them today," she explained.

Reece looked bemused, but followed her lead and grabbed his shirt, buttoning up his jeans.

"You mean, tree, singular?"

"No, sixteen of them," she said, and washed her hands quickly, grabbing a coat from the hook where she had left it earlier.

"Sixteen?" he echoed.

She grinned, her lusty thoughts fading to the background. "Three for the tasting rooms, a dozen for the decorating contest and one for the house. C'mon, you can help me with them."

As they walked out into the crisp air where two men unloaded a flatbed truck loaded with trees, Abby couldn't help but feel that their arrival might just have saved her from herself. As much as she wanted Reece, and wanted to give in, it would make her life an even greater mess. Right now, that was something she didn't need. As they spent the next few hours setting up Christmas trees, she tried to convince herself she was okay with that.

CHAPTER FIVE

REECE FROWNED AT THE jungle of boxes and bins that crowded the main room of his house. Even more so since there was a huge tree in the corner, by the two front windows, and then more bags of new ornaments Abby had purchased. He looked at the tree again. It had to be eight feet tall. It had taken two hours to get the trees off the truck and in place. Two hours when he could have been making love to Abby, but while he had been helping with setting up trees, she had been hauling out decorations, apparently having forgotten their moment in the kitchen.

Now he knew how much work it had been for his dad, who always brought the trees home and spent hours struggling to erect them, to get the "right side" showing—a tree quality that only his mother seemed able to assess.

"You really didn't have to get a tree for in here," he said, trying to be tactful. He would have skipped it, personally.

"It's your last Christmas in this house. There should be a tree," she said, as if that was the most logical thing in the world.

Luckily, most of Abby's family ornaments and

decorations had been salvageable, contained neatly in plastic bins in her basement where the water from the fire hoses hadn't damaged them.

He'd had to call his mother, but found several boxes of their own, including several that he remembered from childhood. After a fantastic dinner of succulent pork that was one of the best things he had eaten in a long time, they had opened up the boxes and pulled everything out, which created what appeared to be utter chaos to Reece's eyes.

But Abby apparently had that special, female, Christmas sense that told her what ornaments should go where, and why.

Did it really make a difference?

He could tell from the intense concentration on Abby's face and the way she bit her lip—which was sexy, as well as completely endearing—that if she had lost these bins in the fire, it would have been a terrible thing. They were clearly meaningful to her.

It wasn't that he disliked Christmas, but he'd managed to tactfully avoid it this year by staying here, alone, and now it looked like it had found him anyway. Normally he would spend most of his holiday—when he didn't come home—working, and just have dinner with friends on the day, call his family, relax. But it had been his idea to have Abby here, and so he sucked it up.

A few hours later, having strung all the lights, they were now picking through the decorations, deciding what should go where.

"The silver and white should go in the back room,

for the wedding reception, and the grapes will go on the tree in the tasting room, of course," she said, pulling several boxes aside.

"Grapes? You have grape ornaments?"

"There's a little store down on the Commons, the one that sells Christmas stuff all year round—you know the one?" she said, looking at him askance.

"I don't think I was ever in there," he admitted. When he was a student, he spent more time partying than shopping, and in the years since, even when he came home, spent most of his time with his family and never went into town too much.

"Oh, they have the most unusual ornaments. All kinds of characters, food items, just…whatever. And every year we would go down to see if they had some different grape ornaments, or ones that maybe looked like tiny wine bottles—we have fewer of those. Eventually the owner just called us when he got new things in, and he would trade us ornaments for bottles of wine. We had enough to decorate one tree with them."

Reece smiled, enjoying her enthusiasm about such a simple thing. "It sounds great—I can't wait to see it."

"Well, we can do that one first then."

"Tonight?" he said, surprised.

"Yes—I don't know that we can get all four done, but I'd like to try. There aren't any tastings until Friday, thank God, but I have dozens of other things to do."

Reece hadn't been aware he was going to spend the entire evening decorating Christmas trees—he had planned on much more interesting activities, like getting Abby in his bed. But she seemed genuinely excited about the trees, and all things considered, he decided, why not?

"Okay, I'm in."

His agreement was worth the smile it elicited.

So, after all of the ornaments were separated, they hauled the boxes over to the tasting room, which in the case of Winston wineries, was completely separate from the house and a much more modern construction, with shining oak beams and plate glass windows around their sales area.

Large leather chairs were strewn around the actual tasting area, inviting guests to enjoy the view and the wine. There was a fireplace near the bar, behind which the bottles of wine were arranged. Hidden track lighting put a soft golden glow over the room, rather than anything harsh or too bright. There were double French doors at the back that led to a reception area and an outdoor deck that overlooked the lake.

"It's so pretty and spacious here. I feel like our little tasting room was about the size of your closet," Abby said with a laugh, setting down her box of ornaments with a sigh. "I hope I have enough business to justify you letting us use all this space. I'll need to run through a tour with you, too, if you don't mind, so that I can train Hannah and Carl, and we need to set up the wine displays still, and—"

Reece put both hands on her shoulders. "Abby. Stop. Right now, focus on the tree, just this tree. One thing. Tomorrow there will be time to think about the rest."

"I know, but there's so much—"

"I know there is. But we can't do it tonight, and anyway, it's been a while since I've decorated a tree, let alone four of them," he said with a grin. He leaned in to brush a kiss over her mouth when she seemed ready to argue again. "Let's enjoy it."

Taking a deep breath, her cheeks pink from the kiss—something he planned to repeat as often as possible—she nodded, smiling, too.

"Sorry. Once my mind gets rolling, I can't stop sometimes," she admitted.

"I know the feeling. I used to be like that before a race. The day before, the night before, I wouldn't be able to stop thinking of everything, double- and triple-checking every detail. But I had to learn to trust my team, and also, I needed to sleep. A tired driver isn't a good driver. By trying to do everything, I wasn't doing my job as well as I needed to."

"I know. It was easier before, when Mom and Dad were here, and Sarah, but then it seemed like it all just landed in my lap, and I got so used to thinking about it all, all the time." She cast a glance over her shoulder, back toward her burned winery, though she couldn't see it in the dark. "Now I don't know what to think."

"It will all work out," Reece said steadily. "Speaking of your mom and dad, have you talked to them yet?" He guessed that, depending on where her parents were exactly in earthquake-torn Haiti, communication could be a real challenge.

He was sorry he asked, as her face crumpled with distress. “No, I don't want to worry them with vague emails, so I certainly don't want to deliver the news to them that way. I have left messages, and I'm just waiting for them to call me back,” she said, wringing her fingers together. “I'm dreading it. I hate that I let this happen. They'll be so upset,” she said.

“I'm sure all that they'll care about is that you are okay. Everything else can be rebuilt. But it might be another sign you are overworked—you start trying to handle too many things, you miss important details, and that's when bad things happen.”

“Like you were just saying, about racing. I know you don't like to talk about it,” she said quickly, looking away as she pulled some ornaments from a box and turned toward the tree, motioning him to do the same. “But is that what happened with your accident? You were trying to do too much?”

He swallowed hard. In the middle of seducing Abby in the kitchen, Christmas tree chaos and having their wonderful dinner, he realized he hadn't thought about his accident once in several hours, maybe for the first time in a long time. He hated bringing it back up again, but he supposed it was only fair to at least answer her question.

“No, not this time. This was just one of those crazy, unfortunate things.... I actually can't remember the crash.”

“You have amnesia?” she said with some surprise.

He nodded shortly. “They say it's normal in traumatic situations, like car crashes, and I had pretty serious head injuries. You probably know I was in a coma for a while," he said.

She nodded, and as they put ornaments on the tree, it was easier to share the things he didn't normally talk with anyone about, except for his doctors.

"I watched the video footage for the first time a month ago. I blew out a tire and the roads were wet, but I don't know why I lost control so completely, and I guess I might never know. I've had tires go before and controlled it. This time..." he said, trailing off, shaking his head. "I just don't know."

Her hand was on his arm then, squeezing in a way meant to comfort, but he felt his pulse jump. Any touch from Abby seemed to make that happen.

"My dad always says the only control we have in life is self-control. We can control how we react, what we do, and that's it. You were—" she paused, catching her slip "—*are* a fantastic driver. Even if you can't remember, I'm sure you did everything you could. Like you said, sometimes things just happen."

"Your dad always was a smart guy. How would you know what kind of driver I am?" he asked, hanging his last ornament on the tree.

"Uh, um, well..." She took her hand from his arm and reached into the box for more decorations. "It stands to reason, right? You're one of the major players. They said you could be the next Clark or Stewart."

His eyes widened. "You follow racing?"

She paused, leaning into the box, and he realized she'd let on more than she meant to. It warmed him in a whole different way that she had followed his career. He never would have guessed.

"I just caught things on the news. Hometown boy makes it big in Europe, you know, and you came back and drove at the Glen that one time," she said, gathering an armful of ornaments and returning to the tree.

"Did you come to that race?" he asked. It had only been an exhibition run, a charity event, but he'd had no idea she was there.

"Some friends wanted to go, so I tagged along."

"I see."

"You see what?"

He shrugged, unable to resist the temptation to egg her on a little. "You followed my racing, you came to my exhibition…clearly you never quite got over your crush on me," he said with a grin.

Abby's jaw dropped and she huffed something about his "intolerable ego" until she saw the barely restrained glee in his eyes.

Then her gorgeous lips quirked at the edges, too. "You really enjoy getting me worked up, don't you?"

Reece took that as his cue, and stepped around the tree to pull her up close. "You have no idea," he said, serious now as he dipped in for another kiss.

"You're wicked," she said against his mouth, a little breathless. Her cheeks were flushed, her eyes bright, and Reece couldn't seem to get enough of taking her in.

"I know," he admitted. He seemed to be having especially wicked thoughts at the moment.

"I kind of like it," she said with a grin that made

his heart flip inside his chest. "But I…I've never done this," she said, looking nervous.

His eyebrows flew up. He was pretty certain that… but was he wrong? "You mean you've never, uh—"

"Oh, no! I've had sex, sure. But never when I knew it was going to end before it started. Never without at least the vague promise of something more that could happen," she said, and then broke away, looking embarrassed.

"We have a relationship, Abby. We have history, even. We're friends. That won't change."

She smiled a little. "It's already changed. We were barely friends in high school, and we've barely started a friendship now. We're leaping right into being lovers."

He knew she was right, but didn't say a word.

"I want you," she admitted. "But I don't know if I can get into this knowing you're going to sell this place and leave. I know it's stupid, and unsophisticated, but I…um, I—"

Don't want to get hurt, he finished for her in his head.

"I know, Abby. I understand," he said, though he didn't want to. He wanted Abby more than he wanted just about anything except getting back in a car, but he didn't want to hurt her, either.

She wasn't like the women he took to bed and found gone in the morning. She wasn't just using him for a thrill or some notoriety. Abby was the kind of woman you took to bed and then woke up with in the morning—every morning—for a long time.

And he wasn't that guy. Maybe someday, but not now.

"It's sweet, actually," he said, closing the gap between them and pulling her into the circle of his arms. "I can't make any promises about anything, Abby, I can only be as upfront as possible. I want you, too, a lot. But it's your choice, okay?"

She nodded against his chest, her small hands moving over his back, making him crazy, but he reined in his desire.

"Thanks, Reece. I wish I could—"

"It's okay, really. How about we finish these trees?" he said cheerfully, planting a kiss on her hair and wondering if that was the last time he'd ever have Abby in his arms.

CHAPTER SIX

ABBY WRENCHED UPWARD, an unfamiliar noise pulling her out of a restless dream.

The thud sounded again, and she sat up, hand to her slamming heart. Looking at the clock, she saw it was two-thirty in the morning. She'd only been sleeping for a few hours. Living alone for several years now had fine-tuned her senses to any noise in the house at night, and she listened closer.

She didn't need to wonder if she had imagined it when it was followed by a large crash, and glass breaking. She leapt from the bed, opening her door to peek down the hall toward Reece's room, but didn't see him. Had he slept through the noise? Heard it at all?

Moving on tiptoe down the hall, she stopped by his door, lifting her hand, then pausing. She couldn't knock if there was an intruder downstairs, they might hear.

She pushed Reece's door open just slightly, poking her head into the dark room.

"Reece?" she whispered as loudly as she dared.

A loud shout met her whisper, making her jump out of her skin, but also launching her inside the room and closing the door behind her. She saw immediately that the noise she'd heard hadn't been from an intruder, but from Reece, who had knocked the hurricane lamp off of his nightstand. He still appeared to be sleeping, and not well.

Venturing toward the bed, she bit her lip in concern.

"Reece, are you okay?"

He twisted in the sheets, as if trying to push them off, though he couldn't. He was murmuring, then shouting again, then whimpering in a way that told her he was in some kind of pain—or dreaming about it. She rushed to the side of the bed and put a calming hand on his shoulder, saying his name again, only to have him wrench away. He started saying things, his tone low and business-like, something with numbers and other mumbled words she couldn't understand.

Silver light shone through the window, and she could see his face was contorted in the agony of his dream and didn't know what to do. Then her eye caught sight of a small bottle on the dresser. She picked it up and held it close to the window—sleep aids. Those would knock him out and she probably didn't stand much chance of waking him up, she figured.

Still, she couldn't just leave him here like this, even if it was just a dream. Scooting into the empty space next to him, Abby knew she was playing with fire—especially when she realized he wasn't wearing anything but his briefs.

"God help me," she muttered, but settled down

next to him and cuddled up behind, hoping to offer some kind of comfort. Maybe she could not let him be alone through the worst of it and then go back to her room.

Reece would never know. She rubbed his back with her palm, hoping to soothe, and after a few minutes, he did seem to quiet down. Her own body relaxed and her breathing returned to almost normal. Except that she was laying here in bed with a mostly naked, absolutely gorgeous man—still, she focused on just helping him back into a restful place.

Soon, his breathing evened, the mumbling stopped and his tight muscles softened under her hands.

"That's better," she said, intending to go back to her own room, but she was warm, comfortable and exhausted.

It didn't take much for her to drift off, too.

REECE WAS HAVING THE time of his life.

All drivers dreamed of the perfect race, and in his case, he was living the dream.

He was strapped into his Ferrari F60 so tightly that he could only just about breathe. The heat was intense, the wind bruising and the G-forces flattened him against the seat.

He was in sheer heaven—and he was in second place.

There was nothing in the universe except for his car, the road and the car in front of him. Adrenaline fueled his laserlike focus, strategy a constant clicking in his brain. Second would be his best in a World

Cup race, but second wasn't good enough. Reece was pulling out all the stops and racing for first.

It had been raining. The roads were wet, but that was nothing. He knew this car like his own body, and when he was driving it, there wasn't any difference between the two, the way he saw it.

He edged up on his competitor. Overtaking wasn't common on Formula One tracks, but he had a shot as they came around the final turn. He hit the accelerator as they rounded, positioning himself to make the most of the aerodynamics of the high-tech car he drove. The back wheel of the guy in front of him was spinning close by when Reece heard the whining noise, but he didn't catch on at first that something was wrong. He'd blown out the front driver's side tire.

He'd skipped that last pit stop. A calculated risk. A mistake.

His car could go on three tires in some conditions, but not rounding a curb, not at his speed, not on wet roads. His mind didn't anticipate the worst—he adjusted and focused on cold calculation of how to maneuver, still thinking about the win as he felt himself propel sideways, lurching hard.

Reece sometimes felt like he was flying when he drove, but something told him that for a second, he was actually airborne.

Everything was black, and then it was very, very bright.

The pain was intense, and he was trapped. He fought to get out, at least, he thought he did. He had no idea where he even was.

He couldn't seem to open his eyes, no matter how hard he tried. He wanted to speak but couldn't, and while there was noise in his head that wouldn't stop, he couldn't make out anything understandable.

Panic set in, fear clawing at him, and he tried to calm down, but it just made it worse. He lunged forward, reaching out, trying to get through the blinding brightness, the deafening noise, but he couldn't.

Was this what dying was like?

His heart felt as if it would explode from his chest when he felt something, finally. Someone touched him, and he reached, finding a hand he could grab on to. He held it like it was his only connection to life, and maybe it was.

He still couldn't speak, or hear, but he could touch.

His heartbeat slowed, the panic subsiding slightly. He was alive, connected to something.

Not alone.

For that moment, it was enough.

BEFORE SHE EVEN REALIZED IT, Abby opened her eyes to the soft, pre-dawn light, and to Reece's silver eyes watching her.

"Change your mind?" he said softly.

"Hmm?" she said, not sure what he was saying, or why he was in her bed, or… Her eyes flew open and she started to push up, but Reece's arm was over her, holding her snug against him.

"Steady," he said.

Morning brain-fog assaulted her, and she fought for words, but ended up sputtering, becoming increasingly aware of the warm, hard male body aligned with hers, both buried under the soft quilt and blankets.

"You were dreaming," she finally managed to say. "You broke your lamp. I thought you were an intruder," she explained, hoping he was awake enough to interpret her garbled, simple sentences.

As she shifted, it brought her closer to him and she knew he was *very* awake.

"You thought there was someone in the house, so you decided to crawl into bed with me?" he asked, his brow furrowed.

"No, I thought there was an intruder, but when I came to get you, I saw you had broken your lamp and were having a nightmare. Do you remember?"

He shook his head, then closed his eyes. "Vaguely. I've had it before, or other nightmares anyway. I don't know if it's the same one. I can never remember the details."

"You were thrashing around, so obviously it was… bad. I tried to wake you up, but you were out cold, so I thought maybe if I just sat with you for a while you'd be okay," she said, shrugging.

"You could have been hurt. Stepped on glass," he said, frowning.

"I was fine. You were the one hurting, apparently."

"And you helped," he said softly, looking at her strangely, like he was remembering something, but he didn't say anything, so she did.

"I meant to go back to my room, and then I guess I fell asleep."

"I see," he said, his eyes warm on her face.

"I should probably go," she said.

"Do you really want to?"

Did she?

Of course she did, but…but what?

All of her reservations seemed so flimsy. Sure, she might get hurt, but she was a big girl. This was her chance to experience something wonderful, and there might never be another chance.

Reece would sell this winery, leave, and the odds were that she'd never see him again, except on TV.

Already, it hurt her heart a little to think about that, but so what? She'd survive, and she'd have some great memories. Maybe it was impossible to live your fantasies without some risk of being hurt. Maybe that was the price.

"No, I really don't," she said.

"Good, because I really want you to stay."

Her decision made, she smiled and slid her arm around him, too, enjoying how he pressed fully against her in a move that left her in no doubt that he wanted her—a lot.

The look of sheer hunger on his face made reason disappear. His lips were just a scant breath from hers, and she could hardly believe this was truly happening.

"Here's the thing, sweetheart," he said against her lips. "I don't care if an asteroid hits outside the window, nothing is interrupting us this time."

"Got it, no asteroids," she managed to say before he was kissing the life out of her, pushing her back until she was pinned between the warm, soft mattress and about six feet of hard, delicious man.

His mouth rubbed over hers erotically as he stopped to nip at her lower lip, his tongue darting out to lick the spot he bit before plunging deeper.

She arched into him, kissing him back with every ounce of passion she'd been holding back, tasting him as deeply as he tasted her. The faint scent of cedar, pine and smoke clung to his body from the night before, and she inhaled, loving how it mixed with his natural manly scent.

She barely recognized herself as she clung to him, wrapping a leg around his hip, arching into his hardness, rubbing and moaning into his mouth. She enjoyed sex, but she'd never felt so voracious about it. But right now, she wanted skin-on-skin, and pushed at the elastic band of the shorts between them.

He was of like mind, sliding his shorts off, then reaching for the edge of her flimsy cotton nightgown and pushing it upward until there wasn't anything hiding her from his gaze.

"Oh, sweetheart, this has been so worth waiting for," Reece said as he took her in. His hands drifted over her, learning her softness, studying her body so intently that she would have felt self-conscious if his touches weren't rendering her mindless.

"Um, I'm on birth control and I'm, you know, healthy. I haven't been with anyone in a while," she admitted, feeling a little awkward. But while they were old friends, they were new lovers, and certain things had to be said.

He nodded while nibbling at her shoulder, sending shivers everywhere.

"Me, too. Like I mentioned earlier, there's been no one since before the accident, and I've been thoroughly checked for everything with all of the time I spent in hospitals," he whispered against her ear.

She remembered how hard and urgent he'd been the day before when she'd stroked him to orgasm in the kitchen, and it was enough to make her shudder, reaching for him, wanting to make it happen again. The idea that she was his first lover after such a long time was important to her. Maybe that meant he wouldn't forget her later, either.

"Good, so we know we don't have to worry about *any* interruptions," she said with a smile.

She didn't want anything between them, and let him know by reaching down to find him, closing her fingers around him with a sigh of satisfaction. She opened her thighs and used her hand to slide him against her already slick sex, arching and then closing her legs to trap him there.

"I love how you feel next to me," she said, moving her hips against him, enjoying the slippery friction of their bodies. "But I bet it's not as good as you'd feel inside me."

"You make it tough to go slow," he said, pushing against her, sliding along the wet V of her flesh in a way that made her whimper and dig her fingers into his shoulders.

"Who wants slow?" she said, biting his shoulder. "Aren't you supposed to like speed?"

She yelped and then laughed as he found a ticklish spot and capitalized on it, then grabbed her hands and pinned them up over her head. She struggled slightly, and he could see it just excited her more when he pressed down, holding her in place.

Another little discovery about Abby.

"Now I've got you right where I want you," he said with a delicious smile. "And I plan to take my time. Maybe some guys make love like they race, but I think women and wine are more alike, they need to be savored," he said against her lips, catching her lower one between his teeth, then drawing it in and sucking before taking her whole mouth in a deep, carnal kiss. "We have time. Let's get to know each other," he said softly.

"But I want—"

"I know, me, too, and we'll get there. Promise," he said.

"You're such a tease," she accused, the last word ending on a moan as he ran his tongue along the shell of her ear, his cock still prodding and sliding along her sex, but not even coming close to where she wanted him.

"Can't help it when it comes to you," he said, moving lower to draw a nipple between his teeth, nipping lightly and making her arch, the slight pain making the drawing pleasure of his mouth a moment later even more intense.

He let her arms go and looked at her, his voice stern.

"Leave your hands there. Don't move them. I want to find out what you like, what you want," he said, his hands moving over her experimentally, lingering in places that made her react, moving on past the ones that didn't. "But if you move, I have to stop."

She nodded, moaning a little.

He was studying her body the way he must have studied a race course, or more accurately, tasting her like a good wine, she thought hazily, too immersed in sensation to argue. She'd been *done* plenty of times, but she'd never been paid attention to like this.

He dragged his lips down the inside of her thigh, and worked his way back up, nudging her legs apart with his shoulders.

His tongue found her, but only lightly, flicking at her clit, a butterfly touch that had her nearly screaming, writhing on the bed.

"Reece, please, I need you," she said, panting, but she obeyed, leaving her hands where he'd put them. It was driving her crazy, in the best possible way.

He licked her a little harder this time, and his fingers found their way inside of her—one, then two and then, making her eyes widen, another teased the other opening to her body, penetrating slightly. She tensed at the unexpected sensation, then relaxed. Her entire body shivered with the pleasure of his fingers and mouth everywhere.

"That feels so good," she said.

"And this?" he whispered against her sex, so softly she wasn't sure he really said anything before he kissed her again on pulsing, sensitive flesh.

"Yes," she said desperately, wanting more of everything, thrusting against him. "Please," she begged.

Reece was someone she'd known for so long, but

she knew in that instant that she didn't know anything about him at all. He seemed to know what she fantasized about, what she wanted that maybe she didn't even know to ask for. He continued to press, to lick and to thrust until she cried out, arching off the bed, her body bent in ecstasy.

He moved back up, and levered over her, pulling her legs up over his shoulders.

"I need this so much," he said roughly, staring down into her face as he poised himself before her, rubbing and teasing her sex with his cock until both of them were mindless. When she was about to beg, he eased forward, sliding inside and filling her deeply, adjusting her legs so that he could go even deeper.

Oh, thank you, Abby thought, her entire body expressing a sigh of wonder as he started moving.

"You're so wet," he said, his jaw tight with the effort of control he was exerting. "So hot inside," he said, continuing to describe what he felt, what he wanted to do to her, in exacting detail until she wanted to just beg him to make it all real.

There was little she could do to control the pace at her angle, so she traced her hands and lips over hard lines of his chest, shoulders and hips. Every muscle was tense as he rocked into her in a steady rhythm.

She ran her fingers over his scars, exploring the different textures of his skin, then across the light hair on his chest, and over male nipples that beaded, drawing a groan from him as she pinched.

"You moved your hands," he said breathlessly.

"Do you mind?"

"Not at all."

He turned his face to the side, planting wet kisses on the side of her knee, and she whimpered as the sensation traveled all the way back down through her thighs to the eddy of pleasure between her legs.

It was all too good, but she needed more. She was so close, and reached down to touch him as he moved in and out, her fingers firm around the base of his erection.

"That's so hot, Abby," he said, watching.

She pressed on her clit then, rubbing, knowing what she needed and liking the way he watched so greedily. Hot sensation immediately coursed through her body, everything tightening, her muscles clenching down on his cock so hard it almost ached.

"Oh, yeah, Abby," he ground out, thrusting faster, deeper.

Suddenly all of the tightness melted, her climax overcoming her and drawing him along as well. Abby had never felt anything quite so pure in her life, she was sure of it.

Minutes later, Reece released her legs and fell to her side, pulling her over next to him as they both caught their breath, calming down from what Abby was sure had to be the most intense, incredible sex she'd ever had.

"I may not be able to move from this bed today," she said jokingly, though when she did try to move her leg, it felt like spaghetti. Her muscles felt as if they actually had melted.

"You'll get no arguments from me," Reece said

with evil glee, propping up on one elbow at her side. He ran his finger along her sternum, down her belly, and stopped at the edge of her sex. "I thought about tying you to it at one point."

She was surprised, then she smiled.

"Maybe we could take turns."

"Sounds like a plan."

"I still can't feel my legs," she admitted, laughing.

"I'm a bit dizzy myself, but even so, I want more," he said, leaning in for a kiss.

"Me, too," she said, touching his face, running her finger along his lips. He darted his tongue out to taste her. "I want more, too."

"We can do anything," he said. "Everything. Whatever you want or need. Just say so."

In the years since her few crazy experiences in college, her lovers had been nice but uncreative men, the sex more or less vanilla, and she hadn't realized how many fantasies she had packed away. If Reece was willing to explore them with her...?

"Maybe I should write up a list, you know, like for Santa. All the things I want you to do to me, and what I'd like to do to you," she said naughtily, grinning.

"Hmm...that could be interesting. We could make it our goal to make sure every item is attended to," he said, trailing his hand over her breast, in long strokes up and down her torso, down her arm, back up again, back over her breast until she trembled.

She wanted him again, right now. Amazing.

"Roll over."

"Why?"

"Just do it," he said, commanding but gentle.

With a little shiver of pleasure, she did, snuggling down into the soft material of his comforter. It was warm and soft, smelling like sex, and she was in heaven.

Reece pushed up, balancing himself as he levered over her, straddling the backs of her thighs, and then she felt the next-best thing to sex that she could imagine as his hands slid up either side of her spine and continued to massage in slow, thorough motions.

"That feels amazing…where did you learn to give massages?" she said.

"Here and there…but giving a massage can feel as good as getting one," he responded.

As he worked her neck, she sighed. "Somehow I doubt that," she said on another sigh, followed by a moan as he leaned forward and was inside of her again, moving in a lazy rhythm that matched the motion of his hands.

She'd never even imagined so much physical sensation being possible. He kept rubbing, moving over her and inside of her until she was clawing her fingers into the quilt and rotating her hips beneath him. It was so slow, it was torture. It was perfect.

His hands slipped down to work their magic on her derriere, massaging and squeezing. She pushed up on her elbows, thrusting back against him, seeking more. He kept up the constant gentle rhythm, a steady beat of pleasure, as if making love to her was a song. She fell to the bed again, giving herself up to him and enjoying every second of it.

He never stopped touching her, through her orgasm and then through his own. Abby drifted off to sleep later, thinking that she'd definitely given herself the best Christmas present she could have ever imagined.

REECE HADN'T FELT SO good since, well, since he couldn't remember. He'd slept some more after making love to Abby, and it had been a deep, dreamless, drugless sleep, which he hadn't known in quite some time.

When he saw the mess he'd made of the nightstand, breaking one of his mother's antique lamps, he wished he could remember the dream. The only impression he was ever left with was that of being horribly trapped, dying, until someone touched him. Abby. As if she had reached directly into his terror and made it stop.

He cleaned the mess while she was still sleeping, liking the way her foot dangled over the edge of his bed. A silly thing to trip his heart rate, but nearly enough to make him slide his hand up the arch and crawl back in with her. He'd lived in France too long not to have developed at least a little bit of a romantic streak, he guessed, as he smiled at her pretty pink toes.

Instead, he pulled himself away and pushed through a punishing workout, especially after the wonderful but rich dinner Abby had cooked the night before.

He'd been way off the nutritional regimen that he usually adhered to during the year, but things were always a little more slack around the holidays—more sweets, more wine—and so he had to make up for it with exercise.

Racing was more punishing on the body that most people imagined, requiring a lot of strength to turn a car that was pushing down three Gs. He had to work twice as hard now.

He was feeling strong today, though. Energized. There was no numbness, no pins and needles. A second round of push-ups was interrupted by the doorbell, and he went quickly to answer, hoping not to wake Abby. Much to his surprise, Charles stood at the door, frowning through the ring of the wreath Abby had hung over the panes of glass the day before.

"What the hell is all of this?" Charles asked, looking back at the trees set up on the large front lawn as he stepped inside.

"Good morning to you, too," Reece said dryly, not offering to take Charles's coat. "To what do I owe this impromptu visit so very early in the morning?"

Charles glared. "It's not impromptu—we have an appointment with the Keller rep in a half hour, and I thought we had talked about staging? Why all the trees and lights? What's going on?"

Reece had been remiss in telling Charles about Abby moving in, and so he proceeded to do that, watching the real estate agent's face redden as he spoke. When he was done, Charles didn't say anything, but went outside, peering over across the field past the trees on the lawn to the blackened buildings on the hill before he stomped back in.

"Okay, okay, let's not panic. This could work for us."

"What do you mean?"

"Well, we'd talked about her selling, in a package deal with you, right? Maybe now that would be even more appealing—certainly more appealing than having that right in the line of view from the front door. And that barn—that alone would bring down the property value—"

Reece held up his hand. "Stop right there. The barn is fine, she keeps her horses there, and I can guarantee you there's no way she's selling. And I know she'd regret causing us any inconvenience by having her home almost burnt to the ground," he said, not bothering to hide his sarcasm, "but I'm letting her work through the end of the holiday season here, period. It's good for us, too, since I have inventory to clear out."

"So why all the trees? You selling those, too, now?"

"It's for a tasting event. They are having a tree-decorating contest and giving away a case of wine and a weekend at their inn, when it's rebuilt, to the winner."

"Cute. But we can't have this all going on while we're trying to show the place—she'll have to be willing to clear out when we're bringing prospective buyers through."

Reece pushed a hand though his hair, and didn't have time to argue as another car pulled up in front of the house, and a burly man in a black suit approached the house. He stopped and looked out over the land,

and Reece could see him bulldozing just by how he surveyed the property.

Reece didn't bother to grab a jacket and the three of them walked the property, the Keller rep obviously liking what he saw. Reece liked what he saw, too. It had been a while since he'd walked the land, taking in the view of crystal blue Cayuga Lake, breathing in the clean air.

Standing among the rolling hills of vines, snow bright on the branches of trees that marked the boundaries, he wondered how he'd never noticed how similar the place was to where he lived in France. Just as beautiful, just as pristine. Showing it to the Keller sales rep was like seeing it himself for the first time.

"We'd be willing to offer you top dollar, Winston. This is a great location, driving distance to the city, and having bought it from a famous local celebrity can only add to its draw. We're thinking we could use the local vineyards as a jumping-off point, give the development a vineyard theme, all of the streets named after certain kind of grapes, maybe name the place Vineyard Hills, or something to that effect," the man said, obviously getting way ahead of himself.

"Yeah, I always wondered about that," Reece said. "Why developers come into a place, clear out all the pine trees and then name them all after what they cleared out…"

Charles glared, but the Keller rep laughed and slapped him on the shoulder. Reece had expected some slimy sales guy, but this man was local and down-to-earth in a way a lot of central New York people were. He didn't take offense at all.

"Just the way of the business, I guess."

Reece liked him, which made it harder to think of Keller as so bad. He was a businessman looking to do business, and so why did it all irritate him so much?

"The property down the line might be for sale as well," Charles added as they stood on the front porch again, nodding down toward Abby's place. "Maybe we could work out some kind of package deal?"

"Charles—" Reece interrupted, but he didn't get far.

"I'd have to talk to the boss, but that could be a very appealing prospect," Keller agreed. "I know you want to sell, and we'd be happy to talk about some kind of package, but we're also looking at a prime piece of property over on Kueka, so we'll decide which way we want to go, but we won't wait indefinitely," he said.

Reece nodded and bit his tongue as he noticed movement inside the window. Abby was up. He wasn't going to get into this now. They shook hands with a promise to stay in contact, and the Keller guy left.

Charles looked disgusted. "He wants it, Reece, and if you know what's smart, you'll move your friend out of here as soon as possible and off-load this place, and hers, if you can get it. If not, you're going to have it shackled to your ankle for some time, or take a huge loss," he warned before walking down toward his own car.

Reece's good morning vibe evaporated, and he stood on the porch watching Charles leave. There was no way he was asking Abby to leave before the holiday season was over, and he had to hope that wouldn't get in the way of a deal. He knew he should be putting the sale first—Abby was a big girl—but he'd made a promise, and he intended to keep it.

Walking back into the house, the warmth and the scent of coffee and pine trees wrapped around him in welcome. The strong sense of being *home* was disconcerting, making him stop in the entryway and look around the room. Maybe Charles was right about the staging. When the house was empty, his parents gone, no decorations, he could look at it as a building to be sold.

Now, with Abby's coat over the back of the chair, her bag on the table, the tree in the corner, and some boxes of ornaments still stashed by the wall, the place looked…lived in.

Was he making a mistake?

He heard her talking in the other room, on the phone, and wondered how what had been so black and white just the day before was now not clear at all.

CHAPTER SEVEN

ABBY AWAKENED FEELING like a cat, warm, loose-muscled and well-tuned, but the minute her feet had hit the floor, doubts had set in and chaos followed her every footstep right into the shower.

She'd slept with Reece. That seemed like a tremendous understatement. The luscious, carnal hours made her warm with arousal even now and blew her previous idea of what "good sex" could be right out of the water.

It had been *great* sex.

Still, in the very bright light of day that was glaring off the snow-covered ground, they would have to face each other and the realities between them.

The morning began with a second call for Reece from Danielle, which Abby overheard while making coffee. The woman sounded irritated as she left her message on the machine, and guilt assailed Abby for forgetting Danielle's first one.

Jealousy also kicked in, and Abby knew she couldn't afford that. It was just sex, and being jealous wasn't part of the bargain. She'd make sure he knew about Danielle's calls as soon as she saw him, which made her wonder where he was.

She looked out the front window when she heard voices and saw a black sedan parked out front, Keller Industries written in neat, white lettering on one door.

Her hands turned cold as she saw the three men round the corner of the tasting rooms and come up to the house. They stood on the porch, apparently enjoying their conversation, looking over at *her* property, once, at least, their expressions speculative.

Coffee turned to acid in her stomach as she watched Reece smile and shake hands with the guy from Keller.

Her cell phone rang, and she turned toward the table near the Christmas tree they had decorated together the night before, her mind still on Reece even as the speaker on the other end addressed her. The whole incredible evening was starting to feel like a lie, a huge mistake.

Then, what she was hearing made those concerns seem like mere annoyances, her mind snapping to attention. "What do you mean the insurance payments have been halted?" she asked, setting her cup down on the counter before she dropped it.

"The complete fire investigator's report showed that while the fire was caused by an electrical short, it came closer to the wall by where one of your trees was plugged in, not at the source of your wiring problem in the ceiling."

Abby blinked. "So?"

"There is some indication that the wires could have been tampered with when the tree was set up."

Abby's jaw dropped, and her mind blanked with disbelief.

"Are you saying you think the fire was intentionally set?"

"It's not certain, but any doubt creates the need for a larger investigation before we can pay out. We have to make sure there's no fraud concern, you understand."

He said it so politely, accusing her of setting fire to her own home, as if it was just business.

"They're bringing in another investigator to make a new report, but until then, any progress on rebuilding or payment has to be stopped. We're very sorry for the inconvenience," the insurance agent said.

"How long will this take?" Abby knew the fire was an accident, but any delay on scheduling new construction would further eat into her reopening the following year.

"The investigator will be there Monday, but the report could take a few weeks. With the holidays, everything is slowed down, but I'm sure they'll get on it as soon as possible. Can you also supply them with the names of the company that brought in the trees?"

"You think they might have tampered with my wiring? I can assure you, they didn't. No one did. This was just an accident. My family has done business with them for years. This is just some stupid misunderstanding."

"Either way, they'll be conducting interviews and getting all of the information they can."

Abby was numb as she hung up the phone and heard the front door open.

Reece.

She had to compose herself, to hide her distress. She didn't want to talk about this new mess with him right now.

But as soon as she moved, her phone rang again.

Looking down, she closed her eyes when she saw her father's name on the caller ID.

Tears stung behind her eyelids seeing her dad's name. She wished so much they were here, and at the same time, she was glad they weren't. In spite of what she had to tell them, she was relieved to hear her father's voice on the line when she picked up the call.

"Hi, Dad," she said, her voice breaking immediately even though she promised herself she'd remain stalwart. She tried, only crying a little as she told them everything, including the new trouble.

As Reece and Hannah predicted, her parents were shocked, but their first concern was her safety, and they were clearly not as worried about the property, to an extent that left Abby somewhat surprised.

"I guess I thought you'd be more upset," she said to her dad, somewhat confused. "You built this place. You devoted everything to it."

"Oh, honey, we are, but more so that you have to deal with all of this alone. Should we come home?"

"No, no, please don't. I'm not alone. I have Hannah, and Reece has been so generous," she said, wanting them to know she wasn't completely on her own, as much as she missed them. "And besides, there's not much I can do until the insurance works itself out, I guess, and they do this new investigation."

"Well, that's just absurd," her mother said, joining in the call on conference. "Dad will make a call to Harold this afternoon," her mom assured. Harold was their longtime insurance agent who had retired, but probably still would have some good advice.

"I'm glad you're taking it okay," Abby said. "I was so worried about telling you."

"Sweetheart, all we care about is that you are unhurt, and it's so good to know Beau and Buttercup and the other pets are safe. When you see the kinds of things we've seen here in Haiti, helping people rebuild when they have so little, or just getting clean water running, it tends to help straighten out priorities," her mom added, and Abby heard her father's murmured assent in the background.

"You just say the word, and we'll come back if you need us. You're our first priority and always will be," her mom said.

"I'm fine, Mom, really. I'm good here at Reece's through the season, and hopefully after that, things will be more settled. I can stay with Hannah until the house is back to rights," she added.

"I'm so impressed that Reece stepped up like that," her mother said. "Not that he wasn't always a nice young man, and I think he did have a bit of a crush on you," she said, and Abby's eyes widened as she heard the smile in her mom's voice.

"Reece? Have a crush on me? Hardly," she scoffed.

"He was a handsome boy," her mom continued. "I

take it he's recovering from that awful accident? And his father is doing well?"

Abby filled her mom in on everything. Okay, not *everything,* although she had that sneaking feeling that her parents could sense something more than being neighborly was between her and Reece. She did nothing to encourage that idea—there was no point when she and Reece were clearly just having a holiday fling that would be over soon enough.

She stared at the blinking red light on the phone to her left. Danielle.

Nevermind, that. She was here, now, and some woman an ocean away was not her concern. She felt marginally better. At least telling her parents hadn't been as terrible as she thought it might be, and her parents were right.

When she hung up, Abby felt more in control of things. As her parents pointed out, there were people in the world with much bigger problems than hers. She was alive, healthy and able to deal with whatever life put in front of her.

She wished she felt so confident about her emotions concerning Reece as she heard him in the front room. Taking another deep breath, she went out to meet him. No sense in avoiding it.

She stepped through the hall and stopped in her tracks the minute their eyes met, her composure flying out the window as she remembered every single touch, kiss and more. She wanted to cross the room and throw herself up against him, to feel the warm solidity of his body and forget everything else.

His brow lowered, and he looked at her, concerned. Probably because she was just standing there like a moron.

"Abby, you okay?"

"I talked to my folks" was the first thing out of her mouth, and while she didn't move, he did, crossing the room to pull her in. He was so warm, even though he was only wearing a heavy sweater coming in from outside.

"How did it go?" he asked.

She nodded, her cheek rubbing against the rough wool that covered his chest, his warmth seeping through, comforting her.

"They took it better than I imagined. I guess they've seen so much devastation, they have a different perspective on things," she said.

This wasn't going at all as she had planned. It was wrong to feel so good being able to talk to him while he stood there, holding her. His hands were rubbing over her back, and the comfort started to turn hot as sparks of desire leapt between them.

Should they talk about the night before? What was there to say? She pushed back gently, trying to rein her reactions in.

"Um, I don't know if you noticed, but you have a message on the kitchen phone. And I forgot to tell you last night," she said, feeling her cheeks heat annoyingly.

"A woman, Danielle, called yesterday, and I picked up the phone without thinking, and I promised her I would give you the message, which she said you would know who it was, and then I forgot to let you know, with everything that…happened," she babbled, lowering her gaze to his mouth.

He had such a great mouth.

"Danielle called?" he said then, sounding pleased. Her heart sank.

"Yeah, um, I just thought you should know. I didn't know if you checked the machine, it's hard to notice that little blinking light on your parents' phone unless you are standing in there right by the sink, and so I wanted to make sure you knew," she said, babbling again in the face of her discomfort. "I'm sorry I forgot yesterday."

Was the smile on his face because of Danielle?

"No need to apologize. I miss calls on that all the time—I'm surprised she didn't call my cell, but she might not have international minutes, I guess. Thanks," he said, not elaborating. Why would he?

"Old friend?" she asked spontaneously when he didn't offer more, then bit her lip and looked away, regretting giving in to the urge.

"Yeah," Reece said easily, apparently thinking nothing of it. "Actually, her brother, Gerard, was a driver and a good friend of mine since I'd moved to Europe. He was killed in a nonracing crash a few years ago."

Abby lifted a hand to her mouth. "Oh, no, that's awful. I'm so sorry."

"Yeah, it was hard on all of us. He was a great guy, helped me get into the sport. Danielle was his only sibling, and we spent some time together after he was gone. She helped me a lot last year," he said, shaking his head, remembering.

"There were days I might not have gotten up to bother with my physical therapy if she hadn't been there, cursing me out in three languages if I whined about it," he said, laughing at the memory.

Abby was silent. And she thought they had history? How could she compete with something like that? Danielle had been with Reece day after day through a time in his life he didn't really even want to talk to Abby about. It made her feel on the outside, in spite of the closeness they'd shared just hours before.

"I'm glad you had someone there for you," she said slowly, and she meant it, even if it cost her something to admit.

"I guess I was, too, even if at the time I didn't always like her very much for ranting at me and pushing me. I guess she figured she'd fill in for Gerard, at least, that's what Tomás told me once."

"Tomás?"

"Danielle's husband. She spent so much time at the hospital with me, he said he felt like a single parent," Reece said. "But I was grateful for her pushing. She convinced me I could do anything I wanted to do, even go back to racing. It took some of the worry off of my parents, too, knowing she was there."

Danielle's husband. The words rang in Abby's mind. She'd been thinking the sexy-sounding French woman had been a lover, picturing a svelte vixen who warmed Reece's bed when he was in Europe.

In fact, she sounded like a good friend, and a wonderful person—a much better person than Abby felt like at the moment.

"Why are you frowning?" Reece asked, watching her closely.

"I, uh…never mind," she said, not about to confess that she'd been jealous of a woman she not only didn't know but had absolutely no good reason to be jealous of.

"I saw you were meeting with the Keller rep this morning. And the man you were at the café with the other day?" she asked, changing the subject.

His mouth flattened. "Yeah, he's interested, but we're not making any deals yet."

"Yet," she echoed softly. "When?"

"They haven't made a formal offer. They're considering a couple of other properties as well."

"Including mine?" she asked.

He blinked in surprise. "Why do you say that?"

"I happened to see you all looking over there, and the man you were with pointed to my buildings. So I wondered what that was about."

Reece was notably uncomfortable. He turned, talking as he randomly reorganized some boxes that were in the path of the hallway.

"They saw it and wondered about the fire," he explained haltingly, then sighed. "But, yes, it would be more attractive to them to get both properties in a package deal. They thought that since you had the fire, you might be interested in selling, too."

"I'm not."

"I told them that," he said, making eye contact. "I

know you don't want to sell. I know this affects you, too, my selling. I can't promise I'm going to sell to someone you'll approve of—"

"Keller," she said woodenly.

"Maybe. If there are options, we can talk about them."

"Okay."

"But Abby?"

"Hmm?"

"I am going back to Europe and back to racing, sooner than later if I have my way. I need you to know that."

She knew it, but she couldn't help asking what was on her mind since she'd seen him in the café. "I thought the news said, I mean, they said the doctors said..." She faltered, hating to say it out loud.

"That my injuries were too severe, I know. That I would probably never make the full recovery needed to race again," he bit out, looking away, bitterness and determination carved into every line of his face. "I know what they say." He pushed a hand through his hair.

He looked so tense, she took a step closer, trying to find something encouraging to say. "Well, you seem pretty healthy to me," she said with a smile. "What are they waiting for?"

He looked up and seemed to relax a little.

"I have relapses, numbness, some pins and needles, and my reflex time has slowed down. I can build it back up if I can get back into proper training. The longer I'm here..."

She nodded, keeping her tone neutral. "The harder it is for you to get back in."

He sighed. "I'll be easily forgotten, replaced, if I don't get back in soon. I have to show them I can do it."

"Why?" Why did he want to return to a sport that almost killed him and might not take him back?

He stared at her in surprise. "I love it. It's the one thing I have ever really loved doing, really excelled at."

She frowned, thinking back. Reece had been an excellent student and athlete.

"I find that hard to believe."

"It's true. I was good at a lot of things, but nothing was my passion. Sometimes I ever wondered if I would have one. My dad would always say how he'd had wine in his blood and he felt so connected to this place. Ben knew what he wanted to do, to design golf courses, since he stepped foot on one when he was ten. I never had that focus, that desire, until I found racing. I can't even think of what else I would do with myself," he said, sounding slightly hollow, and her heart went out to him. "It's all I know."

"I can understand that," she said, and she did. She loved her home, her business, and she couldn't imagine any other work, either.

She took a deep breath, closing her eyes, then opening them again. "Give me a week. I'm meeting with Hannah to see if there's any way for me to liquidate assets and maybe buy you out. I don't know if it's possible, but maybe we could work something out, if you're willing."

He nodded. "I'd love you to have the place, and if there's a way we can do that, I'm all for it. I know my parents would be thrilled, too. We don't want to sell to Keller, but the market is so hard now, and we can't keep this place running for long."

"I'll do what I can," she said, but hope faded as she thought about the insurance money not coming through.

It had been feasible that she could have used that as a down payment, but she didn't tell Reece that. "And if we can't, and if you have to sell to Keller, do it. Maybe you can even leave earlier, get back to your life, your training," she said, proud of how calm she sounded.

"Trying to get rid of me, Abby?" He offered a small, slanted smile, but it didn't reach his eyes.

"No, but you obviously need to get back. The sooner the better, right?" She sounded brittle to her own ears.

He stood close again, and she resisted the urge to lift a hand, to touch him. How had this become so difficult so quickly?

"And until then?"

She didn't want to talk. She didn't want to debate the options and treat what was between them like a contract, discussing the terms and what-ifs.

She wanted him, and she had the chance to spend some time with him over the holiday. She'd be too busy to deal with a broken heart later, she figured.

Reaching up, she slid her hands around his neck, linking her arms behind and pulling his mouth down to hers.

"In the meantime, we have this," she said, kissing him until talking wasn't what either of them was interested in.

CHAPTER EIGHT

ABBY KNEW REECE WAS avoiding her, she just didn't know why.

In the three days since their talk, their last kiss—a kiss that hadn't led to a night in his bed—they'd both been busy and preoccupied.

When she was at the house, he seemed to be gone, and she was too busy even when he was there, working in the tasting room until late hours, getting things set up, preparing for the upcoming wedding and Christmas events.

As before, she'd come home to find him already in bed, his light shining under the closed door, or in the workout room going through the punishing routine that he did two or three times a day now. She didn't want to interrupt.

She hadn't slept well for those lonely nights, and so maybe this was best. She had too much happening to lose sleep over relationship drama.

Like right now, Abby was trying to get the supplies out to the yard where the Christmas trees waited. Hannah was supposed to have come with help an hour ago, but called to say she had a bad tire and had to have it changed before she could pick up their other part-timer for the day and get out there.

So Abby was on her own. Again. She didn't like to complain—she loved her work—but so much of it had come down on her shoulders recently, she was starting to feel it more than ever.

In a short while, the yard would fill with parents and children for the Christmas tree-decorating contest. Tasting was set up for the parents, with cases of both Maple Hills and Winston Vineyard wines up for first prize, with single bottles for second and third, along with fun prizes for the kids, who could also take part in a snowball-throwing contest and a snowman build-a-thon. The first-place winner would also get a free weekend at her inn next summer as a way to promote future business, and to ensure people would know she was rebuilding.

Boxes of lights, garland and unbreakable ornaments as well as popcorn were ready to be strung, along with other creative decorations that had to be hauled out to the yard and set up. Everything had to be ready to start just past noon. She'd been running behind all morning and could have used a hand, waiting for Hannah and her other helper.

Reece's truck was over by the barn, but she hadn't seen him yet. He had come in late the night before and was probably sleeping in. Besides, he'd been clear that he didn't want to be too involved with the everyday business of the winery. He was handling the Winston inventory and sales, and answered any questions she had, but otherwise, he stayed out of it.

Now that seemed to include her, too, apparently. She didn't understand it, but something had changed after their talk. Maybe he realized he'd made a mistake, or maybe he had simply gotten what he wanted.

She had, too, right? So why did it hurt so much now? She'd gone into it with her eyes open. They hadn't made any commitments. No promises. Reece had made it clear he was still poised to leave, and she had been the one throwing herself back at him. Maybe, in his way, he had been trying to back away, but she just didn't get it. Why couldn't he just tell her so instead of avoiding her? Or maybe he had only meant it to be a one-night thing, and she had misunderstood.

She was about to pick up another full box and bring it out to the yard when she heard footsteps, Reece coming down the creaky hardwood stairs from his room. He turned the corner, pausing when he saw her. She was grateful to see him, but also worried. He looked like he hadn't slept all night, either.

"Hey," she said, unable to ignore the way the brown hair mussed, the five o'clock shadow thick on his jaw. His body was probably still warm from sleep, and the magnetic pull toward him was hard to resist. But she did. She leaned down and picked up the box instead, holding it in front of her like a barrier.

"Hey," he said back, looking toward the kitchen.

"There's still coffee if you want some," she offered.

"Thanks," he said, taking a few steps in that direction, and she noticed him wince, a hitch on his left side.

"Are you okay?"

"I'm fine," he said. "Just had a rough night."

There was no warmth in his voice, and she felt awkward and exposed standing there, even though she was dressed in her winter coat and sweater. None of it seemed enough to keep the hurt his tone caused from penetrating into her chest.

She told herself to stop being stupid. He'd had a bad night and was tired and a little grumpy, that was all. Maybe he just needed some downtime, or some fun.

"Okay, well, we have the tree-decorating contest today. It's going to be a good time, and you're welcome to join. In fact—"

"Listen, Abby, I don't think I can do this. It's too complicated," he said wearily.

"It's just trees, Reece, we're going to—"

"I don't mean the trees," he said abruptly and shuffled off into the kitchen.

Abby took the box outside without another word, hoping the cold slap of air on her cheeks would freeze the tears stinging behind her eyes. So, he had been trying to break things off, and she hadn't understood. Now she did.

Still, did he have to be so harsh? What had she done to deserve that?

Whatever warmth was between them seemed to have evaporated. Maybe it was better. Being together like they were would only make it harder, and she couldn't say he wasn't honest about things.

Yes, this was better, she thought, her heart aching as she dropped the box by the Christmas trees and turned to get another one, pulling her coat tighter as the sun dipped behind a cloud.

Then anger set in. He might be having a hard time of it, but that was no reason to treat her badly.

Whatever was going on, she deserved better treatment from him than being so easily dismissed, she thought as she walked back in for another box and stepped past them and into the kitchen instead. She stopped in the doorway, hearing two voices, realizing Reece had turned on the speakerphone.

She should leave, she thought, but her feet didn't seem to move.

"I can do it, Joe, give me a chance to show you. Whatever little things are still bugging me, I can ignore them. It's not a big deal," Reece said, tense.

"If it were just up to me, I'd give you a shot, but it's not. Something happens to that car this early in the game, I don't have to tell you how bad that would be. I'll be out of a job, and we'll both have lawsuits landing on us. The doc says no. Sorry to say it, but you're out, Reece. It's just a shitty break."

"I don't give a damn what he says, how the hell can he know what I'm able to do?" Reece's voice rose.

The other man sighed audibly over the phone. "Reece, you need to accept reality. It can't happen. You're one lucky bastard as it is, having survived that wreck. What's still wrong with your body is enough to take you out at two hundred if something goes wrong, and you know it. Why go take a second chance at killing yourself?"

"I'd be fine. Just let me do some test drives in January, I'll show you."

Abby's heart squeezed painfully for him; he wanted this so much, and it didn't sound like things were going his way.

"I'll see what I can do, Reece. But you haven't been

cleared on the post-traumatic stress issues, either. The doctor said you stopped the counseling."

Abby froze. PTS? She'd heard more about that in the news lately, with returning soldiers, but she hadn't thought about it in terms of things like a car accident. But it made perfect sense—anytime someone almost lost their life, especially if there were violent circumstances, post-traumatic stress would be an issue.

She put a hand to her lips. Maybe that was why Reece was acting so erratically, having nightmares and so forth. Her anger melted in the face of new information.

"I'm fine. Take my word for it."

"Well, the sponsors are looking at a new guy, an up-and-comer, got a hot record so far, and..."

Abby didn't hear the rest of what the guy had to say. She watched as Reece's head fell forward in a clear expression of his frustration and unhappiness at the news.

She took a step, then another, needing to comfort him in some way, his earlier surliness forgotten. None of that mattered. All that she cared about at the moment was being there for Reece, the way he'd been there for her lately.

REECE HAD SO MANY emotions crashing together inside of him, he didn't know which one to deal with first. Anger that they wouldn't listen and that the damned doctors wouldn't clear him. Betrayal that they wouldn't trust him to do what he was so good at doing, that they were just writing him off.

Fear that he'd never get to drive again, or maybe

he was way past fear and closer to panic. Joe said the team was already lining up someone new.

When he looked up from where he had braced his hands against the counter over a cooling cup of coffee and saw Abby looking at him with her heart in her eyes, he added embarrassment to the mix.

"Joe, I have to go. See what you can do, I'll be in touch," he said, hanging up abruptly.

"Reece..." she began.

"Eavesdropping, Abby?"

"No!" She closed her eyes, blowing out a breath. "I mean, not on purpose. I came back in to talk, and you were on the phone, and I just...heard," she explained.

"I see."

He knew that he'd growled at her when he came downstairs, still groggy from the painkillers he was taking to help him sleep through the pain in his left leg that had been torturing him for the last few days.

He hadn't touched Abby since their conversation about the sale, and he didn't intend to. While she had come to him even after he told her it could never be more than sex, he decided to put some distance between them, to cool things off, for both of their sakes. It didn't matter that he wanted more, too. He knew they were getting in too deep, too fast, and it wouldn't be good for either of them in the end. Better to hurt her now, the way he saw it.

He hadn't counted on it, but he missed her like hell, and that pissed him off, too, unaccountably. He'd avoided emotional complications with women, and this was why.

The first two nights he'd been awake, he'd only been able to think about her being a few yards down the hall, and how much he wanted her. He'd paced, tossed and turned, worked out and then, probably due to anxiety and lack of sleep, his left side started acting up worse than ever.

So last night he'd turned to the painkillers to smother the pain, which was now accompanied by a burning sensation that was a new kind of agony. If it kept up, he knew he'd have to go in to see the doctors, but he was determined to make it stop or to learn to ignore it. He was trying hard to ignore it.

Abby chewed her lip, watching him, looking unsure. He grabbed the coffee and then set it down, his fingers curling tightly as he fought the urge to go to her, to smooth over his harsh words.

"I'm so sorry, Reece."

"For what?"

"That they don't want you to race anymore," she said, her words soft, pained, for him.

He frowned, not wanting her sympathy. That was the last thing he wanted. "Don't waste your pity on me, Abby. I am going to drive again, and soon."

"But he said—"

"I know what he said. They might have some new hotshot lined up, but I can talk to the sponsors myself. I have a strong record, a following, and there's nothing fans like more than a comeback. I will make a hell of a lot more money for them, and get more wins, than someone green out of the gate," he said, almost convincing himself.

"What about the post-traumatic stress?"

"That's nothing. A few nightmares, some lost sleep. It will pass. The rest I can handle."

"Maybe dismissing it too easily is part of the problem," she offered.

Reece put a hand up. Abby was a good friend who meant well, he knew, but her words got his back up. He wanted to keep their friendship in place, but he also wasn't going to have this conversation with her.

"Abby, listen. I care about you, and I want us to be friends, but there's a lot you don't know about me. I know my own limitations."

"You have to talk about it with someone," she countered.

"Not you."

"Why not?"

"Abby, we slept together. That doesn't give you a free pass into my life," he said. "Besides, it's not like you don't have your own agenda. The longer I stay, the better for you, putting off the sale, right?"

He regretted the words as they passed his lips, but was unable to resist the urge to push her away.

Why? Because she was right? Was Joe right, too?

He couldn't deal with it and turned to leave, surprised when he felt her hand on his arm, pulling him back around.

She was furious, her eyes were mossy green, darkened by emotion. Her hand left his arm to settle on her hip, but he'd missed her so much that even such a quick touch left its impression.

"Are you serious? You think I am sleeping with you to stall you from selling?"

He didn't, he never thought that, but he didn't say so. If she hated his guts, things would probably work out easier for both of them. She had enough to think about without worrying about his problems, too.

She shook her head in astonishment. "I'm not sure who that is more insulting toward, me or you," she said.

"I'm sorry, Abby, it's just that I've been here before. I've been with women who think sex is more, and I know the signs."

Now her mouth was gaping at him.

"Need an ego adjustment, Reece? I have a lot going on, and yes, I don't want you selling to Keller, but I've accepted that you might. I've known from the start what we have…had…was temporary. Don't think I am hanging my future on you. My future is over there." She pointed out the window to her winery, and he saw her hand tremble. She was clearly furious, and she was right.

"I'm sorry, Abby. I just didn't want you getting the idea that I would stay, or that sleeping together means more than it does."

She shook her head, looking at him like she'd never seen him before.

"Don't worry, Reece. As far as I'm concerned, it didn't mean a damned thing."

Reece closed his eyes, wishing he knew a better way to handle this, but he was fighting on so many fronts, he didn't know what else to do. He felt as if he was fighting the whole damned world and himself, and he was tired of it.

He started to say something, he wasn't even sure what, but she'd already started to leave the room. He stepped forward, thinking about following, but instead he grabbed his jacket from the hook by the door and went out the back door to the barn with his cold coffee.

"HEY, WHERE'S REECE?" Hannah asked Abby, smiling at a young girl who stood with her father, waiting on a paper cup of hot chocolate. "Anything interesting progressing there?" she asked slyly.

The father took a small tasting glass of Baco Noir, and Hannah marked his plastic bracelet with a second check—no one got more than three tastings in the course of an hour, even if they spat between tastings, so that they were okay to drive when they left.

Abby hadn't filled in Hannah on everything going on, but that was because she had an event to focus on, which was good. Having a couple dozen people flying in every direction and Christmas trees being decorated kept her from dwelling on what had happened that morning.

She was still furious, though maybe with herself as much as anything. How could she have been so stupid?

"Hardly. He's around here somewhere," she said vaguely. Reece hadn't left, and he hadn't been in the house the last time she went inside, sparing them both another awkward moment.

She'd heard some noises coming from one of the barns, the sounds of power tools. He must be working on something, though she didn't go to find out what. She didn't care.

Well, the sad fact was that she *did* care, but she had to stop. The ache that had been dully thudding in the background of her heart all afternoon became so sharp as she replayed his words in her mind that she swallowed hard and pushed it back down. This was not the time.

Hannah watched father and daughter walk away, her eyes clearly focused on the man's butt, distracting Abby enough to make her smile.

"Why are all the cute ones married?" Her friend sighed. "What I wouldn't give for just one night of unbelievably hot sex right now."

Abby coughed, looking around to make sure none of the children or parents had overheard Hannah's heartfelt wish.

"Weren't you dating that lawyer?"

"Yeah, that was over weeks ago. He was boring. I could hardly get through dinner on our first date without falling asleep in my spaghetti. That was enough for me."

"Oh."

"Yeah. And it's getting pretty sparse out there. I can't date the guys I work with, of course, and most of the other men our age I've known since we were kids. If I slept with one of them, everyone in town would know and my mother would have us married."

Hannah sighed, pouring herself a larger glass of

the noir. "What I need is some wild, kinky sex with someone who's not local. I'd settle for just one night with a guy whose mother or friends I might not bump into the next day at the store."

Abby shook her head, grimacing. "Watch what you wish for."

"I'm willing to risk it," Hannah said. "But I take it things fizzled between you and Reece?"

"More like they imploded," she said, closing her eyes at the hitch in her voice.

"Oh, no, honey…you fell for him, didn't you?"

"Not really. Well, a little," Abby admitted. "It's not like I am madly in love with him or going to jump off a cliff, but I thought we had something. Then he—he just decided that we didn't. I didn't see it coming, not really. I knew it was temporary, but he just ended it and let me know later," she said, filling Hannah in on the gruesome details of that morning's conversation.

"Jerk."

"It's complicated for him, I know, but I can't believe he actually thought I would be so naive," she said, and told Hannah about the phone call she heard and their resulting argument.

Hannah looked thoughtful for a moment. "My Aunt had PTS after a bad car accident—she couldn't even ride in a car for a long time, let alone drive, and it can make people act very strangely, but it sounds more like Reece's ego is just too big for his body, nice as that body is. You have to watch out for yourself, too. You were just trying to help," Hannah said, giving her a hug.

"Yes, that's exactly it! He knows all about my life, he helped me with recovering from the fire, he has been there for me every step of the way, which was just…incredible," Abby said, swiping a hand at a tear that snuck out.

"But then, when I reach out to him, when I want to help, he swatted me back. Told me not to mistake sex for the right to care about him, basically," she concluded with a sniff.

"Ouch."

"Yeah."

"Well, maybe in some ass-backward male way he's trying to protect you by pushing you away," Hannah offered, shrugging.

"Yeah, maybe, but it's stupid."

"Well, he's a *guy,*" Hannah said, and for the first time in hours Abby had reason to laugh.

"I guess. A lesson learned, I suppose."

"And you had some great sex, got to live out a high-school fantasy and got back in the game."

"I would hardly call it getting back in the game," Abby said. "Probably heading for another long dry spell."

They both looked over at the people happily decorating trees. She envied their simple holiday cheer.

"Oh, I don't know. I think you might be putting out the sex vibe."

"The *what?*"

Hannah grinned. "The sex vibe. It's probably pheromones or something, but when someone is sexually active, it's like they put out a signal and attract other people who are interested, too."

"Hannah, what the heck are you talking about? Give me that wine, you've had too much," Abby said, laughing.

"See for yourself," Hannah said, holding her glass back where Abby couldn't reach it. "A totally hot guy has been checking you out all day."

Abby had no idea what Hannah was talking about until she spotted two cute guys standing by the far edge of the crowd of half-decorated Christmas trees. One smiled at her boldly.

"Where did they come from?" Abby asked Hannah.

"They've been here the whole time, and that one hasn't been able to take his eyes off you, though you've been too distracted to notice. Good thing you have me watching out for you," Hannah said, smiling and waving back at the cute guy.

"Hannah, *don't,*" Abby insisted, but then saw he was already on his way over.

"Why not? It's the perfect distraction from your troubles. Maybe his friend would be interested in doubling," Hannah said, elbowing her slightly.

Abby sent her a look that promised retribution later on, but turned to the handsome guy—whose name was Derek—and offered him a taste of the Baco.

She maintained her professional composure for the first few minutes, but Hannah was right. Derek was charming and obviously interested. Unfortunately for Hannah, his friend was already making a move on another of the event guests, and her friend winked at her, giving her an "oh well" shrug before leaving Abby alone with Derek.

He was a local business owner, too, running his own computer software shop. He was also about three years her junior, but that didn't seem to bother him any. Maybe it shouldn't bother her, either.

He *was* hot, with wavy blond hair and mischievous blue eyes, and he looked great in his jeans, but Abby didn't feel any sparks at all. For all the attraction she felt, Derek could have been her brother.

But she chatted with him, enjoying the distraction from thinking about Reece.

"I'm glad we decided to stop when we saw all the commotion," Derek said, studying the group decorating trees and stepping back to watch Abby fill tasting cups or dole out hot cocoa as people approached the booth.

"I'm glad you're enjoying yourself," she said diplomatically, wondering if there was a way to discourage him without losing a new customer or being rude. He was a nice guy, but contrary to Hannah's theories about sex vibes, Abby wasn't feeling too flirty or sexy at the moment.

"I am. I've never really been into wines. I mostly like a beer after work," he said, smiling at her in that way that surely sent many a girl into a flutter.

"I like beer, too. Many of the gourmet ones are so interesting," she responded vaguely, and that set them off talking about breweries and beer tasting, which she had to admit, was very interesting. He didn't know much about wine, but he was very knowledgeable about beer.

"It looks like the trees are almost done—I'm going to have to do some judging and hand out prizes," she said, hoping to find her exit that way.

Where had Hannah gone?

"Do you need any help?" Derek offered.

Abby was about to refuse, but then she saw Reece, walking from the barn up to the house. He stood by the front and watched her, not moving.

She felt her annoyance kick in again and smiled brightly at Derek. "Sure. You can help me collect votes," she said, standing close to him as she explained the voting process.

Abby didn't look back, but she heard the door slam in the background and grinned.

Derek was lit up like one of the Christmas trees by her interest, and she had to stop and think while he helped her collect votes for the best tree.

What was she doing? Derek was a sweet guy, as far as she could tell, and she had absolutely no romantic interest in him at all—using him to poke at Reece was ridiculous. She just hadn't been able to help herself. Still, it wasn't fair to Derek.

She watched her new friend smiling with a group of kids as he collected their votes and laughed as he took a snowball to the shoulder from one boy. Abby smiled, wishing she could just flip her emotions off from Reece and on to Derek. But she couldn't.

"You two seemed chummy," Hannah said, appearing back at her side suddenly.

"Where were you?"

"I had to watch over the snowman-making contest," she said innocently.

"Judy is doing that," Abby said knowingly. "You left me alone with him here on purpose."

Hannah grinned. "Did he ask you out?"

"Not yet."

"You going to go?"

"I don't know."

"Then my evil plan worked."

"Reece saw us," Abby said.

Hannah smiled. "I saw him staring at something, and he nearly broke the window in the door when he went inside."

Abby shook her head. "Yeah, I think I got a little carried away and made it look like I was more interested in Derek than I am," she confessed.

Hannah grinned more widely. "Then I would say my evil plan *really* worked. Reece was fit to be tied. Only one thing would get him that worked up at seeing you with another guy."

Hope leapt in Abby's chest, but she squashed it. "I'm not going to count on that. Nothing has changed."

Derek walked back over, and they wrapped up the contest, awarded the prizes and made sure everyone had a little something to take home with them.

It was a very successful event, in spite of her own personal challenges, and Abby felt good about pulling it off.

When Derek asked her out before he was leaving, she regretfully declined, leaving Hannah shaking her head. Derek smiled and gave her his email, just in case, writing it down on a napkin and sticking it in her pocket.

"Why couldn't I have met him a few weeks ago?" she asked Hannah as the yard turned dark, and she sat with her friend on the porch step, looking at a field filled with brightly decorated trees and a crowd of snowmen. If she had met Derek then, maybe none of this would have happened.

"Would that have made a difference, really?"

Abby sighed. "Probably not."

Whatever was between her and Reece, if anything, it wasn't easy, and it wasn't what she'd counted on. Still, she knew she wouldn't trade one second of the fun or passion they'd had, even though it blew up in her face.

"Want to spend the night at my place?" Hannah offered.

Abby shook her head. Even though it was awkward, she and Reece were in this until the end, and she'd handle it. She wasn't sure how, but she didn't really have any other choice.

CHAPTER NINE

REECE'S HANDS OPENED and closed around the leather-covered wheel. His old friend Brody Palmer, who was sitting in the passenger's seat, chuckled. Brody had come up from Florida to see family for a few days, and Reece had really enjoyed a night out with a friend, having a few beers and talking shop. It was also the first time he'd driven anything other than his dad's old, slow truck for a while, and truth be told, he didn't drive that if he could avoid it, relying on friends or public transport.

It felt good, though he was somewhat nervous. That was to be expected, right? His mind went to Abby, distracting him from his doubts. It had been a week since their argument, and they managed to move around each other without a lot of fuss, talking when they had to, but not much else. He had also seen her talking with the fire investigator sent to do the second report, and the strain she'd been under was obvious. He made himself scarce, not wanting to add to it. How could they think she would have torched her own place?

He wondered where she went when she was out.

With the young stud he'd seen her flirting with at the Christmas tree contest?

He'd wanted to punch the guy in the face, but that wasn't his right. Never was. Still, it had been all he could do to keep from crossing the field and claiming Abby as his.

Which left him more confused than ever.

"Stop feeling her up and drive already," Brody said, making Reece laugh.

"Sorry. It's been a while," he said, enjoying the snug fit of the seat and the powerful purr of the engine as he hit the gas and pulled out from the restaurant where he'd met Brody for dinner. Brody had been in the NASCAR circuit for a while and was thinking about retiring, which he'd told Reece over dinner.

"It's like sex. You might be a little rusty, but it will come back to you," Brody reassured.

"You sure you trust me not to scratch her?" he asked with a hint of humor, but his nerves betrayed him.

Brody's new Dodge Charger SRT8 was a nice machine. This was the most car he'd driven since he crashed, and his hands were a bit sweaty, his heart slamming not from excitement, but apprehension.

"It's right to be nervous after a crash," Brody said, reading him. "It's normal, but if you want back in, you have to start working through it. Open her up gradually. See how it feels. You can back off if you need to."

His friend's understanding helped ease his anxiety. Brody was absolutely right—how could Reece expect to return to driving if he couldn't drive a regular road car?

He left the parking lot, and relaxed as the car started moving.

This was familiar. It felt good.

As they hit the lake road heading to the winery, Reece picked up speed, feeling his reflexes kick in, and he laughed with pure pleasure.

"Told you," Brody said, chuckling, too.

Except for when he'd been making love to Abby, he hadn't been this pumped in some time. Her face, her scent, came back to him with startling clarity, and he lost track of what he was doing for a moment, which had him backing off on the gas.

"You okay?" Brody asked.

"Yeah, sorry. I was distracted for a minute," he said, irritated. He still craved her touch, but he couldn't afford any distractions if he was going to drive, and that included women. Even Abby.

Reece focused for the rest of the drive up the side of the lake, turning into the driveway where he found a crowd of cars in the parking lot.

"I guess the party is still going, but we can head into the house, have a few beers," he said to Brody, parking the Charger and handing his buddy the keys. "Thanks for that. It felt good."

Brody stuck the keys in the pocket of the leather bomber jacket he wore, watching Reece speculatively. "I heard they were thinking of a new guy for your team," he said.

"Yeah, I heard that, too. Hope to convince them differently, but it's hard, being stuck here."

"I know a few guys at Daytona. If you want to fly in for a day, I could set up a test drive for you. We could go down there for a few times around the track, do some timed runs, if you want to see how it goes."

Reece knew he should jump at the opportunity, but the sweat broke out on his hands again. He didn't understand why he was reacting this way, and it pissed him off.

"Sure, set it up," he said evenly, though his stomach lurched as they walked up to the house.

His left leg was still bothering him. He was starting to think it might never get better, though he knew it felt worse after being locked into position while driving. Exercise and time would solve that problem, he kept telling himself.

"So what's the big event?" Brody asked, nodding toward the group of cars.

"Bachelorette party," Reece said with a laugh, shaking his head.

"Are you kidding me?"

"Nope."

Reece explained about Abby, and how she was working out of the winery. The bachelor party was at a bar in town, but Sandra had decided to have her party at the winery. Reece had overheard that conversation on his way through the house one day.

Brody stopped, rubbing his chin with his thumb and forefinger, grinning as he looked toward the reception rooms. "Should we crash?"

Reece laughed. "We're not eighteen anymore."

His friend cocked an eyebrow in his direction. "Yeah, we wouldn't have known what to do with a roomful of half-drunk chicks in the mood to party when we were eighteen," he said, making Reece laugh harder, his former tension dissolving.

"And you do now?" Reece teased back, slapping Brody on the shoulder, but Brody was already heading toward the party. Reece followed, reluctantly.

"It's kind of Abby's thing," he hedged. "Maybe we should just stick to the house."

"Gotta get your spirit of adventure back, friend," Brody said with a grin, and Reece gave in and continued to follow. They made their way over to the tasting room, walking in the side door where it was dark in the lobby, moving like spies along the bar and cracking open the door to the reception room out back.

Reece wasn't sure what he expected to see, but it sure wasn't what he saw.

"You sure this is the *bachelorette* party?" Brody asked on a whisper, his eyes wide.

"Yeah," he answered, though he had to admit to a moment of confusion, as well.

At the far side of the room, women all gathered, and Reece had to blink a few times to believe what he was seeing. Abby had been very hush-hush about the party and changed the subject or was vague when he asked how it was going. Now he knew why.

He'd figured the party would either be a bunch of women dancing or talking, or sticking dollar bills in some young guy's jock strap, but instead, a ministage had been set up on the far end of the room, and there was a pole that braced from ceiling to floor.

And the women were taking turns dancing around it. They had their clothes on, of course. And most of them collapsed laughing as they tried to imitate classic stripper moves—some more successful than others—to songs playing so loudly all he could hear was music and shrieks of laughter, along with encouraging comments.

"Women are strange," Brody said. "Don't they usually get mad at us for going to watch this kind of thing?"

Reece laughed, edging the door open for a better view of the merriment. It was all innocent fun and games, and no one even noticed they were there, they were all enjoying themselves so much.

He naturally sought out Abby, who was standing to the side, monitoring the event and making sure all was going well. She smiled and spoke to Hannah, who stood by her side, the two women standing apart from the main action.

The song ended and Sandra, much happier than the day he'd found her screaming at Abby out in the field, took the stage. She definitely appeared to be tilting a bit, a martini sloshing dangerously in her hand.

She took a microphone and grinned at the group of women in front of her.

"This is such a blast—as you know, it's all on video, and I'll be sure to let you know which cuts make it to YouTube tomorrow," she promised. Laughter and a few playful threats ensued.

"But the martinis aren't gone and we're not done yet!" she announced to a chorus of hooting and howling.

"And not everyone has taken their turn, and we said everyone has to take a turn," she warned, turning to face Abby, who was still talking to Hannah.

The crowd cheered again as Sandra said, "Now we know Abby Harper can throw a monster bachelorette party, but can she dance?"

Abby stopped midconversation with Hannah, just then noticing the room's attention was on her. Her eyes widened and she shook her head.

"Oh, this just got interesting," Brody said, leering at Abby and Hannah. Reece elbowed him.

"The one on the right is Abby," Reece told him, but the light warning in his voice was clear.

Brody grinned. "So the one on the left is free?"

Brody was a shameless womanizer, teased in the media as to whether he had more trophies or romantic conquests. About the only thing in life he was serious about was his driving. Behind the wheel, he was all business, but out in the world, he was all play.

"Yeah, bud, go for it," Reece said, thinking it might be funny to see Brody get shot down. He'd known Hannah as long as he'd known Abby, and Hannah was as no-nonsense as they came, and she didn't suffer fools.

Abby was still vociferously protesting, even as Sandra tugged her up on stage, everyone laughing and daring her to do it.

When Abby was left alone by the pole, the crowd

clapping to the beat of some bump-and-grind rock song that started playing, Abby laughed, put a hand to her face in embarrassment and rolled her eyes.

"Oh, my God, she's going to do it," Reece said, finding himself inexplicably breathless.

Abby was dressed in a very simple black dress that seemed conservative next to some of the outfits in the room, but when she kicked her heels off and grabbed the pole, Reece's cock jerked and hardened.

She slid her back up and down the pole, the simple dress sliding down off her shoulder slightly, and rising as she bent her knee to reveal a smooth expanse of thigh. When her head fell back in apparent sexual bliss, Reece heard Brody hiss a breath and elbowed him again.

When she came back up, vamping for the girls, she looked across the room and froze as she saw him.

He smiled, nodding once, and mischief sparkled in her expression. No one seemed to notice them watching but her.

Her eyes stayed on his as she started dancing again. Wrapping herself around that pole like a pro, she bent forward to show the tops of beautiful breasts as she shimmied, impressing him with flexibility that he knew he wanted to learn more about.

"*That's* your high school girlfriend?" Brody said in awe.

"No, she was just a neighbor then, a girl I knew," Reece said, not looking away.

"And now?"

"Not sure," Reece said, wanting to stop talking and focus.

Laughing, Abby held her hand out. All hell broke loose when Hannah strutted up on stage, wearing a classic wool skirt and plain white blouse, but Reece suddenly saw the smart-mouthed accountant that he knew turn into a sexy vixen. She undid a few buttons and her hair swished around her face, making those dark-rimmed glasses downright intriguing.

Brody lost all control and started whistling, cat-calling for more, and the women turned, gaping, a moment of silence falling over the room, except for the heavy beat of the music still playing.

Reece wasn't sure what their reception would be, but he was poised to either apologize or make a run for it.

Brody's eyes were glued to Hannah, and he seemed to care less if they had been discovered, yelling to the women to start dancing again.

Laughter broke out, and some women came back, taking Reece and Brody by the hands, pulling them forward and insisting if they wanted to join the party, that *they* had to dance.

Reece laughed, but "over my dead body" was his silent reply to that. Brody, though, was in party form, grabbing a martini and jumping up on stage with a shocked Hannah, leading her to dance more with him, just as Reece took Abby's hand and helped her down.

"I missed you" was the first thing he said, and he realized it was true.

"I missed you, too," she admitted.

His eyes devoured her flushed cheeks and the rest of the room around them fell away.

"I don't get the dancing thing, but I sure did like it," he said in a low voice.

She grinned. "I don't know, either. It's some stripper fantasy, girl-power deal, I guess," she said, shrugging. "It was fun, though."

They both cracked up when they looked back to see Brody dancing around the pole.

Something clicked for Reece when he heard Abby laugh. He wanted to drag her off to a dark corner and take her now.

She seemed to know what he was thinking. The party had taken on a life of its own, and no one even noticed them anymore.

Before she could find some reason to change her mind, he took her by the hand and led her out of the room, into the tasting room, behind the bar. It was mostly dark, and no one else was there, though everyone was about twenty feet away at the party.

He backed her up against the wall, silencing anything she might say with a kiss that made his need clear. She moaned into his mouth, and as he slipped his hand up under the skirt of her dress, he found her slick, as aroused as he was.

"It's not the hedges, but it will do," he said roughly into her neck, need clawing at him as he picked up the scent of her sweat and sex, her skin hot from dancing and arousal.

"Someone might come out, they could see," she

said, but he knew from her tone it was exciting her more…and she didn't ask him to stop.

"Yeah, they could, so we'd better hurry," he agreed, freeing his erection from his jeans and lifting her hips, cradling her butt in his hands so that she could wrap her legs around him.

Reece wasted no time getting inside of her, pushing deep and hard, taking her in short, quick thrusts that made her arch against him. She muffled a cry of pleasure as she dug her fingers into his shoulders, hanging on. She was hot and tight around him, and he didn't care if someone did come out and catch them, he needed her too much.

He didn't think he'd ever been this aroused. He was starving for her. In fact, he never would have risked this kind of public exposure given his responsibilities to the team and his sponsors, but right now, he didn't have to worry about that.

He leaned down, bracing Abby against the wall so that he could suck a nipple through the fabric of her dress. That sent her over the edge. She sank her teeth into his shoulder as she came, holding on tight and trying to hold back the scream that became a low keening against his neck.

He couldn't stop, either, and found her mouth, plundering it with a deep kiss as he exploded inside of her, the orgasm making his legs weak, but he rode it out, taking every last bit of pleasure she offered him.

When the moment passed, they were both sweaty, sticky and breathless. Reece heard voices coming toward them and they quickly ducked down behind the bar. Abby was illuminated in a sliver of light that angled down from the front windows, her eyes wide and sparkling, hair tousled. She covered her mouth to smother a giggle.

He pulled her in close, wrapping his arms around her as the voices came closer.

It was Brody and—if he was correct—Hannah.

He felt Abby shift in his arms, she must have realized, too, and reached to see. He held her still, putting a finger to her lips until their friends moved on, and Reece heard the grumbling engine of the Charger rev to life.

"Sounds like Hannah is taking home a little Christmas cheer," Abby said, chuckling, and Reece grinned as they both stood up, surveying the area as they fixed their clothes and emerged into the other room.

"Who was that, anyway?" she asked, threading fingers through her hair to smooth it down.

He ran his eyes over her and wanted to mess it right back up again.

"My friend Brody. Palmer," he added.

"Like, *the* Brody Palmer?" she asked. "Are you telling me my best friend just left with *Brody Palmer?* The one whose fan site has a poll keeping track of whether he's ridden more cars or women?"

Reece winced and opted for being straightforward. "Yeah, that would be the one."

Abby groaned. "I don't know whether I should call her to warn her off or congratulate her," she said.

"You can't believe everything you hear in the media," Reece said, chuckling.

Abby eyed him doubtfully, and he caved.

"Well, okay, when it comes to Brody, most of that is kind of true, but he's a good guy, I promise. She'll be okay with him," he insisted.

"If you say so," she commented, smiling, and pressed in close. She kept Hannah's comments about wishing she could find a hot guy to use for sex to herself. It looked like her friend's wish had come true.

"How about you?"

"What?" he asked, playing dumb.

"More cars or women?" she asked with a grin.

"I don't have anyone running polls, but I'm pretty sure I can say cars," he answered, nuzzling her neck. "I'm not a saint, but I'm no Brody Palmer."

"Thank heavens," she said, laughing and wrapping her arms around his neck, sighing.

Bright lights flicked on and they flew apart to find a grinning, soused bride-to-be facing them. Sandra stared at them for a minute, still smiling.

"Sandra, are you okay?"

"I'm *won-fer-dul,*" she said, lurching forward to wrap her arms around Abby in a drunken hug. Abby sagged under the slack weight of the woman, who mumbled praise about the best party ever and being so sorry she had threatened to "shoe" Abby after the fire.

"It's okay, Sandra. I knew you were just upset, and wouldn't really sue me," Abby comforted, trying to support her weight and looking over Sandra's shoulder for help.

Reece came to her rescue, slinging one of Sandra's

arms over his shoulder, bracing most of the weight as they got her to one of the fireplace chairs and gently deposited her in it.

"What are you doing with the not-so-blushing bride?" he asked with a grin.

Abby sighed. "I can find out which of her friends or sisters is most sober, and see if they can get her upstairs to her room. I have all of their car keys over at the house, so no one is going anywhere tonight. Big sleepover," she said, chuckling, and Reece relaxed. "They have a group brunch planned for tomorrow morning, so once I get them set tonight, I'm done."

"What can I do to help?" he asked, and she looked at him in surprise.

"You can't take care of all of this alone, and Hannah is gone for the night," Reece pointed out.

"You're sure?" she said, and he saw the doubt in her eyes. He didn't blame her.

But now that he'd had her in his arms again, he knew that he didn't want to let her go one minute sooner than he had to.

"Absolutely. Abby, I'm sorry I was an ass last week. I guess I thought it would be easier if I put some distance between us, but it wasn't."

"Reece," she said on a sigh, leaning her forehead against him.

"That guy, at the Christmas tree event…did you go out with him?"

God, he felt sixteen, but he had to know.

"No. I was just trying to tick you off."

"It worked," he said with a grin, but then became

serious again. "I didn't mean to hurt you. I just… I don't know," he admitted, feeling foolish. "I was messed up."

She pressed a kiss to the corner of his lips. "I know. Me, too."

Suddenly the world seemed a little more right again, and Reece blew out a breath, looking at his watch.

"You can go see what's what. I can start cleaning up, if you want," he said.

"Thanks. I appreciate it. I'll be right back."

He watched her walk away, all female grace and strength, and knew he couldn't fight what he felt for her anymore, but he had no idea where it was heading, either. Nothing had changed—and everything had changed.

"Abby?" he called out, before she disappeared back into the reception room.

She turned. "Hmm?"

"Maybe we should leave that pole up, though, just for a night or two," he said, imagining he'd like a show for one.

The sexy, mischievous look in her eyes as she smiled told him she agreed.

CHAPTER TEN

ABBY WAS GETTING USED to her life on a roller coaster, and when it meant she was able to wake up in Reece's bed, that was definitely okay with her.

She wasn't interested in fighting it anymore, releasing all the doubt and worry. They were good together. She wanted him, and apparently he wanted her. She shivered, thinking about the wonderful, desperate way he'd taken her the night before, standing up, behind the wine bar. The sex had been fast, a little awkward and…spectacular.

They'd worked side-by-side the rest of the evening, some understanding hammered out even though they didn't talk very much at all.

As much as she wanted him again, they'd both crashed as soon as they hit the mattress, exhausted and wrapped around each other. She remembered feeling a deep satisfaction that he seemed to have missed her as much as she missed him.

Maybe that was foolish, but she didn't care.

She stared at the empty pillow beside her—he'd probably gotten up early to work out. Her cell phone rang, interrupting her thoughts. Hannah.

"Hey," Abby said cheerfully. "I didn't expect to

hear from you today, you wild woman," she teased her friend.

"You know me, I'm an early bird," Hannah said, her voice practically singing with I-had-a-night-of-wild-sex energy. "Even when I was up very, very late."

"Do tell."

"Later, promise. Right now, we were wondering if you'd be interested in brunch."

"We?"

"Brody and I. We're calling for both of you, but if you want, you could just come yourself."

Abby detected the unspoken question in Hannah's voice—she must have seen them leave together, and wondered what had happened.

"I'm sure Reece will want to come, too."

Hannah laughed knowingly. "So your cold spell is over," she said happily.

"Most definitely," Abby said with a smile. "Where should we meet you?"

They named a time and place, and Abby got up, taking off what little she had on and padding to the bathroom, where she had just heard the water turn on. Losing her robe, she smiled, pulling the door open to find Reece waiting.

"I was hoping the noise might wake you up," he said with an unabashed grin, holding out a hand to her.

"Wow," she said, not hiding her awe. He was using the master bath, and she had been using the guest bath attached to her room. Hers was very nice, she had no complaints, but this was just…sinful.

The entire space was composed of granite with specks of gold, black and dark red lending a warm touch, textured on the floor so as to avoid being slippery, and smooth, but with a matte finish, on the sides. Plants lined a window that set a few feet above them, draping down, obviously loving the high humidity and light. Abby felt like she was stepping into a hidden cave with a waterfall.

There were five jets at different heights, and a bench seat that ran almost the entire length of the shower, with a shelf of soaps, shampoos, body oils, sponges, loofahs and pretty much anything else you could think of. You could even adjust the lighting, bright or soft, and the controls for the water temperature were digital so you could set the degree—no guessing.

"This isn't a shower. This is shower heaven," she said.

"Yeah, it's extreme. My dad always called it 'The Lagoon,'" he said with a laugh.

"That's it exactly."

"It was my mom's pet project. She set out to create the perfect bathroom one year. It actually was featured in a home décor magazine. She was on top of the world."

"She nailed it," Abby agreed breathlessly, and he laughed as she went into his arms under the hot spray.

His hands covered and massaged her breasts

as they kissed, and he added, "Now *this* is shower heaven."

"Mmm-hmm," she agreed, her hands dipping low to stroke his ready erection, making him groan. She was intrigued when he trembled as she reached lower, stroking a finger over his balls and petting the soft skin deep between his thighs.

"Come here," he said as he sat on the bench and pulled her on to his lap, angled slightly so she could kiss him as the water poured over them from seemingly everywhere.

She started to turn to face him, to straddle him, but he shook his head. "You'll punish your knees on the stone. Like this," he said, stretching out his legs straight and moving her over him.

"Oh…*oh,*" she gasped as he slid deep inside.

He held her there against him, kissing her ears, her neck. His hands covered her breasts, plucking and rolling hard, wet nipples between his fingers until she was writhing.

She had a feeling he'd planned that, and she liked a man who thought ahead. The throbbing of the hot water against her flesh and the sensation of him buried deep inside had her moaning as an easy orgasm rolled over her. Reece whispered hot, raw things in her ear as she came, and then came again.

Breathless and panting, she pushed forward, still poised against him, bracing her hands on his knees, looking back with a sexy wink.

"I like this," she said, enjoying how his hands covered her bottom, his fingers digging in a little as he brought her down the way that he needed.

"Me, too."

She moved her right hand from his knee to stroke herself as she took him deep and ground against him in a way that had him yelling her name, arching up and pushing even deeper as they came together.

She relaxed back against him, turning her face into the strong column of his neck.

"That was so good. It's always good with you," she said, wrapping her fingers in his as the water washed over them.

"I'm glad you think so."

"I do."

He helped her up and stood with her, grabbing a soft natural sponge and some soap. He washed her carefully, tenderly, and she nearly purred. She'd never felt this cared for, and the intimacy was stunning as he bent before her, washing her legs and between them, planting kisses where the shower washed away the soap. She was feeling sparks again before he was back at eye level.

"Do you like games, Abby?"

A flicker of anticipation teased her.

"Like Monopoly?" she asked innocently.

He smiled, and pulled her closer, whispering in her ear. Her breath hitched. How was it that her fantasies seemed to be his?

"I love those kinds of games," she said, finding it hard to breathe.

"Come here then," he said, pulling her upright.

He positioned her by the edge of the spray, and she looked up, seeing the two ties that hung limply from the shower rod. Realization dawned.

"Oh. I thought you had just left your laundry in here," she said, her heart stuttering as he lifted her arm and pulled one tie down to her wrist.

"Make sure the ties won't give," she said, daringly, and saw his eyes darken as they met hers.

"Is this comfortable?" he asked, securing the tie.

She wiggled her fingers, and pulled. The knots were solid. A slight edge of apprehension rose, but curiosity and excitement outweighed it.

"I'm good," she said, watching him step back and look at her.

"We're going to do what I told you, and you're okay with it? My rules?"

"Yes," she said, as submissively as she could.

"Good," he said, his eyes dark and passionate on hers as he stroked himself to semihardness.

She watched, fascinated, unable to take her eyes away from him. She'd never watched a man pleasure himself, and felt herself get wet from more than the shower.

"You'd like to watch me finish this, wouldn't you?"

She struggled, flexing her fingers, wanting to touch, to go to him, but he was out of reach. And if she couldn't touch him, she wanted to touch herself, suddenly craving release again.

"I'd like that very much," she admitted. "But there's a problem."

"What?"

"I want to come again, too."

"Well," he said, teasingly, softly, "we'll both get there, eventually."

She frowned. "Eventually?"

He walked over to her, leaning in to nuzzle her neck, and she whimpered, needing the touch.

"You'll see."

He kissed her sweetly, then moved down her body in a string of butterfly kisses, leaving sparks of heat everywhere, but not giving her anything near what she needed. He brushed his thumbs and then his lips over her nipples, lightly, teasing some more, until she was almost limp and begging.

Then he went down farther, and she braced for his kiss between her legs, but he only ran his hands up and down her legs, kissing and nibbling at the insides of her thighs. She opened herself as much as she could, trying to show him what she needed.

"You want my mouth on you, Abby?"

"Please, yes," she said weakly. Desire was a hot weight in her abdomen, a bomb needing to explode.

He nodded and whispered, "Okay," against her skin, then used both hands to spread her slick flesh, but rather than planting his mouth against her, he flicked his tongue against her clit, the sensations intense but fleeting, not constant enough to push her over. She tried to press against him, to find the pressure she needed to come, but he would move and she cried out in lust and need.

"Please, Reece. I don't think I want to play anymore," she said.

He stood, his jaw tight, his eyes dark. "Abby, I'm hard as rock, ready to explode—again. I haven't felt need like this in years. I want to pull you up and fuck you until we both dissolve under the water," he said, and his raw language only excited her more.

"Do it," she urged, wanting exactly that. "Just think how good it would be, Reece. You could take me any way you want…and I want you to," she tempted, trying to break him. "Whatever you want, however you want me," she whispered.

By the look on his face and the way his cock jerked at her words, it was working.

He came up close to her, and she cheered inside her mind, celebrating her win.

He smiled and then did something she never expected, bringing his hand down on her bottom in a stinging swat. "Stop that. We both have to wait. Those are the rules."

The sting from the swat turned to heat on her skin, and she found she craved more, anything that would relieve the torturous pressure of arousal inside of her. They'd just made love minutes before, but it had been too long, and her body was on fire for more.

He rubbed his hand over the spot where he had spanked her, and brushed his lips against hers, then kissed her more deeply.

Their bodies were hardly touching, though their mouths tried to make up for it, mating furiously.

"Reece, I need you," she said, breaking the kiss to breathe.

"I need you, too, Abby," he said roughly. "So much."

He reached up past her, the length of his body touching hers, making her shudder, and she heard a noise. One arm fell free, then the other.

She looked down at her wrists, and he reached over to shut off the water.

She stared at him, stunned. "You really mean it, don't you? You're going to make us both wait?"

He nodded, stepping away and coming back with a heated towel that he wrapped around her. She was dizzy with arousal, and he pulled her up close, rubbing her back soothingly.

"That's right. That's the game."

"What if I don't want to wait?"

"You already agreed to play," he said, pulling her behind him and grabbing a towel for himself. "Don't worry. I'm just as hot as you are, and you'll have your turn later," he promised. "Didn't you say we have to go meet Brody and Hannah for breakfast."

She almost groaned in dismay. She'd almost forgotten. How was she going to get through brunch with friends, as wound up as she was? She couldn't even think straight, she was so turned on.

It was wonderful.

She was tuned into him more closely than she had ever been to anything in her life, as if she was aware of every movement, every breath. She rubbed her wrists.

"You okay?" he asked, clearly concerned.

"Yes. I liked how it felt. I wanted it to last longer," she admitted, starting to calm down a little. She was on edge, certain that so much as a touch from him might send her into climax, but now…now she also wanted to see how long they could last. How crazy they could make each other before they gave in.

And she was very much looking forward to her turn to push Reece to his limit.

He smiled at her, as if he'd read every thought. It was incredibly intimate, linking them together in a way she hadn't experienced with anyone else, ever.

As they got dressed, he leaned in and planted a kiss on her lips, whispering, "It's going to be worth every second we wait, I promise," he said.

She believed it.

REECE SHIFTED IN HIS chair at the table, dealing with an on-and-off hard-on all through brunch. Abby was a clever lover—and a little mean—he thought with a smile.

When he'd told her he wanted to tie her up and tease her until she begged, she'd been all for it. When he told her he was going to leave them both on edge, not give in, she'd doubted him, but it was perfect. The constant potential for satisfaction—or not—was like live electricity crackling between them.

He'd read about extended sexual seduction practices. They included but also went beyond Tantra to create arousal that lasted for days, resulting in climax for both partners that was off the scale—but he'd never been with anyone he desired enough to actually try it. He imagined him and Abby seducing each other with baths, massages, meals and light sexual teasing for days before having sex. He'd always wondered what that would be like.

Now he knew.

She became adept at the game very quickly.

Small touches to his knee or his thigh were bad enough, but the way she innocently worked bondage references into her conversation taunted him, reminding him of how incredibly erotic she had looked hours ago, and how close he had come to taking her again.

But this was better. The play was demonical, but fun.

His focus was on her hand as she appeared to absently rub her wrist as they ate and chatted—not because it hurt, but because she knew, the little minx, that it would be driving him out of his mind to think about tying her up again. The first time had been an experiment, and way too brief.

"So anyway," Brody said, stretching back in his chair, grinning and eyeing Reece speculatively as Brody's hand landed on Hannah's nape.

It was an oddly possessive gesture, Reece thought. He'd been surprised enough that Brody was at a brunch with a woman he slept with. It might be a first. Reece certainly didn't know the details of Brody's love life, except that most of his stories of the women he met included a hasty exit before morning light.

Hannah seemed quite happy with herself this morning, too. Interesting.

"Anyway," Brody started again, "I talked with a friend down at Daytona this morning. If you're interested, we could fly there later today, do a test run tomorrow, see how it feels, get your legs back under you," Brody announced.

Reece hadn't seen that coming, either. Brody was full of surprises. He knew he'd told him to set it up, but he thought it would probably be weeks, not hours.

"Wow, that was fast," was all he could say.

"Strike while the iron is hot," Brody said, chugging back his orange juice. "We'd have to leave later today, but I can get us down there. Friend of mine has a private plane and pilot here that he's willing to loan out."

Reece was dumbstruck, and he knew his response should have been immediate. Brody's eyes narrowed as he watched him, but he didn't say anything else.

Reece was dealing with the fact that his first response had not been *hell, yeah,* but that he didn't want to leave Abby, not when they had just found their footing again.

Which was ridiculous. He'd be back after a day or so. She'd still be here, right?

"Reece, you have to get back behind the wheel before they're even going to look at you for the new season. You have to get your mojo," Brody added.

Reece knew he shouldn't need arm-twisting, and jumped when he felt Abby's hand cover his in a visible show of support.

"You should go," she said, her voice sure.

He looked at her and she didn't waver, just gave him a single nod before squeezing his hand and returning to her breakfast.

He wasn't sure how to respond to that, either—was she able to let him go so easily? Why did that bother him? He'd done nothing but tell her that he was leaving since they first met.

"You should come with me," he said to her, the words leaving his lips almost before the idea had fully formed in his brain. It made sense though. For one thing, he felt better when he had Abby with him—he'd slept peacefully for the first time last night, and his legs or arm weren't bothering him at all this morning.

Maybe it was the sex, the release, the stimulation or just her personal magic, but she made him feel good. And he needed to feel good if he was going to get into a car and hit a track at one-eighty plus for the first time in months.

"Oh, I don't know…." she said, frowning. "The wedding is only ten days off—"

"You have most of that prepped," Hannah interrupted. "Anything else is up to the families, except for the decorating, but you don't need to do that now. I checked the schedule, and the next thing you have is the Christmas and Chocolate party this Friday night. You can manage to take a few days off. C'mon Abby, let's take a little vacation," Hannah urged.

"You're both going?" Reece asked, looking at Brody with even more surprise.

"Yeah. Hannah says she wants some excitement, and I can't think of anything more exciting than being at the track. So she's coming with me for a month of preseason."

Abby and Reece were both struck silent with surprise. Hannah's cheeks were warm, but her eyes were bright with pure joy.

"I hope that's okay, Abby, I was going to talk to you before Brody decided to just leap in and volunteer the information," she said, sliding him an affectionate look. "But January is always slow, and you can take my apartment while you're working on getting things done with the winery, I mean, you know, if you're still not at Reece's after the New Year," Hannah said.

Abby nodded, and didn't appear to know what to say. Reece put his hand on hers this time and squeezed, turning to her so that they were only looking at each other.

"I'd really like it if you could come with me," he said. "It would mean a lot, but I also understand if you can't."

Abby, looking slightly cornered, shook her head, as if trying to clear her thoughts. She turned her hand over to hold Reece's, an encouraging sign.

"Hannah is right. I can close for a few days, not much happening on weekdays now anyway. I'll have Judy come by to look in on the horses and animals. She's done that for me before," she said.

"So you'll come?" Reece asked, feeling far too hopeful.

She paused for another moment, then smiled. "Yes, it'll be fun," she replied. "And I want to be there for you."

"Great! I'll make the flight arrangements right now," Brody, their man of action, said, planting a quick kiss on Hannah's mouth. He pulled his cell phone from his pocket and stood up from the table.

Reece leaned in to kiss Abby's cheek. "Thank you. This will be a lot less nerve-racking with you there."

She was obviously surprised at his unvarnished admission, and he was, too, but it was the truth. He was developing emotions that amounted to far more than lust for Abby. He had a need for her that went beyond the physical.

She was different than any woman he'd ever known, and he didn't want to lose whatever was growing between them.

What they would do about that, long-term, he had no idea, but for now, he would just take the curves as they came.

Hannah was grinning at them, all dewy-eyed. "I'm so glad you guys made up," she said.

Reece straightened in his chair, realizing Abby would have, of course, told her about their fight, and no doubt what a jerk he was. But the way she looked right now, happy and hopeful, made him a bit twitchy. He was willing to admit that he had some serious feelings for Abby, but he wasn't entirely comfortable having assumptions made about them as a couple.

"So you're going to hang out with Brody at the track for a month?" he said to Hannah, changing the topic.

"I need some adventure. This sounds...adventurous."

"You follow racing?" Reece asked.

"No, not at all. But I guess I'll learn," she said with a goofy smile, picking apart a croissant.

Reece liked Brody. He was a good friend, and a great driver. But somehow, he felt like he had to say something to Hannah.

"I hope you're not putting too much stock into this, Hannah. Just so you know. He's a good man, but, well, you know what I'm trying to say. I'm surprised he was even here for breakfast," Reece said bluntly, drawing a shocked look from Abby, but Hannah just stared, and then burst out laughing.

"Thanks, Reece, but Brody made it quite clear that he's not interested in anything permanent. That's perfect, because all I want is a month of hot sex and something new in my life before I come back to my routine," she said, making Reece choke on his coffee.

"You two should be perfect together, then," he agreed, laughing.

Abby was uncharacteristically quiet, focused on the remainder of her breakfast, but he could practically hear the wheels spinning in her mind. Right now though, all he cared about was that she would be with him.

They'd have a few days in sunny Florida to go to the track, and to hopefully continue their fun and games.

As much as some excitement had filtered through about the prospect of getting back into a car, it was disconcerting to know that the second item excited him the most.

CHAPTER ELEVEN

ABBY SQUINTED AS SHE DEPLANED, walking down the short course of steps onto the tarmac. She hadn't flown anywhere in quite some time, and never in a private jet. It had been a lot of fun. She'd forgotten how much she enjoyed the speed and thrill of take-offs, checking out the landscape below as she flew by and the joy of setting feet to ground again. They'd had a smooth flight, and it was only early evening, the weather clear and warm.

She was also starving and, frankly, so horny she could hardly stand it. The close quarters of the plane had given them plenty of time to play their secret game, with quick touches and teasing talk or glances. She figured she might help him relax once they got to their condo, a place Brody owned right by the track.

But there was more than sex going on between them. Reece had thanked her about ten times since brunch, and it warmed her to know that her presence here meant so much to him. She could also detect the fine tension in him. She knew this was a big deal for him, and she was perhaps more nervous for him than he was for himself.

She didn't want to think about where it was all

leading. They had something new, some kind of deeper connection, an intimacy that had blossomed quickly and almost without her realizing it. It was as if, after the argument, they had come back together more deeply than before.

Or maybe it was just her. Somehow, regardless of all of the external circumstances and doubts, she knew she could trust Reece, and she wanted to be with him, no matter what the future held.

She was dying to talk to Hannah about her arrangement with Brody, and what had happened to make her friend take off on such a wild lark. She seized the opportunity as they crossed the terminal to a large SUV that was waiting for them. Brody had thought of everything. The men walked ahead, and she slowed down, hanging back with Hannah.

"So…a month with Brody?" she asked, opening the door for Hannah to elaborate.

"Yeah, it's crazy, I know," Hannah said, shaking her head, her strawberry-blond hair swinging over her shoulders. "I wanted to talk to you privately first, since I know this affects you, too, with the winery, but Brody, well, he's kind of a force of nature," she said with a grin.

Abby smiled. "Yeah, that's the perfect description," she agreed. "Must have been some night you had with him, but are you sure a month is going to work out? It's a long time with someone you barely know," Abby said.

"Well, I can always come back early if I don't like it, or if things aren't good. But, Abby, he's amazing. If the month with him is anything like the other night, I'm not sure a month would be enough. I could get addicted."

Abby frowned. "That's another problem altogether. What Reece was talking about. These guys…some of them settle down, but not Reece. Not Brody. I don't want you getting heartbroken," Abby said.

Do as I say, but not as I do, she thought to herself. She wanted to save her friend some pain, if she could.

"I won't. I have no interest in love," Hannah continued. "I just want to be free for a while, to get out of my routine and live a little before I come back and probably end up marrying some nice, safe, dependable man and raising our two-point-eight."

Abby couldn't begrudge her friend that, in fact, she understood all too well. She loved their small-town life on the lake, on the vineyards, but it was a relatively ordinary life. Reece and Brody were extraordinary men.

But it was even more seductive for Hannah, Abby imagined. While she and Reece had grown up on the vineyards with parents who were successful enough to provide some of the extras like college and vacations, Hannah hadn't.

Her parents owned a local farm that had become defunct. Most of Hannah's youth had been beyond difficult, her father working too hard and dying of a heart attack when she was only ten. Her mom had had to work constantly after that to keep the house, and they had eventually sold and lived in an apartment in Ithaca.

Hannah had lost her dad and her home, and yet she'd never moaned and felt sorry for herself, which is something Abby admired so much. Hannah had spent many nights and weekends at Abby's house when they were kids, and she felt more like her sister than her friend.

Hannah's mother did better now, but that was largely due to Hannah working her way through state college on loans and scholarships, and making life better for both of them.

Abby knew it was no accident that Hannah had studied accounting and that she worked like a dog. Hannah applied the same logic to her love life—she wouldn't marry a man who risked her security. So Abby knew that Brody really was just a wild fling, and if anyone deserved some fun and time away, it was Hannah.

Her friend's sexy brashness made her smile to herself, and she sighed as they were almost to the car.

"Yeah, that's what I thought with Reece at the beginning. Just be careful."

"You two seem more serious now, I take it?" Hannah queried.

"I'm not sure. The other night was…I don't know what it was," she said honestly, with another sigh. "I care about him. I think he cares about me. But as far as I know, nothing has changed. That's why we're here, right? So he can get one step closer to leaving."

"Aw, hon," Hannah said, slinging an arm around her. "Just have faith. If you two are supposed to work out, you will find a way."

Abby didn't want to think about it, really, and she also didn't want to rain on Hannah's fun, so she just smiled and nodded.

Right now, she was just focusing on the moment.

Hannah grinned, nudging her in the side as she ogled the guys' backsides. "They sure are a couple of hotties, though, huh?"

Abby had to grin, taking a long peek at how well Reece wore his jeans as they approached the SUV.

"You said it," she agreed, and they laughed the rest of the way to the car, the guys watching them curiously as they opened doors, climbed in and headed to the track.

THE CONDO WAS SPACIOUS and modern, with a huge picture window that looked out over the racetrack. Abby was thrilled that she had come along on the trip, not only to be with Reece and Hannah, but also because she had never been to a track except for Watkins Glen, which was a great racetrack, but with it being almost in her backyard didn't have the same kind of excitement.

Like some people enjoyed the beauty of baseball parks or tennis greens, she felt a zing of excitement run down her spine as she scrutinized the raceway. The track wasn't completely empty, though the stands were, but workers were getting ready for preseason events, and she'd seen one driver out on a test drive earlier that morning.

She couldn't help but shiver, watching. She enjoyed the thrill of the speed and the noise, but it had all been so distant before. Now it was real, and it would be Reece in that car, speeding around the curves.

"You're like a kid in a candy shop," Reece said, smiling as he slipped his hands over her shoulders, enjoying her excitement at being involved in his world. This wasn't Formula One, but people who were in racing and who really enjoyed the sport had to respect both circuits, regardless of the debates that always raged among fans about which was superior.

"It's pretty amazing," she said, snuggling back against him. "I'm glad I came."

"Me, too," he murmured.

The night before, they'd gone for a late dinner with Hannah and Brody and then out to walk around the town, as neither Hannah nor Abby had ever been to the area.

It was quite an experience, as they ate in a restaurant that had Brody's picture on the wall, and as they were interrupted by fans of both drivers for pictures and autographs. Both men were gracious and friendly, and Abby had watched in wonder, seeing a whole new side to Reece. He was a well-known public figure. She knew that, but it had never really hit her until now how famous he actually was in this world. And he was here, with her.

It was hard for her to get her mind around it, but she was learning not to second-guess everything.

Brody's condo was huge and, luckily, provided three large, separate sleeping quarters, which Brody often lent to visiting friends and family, or his team. It was immaculate, but not homey, obviously more of a practical investment for Brody than a place he had any emotional attachment to.

"Shouldn't you be at the track with Brody?" she asked, not wanting him to leave, but also wanting to support him, not become a distraction.

Reece seemed to have other ideas, sliding his hands over her hips and up her stomach to cover her breasts, and she couldn't deny the wave of lust that shook her to her toes as they stood before the large window.

They weren't very likely being watched by anyone. The scattering of people who were on the track were busy with their own concerns. Still, the idea of being here, so visible, turned her on.

"You have to drive today," she said on a groan as he nibbled her earlobe.

"I know, and I'm kind of on edge. I need to relax, burn off some energy. You have any ideas?"

She had nothing but ideas.

"What about our game?"

"We can just let off steam, maybe," he said, nipping at her neck and easing her shirt up, sliding his hands beneath as he pressed his hardness against her bottom.

"Oh, okay, then," she said, happy to pursue the satisfaction that had been keeping her in a constant state of wanting. The night before, she had done to him as he had to her, kissing him everywhere, taking him into her mouth and bringing him to the edge, but not finishing. They'd come back down to earth with kisses, eventually falling into an exhausted sleep.

In a strange way, she liked it. What had been frustration turned to something else, a kind of constant promisc of intimacy that she had never imagined.

She turned in his arms, pulling his head down for a kiss, after he got rid of her shirt and undid her bra. "One of us has too many clothes on," she said, reaching for the buckle of his belt and undoing it.

Things were getting hot quickly, and she didn't recognize the sound filling the room, but then realized it was her phone.

"Let it go to message," Reece said, drawing on her breast so sweetly she gasped.

"I can't," she said breathlessly, pulling away gently. "I'll see what's up and be right back," she promised.

When she grabbed her phone, she saw it was her insurance agent. She answered immediately.

"Ms. Harper?"

"Yes?" Her heart was in her throat and she couldn't say more.

"Good news. The second fire inspector deemed the fire accidental. We can continue with paying the claim, as planned."

Relief made her hands tremble, and she felt tears sting her eyes. "Oh, thank you so much. Really, I appreciate you doing this so quickly," she said, her voice thick.

"You're very welcome—we do try to do the best for our clients, and a call from your father's friend helped me speed things along," he said with a smile. "Merry Christmas, Miss Harper. We'll be in touch."

She put the phone down and tried to compose herself before she turned back to Reece, but he was already there, turning her to him, taking in her tears. "What is it? What happened?"

She bit her lip and told him everything. He looked surprised, concerned and confused.

"Abby, why didn't you talk to me about this? It has to have been worrying you sick," he said, pulling her in next to him, his chin resting on her head as he rubbed her shoulders.

"I just never could. The timing was always wrong. I worried, at the start, that you might go ahead and sell to Keller if you thought that I wouldn't be financially viable, and then we had our blowup, and now we're just back together, and it's all been crazy," she said, hoping he understood.

He tipped her face up to meet his gaze.

"I guess I can understand why you'd think that, before, but I hope you trust me with more than your body by now. I wouldn't do anything to hurt you, Abby, ever."

"I know. It's just been...intense. But when they pay out, I might be able to use the funds as a down payment on your property. It'll take everything I have, but if you're willing to work with me, I could do it," she said, holding her breath again.

He nodded, though there was a strange glint in his eye that she couldn't quite read. "I'd like nothing better than for you to have that land. I'll do whatever it takes to sell Winston Vineyards to you," he said. "But what about your own property?"

"At some point I'll repair our house, go back to

living there. It's my home, but I won't build new tasting rooms. Yours are so much larger and nicer. If it's okay with you, I thought I might change your house into a bed-and-breakfast," she said, gauging his reaction. "That way it maintains the house, and puts it to good use."

He nodded. "That's smart."

"I'm glad you approve," she said with a smile, feeling lighter by the second. "I would keep your family's vines, too, though I would probably slowly transition the entire operation over to organic."

"Mom and Dad will love hearing that," he said.

The lightness of having things worked out made her dizzy. Reece was going to sell to her. It was going to be okay.

It would be financially tight for many years, but she'd be able to keep her legacy—and his—in place. That was worth everything.

"So, where were we?" she said, sliding her hands up under his shirt, and watching his eyes darken with desire. "I think we were loosening you up for your drive this afternoon?"

He groaned, looking at the clock. "I really do have to meet Brody. I suppose we'll have to…wait."

She smiled, kissing him again. "That's okay. It can be our celebration after you finish your drive."

Her heartbeat raced as she said the words, determined to be supportive and appreciate what they had, for now. The good news from the agent didn't reduce her anxiety about Reece driving, or about him eventually leaving. After all, that was why he was here—to get a second chance at his old life, even if she couldn't be part of it. She was with him now, so she shut out the rest and focused on that as he erased her thoughts with one more scorching kiss before he left.

REECE RAN HIS HAND OVER the hood of the car—it was a beauty, and he was anxious to get out on the track, his nerves banished. He felt great.

The stock car was heavier and built out far differently than those he drove for Formula One, not as low or aerodynamic, but it was a powerful beast, and it would put him to the test.

He knew he could do this. He was ready.

"Feeling good?" Brody asked, walking up beside him, handing him a helmet.

"Yeah. Yeah, I am."

"Let's go then," his buddy said with a slap on his shoulder. "They have everything set up and won't time the first run, so you can get a feel for it, but we'll time a second and third."

He tried to pretend this was as informal as Brody said, but Reece knew a couple of reporters had caught wind of this drive, and asked to come on site. He'd allowed it. It was risky, but he had nothing to lose at this point.

"Sounds good," Reece said, pulling the helmet on, adjusting and testing the microphone as he prepared to slide himself into the tight spot, the men suddenly gathered around him ready to strap him to the seat.

Before he did so, however, he glanced up and saw

Abby, waiting just beyond the perimeter with Hannah and a few other onlookers.

He waved, and she blew him a kiss back.

"You ready, Romeo?" Brody teased and Reece slid into the seat and got prepped.

Minutes later, all systems checked and ready, it was up to him now. Reece had driven this track once or twice before, never officially, but as he looked ahead, everything fell into place.

The world outside of the car dropped away as he pulled forward and got a feel for the smooth, powerful growl of the engine. Something very close to arousal flowed through him, and he became completely focused as he started a first lap, taking it slow at first, getting into the groove.

"God, this feels good," he said with gusto into the mic.

"You're looking good," he heard Brody respond with a knowing laugh.

Closing one lap, Reece got serious and picked up speed, moving the tach up to about 7000 rpms. He took the next corner perfectly, smiling.

This was right. This was where he belonged.

He did a few more laps and pulled in, signaling that he was ready for a timed run.

A short while later, he was off again, punching up the speed, testing the car, his reflexes and his body.

All seemed in working order, and he pulled in a few seconds later, listening over the radio for his time.

"I can do better," he said, to himself as much as to the guys on the other side.

This time, he went for it, watching the yellow light come on that told him he was pushing into the higher area of speeds that could disqualify a driver from a win, but he wasn't competing with anyone but himself and the clock.

He pushed it a little more, coming into the last lap, and caught his breath, cursing as a sharp pain shot up his calf to his knee, causing him to lose focus slightly, and the car wavered on the track.

Cold sweat broke out as he controlled the car, fishtailing slightly, trying to ignore the pain.

"Again," he ground out over the mic, even though Brody was saying no.

"One more."

He managed one more set of laps, clocking a decent time, though slower than he'd have liked.

But he had to stop, he knew, because the pins and needles were so intense, he couldn't feel the accelerator with his foot.

The frustration was more painful, but he swallowed it as he unbuckled himself and was pulled out. When he was set on his feet, his left leg faltered slightly, and he caught it in time to save himself public humiliation.

Brody noticed, and did him the favor of distracting those who were watching.

Abby noticed, too. She was as white as a sheet, staring at him with dark eyes.

A second later, she launched herself at him, and if not for the car behind him they would have both gone down.

"You were wonderful," she said, but she was trembling from head to toe.

"Hey, what's wrong?" he asked. "You're crying."

"I'm so happy for you, and that you are here again. I thought you were going to crash when you fishtailed—it scared me," she said. "But you didn't. You did it," she said, hugging him tightly again.

"My leg went buzzy on me," he said, disgusted with himself, adrenaline still surging through him, his own hands shaking. "I needed to do better."

He figured this was it. He'd made the drive, but his warble was going to be the thing everyone focused on. The thing that would convince the sponsors not to take a chance on him.

"It was respectable, considering," Brody interrupted. "What happened?"

"Lost feeling in my leg—or rather, pins and needles were too intense for me to apply as much pressure as I should. I lost focus for a moment," Reece admitted.

"You controlled it, and your time was decent. Still, your cars and tracks are a lot different, more unpredictable," Brody said, sliding one arm around Hannah and the other rubbing the back of his neck in an obviously nervous gesture. "Maybe if you rest one more season and let your body heal, you'll be in better shape next—"

"I can't do that, Brody, and you know it," Reece said. His leg was a little better now that he was out of his cramped position, but it still bothered him. "This will either convince them or not," he said, thanking his friend and shaking his hand. The chance to prove himself was all he could ask for, but even Reece knew the drive hadn't gone as well as he needed it to. Not well enough for sponsors to risk millions of dollars on him.

Still, he had done it, and he was going to celebrate, like he had promised Abby.

"Hannah and I have plans tonight—you two are okay on your own?" Brody asked as they left the track.

"Yeah, we'll be fine. You guys have fun—we fly out early?"

"Yeah, see you in the morning."

They parted ways out in the lot after Reece had changed and met Abby where she waited for him outside.

"So, you want to go out and celebrate that I didn't completely wipe out?" he said with humor he wasn't completely feeling.

She touched his face, her eyes fierce. "You did better than that—you had one lapse, and I've seen drivers do a lot worse. We should celebrate because you did *well.*"

Reece pulled her in, hugging her tight to his chest, a feeling of warmth and a tangle of other emotions washing over him. To keep himself from thinking about it, he found her mouth, nibbled at it, then kissed her more deeply, soaking up her warmth and her taste and everything that was Abby.

He wanted to hold on to her forever. He loved her, he thought, gazing beyond the open track. The realization didn't come as a surprise, more of a relief. He'd been struggling with his emotions for days, and it felt good to just set them free. He didn't know if he had room for both loves in his life, but he wanted to try.

CHAPTER TWELVE

BACK AT THE ROOM, Abby was relieved that her stomach had settled and her hands had finally stopped shaking. She hadn't realized how afraid she'd been for Reece until he actually started to drive.

As she watched the bright blue car covered with logos make laps, she'd relaxed and cheered him on, and when he'd lost control for that handful of seconds, her heart thudded in her chest, and she'd found herself propped up by Hannah.

All she could think of was him dying in that car, and it had flattened her.

The thought of life without him was suddenly impossible.

She loved him. It was a mistake, but she knew it clear down to her bones in the second that the car had fishtailed, and she knew she couldn't stand the idea of losing him, or of him being hurt again.

Lost in her thoughts as they entered the condo, she wandered into the bedroom with the idea of freshening up and maybe taking a nap, and saw several large boxes, all wrapped in bright Christmas wrapping, waiting on the bed.

"What's all this?" she asked Reece, who stood just behind her.

"For you. Open them. This one first," he said, handing her a large, flat box.

"But…it's not even Christmas yet, and I didn't buy anything for you," she objected.

"Just open it, Abby," he said, giving her a patient look.

She did, and set the box down, pulling out the most lovely emerald-green silk dress she had ever seen. A modest scooped bodice was held by lacy spaghetti straps, nipping in at the waist and flaring out around the knee in an ultrafeminine way.

"Reece, it's gorgeous," she breathed, and she sucked her breath back in, coughing as she saw the name of the designer. "Oh, no…this is too much."

"It's what I wanted to buy you. I saw it when we were out yesterday, and I knew it would be perfect on you. And it's warm enough to wear it down here," he said.

"Now?"

"We're going out tonight," he said. "On a date. We haven't had time for that. We need to make time."

"Oh. Reece, I'm so—I'm so…" She tried to find words, but she put the dress down and didn't know what to say. She didn't know what this meant, and she hated the confused rush of thoughts, hopes and doubts that crowded her mind.

"Open the others," he said, pushing her back to the pile of boxes.

"It's too much. The dress is enough."

"What, are you wearing it barefoot or with your boots?" he teased.

She noticed the size of one of the boxes was perfect for shoes, and leapt on it. She couldn't resist shoes, and he was right, she had to have something for the dress.

When she pulled out the sexy, strappy black stilettos, she groaned. "I think I am in lust," she said, petting the soft leather.

"I can't wait to see them on you." He handed her another smaller box, grinning devlishly.

Seeing that he was enjoying her opening the gifts as much as she was enjoying receiving them, she unwrapped the next one, and paused. The box itself was made from black leather with the word *Naughty* embossed on the top.

Taking the lid off, she saw a pair of shiny new handcuffs.

Her heart began to race.

"I want you to wear those tonight, too," he said. "Later," he corrected, his eyes burning hot.

She looked up at him. "I can do that."

The last box, also black leather, said *Nice* on the top.

She smiled. "How can nice be as fun as naughty?"

"Open it and see."

She did, and saw a small bottle of cinnamon massage oil—edible—and she smiled. She lifted it, opening the bottle, the spicy scent greeting her, and she put a dab on her finger, then tasted it, meeting Reece's eyes.

"That is nice," she said, drawing her finger out from between her lips in a sexy gesture, watching his jaw become tense with desire.

But there was one more thing in the box, and she pulled out a small black satin bag, from which a sparkling silver chain fell out into her palm. She lifted it with shaking fingers, a flawless emerald teardrop winking at her in the low light of the room.

"It's beautiful, but I can't possibly accept this, Reece," she said, looking up at him.

He pulled her to her feet, and into his arms for a tight hug followed by a deep kiss.

"Please, I want you to. I want to see you in that dress and the necklace, and then we're coming back here, and it will be my turn to unwrap you," he said, trailing his tongue down her neck, making her shiver.

REECE KNEW HE WAS PLAYING with fire. It'd be hours before he could go back to the room and enjoy Abby's body in every way he imagined.

They sat at a private table at the back of one of his favorite restaurants, the lush bougainvillea and palms surrounding them, a half-finished bottle of wine on the table between them.

Abby was beyond gorgeous in the dress he'd picked out for her when he had snuck out earlier in the day, his plan in place. Hannah had been his coconspirator, and he felt a serious wave of pride and possession as he and Abby had entered the restaurant. He knew every man there envied him, and rightfully so.

Her eyes were as bright as the emerald that lay

against her skin, and he got hard every time he thought about their using his other gifts.

"Would you like to dance?" he asked, as the band started to play a slow romantic tune.

She smiled, her eyes soft with the effects of wine and their relaxing time together.

Though she kept silent, he stood. "Dance with me, Abby," he said, his heart hammering in his chest. He wanted to give her everything, which was the source of his dilemma.

She put her hand in his, and it was like a fantasy as they walked onto the dance floor. Amid other couples who swayed together under the Christmas lights hung round the room, they danced to a sexy jazz version of "Have Yourself A Merry Little Christmas."

He pulled her close, pressing his lower body against her and letting her feel how aroused he was. He smiled into her neck as he felt her fingers curl into his jacket.

The dress was a mere scrap between them—another reason he'd picked it out, and he felt her nipples bead under the thin fabric. He moved to the music, letting his chest brush against them, and felt her shudder.

"Reece," she breathed, burying her face against his chest, sounding like she was barely holding on.

It was the sexiest moment of his life. They were in the middle of a crowd of people, and he discreetly leaned in to kiss the curve of her neck, while letting his hand brush her pebbled nipple. She came apart in his arms as they danced.

He captured her surprised gasp with a kiss, the shock of sensation moving through her as she moaned into his mouth, the music offering some disguise. He nearly lost control himself, but somehow managed to hold on.

Later, he thought, smiling at the idea of peeling this dress away, using the handcuffs and the oil. However, he wanted her to leave the necklace and stilettos on.

"Reece, that was..." She paused, looking up at him with smoky eyes and flushed cheeks.

"I know," he murmured, dipping to catch her mouth in another kiss, and keeping her in his arms for several more turns around the dance floor.

He really didn't want this to end—ever—and that was where the danger lay.

The day had been one he wouldn't soon forget—the drive, even though he had had a lapse, was more or less successful, but it was Abby's support that made it shine for him. She made him feel like he could do anything.

She knew he had to leave, that he would go back to racing, and yet she gave herself to him completely, and supported him completely, as well.

He loved her, and he wanted it all—he wanted to race, and he wanted Abby, for good.

He barely noticed the music had stopped, until light applause from the group shook him out of his deep thoughts.

"This has been wonderful," Abby said, looking

up at him. "But can we go back to the condo now? Please?"

Her sexy plea shook him with desire, and he nodded, retrieving her shawl and paying the bill. She was the only Christmas gift he ever wanted.

REECE SET FORTH, paying great attention to every aspect of Abby's body. He loved how he could find some new spot that would make her whimper or gasp and when she insistently wove her fingers into his hair, directing him as to what she needed.

She was beautiful but real, smart but modest, sexier than hell and everything he could ever imagine wanting in a woman.

Limp from his intimate kissing, he carried her to the bed. Slowly he took the sexy shoes off, kissing her ankles and massaging her feet, still sifting through his emotions as he stood to take his own clothes off and join her on the bed.

"No talking," she said, putting a finger against his lips. "Just make love to me, okay?" He was glad to oblige, covering her completely as he drove deep inside. Bodies moving in harmony, their patience and seduction paid off in a series of powerful orgasms that left them both breathless and hanging on to each other.

"I love you, Abby," he said, feeling the truth of what he told her as much as anything he had ever known in his life.

She studied him, as if wondering if she had heard correctly.

"Reece," she said, sighing. "I love you, too."

He had not realized how he'd been holding his breath.

Joy coursed through him. "I've loved you forever, Abby, it just took me a long time to realize it," he said, leaning in to kiss her softly, tenderly, trying to communicate everything he was feeling. It seemed impossible. "Come back with me. To France. Please."

His question hung in the dark between them, and he knew her answer before she even said it.

"I can't…you know that. I mean, I could visit, I could come to see you, but I can't leave the vineyards."

Everything inside of him sank. "You can. We can make it work."

They parted, and pushed back on the pillows, facing each other. He had to convince her, somehow.

"Reece, you know how you said racing was your passion, the thing you loved?"

"Mmm-hmm."

She shrugged her shoulder slightly. "That's what the vineyards are for me. I love it there. It's my home, but it's also my passion, and it feels important to preserve that legacy. My parents left me the business they spent their lives building. I can't just abandon that."

"We could work it out. You could get a manager, and we could come back as often as we needed to—" he said, but she interrupted.

"And what would I do in Europe? Follow you around to the races? As much as I want to be with you, that's not a life I want. And…I don't know if I could do it. It was hard, watching you drive today. I was proud of you, happy for you, but I don't think I could stand there and watch if something bad happened again. I just…couldn't."

He pulled her in, not wanting her to see how disappointed he was, though he knew she was right. He shouldn't ask her to make this sacrifice for him.

"It's selfish of me to want you to come with me, you're right, and I suppose it's time I face facts. They aren't going to take me back," he said, weaving his fingers through hers and not wanting to let go. "Maybe Brody is right, maybe another year, or maybe not. Maybe it's time for me to move on to other things."

"Do you mean…are you saying…?"

"I'll stay. I want to be with you, Abby, and I think today proved that it's the right choice for me to make."

She was quiet in his arms, and he wanted to see her face.

"You okay? I thought you would be happier."

"I am," she said, looking at him closely. "I just don't want you giving up on your dreams for me."

"Maybe it's just time I learn to chase a new dream, don't you think? One you and I could share together?"

She smiled then, and reached up to kiss him.

Reece let the passion rise again, losing himself in Abby, and setting his doubts aside. He loved her. He was making the right decision. He had to be.

CHAPTER THIRTEEN

ABBY PANICKED WHEN she walked out of Reece's kitchen, the scent of fire meeting her nose. Following it, she found Reece down behind the lower barn on his property, a fire burning in an area he cleared, and some contraption built above that held a wine barrel in place.

"I wondered what you were up to," Abby said. He'd spent most of his time here since they had gotten back from Daytona the day before. She'd been constantly busy, too busy to investigate before now.

"It's a wine barrel," Reece said, grinning.

"I see that. I knew your Dad was a cooper, but I didn't know you were."

"I'm not," Reece clarified, rubbing his hands together and leaning in for a kiss before he nodded to her to follow him into the barn. "Dad always tried to get me into it, but I was never interested. I forgot he had this workshop. I figured I'd see what I could remember, and looked up the rest on the Internet." He checked the steaming barrel suspended above the fire. "That's my first one. We'll see what happens."

"Wow, I am impressed. You are a man of many

talents," she said, reaching up to kiss him again and loving the smoky, earthy scents that surrounded them.

Still, something was off, and she'd felt it in the four days since they had returned. Since he had told her he was staying, she knew. It was what she wanted. She loved him, and she wanted him here, but some undefinable layer of tension seemed to run underneath them now, and while she thought it was good for Reece to get back in touch with his family's history and pursuits, he himself had said this was never his passion.

Driving was his passion, and he was giving it up, for her.

So she had made a few calls herself, namely, one to Joe, the man Reece had been talking with before. His number was left on Reece's phone, and Abby called, and talked to him, to find out if Reece really was out of the sport.

As it turned out, just the opposite.

News of Reece's test run had spread and, true to form, fans were cheering him on, wanting him back. Joe knew it, and sponsors knew it, and they were willing to give him some test runs in Europe, to see how things went.

They wanted him there soon, and they had been going to call him, when Abby had taken the tiger by the tail and contacted them.

Her chest tightened as she pulled back from Reece's increasingly passionate kiss.

"I have something to tell you," she said, trying to sound normal, but her heart hurt a little, even though she knew this was the right thing to do. She loved him, and that meant not having him just walk away from his dream for her.

"Yeah, can it wait?" Reece said teasingly, dipping in for another kiss.

She laughed, evading him, and putting a hand on either shoulder, she made him listen as she told him about her phone call to Joe.

Everything from confusion to disbelief to excitement passed across his face, and finally, he shook his head and pulled her in closer.

"I can't believe you did that," he said huskily against her hair.

"I didn't do anything. They were going to call you anyway. And you know you have to go. Reece, you have to."

He didn't say anything, but she'd seen the light, the hope, in his face. She wouldn't let him stay here and give it all up.

"So what do we do, then? I don't want to lose you," he said, the emotion in his voice sincere.

"I guess we'll just have to see what happens. Maybe we can visit each other, definitely we'll talk on the phone," she said. She feared her tone betrayed her, that maintaining a relationship that way probably wasn't realistic. "It'll only be for another few years, and then we could make some decisions about being together for good, right?"

REECE HELD HER TIGHT, his mind spinning with the news. They wanted him back! But he also wanted to be with Abby. Conflicted, he didn't know how to answer her question.

He was on the circuit for months at a time. Some of the guys' families did stay home, especially when there were kids and other considerations. Not all of the wives traveled with their husbands, but a few did.

Still, those couples had the deeper connection of years together, a marriage to return to. He didn't know if what he had with Abby was too new, too tenuous to endure that kind of separation. The realization hit him like a ton of bricks, and he lifted her face up to his, kissing her.

"Aw, Abby, don't cry."

"I can't help it. I love you, and you love me, but I can't see how we can make this work," she said, her voice tight and pained. "I want to, but…"

He held her tight, unable to stand that she was suffering, even a little, because of him.

He knew how to make it right. They could make it work—and they would. He was going back to Europe, and he had no idea what the future held, but he knew two things for sure: he had to at least try to get back to racing, and he couldn't lose Abby.

The answer to both seemed clear.

"Abby?" he asked, his heart thundering.

"Yeah?"

"Will you marry me?"

ABBY WAS UP TO her ears in satin, flowers and bridesmaids.

Two days before Christmas, the winery was decorated, and everything was ready for the wedding reception. She'd been working overtime—an understatement—to make sure it was all perfect.

Looking around at the young women in beautiful, deep red satin Christmas gowns, it put to rest the notion that bridesmaids wore ugly dresses. These were chic and stylish, and Abby thought of the beautiful silk dress Reece had given her. It was far too light to wear, even indoors, in this climate, but she felt very proper back in her basic black business dress.

She lifted her hand to the emerald that lay against her throat. She hadn't taken it off since Reece had put it on for her that night in Florida.

The winery looked magical. Christmas lights were strung everywhere along the reception-room ceiling and through the entryway. He'd helped her string them before he left. It had only been four days and it felt like so much longer.

A fire crackled in the fireplace. The tables were set with fine white china, the glasses were sparkling crystal and Christmas bouquets of holly, poinsettias and white roses decorated each table.

The small band the bride and groom had hired was setting up in the reception room. Specialty bottles of different varieties of both Winston and Maple Hills wines, uniquely labeled for the bridal couple's special day, looked elegant on the tables, ready for each guest to take one home.

All they needed now was the bride and groom, who were taking a little longer arriving, so the bridesmaids and some of the groomsmen—also handsome in gray tuxedos with deep red cummerbunds—milled around, tasting appetizers and enjoying some drinks.

Abby felt incredibly alone even though she was in a roomful of people. Her throat tightened with emotions she had been fighting off since Reece had left for France.

He'd had to go. She wanted him to go. His sponsors were asking him to come back. No promises, but they were giving him a chance. It was exactly as Reece had predicted—everyone loved a comeback.

She wasn't about to stand in his way, and she made that clear by refusing his proposal. It had been the hardest thing she'd ever done. He wasn't angry, but he also told her he intended to keep on asking.

She figured he would, maybe, for a while. Then his life would take over, and he would know they'd made the right decision. Maybe, in a few years, things would be different, she thought, but found it hard to believe. So many things could happen in that time.

On top of that, Hannah was gone, too, staying in Florida with Brody. She had offered to come back, but Abby had released her from that responsibility. Abby was glad to take it on by herself, to have so much work to do that maybe she wouldn't think too much.

That would come to an end after the wedding, when she would close down through New Year's.

And do what? With whom?

Well, she thought, she had Beau and Buttercup.

She couldn't even move forward on plans for the reconstruction, since the city more or less closed down between Christmas and New Year's.

Reece had asked her to come to France for Christmas and stay the week. She was tempted. She'd never seen France, but would it just be extending the torture for both of them?

She didn't know if she'd be able to leave if she went there to be with him.

The fact was, though they loved each other, they had both chosen their individual passions over being together. Who was going to budge? Who should give up what they loved? What kind of foundation was that for a marriage? And how could they even think of getting married when they had only been lovers for less than a month? It was so unfair. It went against every grain of common sense she had, and at the same time, she knew he was the only one for her.

She was shaken from her reverie as applause scattered around her, growing louder with hoots and whistles as the bridal couple arrived, and Abby joined in. Sandra looked absolutely gorgeous, and as the party started, she took her place with the caterers and other party organizers, making sure all went well.

Seeing Sandra and her new husband so happy filled Abby with doubt—had she made the wrong choice?

Was being here more important than being with Reece, and supporting him as he made his way back onto the circuit? He would only be racing for another few years at most, and then they could open their own winery, wherever they wanted. Everyone else in her life was gone, out living their lives, but this was her life, her dream—wasn't it?

She didn't know anymore. What was the right thing to do? She had so many plans to revive this place, and at the very least, she needed to be here during the rebuilding to see that through.

Her heart was heavy, and she was exhausted as the hours wore on. Late in the evening, the caterers gone, the party was still lasting long past her ability to stay. She needed to be alone, to go off and lick her wounds in private.

As she started back toward the house, she saw headlights turn into the drive. It was very late for anyone to be arriving—a late wedding guest maybe?

The car came closer, and her heart leapt as she recognized the driver. She ran toward the car as the door opened, feeling happy for the first time in days.

"Oh, Mom, Dad! I'm so happy you're here!"

Her parents had no idea what to do when she launched herself at them and broke down in tears.

THEY WANTED HIM BACK.

While the younger guy who had been in line to replace him had been close to doing just that, the media coverage of Reece's trial in Florida, coupled with an interview that hit the French and U.S. papers, had fans insisting they wanted Reece back on the track. The response was overwhelming, especially online, and Reece had as hard a time believing it as anyone.

He should have been thrilled.

Snow was falling in Paris as he sat in a conference room with his manager, the car's owner, the sponsor reps and God knew who else. They had been talking incessantly about new acupuncture methods, hiring him a personal physical therapist and doing whatever was necessary to get him back in a car, winning races.

It was what he wanted, so why was he sitting here thinking about what Abby was doing? Today was the wedding, and she was probably so busy she hadn't even thought of him. He'd sent her an e-mail, left her a phone message earlier, but hadn't heard back.

He still couldn't believe she had made that call—she hadn't set any of this in motion, of course, but the fact that she had been willing to let him go, to put his dreams first, still stunned him. If it was possible, he loved her more every time he thought about her.

He didn't know how he was going to manage it, but he wasn't going to lose her. She'd said no this time, and that was fine. She was right, again. It was too soon, maybe he had proposed for the wrong reasons. He had been desperately trying to find a way to make it all work, but he knew he really did want her, and only her, in his life. Maybe she'd say yes the next time, or the time after that.

He didn't plan on giving up.

"Reece? Can you be in Italy in two days? You can start training now. We want you back in shape and ready to go as soon as possible," his manager said. Tony was a good guy, but Reece swore he saw dollar signs flashing in his eyes for a moment.

Reece wasn't a person—an actual human being—to anyone gathered in this room. He was a commodity, a product.

He listened as they discussed liability issues, if

the car would be covered, how much they stood to lose if he crashed again, what the risks were with insurance if anyone thought he wasn't up to racing in the first place.

He was. Even with his problems at Daytona, he knew he could do it. No more cold hands or nerves at the thought of getting behind the wheel, but what if the worst happened?

He could care less about the car, or anything else. His doubts weren't borne of fear of dying, but of fear of never seeing Abby again. Could he live with that?

No.

"Reece?" Tony asked again, sounding irritated. "I hope your focus is better when you get back in a car," he said.

Some muffled laughter and commentary met the remark, and Reece smiled. He couldn't believe what he was about to do.

"Two days from now? That's Christmas day," he said, sparking off a round of confused glances around the conference table.

"So what? You need to be on this ASAP and 24/7 if it's going to work. The docs will clear you, but only if you sign a contract and follow the physical regimen to the letter."

Reece looked out the window at the snow, thinking, of all things, about Abby's pork roast. That was certainly not going to be part of his training. He'd invited her to come see him next week—but now he would be in training, out of touch twelve to eighteen hours a day, every day.

He wouldn't ask her to do that. No way would he say she had to come all the way over here and then form her life around his crazy racing schedule, content to see him in whatever cracks of time he had left.

It was why he'd never gotten into relationships in the first place.

"Reece, what the—"

"I'm sorry, Tony, I can't do it this week. I have other plans for Christmas," he said, amazed at how easy it was. Abby had given him the gift of going after his dreams, after what he really wanted, and that was what he was going to do.

"You...you *what?*"

"Listen, I appreciate this. I thought it was what I wanted, but I need to be home for Christmas."

"Home? Reece, you are home. This is home."

He grinned again, feeling incredibly giddy as he torpedoed his racing career for good.

"No, home is where Abby is."

"WHY DID YOU DECIDE to come back?" Abby asked, wrapped up in a blanket that smelled like Reece, having a very late-night cup of hot chocolate with her parents.

Her mom and dad shared a somewhat guilty look, and Abby peered at them over her mug. "Tell me."

"Well, to be completely honest," her mother began, "Hannah called us."

Abby groaned. "I'm sorry, she shouldn't have done that. I'm fine."

Her mom looked at her, and Abby felt like she was ten again.

"She told us Reece proposed."

Abby groaned a second time, closing her eyes and planning what she would do to her friend the next time she saw her. It wouldn't be pretty.

"We had no idea you and Reece were an item, let alone so serious," her dad said.

"We…it's complicated. He has his life, I have mine. The two don't match up so well."

"Why is that?"

"He has to be in Europe, racing, hopefully, and I have to be here, rebuilding and running the vineyards."

"Is that really what you want, honey?" her mom asked, as if seeing right through her. "It's clear just by the look on your face, and how you cried your heart out a little while ago, that you love him. So why aren't you in France with an engagement ring on your finger for Christmas?"

Abby opened her mouth, gaped, started to say something. "Mom," she began, "I love it here, and I have responsibilities, and—"

"They sound more like excuses than reasons, Abigail," her father said.

"Wait," she said, putting her hand up. "You know how much work this is, and it's even more so now with the fire and the reorganizing. I have to be here…right? And besides…" she said, but didn't finish her thought.

"Besides, what?"

"I don't know. There was this moment, when Reece lost control of the car for a minute, down in Daytona."

"We saw it on the news. He pulled it back."

"I know. But it scared me to death. What if he hadn't? What if he died, right there in front of me? I don't know if I can handle that."

"Would you rather it happens when you're not there? When you're not the last person he sees before he races? The person he woke up with that morning? I'm sorry to be harsh, honey, but your father and I have seen a lot of pain and suffering in the last few months, and one thing I can tell you is that you can't avoid it. If Reece crashed, would your pain be any less for staying here? Would it be better not to have married him and had that time together?"

Abby gaped, wordless in response to her parents' questions. That Reece could crash, could get hurt or worse, knowing that she hadn't wanted to be with him, had said no to marrying him. Had let him go…

And what about when he won? When he wanted to celebrate and enjoy life? Didn't she want to share that with him, too? The good and the bad?

"Oh, Mom," she said, a fresh batch of new tears at the realization flooding her eyes.

"It's hard to figure out on your own sometimes, I know," her mom said.

"But if I go…what about here? What about the wineries, and the rebuilding?"

"Well, that was kind of the miracle of Hannah's call. She gave us an excuse to come back."

"She…what? I thought you loved your travel and your work?"

"Oh, we did. It was wonderful, but it made us also realize how precious home was, and how long we had been away. We wanted to come back, to come back to running the vineyard, but we didn't want you to feel like we were intruding or suggesting you weren't doing just fine. When Hannah called, we knew it was the right time to come back. For us, and for you."

"You want to run the vineyard again?"

"Yes, and we have a bit more money in investments set aside, so we can, we think, with the insurance, probably buy Reece out, instead of you doing that and going broke trying." Her mother shook her head. "Really, Abby, didn't we teach you better about leading a balanced life?"

Abby fought the urge to smile. "Hannah really did tell you everything, huh?"

"Yes."

"Remind me to thank her."

Her parents' grins broke out wide, and so did hers. "We'll do that. But you have to get ready."

"Ready? For what?"

Her parents chuckled conspiratorially and her father handed her an envelope with a red ribbon on it.

"You have a morning flight to Paris. Our Christmas gift to you. Go pack."

REECE TURNED INTO the driveway of the house and parked at the edge, partygoers apparently still sleeping from the wedding reception. It was Christmas Eve morning; he had made it home, just in time.

He couldn't wait to sneak in and wake Abby up—he fully intended to make love to her until she agreed to wear the ring he had in his pocket. It was his mission, he thought with a smile.

As he climbed the steps to the porch, he paused, looking out over the snowy fields down toward the grapes. All of the trees Abby had put in the yard sparkled and were lit, and Christmas was in the air. He never really understood what people meant when they said that, but he could feel it, right now, and he knew. Some of her Christmas magic must have rubbed off on him, he guessed.

He heard the door open behind him and spun, expecting to see Abby, but found himself facing an older man instead.

"Uh, hi," Reece said, peering at the man more closely. He looked familiar. "I'm Reece, I live—"

"Oh, I know who you are," the man said, letting out a belting laugh. He was then was joined by an older woman, whose eyes went wide.

Reece's did, too. He could see Abby in her mother's face and laughed as well.

"Mr. and Mrs. Harper! What a surprise," he said. It *was* a surprise. His sneaky seduction of Abby would have to wait, he supposed. "It's so nice you made it here for Christmas, and not to be rude, but where is Abby?"

CHRISTMAS AT HANCOCK INTERNATIONAL AIRPORT wasn't exactly what Abby had counted on, but she was going to wait out this flight delay no matter what. It would figure. She had nearly killed herself getting here, unable to fly out of the smaller, Ithaca airport, and now her flight was delayed for weather.

She was going to call Reece and let him know she was coming, but then she thought she would make it a surprise instead—hopefully a happy one. He had invited her, so she hoped he'd be glad to see her.

So, she gave up her seat to a young mother carrying a baby, and paced in front of the gate, willing the delay to be lifted. She couldn't sit still anyway, in spite of getting no sleep, she was wired and eager to get going. The place was crowded, flooded with holiday travelers, and she felt sorry for the mom with the crying baby, and for kids napping against the posts and harried parents.

She paced to the vending machine and looked over the candy selection, and grabbed a chocolate bar, then headed to the Starbucks to get another double-shot expresso.

Her phone rang, and she looked.

Reece.

Her heart trip-hammered in her chest, and her hand shook as she clicked the talk button, though it could have been from the caffeine.

Right.

"Abby, it's Reece," he said.

She laughed. "I know."

"Oh, right. Listen, I just wanted to let you know I've had a change in plans, and I won't be able to meet you in France for the week."

She paused. "What do you mean?"

"Listen, I know you probably weren't planning to come anyway, but I have to be somewhere else, and I didn't want you coming here and ending up finding me gone."

Her heart sank. She looked at the lines of people suddenly in motion as they flooded the gate. The flight was boarding.

Of course it was.

She took a deep breath and got a grip.

"So, where will you be? I'll meet you there. Wherever," she said, determined to make this work.

"Really? You'd meet me anywhere?"

"Yes. Reece, I have a lot to tell you, but things have changed, and…I want to spend Christmas with you, and tell you everything that's happened. I don't care where you are, I just want to be with you."

"I can't wait," he said, but this time the sound of his voice didn't come from the phone, but from right behind her.

She turned, and found herself nose-to-nose with him, and let out a screech that stopped just about everyone around them in their tracks. Throwing herself at him, they nearly both fell over until he got his balance and set her on her feet, saying nothing until he kissed her thoroughly.

"Hi, sweetheart."

"When did you come home? How did you know…?"

He smiled. "I didn't. I was at the house, and your parents said you were taking a flight. I couldn't believe it. I was breaking land-speed records getting here, I think, because I thought I would miss you," he explained.

"You mean...at our house?" she asked, slowly putting two and two together.

"Yeah. I'm back. I didn't want to go through Christmas—or my life—without you."

She was stunned, and lack of breathing threatened to steal words from her, the emotions hitting her too hard, the questions all rising too quickly.

"Breathe, Abby," he said, kissing her again, and making sure she did.

"It was all happening, just as I hoped for," he explained, "but none of it felt right. It wasn't like before. I didn't feel like I was home or happy or doing what I wanted to be doing. I didn't expect it. They were offering me everything I wanted, and all I could think of was that I wanted you. I wanted to be here. I wanted to wake up in bed with you Christmas morning, for the rest of our lives."

Abby almost wondered if she had fallen asleep and was dreaming all of this. She must have said so, because he assured her he was real.

"I love you, Abby," he said, his voice low and full of emotion. "I'm yours, if you want me."

"I love you, too, Reece. And Christmas in bed sounds perfect to me," she whispered, sliding into his arms once and for all.

EPILOGUE

ABBY BUSTLED AROUND the kitchen, making Reece the most amazing anniversary dinner he could imagine. They ate out at restaurants so often when they were on the road with the new team that she wanted to do something special, and something private. Her parents had gone on a vacation to the house in Talence, leaving Abby and Reece home to watch over the vineyard and enjoy their first anniversary alone together. With that amazing bathroom, she thought with a grin.

She loved the house, and their new life following the races around the U.S. and traveling and working the vineyard in between. Reece and Brody were co-owners of a new racing team now, and they were often surrounded by crowds and people, which was fun and exciting, but Abby wanted her husband to herself tonight. The team was doing very well, and Brody was in charge while Reece took the week off.

It was their first anniversary, after all, and she looked out the kitchen window at the pristine summer countryside. She loved Christmas, but was happy they had waited for a summer wedding. The vineyards were so lovely, and they had been married out among them, overlooking the lake.

She had plans for her husband, who had been teasing her mercilessly for a week, keeping her on edge, doling out his seductions with practiced patience. She was intent on doing whatever was necessary to make him give in to her tonight.

The thought put a sly smile on her face. She didn't think he'd mind. They'd honed the practice of extended sex play and seduction to a fine art.

She checked all of the food, and took another peep at the delectable pastry in the refrigerator that was one of her favorites.

Her plan started now.

Shucking her clothes, she grabbed the sexy apron he'd caught her in that first Christmas and donned only that, taking her coat from the hook and heading down to the workshop Reece had remodeled to continue perfecting his cooperage. The craft had created a new bond between Reece and his father, as well, which both of them enjoyed, and now many of the barrels in which they aged their wine were made on premises.

She walked into the workshop, which smelled of oak and the delicious scents of wine and burnt wood, and she had come to find the aroma incredibly erotic. Reece was bent over an almost finished cask, cauterizing the opening through which the wine would be poured. She waited for him to finish, enjoying watching him, appreciating every sexy muscle in his body as he leaned into his work.

When he finished, he looked up and was unsurprised to find her there.

"Hey," he said, taking off his safety glasses and crossing to a sink to take off his gloves and wash his hands before he crossed to her, kissing her soundly. "How long have you been there?" he asked.

"Just a minute," she said, love filling her just looking at him. "Dinner is almost done."

"Do we have a few minutes?"

"Sure."

"Isn't it a little hot for a coat?" he said, his eyes drifting down over her bare legs.

She smiled and wiggled her eyebrows. "I didn't think you'd want me walking down from the house in only this," she said as she dropped the coat and watched his eyes darken with lust. "So what did you have in mind?" she asked innocently, raising an eyebrow at some ties attached to a beam that had been put to very good use the evening before.

"I have an anniversary gift for you," he said, his voice a little raspy.

She smiled. "I have one for you, too, back at the house—but it's something we'll want to use there," she said, sending him a sexy look.

"Mmm. Maybe we can come back for yours then," he said, grabbing her by the waist and pulling her up close, where she could feel the extent of his excitement.

"Nope, I'd like mine now, please," she said, poking him in the chest playfully.

"Okay, vixen, come with me," he said, bringing her to a set of newly finished barrels. He opened one bottle and drew two glasses from the tap, a rich Baco that he sniffed, swirled and tasted, then handed hers to her.

"It's perfect, just like you," he said, toying with the apron tie at her neck.

She sipped the rich, fruity wine and groaned in appreciation as the flavors washed over her. "I don't think I have ever had a wine this complex—how did you get those sorts of sweet, smoky notes in there?"

It was a sexy, sensual wine, and she took another sip, feeling the tie at her neck pull loose.

"I've been experimenting with the barrels. This wine is ours. Like your mom and dad always did, I named it for us, too. Our story," he said. "Happy Anniversary."

"Oh, Reece. This is lovely. What did you name it?"

He put his glass down and pulled her in close as the apron fell away completely.

"Christmas in Bed."

She smiled, so much in love she didn't think she could ever express it, so she just let herself be carried away by his kiss, because Reece was right. It was perfect.

* * * * *

Save $1.00

on the purchase of any Harlequin Series book.

Available wherever books are sold, including most bookstores, supermarkets, drugstores and discount stores.

Save $1.00 on the purchase of any Harlequin Series book.

Coupon valid until December 31, 2014. Redeemable at participating retail outlets in the U.S. and Canada only. Limit one coupon per customer.

Canadian Retailers: Harlequin Enterprises Limited will pay the face value of this coupon plus 10.25¢ if submitted by customer for this product only. Any other use constitutes fraud. Coupon is nonassignable. Void if taxed, prohibited or restricted by law. Consumer must pay any government taxes. Void if copied. Millennium1 Promotional Services ("M1P") customers submit coupons and proof of sales to Harlequin Enterprises Limited, P.O. Box 3000, Saint John, NB E2L 4L3, Canada. Non-M1P retailer—for reimbursement submit coupons and proof of sales directly to Harlequin Enterprises Limited, Retail Marketing Department, 225 Duncan Mill Rd., Don Mills, Ontario M3B 3K9, Canada.

U.S. Retailers: Harlequin Enterprises Limited will pay the face value of this coupon plus 8¢ if submitted by customer for this product only. Any other use constitutes fraud. Coupon is nonassignable. Void if taxed, prohibited or restricted by law. Consumer must pay any government taxes. Void if copied. For reimbursement submit coupons and proof of sales directly to Harlequin Enterprises Limited, P.O. Box 880478, El Paso, TX 88588-0478, U.S.A. Cash value 1/100 cents.

HIINC0413COUP